IT WAS CORPORATE WAR . . . TO THE DEATH

Luna Inc. would live, he promised himself dourly. Even if he, the last of the Schollanders, died in the survival effort.

It was in his genes, maybe, as Auntie Elaine had once said. But it was in his heart and mind as well.

What had that long-dead mercenary rally cry been? Grab 'em by their balls—their hearts and minds will follow?

Nakamura sure had balls. He had to give him that.

But that was okay, too.

It gave him a target to grab.

And squeeze. . . .

SINGULARITIES

W. T. QUICK

A ROC BOOK

ROC
Published by the Penguin Group
Penguin Books USA Inc., 375 Hudson Street,
New York, New York 10014, U.S.A.
Penguin Books Ltd, 27 Wrights Lane,
London W8 5TZ, England
Penguin Books Australia Ltd, Ringwood,
Victoria, Australia
Penguin Books Canada Ltd, 2801 John Street,
Markham, Ontario, Canada L3R 1B4
Penguin Books (N.Z.) Ltd, 182-190 Wairau Road,
Auckland 10, New Zealand

Penguin Books Ltd, Registered Offices:
Harmondsworth, Middlesex, England

First published by Roc, an imprint of New American Library, a division of
Penguin Books USA Inc.

First Printing, September, 1990
10 9 8 7 6 5 4 3 2 1

For
Dick Sanders

Chapter One

The assassin came down the side of the mountain a few minutes after sunset. He was a short, compact man dressed in black. His face was covered with glare-suppressant grease, except for his eyes. His eyes were blank, dark circles, light-gathering inserts which made his night vision almost as good as day.

He had left his shadow glider near the top of the mountain. It had been a tricky flight in, buffeted by uncertain winds and sudden updrafts, and for a few moments he'd worried about the house radars picking him out against the general clutter of the neighborhood. They'd told him the glider was stealthed, proofed against casual radar observation, but long experience had taught him not to trust the experts with everything. Particularly not with his own life.

The landing had gone without incident. He'd activated the tiny capsule of tailored carbon-phage bacteria incorporated in the feather-light main spar of the almost weightless craft and, within moments, the butterfly wings had begun to dissolve. Now nothing remained to mark his arrival but a faint dusting of black grains across a thick layer of brown leaves.

He pulled up just before the tree line, where the forest of pine and oak stopped abruptly. Down below a few cattle grazed peacefully in a broad field, brightly silhouetted in the strangely sharp light of emerging stars. Beyond the cattle was a low wall and beyond that, the stark, Oriental plantings which surrounded a wide rock garden.

He hunkered down and scanned the back of the house which abutted the rock garden. A wooden patio ran the entire length of the very large house. Clumps of outdoor furniture dotted the patio, shaded by brightly colored umbrellas which proclaimed Cinzano and OptiTek and Coca-Cola in heavy luminescent strokes. Along much of the patio were tall glass doors divided by intricate wooden traceries, but the doors were shielded by thick curtains. Only here and there could he see faint yellow lines of light. It was late, but someone inside was still awake. The assassin sighed and settled back, concealing himself beneath a rank growth of some kind of flowering bush. He could smell the heavy odor of the blossoms on the chill night air. It reminded him of home.

Of course the inhabitants of the house were awake, he told himself. They were at war, just as he was. He suspected his chances of carrying out his mission were slim. His target was well guarded. The assassin was mildly surprised he'd made it this far. Perhaps the security here was not as good as he'd been told, although, in war, the first rule was that everything went wrong. Sometimes it went wrong for the enemy as well.

Whatever the reason, he'd managed to penetrate this far. His briefings had been explicit—watch and wait. The target always comes to his patio in the morning, to sit and meditate on the silence of his rock garden. That would be the time to take him.

Stupid, he thought. If you are a potential target, habit becomes a liability. Never do the same things in the same way at the same time. Predictability is the key to death.

Perhaps this man feels safe, he thought. A man often feels safe at home. That is why so many men die there.

The assassin closed his eyes. Morning would come soon enough. The sharp-edged bulk of a Little Man rocket launcher, only twenty inches long, scraped against his fabric-clad thigh. He moved slightly to arrange the weapon more comfortably. It was a joke, of course. He liked that kind of humor. The Little Man was manufactured by TriDiCon, an arms maker which was a subsidiary of TechSYSTEM, which was itself wholly owned by Nakamura-Norton. And the man down below who would come to meditate on the gray morning light of his garden, if the spies were to be believed, was Shigeinari Nakamura. If this all came to pass, then Shag Nakamura would die by his own weapon and that, the assassin told himself, was a great joke. Such a success would please his ancestors and his Temple. He wondered if Nakamura would enjoy a joke like that.

Probably. Some things were universal.

He opened his eyes and stared at the stars overhead. A faint breeze crept around the mountain and rustled the fragrant branches of the shrub which concealed him. Only a little more time. He muttered a short prayer to his own personal war god. That was a joke too. He didn't really believe in gods.

The assassin didn't much believe in anything.

Nakamura had been dreaming. He thought it was a terrible dream but, as he opened his eyes, the thin bloody rags of it flapped away and only a bitter mental aftertaste remained. It left him feeling violated. He reached up and touched his cheek and felt a sheen of sweat.

"Shag. Mr. Nakamura. Wake up."

"Don't touch me."

The man bending over his desk withdrew his hand. He was a tall blond man, hair cut short, gray suit impeccable. He had a sort of open Southwestern American face which, at first glance, seemed appealing. But his brown eyes were utterly blank and Shag was struck once again by the frightening mystery of this man he'd created through torture and betrayal, both his and Oranson's.

"Sorry," Frederic Oranson said.

Nakamura waved him away. "What is it?" He felt terribly tired. He'd been up into the late hours trying to keep track of this war he waged against most of the rest of the world. It was a war of murderous shadows, where death came silently by knife or poison or worse, didn't come at all. Some of the ones who survived would wish they had died, he promised himself. It would be a mercy.

"It's all right. I'm—" Nakamura almost said "tired," but that would have been an admission of weakness he could not allow himself. "I'm irritable. It's been a long night." His smooth tenor dropped slightly, became brisker, more businesslike. "Catch me up. I dozed awhile."

Oranson stared at his boss for an instant. Shigeinari Nakamura appeared young for a man who controlled the single most powerful conglomerate on earth. But if he turned his head just so, the morning light slanting through cracks in the thick draperies revealed a network of fine lines that even the best surgical and monoclonal Retin-A treatments couldn't entirely eradicate. Shag Nakamura was older than he looked. Oranson wasn't deceived. It was only another weapon, as everything was to his driven Japanese master.

"Yes," Oranson said. He gestured toward a pair of video monitors inset into the top of Nakamura's priceless antique mahogany desk. "Have you been following the fine details?"

"As much as I can. Given the strategic situation. What happened in Old Bonn, for instance?"

"We sent in killer teams," Oranson said noncommittally. "Two teams made it back out."

A shadow passed quickly across Nakamura's smooth features. His black eyes snapped once, then were hooded again. Oranson continued quickly. "The teams achieved their objectives. The Chancellor is dead. Long live the new Chancellor."

Nakamura permitted himself a small, satisfied smile. "I would have liked to have seen that. The German was a pig. An arrogant one, as well." He paused. "Like all the rest. What about the new man?"

"In our pocket. Bought and paid for a long time ago."

"Certainly. But the question is, will he stay bought?"

Now Oranson allowed his own lips to quirk upwards. "You didn't see the late Chancellor's demise, but his successor was . . . permitted . . . to observe. The reports say he was quite impressed. There are tapes, by the way. Would you like to see?"

The Japanese pushed the fingers of his right hand through his stiff brush of shiny black hair. He tilted his round head back and stretched his neck. "No. Business before pleasure. But keep the tapes."

"Of course," Oranson said.

An insistent, silent pricking in the ball of his thumb woke the assassin an hour before dawn. He tapped the face of his nailtale to shut off the alarm and permitted his eyes to open into slits. False dawn turned a silver line along the distant horizon. Mist smoked across the silent field below, swirling and bunching like ghostly fists above the bulky specters of the cattle. He could hear the soft, plaintive noises they made.

The lights were still glowing behind the curtains of the house, but he had the feeling nothing moved in the room beyond. It was only an intuition, but he trusted such hunches. Not everything could be explained.

Then his mind turned to immediate problems. He had landed black in the dark of night, a shadow on shadows. The surface of his camo suit was stealthed, designed to soak up everything from infrared to radar. At night he should be safe from everything but visual observation, and even that was nearly impossible. But daylight was another story. Soon morning would burn down, and even hidden beneath shrubs he couldn't be certain of escaping detection in the footprint of an overhead spysat on routine patrol. This estate would almost certainly be closely observed. His masters had planned for that as well. Their minds were insectlike in thoroughness and hunger for detail.

Grunting quietly he began to slip out of his night camo suit until he lay naked on the ground. He was careful to muffle any clink or chink of metal, and prudent as well of sudden movement. It was hard to guess what kind of detectors might be spotted in the forest, but insane to suppose that nothing guarded the silent trees.

He lay for a moment on his back, feeling the slow, damp wind roll over his body. False dawn was becoming real. Only a few of the brightest stars still glimmered overhead. He breathed in and out slowly, willing a certain calm. The calm was necessary, for he knew he was about to die. This would be his last dawn, unless he was wrong about the shared joke of gods and men, and there was truly something beyond the gates of death.

He couldn't allow that to interfere with his mission. A sure hand, strong nerves, a calm mind. Death was only a minor distraction.

Thinking such thoughts he began to turn his camo suit inside out. The inner surfaces of the suit were coated with a thin layer of pressed mimetic carbon fibers which imitated any background. As he slid into the reversed suit he tried to think of himself as a chameleon of the technological age, placid and certain as the lizard itself.

He had to get closer to be sure of the kill. Across the field would be best, but halfway would do. He pulled Velcro fasteners shut and blinked thoughtfully. The Little Man launcher was a comforting weight beneath his hand. It would be his last mission. He didn't intend to botch it.

Dreams of life and death. Was there a difference? Only his ancestors knew. He sighed and continued the wait.

Nakamura took a light breakfast in the great room where he'd spent most of the last three days. It wasn't any hardship. The house itself was a rambling wooden design that somehow contained forty-three rooms. A wallpaper baron had built it for his mistress almost two hundred years before, when houses like it were called cottages. Nakamura ate his cold cereal and skim milk alone at a table in front of a huge fieldstone fireplace across from his desk. Oranson kept watch on the various monitors and screens which were dotted about the vast room. Most of the screens were inset into the paneled wall behind Nakamura, usually concealed by Van Goghs and Monets gathered up in the frenzied corporate bidding of Japanese conglomerates the century before. Nakamura-Norton, Double En, had then swallowed the conglomerates, in some cases simply because Nakamura coveted the art that hung on their home office walls.

He ate slowly, without passion, chewing his cereal thoroughly before swallowing. His black button eyes shifted from one screen to another. Some screens showed videos. Snippets of short, bloody action or longer shots of distant explosions and fires. One screen was full of distorted, shouting faces—a mob in full cry. He watched for a long moment. The picture shook, jittered, and fell away.

"What happened there?"

"The cameraman got too close. Stupid."

Nakamura nodded and spooned up the last of his skim milk, then pushed the empty lacquer bowl away. The bowl was worth more than the table it sat on, and the price of the table would have built the house that sheltered it. Nakamura didn't look at the bowl after he was done, though it was exquisite. He had no idea how much it had cost. He never knew how much things cost anymore. He never bothered to ask.

"Arius?" Nakamura said.

Oranson paused. He stopped moving for an instant, and then he moved again, turning his blank eyes toward a distant screen that was as empty as his expression. "Nothing."

"Three days now?"

"Yes," Oranson said.

"Too bad." There was an unholy glee in Nakamura's voice.

"Yes," Oranson said again. But there was nothing at all in his voice. It was dead.

The assassin had removed his light-gathering vision inserts and replaced them with thin polarized goggles made of a pressurized liquid plastic sealed between two polymer lenses. He tightened the muscles of his forehead and, obediently, the tiny chip embedded in the frame of the goggles sensed the movement and activated an invisible pump. The liquid between the lenses swelled slightly. He kept moving his forehead until he could watch the patio behind the house with a thirty-power increase in his eyesight.

The sun was over the horizon now. It was at his back, but a layer of low-lying clouds ringed the far horizon in a bloody, swollen line. He tried to remember the old Western axiom. Red sky at night, sailor's delight. But what was the morning? Something warning, he thought, but wasn't sure. He pushed the riddle away.

Ah. Yes. Two uniformed guards sporting Aachen-20 machine pistols appeared at the far end of the patio and began to march down its length. They moved briskly and seemed alert. He glanced at his nailtale. Right on the money. This little patrol passed by every twenty minutes. Evidently their post was nothing more than a circle around the house. Predictable as sheep.

They didn't bother him. But now he saw something that did.

The tiny figure ambled slowly across the center of the patio. He moved silently, because neither of the guards showed any awareness of his presence. The assassin knew what kind of skill it took to cross creaking wooden floorboards and give no hint to listeners only ten feet away.

The little yellow man on the patio moved with a slow fluidity, as if his muscles were made of some kind of cold but elastic metal. The assassin pressed himself closer to the earth and risked a glance at the sleeve of his camo suit. It was working. His arm mimicked perfectly the colors of the earth on which it rested, even to the few blades of yellowing grass which he'd crushed as he burrowed in.

Even so he felt a twinge of nerves as the small yellow man

13

paused in his quiet pacing. He turned his face away from the house and for an instant looked directly at the assassin's hiding place. The assassin held his breath and tried to think long, innocent thoughts. Some of those who resembled the man below had hunches—intuitions—as good as his own. He might survive a struggle with one of those, but his mission would not.

After what seemed a long time the figure lowered its head and turned back to the house. The assassin tried to follow his movements, but when the little man disappeared, the assassin couldn't quite see how he'd done it.

Good. Very good.

He hissed the thought to himself. The Blade of God was a traitor to the Temple. Yet he was as close as anything the assassin might call brother. Too close.

The assassin would have enjoyed killing him if he could. But it wasn't likely he'd get the chance. He checked his nailtale one more time as a bright blue bird flew overhead with a flap and a harsh cawing croak. Where was the target? Why was he late?

Would that be what went wrong?

Nakamura clasped his hands behind his back and wandered in the direction of the windows. His face was impassive. "Already morning." He peered through a place where the heavy drapes were cracked slightly open and sighed.

"You should rest," Oranson said. "Real rest. In a bed."

"I can't." Nakamura said nothing more, but there was a world of explanation in the two words. Oranson understood. He'd been with the man a long time, through service and betrayal and service again. And while no one could say they were friends—there was too much of a gulf between them—they had a working knowledge of each other.

Oranson watched his master without appearing to do so. Shag seemed sharper these last few days, as if the long hours of battle had awakened him, made him more clear and decisive. Something had happened awhile before, and for a time Nakamura had seemed almost in a trance. The incident had involved Arius, the bizarre fusion of man— William Norton, Nakamura's former partner—and machine— the runaway Lunie Artificial Intelligence which had manipulated them for so long. The fusion called itself Arius and took human form as a stunted, weirdly deformed child.

This war was the work of Arius. But Arius had not been seen or heard from since its beginning, and now Nakamura was blooming as he had not for months.

Oranson was sure it was connected. He wondered how it might affect his own future. It was a question to consider, but the greater conflict had to be resolved first. Nakamura had always been a dangerous man. He was still dangerous.

"We will win," Oranson said quietly.

Nakamura turned away from the window. The epicanthic folds of his eyes hid any meaning. His face seemed bisected by black lines. "Yes, I think so. I might have thought differently two days ago, but now I agree." His bulky chest rose and fell once.

"Perhaps I should rest. But it will be over soon. That will be the time."

"Of course," Oranson said.

"Have you tried to find out about Arius?"

It was a tricky question. Oranson considered his answers. If he said he had, which was the truth, then Nakamura might be angered. Arius had never brooked meddling in his affairs, and his vengeance could be terrible. On the other hand, to deny any effort might be construed as failing Nakamura's own interests, and that could be dangerous as well. Oranson told the truth. It was safer.

"Yes. Mostly direct queries. I've dispatched a team, but they haven't reported back yet."

"To Chicago? The Labyrinth?"

Oranson nodded. "Yes."

Nakamura walked slowly to his desk. He ran his fingers lightly across the polished wood, as if the tactile contact gave him pleasure. Oranson knew it did. He wondered when Nakamura would seek other tactile pleasures, and made a mental note to have such things in readiness.

"Is there any possibility Arius is . . ."

They glanced at each other. Each filled in the missing word, but neither spoke. The death of Arius would be a wonderful thing. But acting on, even speaking of such a consummation might bring horrible results. They let the silence remain between them, acknowledged and understood.

"I'm going outside for awhile," Nakamura said.

Oranson had been expecting it. While the Japanese could go a long time without sleep, he needed something to maintain his energy level. In Nakamura's case, it was a short time of meditation. Oranson didn't understand the pleasures of the rock garden behind the house, but he accepted them.

"A moment," he said, and touched a button set into one of the wood-and-glass doors. The drapes slid back a bit, until two of the doors were completely revealed. He pushed the doors open and stepped out onto the wooden patio.

The morning air smelled damp and fresh. Dew had not yet evaporated from the field beyond the garden wall, although the cattle were beginning to move about. He caught a sharp whiff of their animal smell, a mixture of hide and shit and grass.

It was a peaceful scene, but Oranson was not deceived. He scanned the dark line of the forest further up the mountain. The forest made him nervous. It was public land and Double En had never been able to purchase it. He'd scattered what precautions he could among the trees, but had no confidence in his ability to secure the area against any professional penetration. The meadow and its innocent-looking cattle, however, was a killing field.

Far overhead a flight of ducks winged by. He heard their distant cries. Bootsteps crunched and he turned. The regular guards approached. They saluted him as they passed. He followed them with his eyes until they turned a corner and disappeared.

One more time he scanned the area. The jagged rocks in the neatly raked gravel of the garden cast long morning shadows. There was a rhythm, a serenity to the arrangement that he sensed but didn't fully comprehend.

Which was a new turn. Perhaps he was changing as well. Before, the garden had only been rocks and sand to him. Now it was becoming something else.

An interesting thought.

He turned. "It's okay. Come on out."

Nakamura stepped out into the sunlight, blinking. He walked slowly over to a wooden bench and sank down, facing the garden.

"Leave me alone," he said.

Oranson nodded and wandered away down the patio. Already his mind was turning to the impending victory and

16

what it might hold for him. Particularly if Arius had in some unimaginable way become a non-factor.

Would Nakamura style himself emperor of the earth, or would the power alone be enough for him?

The assassin breathed a small sigh of relief to himself when he finally saw the drapes part on the long wall of glass doors. A tall blond man he'd never seen before stepped out on the patio and gazed around.

He searched his mind for a picture, but nothing came. Perhaps it was Oranson, the mystery man who supervised the uglier, more pragmatic aspects of Double En's vast empire. He wasn't certain. His briefing hadn't included this man.

He scented danger, but after a time the feeling subsided. The man sensed nothing. He turned and said something to somebody inside the house, and then Nakamura appeared.

The assassin watched the Japanese walk slowly to a bench and sit. He cranked up the power of his visual inserts until he could almost see the faint lines at the corner of Nakamura's dark eyes.

He looks tired, the assassin thought. His lips curved into a bleak smile. Very soon this target could rest.

We can rest together, he thought.

Already he was beginning his breathing discipline. He could feel his body respond. It was almost as if he were filling up with pure light. The Blade of God he'd seen earlier had not reappeared, which was good. He feared the Blade. But he saw nothing else that could stop him. Certainly not the blond man who had ambled off down the patio and was facing away from his position. He didn't even think about the guard patrol and their machine pistols.

Instead he concentrated on his target. At first he'd thought he might have to make his shot from the woods, but given the peacefulness of the setting he decided he could rush the middle of the field to increase his certainty. The heavy bodies of the cattle might shield him, and he could be there in fractions of a second. There would be no time for reaction.

Just to be on the safe side he muttered a short prayer to gods he didn't believe in. Then the killing frenzy took him and he began to rise from the earth.

Like a hero, he thought, full of light. Like a hero.

* * *

Nakamura felt the seat of the bench beneath his bony buttocks. He was a wide, solid man but not fleshy, and the wood was hard. He remained still for a moment, then consciously willed himself to relax. It always took a few moments before he began to sink into the garden, began to savor the simple patterns which took him away from the complexities of his life.

And what a long road it had been. If he allowed it, the incidents, treacheries, triumphs of it would overwhelm him merely with their numbers.

He pushed his back against the bench as if to push the weight of memory away, and after a moment he was able to focus on a particular boulder near the center of the raked gravel. It protruded like a rotten tooth but there was a desolate beauty to it that sucked him in.

He let his mind open to the stone, feeling the familiar pounding of his blood in his temples. But he couldn't quite submerge himself. Some nameless thing tugged at his attention.

Slowly he tilted his head back and opened his eyes wider. He saw the meadow and beyond it the black line of forest.

Something moved.

It was shifting and hard to see. The morning sun flared into his eyes. He squinted, but by the time he understood a man was there, where a man should not be, it was already too late.

The cattle began to converge.

Chapter Two

Karl Wier glanced up, momentarily distracted by a sudden gush of noise from the rim of Kennedy Crater. He squinted, sighed at the horde of new arrivals clustering at the top of the chain lifts, and turned back to the small, tense group of men and women seated round the table with him.

"We're getting awfully crowded," he remarked.

Elizabeth Meklina, her smooth black features chill and distant, said, "Refugees." A world of distaste colored the single word.

Wier nodded. "There will be more, of course." He sounded tired. "Nakamura is terrorizing whole nations down there in his efforts to root out the New Church."

Meklina gestured to the waiter for a coffee refill. Overhead the crystal dome of the crater was mildly polarized, but still admitted a blaze of raw sunlight which caught her tight-packed silver curls and turned them molten. "Let them die."

"Drastic."

"We can't absorb refugees indefinitely. We have our own problems."

"Which some of these people may help with. We haven't been entirely unselective."

Meklina nodded minutely, her golden eyes slitted with distance. "We take the rich ones, yes. And the high technicians. But Nakamura isn't letting the real prizes off earth. He may be a hog, but he's a smart hog. He won't give us any advantage he can avoid. When he's finished consolidating his position downwell, then his next move is obvious."

"Us," Wier said. His voice was somber. "But we knew that anyway. Didn't we?"

"Fucking aye." She shifted slightly in her chair. "Does he, though?"

"That depends."

19

"Where's the goddam coffee?" Meklina said, glancing over her shoulder at the waiter's back. She turned. "Depends on what?"

"Whether he'll be satisfied with a single planet. Or whether he wants it all."

The coffee arrived.

The man and the woman seemed to fit in well with the mob of refugees choking the space at the top of the lifts. They had the slightly harried, vaguely frightened air of intelligent, middle-class technocrats rudely uprooted from their settled existence and thrust willy-nilly into an uncertain future. He was tall and slender, with a forgettable face and lines of wiry muscle on his hairless forearms. She was shorter, pudgy, and had scratches of earnest worry engraved on her snub-nosed features. She looked like a mother balancing a career and home life and not succeeding entirely at either. They made an obvious couple; he held her elbow as he steered her through the crowd, and she looked at his eyes when he spoke. Yet there were no children in evidence. They were a pair, but alone.

"Henry," she said. Her voice verged on shrillness. "Henry, I don't know about this chain thing. What if I fall?"

He smiled down at her, and his long, horsy features lost their tension and became almost attractive. "Not to worry, Madge. I'll keep hold of you."

Reassured, she let him lead her farther toward the rim of the precipice overlooking the vast hole of Kennedy Crater itself.

Three calm Lunies rode herd on the crowd, superior in the ease with which they negotiated the lesser gravity of Luna while unsorting various clots of confusion. Henry and Madge finally reached the edge and looked over.

"Oh, my," Madge said.

"Pretty spectacular," Henry replied.

Down below, and inset into the cliffs surrounding the floor, the glittering panoply of the solar system's largest company town went about its business. The floor of the crater was covered with hundreds of roofless buildings. Here and there were a few covered structures, and Henry supposed they were for privacy. The weather was controlled here. There was a regular grid of streets bringing some order to the small metropolis, and more people than he'd expected prowled there, moving with the trademark Lunie glide in the lowered gravity. Madge made soft cooing noises with her rosebud lips at each new wonder. "Look. They have wings."

He followed her pointing finger. "Kids. Microlite kites. And wingsets. They make them out of stretched carbon sheets reinforced with monomole threads. Very strong."

"But Henry, flying. How wonderful!"

"I suppose."

"Do you think?"

He shrugged. "We have to get settled first. We were lucky to get here at all."

She shivered and moved closer to him. "That awful Nakamura. He's a terrible man."

Henry nodded. The Lunie proctor who happened to overhear this bit of conversation grinned to himself. These groundhogs—hogs, as he thought of them—seemed to have the proper grateful attitude. Perhaps eventually they might make good Lunie citizens. Not true Lunies, of course, but reasonable facsimiles.

He wondered what their specialities might be. Something high tech and valuable. They wouldn't have been admitted, otherwise.

"Look, Henry. What's that? That place with all the pretty umbrellas?"

Henry squinted, then took a minioptic from the complimentary tourist packet he'd been given on the shuttle. "A restaurant, looks like."

"Really? Maybe we could try it when we get down. I'm hungry."

He stared at a large table near the front of the place. "Maybe," he said.

Wier watched the waiter leave the table after serving more coffee. His eyes were hooded and thoughtful. The waiter was young, fresh-faced, and seemed not at all awed by the lords of Lunar technology whom he served. But then, Wier reflected, there was no reason he should be. And thought once again what a shame it all was. He sighed and turned back to the group.

"Franny, what about you? Good news or bad?" Wier

received a morning *précis* which summarized anything of note occurring in the previous twenty-four hours, but he preferred these morning *kaffeeklatches* as his real source of information. The hardcopy reports never included the raised eyebrow, the shift in voice tone that signaled true importance.

Franklin Webster, a roly-poly man whose cherubic face belied a tendency toward savage sarcasm, sipped at his fresh coffee and raised his eyebrows innocently. "You're talking about the Low Energy Variable Input Nanocomputer, I presume?"

"Yes, asshole, I'm talking about Levin. Anything new?"

Franny shrugged. "Buttoned up tighter than Yahweh's sphincter," he said. "Nothing in, nothing out. Not since the power input redlined and blew out half the comm system's surge protectors."

Wier pulled at his cheeks. The flesh there was like rubber, gray and doughy, and his fingers left red marks that slowly disappeared. "Wonderful. But everything's online again except Levin himself?"

"Sure. Even Levin, actually. The bugger's there, all right. Just not loading or downloading. Staring at his fucking navel, for all I know." Franny seemed disgusted.

"Should we anthropomorphize the damned thing?" Meklina broke in. "All this he and his bullshit? It's a fucking machine."

"It refers to itself as 'he.' Maybe he'll show me his balls someday. Now that," Franny went on dreamily, "would be a sight."

"Yeah. You'd think so."

"As would you, my dear."

"Lovely," Wier said sourly. "Why don't you two go off in a corner and compare your sexual proclivities? The rest of us can try to get some work done."

"Oh, we wouldn't agree on anything," Franny said. "Lizzybet is aptly named."

"Fuck you," Meklina said.

"Not on the best day of your life, dear. I like my machines straight."

"You don't like anything straight."

"Children," Wier said, "calm yourselves."

Meklina subsided, her black face nettled. Franny grinned beatifically.

"Okay," Wier continued. "So we're well and truly hung, is that right?"

Franny's grin widened. "Not an uncolorful phrase, but accurate. I wish we could find out just what that band of crazies is doing inside our computer. We can make inferences, of course."

Wier nodded. "Make some."

Franny raised one fleshy hand and began to tick down fingers. "First, we presume Berg was successful in his primary objective. We've seen no evidence of any activity on Terra from Arius. Even that pocket Hades he set up under Chicago seems abandoned."

"That's something," Wier said. "And if Arius is out of the picture, it would explain Nakamura running wild. But is Arius gone? And what about Berg and Calley? Did they all destroy each other, and Levin along with them? Or what?"

"Beats hell out of me, chief."

Wier sighed. "Keep trying."

"Of course."

"Anybody got anything else?"

Nobody answered him. He thought about the improbable contents of the metacomputer named Levin. Then he shook his head. "That's it, then," he said, beginning to rise.

A small band of refugees, cut out from the main herd en route to temporary quarters, stumbled and lurched past the restaurant. For one moment Wier locked eyes with a tall, thin man who held the arm of a smaller, chubby woman. It was only an instant, but Wier felt suddenly uncomfortable.

The man had seemed to know him.

But it was barely a flash. Wier shrugged and turned away. All this uncertainty was making him jumpy.

"You're lucky to get a cubicle to yourself," the proctor said. "Private cubes are hard to come by, what with all you hogs pouring in."

Henry surveyed the tiny room, barely three meters on a side. A throbbing hum, so deep it was hardly audible, quivered in his bones. "What's that?"

The Lunie blinked. "Oh. You mean the diggers. This is a new tunnel, just started a few weeks ago. Half a klom farther down is bare rock. That's why these cubes are available now. We don't like the noise much."

"But it's okay for us," Henry said innocently.

"Well, of course." The proctor seemed puzzled.

"Of course."

After the door was safely closed, Madge said, "I don't think I like that young man."

"He's an insular, chauvinist jerk," Henry replied. "Which is to say, he's a Lunie." He examined the room. There was a bed that might be wide enough for the two of them, if they could sleep unmoving. A small table and two chairs. A cupboard-closet inset into an unfinished rock wall. And a standard comm monitor and keyboard. He went to the monitor and examined it. "Voice activated, too," he said. "Only the best for us huddled, miserable hogs."

"What a nasty name," Madge said.

"I've been called worse," Henry told her. His fingers found her palm and began an intricate, unobtrusive dance.

The small man with muddy eyes and a dirty fringe of dark hair overhanging his big ears stared at the tiny chip. It had magically appeared inside a small envelope on the top of his message box. He felt his pulse rise slowly. He didn't bother to plug in the chip. Whatever it carried was totally innocuous. The chip itself was the message. He blinked three times, an autonomic mechanism that came into play whenever he felt tense. Then he tossed the chip into a shredbasket and stood up behind his minuscule desk. The other technician with whom he shared his crowded, cramped office, glanced up.

"Something wrong?" she said.

He forced himself to smile. "No. Nothing." And there wasn't. He'd always known, even from the day he signed on, that it might come to this.

Wier entered the main lab complex with a sense of foreboding. Webster had his usual coterie of assistants gathered around the banked monitors governing the Levin. The older man, his jolly, mocking air gone, instructed them in yet another attempt to break through the guardian wall with which the metamachine had surrounded itself.

Of course, Wier thought, we could always turn the motherfucker off. He shook his head. It wasn't a viable option. Yet. And there were other problems. . . .

24

He walked slowly past two of them, paused, and stared down at the tanks. Dimly, through the smoked shields inset into the top of the tanks, he could see their faces. Calley smiled an enigmatic smile that never changed. Ozzie, on the other hand, seemed to shift expressions slowly, like a face seen beneath deep water. He tapped lightly on the top of Ozzie's tank. No response. Thoughtfully he leaned over and checked the basic readouts. As far as he could tell there was nothing new. The two corpsesicles inside might well have been dead, but they weren't. Not dead, just on vacation. Visiting the one that didn't have a body at all.

He shuddered and walked on.

Lizzybet Meklina awaited him in his office, her feet on his desk as she lounged back in his chair, a sheaf of hardcopy in her large, stub-fingered hands. "Uhm. This mean you're taking my job?" he asked mildly.

She glared at him over the top of the printouts. "You get a look at this jive bullshit, man?"

"Not yet. You haven't showed it to me. Now get your fucking feet off my desk."

"What? Oh. Sorry." She heaved herself up from the chair, a startlingly graceful motion for a woman who seemed to be made of partially congealed cinder blocks. Her face was shiny with sweat and her eyes seemed to bulge. Wier ignored her. She always looked like that.

"Okay, which jive bullshit?"

She hooked one massive haunch over the edge of his desk, leaned over, and breathed on him. She'd somehow had something with garlic in it since breakfast. He wondered what it might have been, and pictured her eating a pizza with both massive hands. Then he closed his eyes and made the picture go away.

"Projections, Karl. Thank God we still have some machines that work. I told you not to hang everything on that goddamned Levin thing. Look what happened to Nakamura-Norton when their database went up the tubes."

"And you were right, Lizzy. You were right." He rubbed his forehead. His eyes were flat, surrounded with a tracery of tiny broken capillaries, and seemed empty as a mountain lake in winter. "So what kind of projections have you got? A little something to cheer me up?"

"Nakamura will win." Her voice had a tiny growl of fear in it.

"That certain?"

"Dead fucking aye," she said. "He's just about got it wrapped up. Mean, shifty little fucker, that one. All that samurai background, maybe."

He leaned back and stared at her blankly. "Does that strike you as a tiny bit racist, darling?"

"Piss on that. Of course I'm racist. I'm black, aren't I?"

But she glanced away for an instant. "I don't have much use for hogs, either."

He burst out laughing. He couldn't help it, and he couldn't stop. She watched him warily. Then her own thick lips began to quiver. Finally she pounded on one thigh with a thud like a cleaver slamming meat and began to make sounds that reminded him of country dogs he remembered from his youth.

"Oh, God," she snorted. "Honey, you do make me laugh sometimes." She inhaled, coughed, and spit on his floor. "Damn."

"Well. Look here, Karl. We got to do something, anyway."

He wiped his eyes. "Why do we got to do something?"

"Projections say so. Here. See for yourself."

He glanced at the digital readout on the wall. Barely past morning break, and already the day was a total write-off. He blinked and began to read. After a while he felt something greasy on his lip and realized he'd chewed the tip of his tongue almost in half.

"Here," Lizzybet said. "Use my hanky."

He worked in the main labs and had made it his business over the years to learn the habits of every major player in the Lunie technological establishment. Now, watching the chiefs move among the Indians with long faces and fast, muttered conversations, he realized there would be a meeting that afternoon at the usual place. He wondered if the meeting would concern whatever had pulled his trigger, but then deliberately put the thought away. He was a weapon. He recalled a byword of the previous century, something that went, "Guns don't kill, people do." He grinned.

He wondered what those vanished reformers would have thought of him.

He gave himself a few moments to summon up the proper queasy expression, then sought his supervisor. "Hey, Candy."

"Yeah?"

"I don't feel so good. Maybe some kind of bug, huh? Something those fucking hogs brought with them."

"Jesus, you pick your times, don't you? All right. Check out. If you can't make it tomorrow, leave a message in my voicemail box."

"Oh, sure. No problem."

He knew it wouldn't be a problem. He wouldn't be making anything tomorrow. Or ever.

The waiter hummed softly to himself as he reset the big front table for the late afternoon reservation. Wier and Meklina and old chubs, Franny Webster. He knew why they hung out at Bobby's Place. It was a spot favored by what passed for the *ancien* aristocracy of Luna, a place where they felt comfortable. It was also tailor-made for his own plans. He was surprised to realize he had plans, after all. He'd thought he could opt out of the formless, gigantic race engendered by his grandfather, but after two years of slinging hash and pouring booze, the amorphous dissatisfaction which had plagued him had begun to crystallize.

Maybe I'm growing up, he thought with sudden wonder.

Then again, maybe not.

He arranged a vase of silk roses in the center of the table and continued his tuneless tune.

"What's the matter with your mouth? You talk funny," Franny said.

"Bit my tongue," Wier told him.

"Oh. Too bad."

"You want me to kiss it, make it well?" Meklina mumbled.

"Kiss this," Franny replied.

Three department heads had joined the triumvirate, but they'd learned to shut their mouths shut and keep their heads down when the weather at the rarefied levels was this unsettled. Meklina, Franny, and even Wier had been known to take notes and act on them later.

Wier sipped iced coffee. His wounded tongue couldn't take heat. He sucked thoughtfully on an ice cube. "Lizzy, you want to lay out that projection you showed me?"

The black woman leaned back in her chair. Even in the diminished Lunar gravity, the spindly metal construction creaked softly. She wasted no time. "We're in deep shit," she said.

Franny stared at her.

"Yeah." Meklina sounded almost satisfied. "Not to say I told you so, but at least you listened. We got two of our own meatmatrices on line, saved up for emergencies just like this. No connection whatsoever to Double En's nets at all, though we think there may still be a way to penetrate them. Depends on Arius, and we got no idea what's happening there. So. Until we do, until Berg and Calley and Ozzie decide to come back, or Levin bothers to drop us a note, it's gonna be a direct face-off between Luna, Inc., and Double En."

She paused. "Any questions so far?"

"Yeah," Franny said. "You going to tell us anything new?"

"Uh, right, jism face. The latest projections show that Nakamura will be able to consolidate the New Church and Double En into a single entity that will, in effect, control all major Terran governments. He may not bother to take an official title, but in effect, he'll be running Earth."

Franny nodded, his eyes vague. "Okay. It's turning out worse than we thought, then. High prob, I suppose?"

"On the order of ninety plus."

"Ouch. So he'll be coming after us sooner than we thought?"

"Looks like."

Franny sighed. "Well, we saw it coming. But with Levin it should have been no contest. What kind of probs without him?"

"Lower orders. Low midrange. Not hopeless, because we swing economic clout far in excess of our size. Without that goddam machine, however, it's touch and go, with the bets moving to Nakamura's side the longer it stretches. We can't fight a war of attrition."

Franny glanced at Wier. "So we go to battle stations?"

Wier nodded. He'd already heard this, and wondered if he'd be able to keep things together. The fate of Luna seemed to rest on the fates of Berg, Calley, Arius, and

Levin. Only one of the four even had a body. It didn't seem fair, having everything turn on a bunch of electronic ghosts.

"We already are." He clinked his ice and saw a vaguely familiar face moving toward their table. Short, big-eared man with muddy brown eyes. Some kind of minor tech. He hoped it wasn't more bad news.

Then he heard Bobby shout behind him: "Karl, look out! He's got a gun!" A Bausch Weapons International .05 needler, Wier noted, and wondered how the fuck he got *that* past customs.

No chance, he realized, as the assassin's lips stretched back to reveal yellowed teeth. Wier's life didn't pass before him. He thought this killer should have brushed his teeth more often. And he wondered why the hog refugee he'd seen earlier, the slender one with the knowing eyes, was coming up right behind the man with the gun.

Chapter Three

Danny Boy MacEwen watched the shadow jitter and tried to figure out what it reminded him of. In the invisible distance water dripped on something hollow and rusty and for one dizzy moment he thought the sound might be coming from his own heart. Faint wisps of moisture curled around his bare toes and sent shivers up his calves. He knew he had to move. It was absolutely essential. His muscles were already beginning to cramp.

But he couldn't move. The shadow was so . . . interesting.

Danny Boy crouched just outside the ruined door of the dark room in the center of the Labyrinth, frozen by a sensation he remembered all too well from his childhood. He'd been the tenth in a seemingly endless chain of MacEwen children. His early years had been a textbook example of the dynamics of tribal infighting for space, food, love. All three, he remembered, had been in short supply in the ramshackle house in New Munster, a quarry town in the rocky hills of southern Indiana. Now, his misshapen muscles were congealed with cold and terror, and he recalled the nightmares that were his earliest memories.

He had lost all feeling in his left leg. There was a long, scabbed gash on his thigh beneath the charred remnants of his jeans. Sometimes he remembered the fight; gods and demons had contended with thunder and lightning beneath the crumbling ceilings of the Lab. The short Rager with the jailhouse face had blown his leg apart—he saw the moment vividly still. Then darkness, and when he awakened, darkness and silence and a feeling of vast emptiness. The infinite weight of the city and the undercity pressed him down, but even so, a spark remained. He'd begun to crawl deeper into the heart of the darkness, seeking the only kind of solace he knew.

The soft white flickering began again and he wanted to

scream, but his tongue was swollen and arid between his jagged, pointed canines. The sound of the water dripping pushed him closer to madness. He knew it had been a mistake to come here, but he'd had no choice. He didn't understand what the fight had been about, but he knew that those in the upper city would only finish what had begun down below. The dark could be terrifying, but the starry night above held death for his kind.

He scraped his raw tongue over his cracked lips and tried to push himself forward. The white flickering was like the times he'd awakened in his childhood, wedged between the sweating bodies of his brothers, and seen the moon fill their shabby room with cold blue light. He'd felt it then, the need and the terror, known even then that something was coming for him. Something just on the other side of the door. Something he waited for all unknowing, a scream wedged in his throat, while the horror snuffled and shuffled just beyond the light.

The sweet monstrosity. His whole life had been an escape from it, but now it had found him at last. Fluids leaked from the edge of his eyes, matted the fur of his face, dripped onto the crusted fabric of his tee shirt.

He made a soft snorting sound. His claws scrabbled on the scarred concrete as he pulled himself forward into the room. Past the door, toward the dancing white light. The light that was a shadow, calling him.

"I don't know," Gloria Calley said, "how much I like this Little Bo Peep shit."

She lounged on the perfect green side of a perfect green hill. She wore skintight, bright red leather pants and a short-sleeved shirt of the same color and constriction. Her boots came to needle toes and heels, both tipped with chrome that flashed in the light of the overhead sun. Farther down the hill sheep grazed, bland balls of white wool and black, slow-chewing faces.

She spit out the stem of grass she'd been gnawing and glanced at Ozzie. "This your fucking construct, boy?"

He wore a headband made of several leather watch straps glued together around his halo of curly blond hair, pulling it back from a pair of horn-rimmed glasses which contained no lenses. He also wore madras-print Bermuda shorts and ancient black wingtip shoes without socks. His bony shoulders had begun to turn an unhealthy rose color. And, if anything, his seven-foot frame, which he was trying to teach himself to think of in metric terms—the number 213 centimeters popped up behind his eyeballs—was skinnier than it had been before he'd left it behind.

"Nah," he said. "This look like Ozzie to you? I think it's Berg, or maybe Levin mirroring one of Berg's fantasies."

She scratched the crotch of her leather jeans. Suddenly the spectacular outfit disappeared entirely and she lay naked on the grass. "That's better," she said. "You think this is one of Berg's fantasies? Sheep grazing? That's really weird."

"Berg is right out of a psychology primer," Ozzie said. "A churning mass of repressions."

She stared at him doubtfully. "We talking about the same guy? Little dude with a big nose?"

"Repressions," Ozzie repeated. "Big nose, lots of repressions. Sheep. It's probably sexual."

A voice spoke out of the air to them. "It's me, not Berg. He doesn't have time for maintenance. What's the matter? You don't like sheep? I think they're kind of restful."

Calley closed her eyes. "Hi, Levin. What's up?"

"*Nada*," the disembodied voice replied. "Slow day at the brain bomb factory."

"They up to their usual tricks?"

There was no reply, but the sky overhead turned into churning layers of fire and fog. Across one half of the heaving dome lay a crystalline sword. A vast, bloated crimson shape obscured the other half. The tableau held a moment, then disappeared. Fluffy white clouds, resembling giant versions of the sheep, rode the blue sky again.

"Working on it," Levin said.

"Jesus," Ozzie said.

"Ain't it just," Levin replied. The voice sounded cheerful.

"Do something about those fucking sheep," Calley told him.

He'd been a beautiful boy. His sisters, even his mother told him so. Some breed of sport, a kind of genetic anomaly in the lumpy, flat chromosomal twists of the MacEwen clan. Pretty as a girl, almost, with long lashes, thin, high cheekbones, and eyes the color of the oak leaves which covered their house in fall. So, of course, his older brothers used him like a girl, because he was handy. Because he was terrified of them, and they liked that. Even, once, his father, stinking of cheap bourbon and week-old sweat, had found him alone in the tumbledown barn.

He'd escaped to Chicago two weeks before his fifteenth birthday, leaving all conscious memory of his childhood behind as easily as he left the slow, rotten days of New Munster in his dust. But the dreams were with him, and the Darkstone Ragers waited to welcome him to the stone necropolis on the Lake. He'd been a slave to one of the Rager gangs for almost two years, performing the same functions for the neon pimps as for his demented brothers. The only difference was the pimps let him keep a little of the money. After two years of hoarding he had enough to purchase the operations. It had been three years now, but he still could hear the sound of his finger claws snapping together like castanets and feel the bunching and loosing of massive muscles in his shoulders, forearms, and thighs as he turned his furry back on the sunlight and clickety-clicked down into the darkness of the Labyrinth. It was the first time he'd ever felt safe. Even the Ragers wouldn't follow him into the lower darkness.

She had welcomed him, but that was no surprise. He'd waited for her all his life.

Pain scraped up his ruined thigh as he inched forward, a joyous suspicion dawning in his fevered skull. The shadow that was like a negative, white on shifting black, seemed familiar as he grew closer.

He'd seen the little Japanese warrior thrust his fingers into the wet redness of her brain. He'd seen her fall, and then, later, heard the explosion. She was dead, no doubt about it. So what was this twisting, beckoning shadow of light that was not light?

Maybe her ghost, he thought suddenly. The thought cheered him. Ghosts had never frightened him.

Only the living could do that.

Chester Limowitz figured that life sucked, and then you died. Nothing much had happened recently to disabuse him of that notion. He'd been camping out in the back lab for almost three weeks now, eating canned beans and tuna fish, waiting for the street riots to subside, waiting for San Francisco to return to what passed for normality. He glanced over at the tank.

Robby and Bobby, the two technicians who had helped him barricade the door to the back lab after a mob of New Church trashers had nearly destroyed the front office complex, were sound asleep, crashed out on surplus cots salvaged from the old Civil Defense shelter beneath the lab itself. Robby snored. Chester wondered how long he would be able to hold out.

The riots were already dying down. On the monitor that was perpetually tuned to Nynex NewsNet he'd seen flying squads of Double En bullyboys sweeping the streets from huge floating platforms, mowing down screaming religious fanatics with wide band rippers and vomitgas bombs. Obviously some kind of new order was emerging, but he couldn't figure out what it might be. He turned slightly on his own cot, feeling every minute of his fifty-six years. Robby and Bobby were younger, more resilient. Whichever way the chips came down, they'd find a way to adjust. Chester wasn't sure how adjustable he was anymore. But perhaps there was a way out. He glanced at the tank again, and this time his eyes widened slightly.

Several tank monitors began to flash amber operational warnings. As he watched, two of the screens slid over into scrolling lines of symbols. One of the laser printers whooshed into action.

Massive input, he decided. He was very tired, but something warm and hopeful began to push through his sludgy nervous system. He propped himself up on his elbows. Maybe things would come to a head now. It was the waiting that got to him.

A faint glow began to circulate, like a band of wandering fireflies, through the thick fluids inside the tank. A pump whirred, and the currents inside the tank quickened.

Groaning softly, he forced himself to sit up, to put his feet on the floor. He wished he knew who he worked for. Then he thought about the chaos outside, and was glad he didn't.

He had so few dreams left.

"Robby," he said. "Bobby. Wake your asses up. Something's happening."

* * *

Ozzie watched her with a mildly bemused expression on his face. She lay on her back, still naked, while chains of jewels appeared, traced odd patterns on her small breasts and tight belly, then disappeared.

"That turn you on?" she asked.

He grinned. "Take a look."

"Mm. Maybe the way to a man's heart isn't through his stomach. My mama was wrong after all."

"Depends how kinky the heart is. Now mine . . ."

"Yeah." She sat up and stretched. Her ribs stood out. The rubies and diamonds and emeralds flashed one final time, and then were gone. "Levin. Those fucking sheep."

There was no answer. She sighed. "Crap. Ozzie, how come we need this blue-sky bullshit anyhow? We took the metamatrix straight."

"Does that mean you're not horny?"

"Just answer the question."

"Uh . . . excuse me. Just let me rearrange something here."

She ignored him.

"You remember those original pee cees?"

"Barely. And you don't at all. You're not old enough."

He leered. "I read. And I'm old enough."

"Not to remember," she repeated.

"I guess you aren't horny." He paused. "Well, they had a hell of a time getting people to use them. If you weren't a nerd or willing to spend a whole lot of energy learning how to talk to them, using a pee cee was a bitch. The computer guys finally figured out that if they were gonna sell any of them, they had to make it so normal people could use computers. So they started to develop interfaces. Software. Pull down icons, all that shit. Pretty pictures. Click and point. That's what this is. This bucolic little world is nothing more than a jumped up interface."

She lowered her arms. Now she wore a clean tee shirt and a pair of cutoff shorts. The tee shirt read, "Kiss My Pass," beneath a picture of a Chicago el train. "Bucolic?" She stared at him, shook her head. "But this isn't the matrix."

"Nah. It's more complicated than that, I think. Berg said it was the human matrix. What did he call it?"

"Gestalt space."

"As good a name as any. Descriptive, at least. Picture seven billion meatmatrices. That's a pretty big metamatrix."

"You buy any of this shit, Oz?"

He scratched at the edge of his nose with one grimy fingernail. "I dunno. Something's going on here. It isn't the matrix, I don't think."

"But how the fuck would we *know?*"

He grinned. " 'Cause Berg says so, babe."

Her eyes, glittering like emerald sand, became thoughtful. "Does that seem," she said, "like enough for you?"

"Oh, fuck," he replied. "Here we go again."

Danny Boy had managed to heave himself almost halfway across the wrecked room. Now he paused, panting, his head whirling, and leaned against the tilted bulk of a huge, thronelike metal chair. He could feel heavy cables trailing away from the base of the chair, tangling his legs and ripping at the soft flesh on his palms. His elbows were greasy with some thick, viscous substance that stank of decay and glowed faintly in the darkness. Bits of her flesh, maybe?

He thrust the thought away. The light was growing brighter, taking on shape and form. An awful thrill ran through his body, squeezed his muscles and jangled his nerve endings. He began to croon, a quiet, random, bubbling sound.

The light danced across a shield of high-tech wreckage; shattered monitors with fanglike shards of glass, towers and decks with gaping wounds that dripped fungi of multicolored wires, soft explosions of yellow and black insulation. He turned his face up and let the light play across it.

The curly hair on his face began to sizzle. "Lady," he breathed gently. "Mother."

Robby and Bobby lived together. They'd shared a two-bedroom apartment out in the Sunset District for almost ten years. They were both of average appearance, the same mouse-colored hair and mouse-crap colored eyes, the same mildly receding hairlines. They finished each other's sentences in normal conversation, and seemed hardly to speak at all when they talked to each other, communicating mostly with small gestures and cryptic glances. They spoke their own private language. Limowitz thought they were a very ordinary couple for that time in that city, except for one thing. Neither of them was gay. Sometimes he wondered exactly what their relationship was, and other times he didn't give a shit.

"What," Robby said, "the fuck—"

"Is going on?" Bobby finished.

"The tank. Look at it."

Everybody stared. The milky fluid inside the monomole enclosure had begun to fluoresce. As it brightened the original glowing motes which had circulated there grew hard and sharp, tiny dots of glittering light which began to converge into a roughly shaped form in the center of the liquid.

"Where's the input coming from?" Robby asked. He stood up and shuffled over to the monitors, rubbed his nose, and leaned over the laser printer. "Satellite transcription," he muttered. Like his roommate he was in his late twenties. He rubbed his nose harder. "It's a black bird. I wonder who it belongs to?"

Limowitz snorted. "Whoever pays us to babysit this lab, probably. Check the protocols. Is there a precedent for this?"

Robby continued to watch the printer while Bobby went to the safe, opened it, and withdrew a ten-cent-thick sheaf of hardcopy.

"Uh, yeah." He ran his forefinger down the paper and licked his lips. "Hey, Chet, it's a red one priority." His movements quickened as he turned.

Limowitz raised his eyebrows. "Red one?"

"Uh-huh. Look, right here . . ."

"Give me that fucking thing," Limowitz said.

More shining dots appeared in the tank. A soft, rising whine filled the room as cooling pump arrays kicked in. The room lights flickered. A lot of power, Limowitz thought. One hell of a lot of power.

"How long you think we've been in here?" Calley asked. Off in the hazy distance a few thick gray clouds began to cluster over the horizon. She squinted and thought she could see a veil of rain beneath them. The air was warm and moist and smelled of grass and sheep. It wasn't really her kind of milieu. She was surprised to find she missed the sharp, cold edges of Chicago, the neon-charged nights, the ever-present sense of danger. This world wasn't hers. It was too soft.

"What do you mean?"

"Well, it seems like we've been here a long time. Weeks. But how much time in the real world? Where our bodies are. You forget about that, Oz? Our bodies are on Luna, in the tender care of good old Karl Wier. Doesn't that make you just a little nervous?"

The amber flecks of his eyes seemed to shift slightly. He blinked. "I dunno. Haven't thought about it really."

Her voice grew tart. "Maybe you should. Maybe we ought to ditch this fucking lotusland and think about it. You know? Those are our fucking bodies there."

He shrugged. "Berg isn't worried."

"Berg doesn't even have a body." She paused. "Besides, are you getting the idea Berg maybe doesn't really give a shit about us? I mean, maybe he's got more important things to worry about right now?"

Ozzie glanced up at the sky, where layers of milk and blood had swirled only a short time before. He sighed. "Not much we can do about it. Berg's the Key. We can't get out unless he says so." He tilted his head back and stretched his scrawny neck muscles. "Not very long," he said.

"What?"

"We haven't been here very long in realtime. We operate on Levin time, you know. Real fast. Nanoseconds. We've maybe only been gone a few seconds. I don't know. Hard to tell, without going back and forth."

"But we aren't in the matrix. We're in something else. This gestalt space. Isn't it a human thing? Maybe the time runs slower."

He stared at her. "I don't even know what gestalt space is. Do you?"

She shook her head.

"Well, then," Ozzie said. He closed his eyes and wrinkled his forehead. "We'll see."

"See what?"

"If I can't do something about those fucking sheep."

When he woke up, he was surprised at how much cooler he felt. The fevers had gone. Slowly, in the dark, he ran one claw down his thigh. The scab there had begun to flake away, and he could feel a ridge of hardened flesh beneath. There would be a scar, he supposed.

He blinked. So dark here. And something had happened. Hadn't it?

Wondering, he placed the palm of his right hand on his face. A memory, vague and formless, began to take shape. Burning. Sizzling. Now it came clearer, and he could almost smell the stench of burned hair, of bubbling flesh.

But there was nothing. He dropped his hand. The hair on his cheeks, his forehead, beneath his eyes, was soft and curly and undisturbed.

Had it all been a dream, then? Some kind of delirium brought on by injury, fear, dehydration?

Slowly, he considered. And finally found the other thing.

It hid deep inside him and fluttered long, white, gauzy wings. It hid inside and it hungered.

The darkness tasted of dust and rust. Far away the water drum pounded slowly, echoing in the empty spaces of his skull.

His black lips spread wide. His fanged grin was ghastly.

He levered himself up and began to feel his way out of the room. His foot claws clicked on the stony floor.

It would be hard, leaving the Lab. But he wasn't, really. She would go with him. Every step of the way, up and out into the greater night.

His tongue lolled. It was all forgotten, his brothers, Indiana, his father, the war between the gods. All jumbled together and all gone.

Only this remained. The waiting stars.

The city.

The hunt.

And the prey.

Robby looked at Bobby and raised his left eyebrow. Bobby looked at Robby and quirked the right side of his mouth. Chet Limowitz watched the tank and ignored them.

They had followed the instructions on the protocols. The directions were simple and explicit. Limowitz knew he was only a technician, a sort of high-tech night watchman, and Robby and Bobby were even less skilled. Nevertheless, they could do what they were told.

Sometimes he wondered why he'd stayed at all. Then he

thought about the chaos in the world outside, and he knew. He had no other place to go.

The sound of the pumps changed slightly, grew deeper and more full-throated. The level of the fluid inside the large tank began to drop.

"Jesus," Robby said.

"Christ," Bobby replied.

Limowitz didn't say anything. He just stared, and wondered what he'd signed up for now.

"Pizza."

"And no mutton, either," Ozzie said. "Anchovies and calamari. You like?"

She nodded, her mouth full, her hands dripping. They sat in the corner of a small walk-up joint at the only table. There was a trash can directly behind her, and a dented metal ashtray next to a mismatched salt and pepper in the center of the table. They had a pile of paper napkins and one plastic fork which they ignored. Through the steamy, greasy windows a streetlight hissed and snapped against the night. The corners of the buildings were hard-edged against shadows like knives. It was Chicago, somewhere on the North Side near the dike, one of the areas reclaimed from the water.

"You do good work," she said at last, wiping her mouth with one of the napkins. He grinned.

"I'm Ozzie. The Wiz. That's what I do."

"I was getting to hate those fucking sheep."

He salted another slice of pizza. "I'm getting the hang of it. You want to stay in Chicago for a while?"

"Sure."

A blast of chilly air filled up the small room as someone opened the door and stepped in. Calley looked up.

The newcomer stared at her. He was short and thin and had a big nose. He wore a patched red ski jacket and black jeans over engineer's boots draped with chrome chains.

His eyes were the same color that old coins turn, gray over glints of silver. The bags beneath them were a darker, less healthy shade, as if the metal had run and tarnished.

"You look like shit," Calley said.

Around his neck he wore a chain. A key in the shape of a sword dangled there. He blinked at her, then walked closer.

SINGULARITIES

"I got a job for you two," he said at last.

"I didn't figure this was social."

"Fuck," Ozzie said. "I was just getting comfortable."

Berg grinned, and patted him on the shoulder.

Chapter Four

As the assassin moved, time slowed down. The morning light took on a crystalline purity in which all details became separate and perfect. He was conscious of his feet moving beneath him, carrying him toward the center of the small meadow, toward the shielding bulk of the cattle. Part of him watched the blond man, who still faced away from him. Another part saw Nakamura raise his head. Those black eyes widened with recognition.

Yet another part of him kept time, splitting seconds with metronomic precision. Nakamura had spotted him, but it was all right. The flank of the largest bovine creature shielded him now, and even though the Japanese below was opening his mouth to shout, he wouldn't have enough time. His time was up.

The assassin felt his lips stretch in a rictus across his teeth. The death smile. He raised the rocket launcher, aiming without thought, his mind drawing an invisible line from the snout of the weapon to Nakamura's chest.

The blond man turned, astonishingly quickly. There hadn't been time for a warning. Nakamura was still silent, rising. But the blond had his hand in his coat and out, a dark, glinting shape in his fist.

The assassin slid to a halt and steadied his launcher. Less than an instant more, a final check and aim, and then—

The huge steer that shadowed him spread its jaws wide. There was the glitter of razors behind the soft, mobile gums. Brown eyes went slow and red. The assassin exhaled as his finger caressed the launch button. And the steer gently, precisely, bit through the heavy bunch of muscle at the top of the assassin's thigh.

He screamed.

He'd been prepared for anything but this. The blond man had a wicked grin on his face as he aimed his pistol.

Nakamura's formless shout echoed among the stones of his garden.

Blood spurted in thick, ropey gouts from the assassin's flesh. Shock set in instantly. He felt no pain, although a pink haze was beginning to gather in front of his eyes.

Fog, he thought wonderingly? But there hadn't been—

The steer chewed through the assassin's kneecap with a moist, crunching snap. He heard a long, humming sound, and a bolt of light sizzled into his shoulder, knocking the Little Man launcher away.

But it was a second cow, dancing with balletic perfection, that actually finished the job with a single quick thrust of steel-shod hooves. The assassin's skull exploded like a wet paper bag filled with rotten tomatoes. The first steer leaned closer and peered myopically at the black and crimson rag. Then, methodically, it began to trample the intruder into thick, liquid mush.

"Oranson!" Nakamura shouted.

"Get in the house," Oranson called back.

Nakamura heard steel shutters slamming down behind him, covering the doors along the back of the great room. The lights automatically brightened, throwing small details into harsh relief. The gold fountain pen on his desktop gleamed silently. Several of the wall screens began to flicker, jumping from picture to picture in frantic confusion. Outside a single siren woop-wooped in eerie rhythms.

Fast moving shapes poured through the double doors opposite his desk. For a moment he raised his hands before he realized the forms were household security forces. A short Oriental man appeared in front of him, bowed perfunctorily, and said, "Mr. Nakamura, sir, please come away from the outside wall." He felt the Blade's fingers take his elbow and begin to lead him across the room, and then a tide of anger washed through him. He shook the man's hand away.

"Oranson's outside. What about him?"

Wordlessly the little man pointed at one of the screens. Nakamura stared. The vantage point was from high on the corner of the house spanning out over the back patio and the meadow beyond. Oranson was crouched behind the low wall, speaking rapidly into microphone beads set into his knuckles. He held a needler in his right hand, but his back was to the wall and he ignored the cattle in the field.

The view slid back toward the meadow, where several of the huge beasts were stamping methodically on a wet, shiny patch of mud. A shadow flitted overhead, hovered, then grew. A Dragonfly attack platform slammed down in a cloud of spattered leaves and armored figures leaped from it and spread into a running advance up the mountain.

The Blade of God touched a control on one of the comm centers and Oranson's voice filled the room.

"—then check the woods up top," Oranson said. His voice was very calm. He might have been reading a children's book.

Nakamura listened as his security chief directed a large part of the estate's defensive force into the area above the meadow. He seems to know exactly what he's doing, Nakamura thought. But then, I pay him for that. And for other things, he realized suddenly. It wasn't a comforting thought.

Nakamura stood quite still for a moment, his eyes closed, seeking the center of himself. The assassination attempt had caught him unawares, at his most vulnerable. The vision of the fanged stone still jangled in his mind, where the peace it offered had been violently ripped away. He tried to recapture the deep feeling of it, but all he could conjure was shadows.

He sighed and opened his eyes. The Blade of God stood in front of him. "Sir?" he said.

"Yes. What."

"Mr. Oranson feels you should go to another part of the house. The armored shelter is what he suggests."

Nakamura glared. "Let Oranson do his job, which is to keep bastards like that"—a quick snapshot of mangled bone and blood flickered in his skull—"from murdering me. And you do yours. And"—he turned back to his desk—"I will do mine."

"Yes, sir." The Blade's eyes were empty as onyx. He bowed one more time and stepped away. Nakamura sat down and began to work his touchpad.

God only knew who was behind it. Perhaps, he decided, it was God himself.

*   *   *

Fred Oranson stared at the flat gray shielding which protected the back of the house and waited for reports. The wall guarding his rear wouldn't stop any heavy stuff, but how could anybody get big guns down without his knowledge? Not within twenty kloms, he decided. He knew how good the house defenses were. He'd designed many of them himself.

He shook his head slightly, feeling the muscles of his calves begin to tighten from the tension of his crouched position. Bursts of static and babble rose and fell like a seashell tide in his inner ear as various assault teams reported in. Finally the data he'd been waiting for arrived and, sighing, he unfolded himself and stood up.

The morning was bright around him. He shaded his eyes with one hand and turned toward the meadow. The cattle, their job done, had wandered away from the coppery smelling patch of mud. The stench of blood was sharp on the morning. He stared at the remains of the would-be assassin and grimaced. Nothing from that one. They'd be lucky if they could reconstruct any kind of eye or print identification, and with a pro, such information would only be a blind alley anyway.

But it had gone as he'd suspected. One of the hunter-seeker teams had found the powdery remains of the shadow glider. It had been a one-man job, and the man was dead.

Oranson grinned. The cattle, bred to kill and armed with steel teeth and hooves, had been his idea. Nakamura had scoffed, but Oranson remembered the look on the assassin's face when the steer had him for lunch. Dogs might have made him more cautious in his attack. But who was frightened of cattle?

He grinned one more time, not really feeling mirth or anything else. Then he climbed over the low wall and began to trudge up the hill. The cattle wouldn't bother him.

After all, they knew their creator.

"You really shouldn't be out here," Oranson said.

Nakamura poked one shiny boot toe at the oleaginous stain on the trampled grass. Technicians in white coats clustered on the scene like maggots, scraping, testing, bagging.

"I won't be a prisoner in my own house, Fred."

"As you will."

Nakamura turned and gazed up at the dark trees which shadowed the upper portions of the mountain. "You found his flyer up there?"

"Yes, sir. He must have come in during the night, evaded the sensors, and waited for you to come out."

Nakamura nodded slowly. "Was he very good, or were we very bad?"

Oranson shrugged. "A little of both. We don't own that ground up there. I did what I could, but you told me to be discreet."

"Yes. I did." Nakamura blinked. "That's over now. Move the perimeter out to include the hill. Whatever you need to make the house secure. Begin immediately."

"Yes. That's government ground. Not ours."

"Just do it."

"Yes, sir."

The two men considered their private demons, each in his own way. Finally Nakamura said, "He knew my habits well."

Oranson didn't say anything.

"Perhaps it was an inside job."

Oranson remained silent.

"Somebody very close to me, who knew my most personal routines. What do you think, Fred?" Nakamura's voice was almost jolly.

"It could have been."

They stared at each other. The Japanese man's features were bland, the Caucasian's empty. The moment held.

"Well, yes," Nakamura said. "You look into it your way, and I will seek in mine. Something will turn up."

"Yes," Oranson said. "It usually does."

Nakamura began to walk away, paused, and looked over his shoulder. "Anything on Arius?"

"No, sir."

Nakamura scraped a bit of shiny pink phlegm from the tip of his boot onto the grass. "Maybe this."

"Anything's possible."

"I'm afraid it is," Nakamura said.

The great room was silent. He had killed all the audio inputs. The blast shields were retracted now, and a watery yellow light filtered through the drapes. Bizarre scenes played themselves out on the many screens in ghostly soundlessness. All over the world revolution was feeding on itself. He had built the New Church better than he'd realized. When the uprising had begun, at first scattered, then a rolling wave of shattering violence that wrecked corporations and toppled governments, even he had been surprised at the thoroughness of the destruction. He glanced at one screen and recognized the silhouette of the Golden Gate Bridge, its rusty orange towers wreathed in smoke from the smashed bubble condos hanging below. Scattered fires burned themselves out on the misty hills of the city by the Bay. He felt a moment of sadness. San Francisco was one of his favorite places. He'd flown in hundreds of armored troops from secret camps in Mendocino, and over a three-day period they'd broken the back of the rioters. But at such great cost. San Francisco had waited more than a century for another great quake, but when the ruin came, it was the work of men.

As ever, he thought tiredly.

Similar stories played themselves out all over the earth. Arius—how he hated that name!—had planned well. The slow creation of the New Church, the nurturing of fanatics, the deep roots sunk into the corporate infrastructure itself. What had the Communists once said? That the capitalists would sell the rope for their own hanging. It was true. Frightening how easy it had been to convince his fellow plutocrats of the usefulness of a tame religion.

But no religion was tame. All gods demanded blood at one time or another.

He smiled at one screen, a slow, contemplative expression full of what might have been pride. One island of serenity remained in the torn and bleeding world. Japan itself, ever suspicious of the outside barbarian, had rejected the new religion. Thus, while fires burned in the night elsewhere, Tokyo, Kyoto, all the great cities of the Rising Sun were quiet.

The Japanese cartels were safe in their island hearts, even though investments overseas had been heavily damaged. But Nippon endured, as it always had, a rock in a heaving sea.

He allowed himself to savor that pride for a while. The white Western cultures would never understand it. No more than they would understand that even as he felt the emotion, he considered other ways to conquer the island of his birth.

Finally he switched off all the screens. The story was old, and would only repeat itself. He got up and walked over to an ancient carved chest that balanced on four sturdy legs. Inside was a bottle of Macallan's eighteen-year-old scotch. He poured a short crystal glass half full and dropped in two ice cubes made from distilled water. The sudden burst of aroma tickled his nose. He sipped lightly and smiled.

There had been nothing from Arius since the beginning. He wondered if anything of Bill Norton existed anymore. It didn't matter, he decided. The scotch warmed his belly. Things might yet work out.

He drained the glass in a single swallow, turned, and threw the heavy chunk of crystal across the room. It smashed the screen where San Francisco burned in the afternoon.

Nothing from Arius, nothing at all.

Perhaps the king is dead, he thought.

Then—

Long live the king.

Oranson felt most like a king in his command center, where he sat in a large, padded, thronelike chair and surveyed the hundreds of inputs that monitored his domain. Here at the estate, under his direct command, were over a thousand men and women. He had technicians and soldiers and assassins and machines, all poised to carry out his least command. Within the walls of his domain the tiniest movement of his fingers carried life and death. And now Nakamura had given permission to enlarge that kingdom.

Although he understood normal emotions were no longer for him—his ravaged brain, sustained only by the drugs Nakamura doled out in gossamer molecular chains, was unable to support what most men called feelings—there were some odd stirrings. The assasination attempt had been a disaster, a direct slap at his own abilities and responsibilities. Yet it had turned out okay. Nakamura's rage—and he had no doubt the man was bursting with it—had not fallen on him. In fact, he'd been given permission to swallow a mountain. Did the cryptic Japanese trust him? He niggled at the question, trying to define his terms. It wasn't trust in the purest sense, he decided. More a kind of confidence in the destruction of his own brain, in the certainty of the deadly tightrope he walked. Nakamura trusted death and the threat of it. He trusted ultimate control.

But did the Japanese have it? That was a question.

Oranson watched the busy monitor screens and spoke softly into surrounding pickups while he thought about it. Arius was the key. Arius and the man Nakamura seemed to have overlooked.

Nakamura dreamed of royalty. He was a man who would be king. And what would his faithful retainer be?

Oranson nodded. Yes, that was another question.

He thought he knew where to find the answers, if that turned out to be his desire.

It all depended on Berg.

Berg was dead. He would know.

"Look at it," Nakamura said.

"Luna," Oranson replied.

The drapes were open to admit the night breeze. Thick scents of pine rolled down the mountain and billowed past softly moving curtains. Almost everything was shut down. A few candles burned here and there, smearing shadows on ancient paintings and polished wood. Nakamura sipped at his scotch, savoring the peaty blend of the single malt as it struggled with the odors of evergreen and darkness.

"We can't wait any longer for Arius," Nakamura said. "Too much is in the balance. What happened to the teams you sent?"

Oranson stood completely still. The flickering lights from the candles and the white orb glowing on the desktop screen caught at his short blond hair and made him look like a mad saint.

"Nothing. They came back. There's nobody left down there. Junk and ruin and corpses."

"No sign of Arius?"

"There was a room," Oranson said slowly. "It looked like it was designed for him. But something had exploded there. There might have been several bodies, but the destruction was too great to tell anything more without a detailed investigation."

"He doesn't need a body," Nakamura said.

"Are you sure?"

"No. Do you know what happened there?"

"An assault force invaded. Local gangsters, street rats. But well armed. We found bodies all over the place. Everybody was dead. Whatever survivors were long gone."

Nakamura's face was golden and impassive, his black eyes glittering in the shifting gloom. "He could be dead. It would solve a lot of problems."

"Yes."

Nakamura tasted his drink again. "He did this to me once before, you know. Set everything up and left me in the lurch. It was part of his plan."

Oranson nodded. "Maybe this time, too."

"I can't wait any longer!"

Oranson blinked at the force of Nakamura's words. His boss rarely showed such emotion openly. Oranson could read him, but Oranson had keys not available to other men. There was an explosion brewing, however. Nakamura had made his decision.

"What do you suggest?"

Nakamura's glance was like a razor slash. "We will continue. We have the people. All those expensive people. The spies and traitors, the soldiers and killers. The fanatics. All mine to use, if he's gone." He paused. "Do you think he's gone, Fred?"

Oranson knew there wasn't any answer to the question. "What choice do we have?"

"Exactly." Nakamura sounded satisfied.

But Oranson, deep within the ruined shell of his mind, wondered. Nothing was ever so easy as it seemed.

He was the living proof.

Danny Boy had grown up in Midwestern hill country, so the forested sprawl of the remote Wisconsin shore wasn't entirely foreign to him. He did, however, understand that his present appearance would be likely to upset the natives. Moreover, his rural reflexes had somewhat atrophied after several years in the Labyrinth, and so he kept reminding himself: take it slow, take it easy.

There was, after all, no rush. The white ghost who possessed him told him so.

He came into the tenuous outskirts of Pale's Crossing a

little after ten at night. There wasn't much to Pale's Crossing; a Shell charging station, dilapidated from little use, only two machines out front new and sparkling in the half-moonlight. Next to the station was a larger building which housed a cafe and a store that sold dry goods and tourist trinkets. Further up the narrow tarmac road a rocky field sloped down to the pavement, ringed by dark, silent pines. In the back of the field he saw the shadowy outline of a shed, and beyond that the rising flank of a mountain. He skirted the charge station, entered the woods, and came on the field from the rear. The soft, moist earth felt good on the callused soles of his feet; soothing and cool. Small night noises filled the air. He thought he heard an owl call. Something scurried through thick leaves overhead, a sharp, flapping noise that receded suddenly. His nose was full of the pitchy odor of pine needles. He widened his eyes, felt the moon on his forehead, and crept forward.

A strand of rusty barbed wire strung from a line of rotten fence posts caught him chest high and pierced his shirt and the fur on his chest. He grunted softly, stopped, untangled himself. Looked around, sniffed, saw nothing. Then he ducked under the wire and made his way through unmown grass toward the small building.

The door was off its hinges but still partially blocked the opening. He got down on his paws and knees and crawled through the widest part. A small, winged creature whistled shrilly and beat a sudden exit through a higher crack, startling him. He jerked up and slapped the top of his head against the edge of the door.

A bat? He grinned whitely. Sure it was. He remembered childhood dreams of vampires. "Dracula," he muttered thickly, rubbing the wiry hair on the top of his skull as he pulled himself the rest of the way in. He wished the bat had stayed. It would have made a classic trio.

The vampire, the werewolf, and the ghost.

Just like a horror movie.

Shag Nakamura woke from his uneasy sleep in the middle of the night. He stared at the horns of the moon through the windows of his bedroom. White, and sharp as knives. His forehead was cool in the faint breeze from the open window. He touched, and felt a sweaty slickness.

51

What did the Americans say?

Like somebody walked on your grave.

Alone, he shivered and rolled over and pulled up the blankets. His own inner beasts told him something was coming. But they didn't say what it was.

Chapter Five

Wier closed his eyes. A lance of fire slammed into his upper chest. Molten agony exploded across his forehead. He smelled his eyelids burning. *What is—?* he thought, but never finished. Just the question. Then merciful darkness.

Bobby Schollander recognized the man. His name was Harry Dougan and he was a third-class technician working on one of the ancillary Levin projects. A part of his mind recalled that Dougan was a longtime immigrant, recruited from one of the Terran megacorps for his expertise in small-body manipulation. Dougan had been on Luna for years, almost long enough to pass for native. Yet there was nothing native about the blank leer on his features, or the blaster in his hand. He swept the stuttering weapon back and forth across Karl Wier's blackened form like a man hosing down a wall.

Without realizing what he was doing, Schollander dived across the table, his trajectory low and flat. He battered into Wier's side and knocked him to the floor. A searing flash of light scraped across his shoulder and he squawked with pain. Then he was on the floor himself, his own frame shielding Wier as he frantically tried to roll them beneath the protection of the metal tabletop.

He heard shouts and screams, saw a jumble of churning legs and feet. The harsh chatter of the needler sawed across the top of the swamp of sound, then shut off suddenly. The silence was like a door slamming. Slowly, then, gingerly, he peered over the top of the table. Became aware that blood had soaked his shirt, was running down, dripping from his fingertips. A lot of blood, his and Wier's together.

A man he didn't recognize held Harry Dougan in a complicated grip. Dougan's face was gray and still. Then Schollander realized that the attacker's head was at a queer, impossible angle. Broken neck, that calm part of him whispered. Dead.

Air erupted into his lungs. "Over here," he screamed. "I've got Karl, over here!"

"Will he live?" Schollander said to the face on the screen.

"I don't know. There's major damage to the thoracic cavity, heart, lungs, you name it. He's running on machines. But that can be handled. It's the brain damage I'm worried about." Schollander knew this man too. He was only a few years older than he, an occasional drinking buddy, a very competent physician. If he was worried, then there was cause to worry.

"Thanks, Gene," he told the face. "Keep me posted, okay?"

"Of course," Gene replied. Schollander switched him off and settled back in his own hospital bed. His right shoulder was swathed in a clear plastic sheath, the jagged, charred track of the burn line vivid beneath. He felt no pain. Three cherry-colored derms placed on flesh near the wound leaked endorphin analogs into his bloodstream, so that all he felt was the hollow, gut-shaking aftermath of adrenaline overdose.

"No problem," he mumbled. Wier was out of it, no matter what happened now. All of Luna's vaunted technology couldn't patch him up soon enough. Wearily, Schollander leaned toward the bedside touchpad. Have to get vocal software online down here, he thought.

He coded the proper instructions. He could use this hospital room for a while, until Gene released him. But not long. What he needed was the shielded safety of his own quarters. The heavy shit was yet to come.

"Dammit!" he muttered.

Gramps had once told him the highest ideal was to serve a great vision. But waiting tables had not been what the old man meant.

Fate, Schollander thought. That, and genes. He sighed and got to work.

He woke to darkness. He wasn't sure how he knew it was dark. Something to do with eyes, and he didn't know what eyes were. Or ears or nose or tongue. All he had to work with was a feeling of space, of openness. He sensed that it was important, this empty space which he occupied.

But if he occupied it, then it couldn't be empty. Could it?

He had so many questions, but there was no urgency. No, he had all the time in the world.

Time?

Another question.

There were so many.

So many questions in the endless dark.

Wier turned away, turned inside, turned and turned. Turned down, turned off.

Was gone.

He wore a pressure suit made of successive layers of silk, gold, carbon fibers, and monomolecular flexcrystal. The flexcrystal was highly polarized, protecting him from the glare of the sun. He cast a long, perfect shadow across the floor of the small crater, up the low ringwall. He stood still and looked down at two neat golden plates set into a pair of slabs made of compressed lunar regolith. There was plenty of space left for more slabs, and he knew that some of the space was for him.

"Father," he said softly. "You were right." He paused. His lips twisted slightly. It might have been a smile. "And you were so certain. How could you know?"

He scuffed a bit of dust, watched it settle. "Well, you trained me for it. You did what you could. Perhaps that was it, the training."

He stood alone for several minutes longer. Finally he turned and walked away from the slabs. Father and grandfather, earth to Luna, but still dust to dust.

"Maybe it will be enough," he said to nobody in particular. He kept walking. The last fluff of dust sparkled on the unwatched graves like a benediction of diamonds.

Dr. Eugene Kilhelm said, "You could do with a little rest and recuperation, you know. But it's not going to do any good, me telling you. Is it?"

Bobby Schollander shook his head. "Everything works, more or less." He touched the bandage on his shoulder. "Just keep those endorphin analogs coming. I'll be all right."

"You're sure this is what you want to do?"

Schollander grinned. His black eyes gleamed slightly, as if coated with a transparent, shiny substance. "It took me awhile to figure it out, but yes, I want this."

Kilhelm nodded. "I never could see you as a waiter. A lot of people couldn't."

"I could then. That's what mattered. But things change. Have changed. What do you think about Karl?"

The young doctor moved his shoulders. "Who knows? Franny Webster says he has a few ideas, if the damage is irreparable. But I can't begin to understand what he's talking about."

"How long?"

"What?"

"Franny. Whatever his idea is, can he do it now?"

"Not a chance."

Schollander took a deep breath. "Then it has to be my way. We didn't have much time before. Now we don't have any at all."

Gene Kilhelm was a serious young man. He considered this. "You mean war?"

"I mean war," Schollander replied. "What do you think?"

"I'd hoped . . ."

The former waiter shook his head somberly. "Not much of that left, either."

The shoulder would be a nuisance, he decided as he walked out into the flat distance of Kennedy Crater. But nothing he couldn't handle. Far overhead a few refugees, awkward as baby birds, wobbled through the sky while their flying instructor called a wingbeat cadence. Schollander grinned. Someday even these fledglings would be part of the Lunie dream. Perhaps sooner than anybody expected.

The cheerful umbrellas of the restaurant came into view. Despite his misgivings about the immediate future, Schollander found himself whistling as he walked through the outer tables and entered the small kitchen area.

"Yo, Suze," he said.

Susan Fujiwara turned from her post at the bread machine and smiled. She was young and cheerfully ugly, with a flat nose and washed-out gray eyes that twinkled inside an epicanthic nest of laugh lines. Her black hair was done in a neat bun.

"Hey, boss. You don't look dead or nothing. When you coming back to work? It's hard to cover your shifts."

"Sorry, babe, but you'll have to manage. I've retired. Officially."

Her mobile features went serious. "Yeah?" She smoothed the fabric of her jeans thoughtfully. "Retired, huh? I can't say it's a surprise. Everybody always knew . . ."

He stared at her. "Not you, too? Gene said almost the same thing. So I didn't make a convincing waiter, hey? Well, maybe not. Maybe I didn't even convince myself."

She didn't answer him. Once they'd been very close, even sharing beds on a few occasions, but that time was long past. Their relationship had eased beyond passion to a vague, comfortable give-and-take marked by the routines of work and chance. Yet she had known him well once, and perhaps still did. "What do you think, Suze?" he said gently. "Am I an idiot now, or was I then?"

She shook her head. "Neither, Bobby. You were never an idiot. But you took some things too seriously, and others not enough."

"Like my father? And maybe you?"

She didn't answer.

"Okay, that's not fair. I know. Forget I asked. But I do need something. A couple of favors."

Her eyes crinkled. "I'm always good for a favor," she said.

"I counted on it. I want you to run this place, okay?"

Her voice was puzzled. "I already do. I input the orders, keep the books—"

"Not what I meant. I mean run it for real. It's yours, Suze. I'm giving it to you."

Her mouth opened slightly. Then it snapped shut. "You aren't an idiot, Bobby, but sometimes you act like one."

"Huh? What do you mean?"

"I'll take the damned restaurant. Part of it's mine anyhow, from all the work. But you'll be paid market value, whatever it's worth. Monthly payments, as soon as we get the details figured out."

He felt warmth rise into his cheeks. She stared at him, her eyes narrowed and waiting. He exhaled. "Sorry. I am pretty stupid, aren't I? I didn't mean to insult you."

She smiled suddenly. "Oh, hell, Bobby. You're one of

57

the good guys. Forget it." She shifted on her seat, slapped a button on the bread machine. The top lifted up to reveal a dozen perfect golden loaves. "So you're retiring, huh? Going back into the physics game?"

"Not exactly."

"Yeah? What's up, then?"

He moved closer. "That's what I wanted to talk to you about. It's the other thing you can help with."

Eaton Vance looked up, his craggy, angular face surprised. "What was that, Mr. Schollander?" he said.

The small room was stuffy. There were ten people seated around the rectangular steel table, each facing his or her own data terminal. Normally, only these ten would be in attendance on the routine, every-other-month director's meeting, but today almost twenty others were seated around the walls on folding chairs. This surprise turnout had obviously caught the attention of the fiftyish, white-maned CEO of Luna, Incorporated. He'd stretched out the reading of his report and twice interrupted himself to whisper to one of his aides, who responded with a look of concern at each question.

Eaton Vance had the only California-style tan on Luna. He worked at it, in the privacy of his office sun room. It had been one of the perks specifically included at his demand when he'd signed his contracts seven years before. Now, beneath the honey chocolate layer of melanin, he seemed tense and pale, but he allowed none of this to enter his businesslike demeanor.

"I want to formally enter a call for a special stockholders' vote," Schollander repeated patiently, his voice low and steady. Most of the men and women who were seated with him at the table were Vance's age. Bobby seemed very young in their company. He knew that it put him at some disadvantage and had done what he could to alleviate the handicap. He wore a somber black suit as perfectly tailored as Vance's own. His thin blond hair was cut short and neatly brushed back over a high forehead. Nevertheless he looked younger than his twenty-six years, and the black suit gave him the air of a polite adolescent vampire.

Eaton stared at him. "Very well," he said. "The documentation, please." Eaton was an old corporate infighter. He kept his hand steady as he reached for the papers.

Schollander passed down a sheaf of hardcopy, then sat back, waiting. Eaton didn't even glance at the printouts. Instead he handed them to the blank-faced aide who hovered behind his left shoulder. Ignoring Schollander he turned back to the table at large. "Any other new business?"

"Wait a second," Bobby said. "What about my call?"

"New business, Mr. Schollander," Eaton said calmly. "The board will consider it, and a vote will be taken at our next meeting."

Eaton spoke from the confidence of two positions. Not only was he President and CEO of Luna, Inc., but he also held the largely ceremonial position of Chairman of the Board. He was legally the dominant force at board meetings and he knew it.

"Not good enough," Schollander said briskly. "I move that the board recess for two hours to consider the matter now, and vote on the emergency election immediately thereafter."

It was a legitimate ploy and Eaton knew it. However, he wasn't about to yield his authority so easily. "New business, Mr. Schollander, will be considered, as always, in due course. Your motion for recess is denied."

At the far end of the table one of the more elderly of the directors, Mason Dodge, a second generation Lunie, slowly raised his hand. "Not so fast," he said. "I second Mr. Schollander's motion."

A red flush began to burn beneath Eaton's tan. But his voice betrayed no hint of anger. "Very well," he said. "The motion has been made and seconded. Any objections?" He searched the faces of the other directors. Some were puzzled. Some seemed irritated. And a few, his finely honed senses informed him, were gleeful beneath their opaque expressions. Some kind of plot, he decided. Maybe it was better to nip it in the bud.

"Let us vote. Madam Secretary, poll the directors, please."

Eunice Ninyiev nodded and ran her fingers across her touchpad. After a moment she nodded and looked up. "The vote is six to four in favor of the motion. The motion is carried."

Vance's hazel eyes, the eyes of a cat, flickered over the table. "I propose a two hour recess, beginning now, to study the new proposal," he said briskly. "Any objections?"

There were none.

"The meeting is in recess," he said. "We will return at fifteen hundred hours." He stood up, glanced at his aide, and left the room.

Bobby Schollander put his hand over his mouth and exhaled slowly. The room seemed very hot. He hoped he wasn't sweating.

Another aide passed out packets identical to the one Eaton had been given. It was all very much out of order. Bobby stood up and nodded at Mason Dodge. The two men moved toward the door.

Schollander's gut was churning, but he felt giddy, light-headed, and as happy as he'd ever been. He whispered to Dodge, "This is what I was made for, you know."

"I always knew," the older man replied. "I just wondered when you would."

"What's the score?" Schollander asked Dodge in the hall-way outside the boardroom.

"You saw the vote. Six to four. Vance voted against, of course, along with two of his cronies. We expected that. The fourth vote was a wild card. Elaine Markowitz. She would normally have been expected to go along with your request, simply out of respect for your name. The, ah, family relationship. But she didn't. You have any idea why?"

Schollander gnawed on one thumbnail, considering. "Auntie Elaine? She's a firster. Jesus, she must be a hundred years old. She knew Gramps, of course. I wonder if—"

"You'd better find out. She's already asked for a private meeting with you."

Schollander sighed. "I don't suppose you'd like to come along?"

Dodge grinned. "This is your show, young Bobby. I'm only along for the ride."

"Yeah. Well, where is the old bag?"

"You might rethink that attitude, before you talk."

"I suppose so," Schollander said.

"I was your grandfather's personal secretary for twenty years, Robert," Elaine Markowitz said. "I powdered your butt when you were—"

"I know, Auntie," Schollander said. "I remember."

"Well. You should. So why do you think I voted against you out there?"

"I don't know. I'd sort of counted on you."

"Just like your granddad," she said. She leaned back in her padded chair, a tiny stick of a woman, all bones and wrinkles and horsy, yellow teeth. Her pure white hair floated long and free from her skull. She wore bright red lipstick. Her blue eyes were sharp and clear as stilettos. "Robert, the first rule of plotting is to inform the participants, if they are expected to help. You took me for granted, and I don't like it. My vote was designed to remind you of that." Her sharp voice softened. "However, I would have gone along if my count showed you losing without me. That young nitwit Dodge should have known better. Did he tell you to keep me in the dark? He is a swine, of course."

Schollander tried to think of Mason Dodge as young, but couldn't make it. He shook his head. "No, Auntie, it was me. I thought it would be better to keep it small. Let me move faster."

"You were wrong," she said tartly. "Do you see it?"

"I guess so."

"You'd better. So, tell me, what bit of mischief do you have up your sleeve, now that Karl Wier is out of the picture?"

His eyes widened with surprise and sudden respect. She gave him a motherly smile that didn't fool him at all.

He told her.

When he finished she said, "Don't teach your Auntie how to suck eggs. Now, here's what we'll do. And oh, get that young fart Dodge in here."

"Your biggest mistake was assuming that you could win your battle in the preliminaries, in these parliamentary maneuverings for the election call. You can't. You will have to win the election straight out, but that can wait. Right now, you have to get the election in the first place. And certainly you realize that two of your initial six votes will switch after this recess?"

Mason Dodge nodded in appreciation of the old woman's sharp words, but Schollander's face went blank. "Those votes are solid," he said.

"No, they aren't," Elaine replied. "Vance isn't stupid.

Oh, he's not a real Lunie, but he's been here seven years, more than enough time to compile some notes. Without going into details, he has certain leverage he can exert. And you can bet your ass he will."

"Shit," Schollander said. "Are you sure?"

"He's not the only one who keeps his eyes open, youngster. I, however, will vote the other way, which leaves us with a tie. And you know what that means."

"He wins," Schollander replied. He thought about it. "Then I'll have to grind it out with a stockholder's vote for the election—an election for permission to have an election—and that will take forever. But we don't have that time! Crap, Auntie, I have to make them understand."

"The only thing you make them understand is that their jobs are on the line. Would you vote to fire yourself?"

"Well, uh, yes. Of course. For the greater good . . ."

"Greater good, my aching ass." She turned to Dodge. "Mason, surely you are cynical enough to explain to this idealist the facts of life."

"You're doing fine, Elaine. Do you want to let him off the hook?"

She blinked. "Whatever do you mean?"

Mason grinned. "He's not old enough, but I remember some of the wildass games you and Bobby Senior used to play."

Her face softened with memory. "Yes, we did, didn't we? Those were the days . . ." She trailed off for a moment, then looked up. "Every old fool thinks those were the days, don't they?" Her voice hardened. "Listen up, young Bobby. I wrote the charter for this lash up. And there are some things in it I don't think Eaton Vance has fully considered."

When she finished, Dodge and Schollander stared at each other. Dodge was the first to speak. His voice was choked with admiration. "What an evil old harridan you are, Elaine."

"Thank you," she said primly. "Now you two get to work. We've got what, about an hour? That should be enough time."

As the two men left the room they heard her cackle softly. "Goddam, I *love* a good fight."

Schollander closed the door. "I feel sorry for them," he whispered.

"So do I," Dodge replied.

Chapter Six

"What kind of pizza is that?" Berg said.

"Calamari anchovy," Ozzie replied.

"Yecch. I hate anchovies."

Calley smiled. "This is our dream, bud. Fuck off or make your own."

Berg grinned tightly and sat down. He stared at her and she stared back unflinching, her green eyes glittering. He nodded and touched the key pendant at his neck. Faint lines appeared at the corners of Calley's eyes and a thin, vertical wrinkle at the bridge of her nose. Ozzie inhaled sharply and pushed his chair back from the table.

"Goddammit, you two. Can't you just say hello like normal people?"

Berg and Calley ignored him. Berg's fingers continued to stroke the tiny silver key. Calley's eyes widened. Suddenly there was a sharp cracking noise, and the smell of burnt tomatoes.

"Oh, shit," Ozzie said.

The pizza in the middle of the table was covered with a mountain of pepperoni and mushrooms. There were no anchovies. Calley sagged back in her chair and Berg let go of his pendant.

"So it's your dream, asshole," Calley said. "And, as usual, you cheat."

"Can I have my anchovies back?" Ozzie said.

Berg blinked, and the steaming pile of Italian meat disappeared. In its place was a fresh, untouched calamari anchovy pizza. The anchovies, however, occupied only one half of the pizza.

"I don't mind calamari, myself," Berg said mildly, peeling up a wedge.

Calley pulled a fresh slice away from the pie and bit off the end. Chewed, swallowed, and said, "I really love this, you know. Catch the headlines in the *Enquirer*. Gods duel over pizza. Prick wins."

Berg burst out laughing so hard he spit bits of calamari all over the table top.

"Good manners, too," Calley said.

Ozzie finally had to pound him several times between his shoulder blades before he could stop whooping and gagging. Calley reached for another slice. "So," she said, when Berg finished wiping tears from his cheeks. "What's the job, massa? Us loyal slaves await your divine instructions."

"Wait a minute," Ozzie said. "I don't feel all that loyal. Or enslaved, either."

"She's bullshit, Ozzie," Berg said. "Haven't you figured it out yet?"

"And you," Calley said levelly, "are a major league motherfucker, Jack." She glanced at Ozzie. "He wins at pizza making. He wins at everything. It isn't our dream, Ozzie. And that was just a reminder. Right, Berg?"

Berg chewed at another slice. "This place got Diet Coke?" he said.

Ozzie stood up. "Sure. You want large or medium?"

"Large," Berg said. "Lotta ice. I like to chew ice."

Ozzie nodded and turned to the counter.

"Berg," Calley said. "What's this all about?"

"Still love me, babe?"

She wrinkled her nose. "I think about it. Occasionally."

"I love you. But there are priorities."

"Berg, you asshole, there are always priorities. How come you and me—us, together—never seem to rank very high?"

He shrugged. "High enough. I told you I had a job for the pair of you. It's voluntary. But it didn't have to be."

She closed her eyes, opened them. "I figured that. From the pizza. Well, thanks. For the choice, I mean."

"You want the anchovies on both sides?"

"No. It's all right," she said.

Morning came chill and full of fogs off the lake. The damp gray tendrils crept across the deserted field, wrapped the shed in a skein of dew, and extended long muffled fingers into the green darkness of the mountain pines. Danny Boy wrinkled his nose and opened his eyes.

At first he didn't know where he was. The smells of the

shed confused him with a welter of ancient earth, rotted wood, rusted iron, molding vegetation. A huge spiderweb draped across the far corner of the hut shivered slightly, dewdrops like tiny jewels ringing, as a fat black spider ventured out into the day.

He watched the spider a moment, his mind blank as an empty plate.

Licked clean. In his mind's eye he could see the hungry tongue and the gleaming emptiness it left behind.

"What," he said.

The silence was heavy as a gravestone. He blinked a leaf-colored blink and forced himself to sit up. Slowly memory began to return.

"Urrruf." It was a slow, whuffing growl, laced with the dead agony of his own joints forced to movement. He raised one paw-hand and stared at it. Claws clicked out, then back. Sharp and yellow-white. He loved his claws. They reminded him of the small carved ivory things his mother had kept in a wooden chest. Nobody was supposed to open the chest, but he had, once, and marveled at the tiny perfection of her keepsakes.

He sighed and lowered his hand. His body felt frozen into slow positions, so that every time he moved, he discovered a new source of pain.

After a while he was able to stand up. He scratched at his armpits and smelled his own pungent odors. He shambled over to the wrecked door and examined it. The cracked wood was still mostly whole. It would be a matter of somehow repairing the hinges. Perhaps if he just leaned it upright it would be okay.

Grunting, he bent over, took one side of the wood panel, and heaved. Sharp, hot sparks shot through his thighs and shoulders. For a moment the door, partly buried in dark, loamy earth, resisted. Then, with a dry sucking sound, it came loose. He leaned it against the jamb, ducked his head, and stepped outside. It was cooler there, where the lake winds that pushed the fog were able to reach him, and sneak beneath his fur.

He stared at the door, picked it up again, and placed it so it covered the opening. Not quite a perfect fit, but he could work on it. He would have the time. A lot of time, he thought.

He rubbed the curly hair above his ears, listening to the faint forest sounds, and the sound of his own breathing. After a while he shook his head and wandered off into the woods. He needed to take a shit. *A dirty bird fouls its own nest,* his mother had once preached. He remembered, and was a clean werewolf.

The milky luminescent fluid drained away. The sound of the pumps ended. Chet Limowitz glanced at Bobby. "Do it," he said.

Bobby punched in several instructions. Slowly, one wall of the tank slid into the aperture in the floor beneath the enclosure. They waited until the last bit of fluid had drained away. Then Bobby said, "Now what?"

Limowitz stared at the figure in the middle of the empty, open tank. He licked his lips. It wasn't so much that the dog danced badly, but that it danced at all.

There was a man standing there. Not an odd-looking man, nothing really out of the ordinary. But from no more than a nutrient fluid the tank had created the man. The mere fact of his existence was a miracle.

"Got me," Limowitz said. "I never seen anything like this before. Is there anything in the protocols?"

Robby looked up from his studies, his expression full of puzzled wonder. "Cheeseburgers," he said.

"What?"

"The protocols say to send out for cheeseburgers."

Danny Boy checked his wristwatch. For obvious reasons he didn't have a nailtale. Clawtale would have been more like it. It was almost eleven o'clock. The time zone here was the same as Chicago. He'd come more or less north to this place, veering somewhat west, but pretty much on a line. Walking most of the way, guided by an internal map he didn't even know he had.

Perhaps, he decided, it wasn't his map at all. He hadn't really followed roads, after all. He had trended toward a point, a distant place, and whenever his path had taken a wrong turning, his hidden hunger had vanished. He had a need to be here, and now that he was, he was starving. Yet he didn't know what he wanted. His hunger wasn't really for food. It was deeper, more pervasive. It was a lust for the hunt, and he had no idea the shape of the prey. Still, there were things to do. Preparations to make. He would be here awhile.

She'd told him that. And when she whispered her thin white messages into the bones of his heart, he listened.

Oh, yes, he did listen.

"Berg, you're slipping away again. The walls are up. The joints are stretching." Calley tried to keep the concern from her husky voice, but she knew she wasn't entirely successful. The unexpected warmth in Berg's eyes told her that. He reached across the table and touched the back of her hand.

"I didn't know you cared," he said.

She shook her head. "Cards on the table, boy. You know better. Or have you forgotten?"

He pulled his hand back. "No. I haven't forgotten. I said we were forever joined." He poked idly at the last piece of soggy pizza. "Sometimes I wish—"

"What do you wish?"

He was silent a moment. "It doesn't matter. Even here, wishing sometimes can't make it so."

Very softly, she said, "Is this one of those times?"

"What do you think?"

"Jack, do we come out of this?"

"I don't know."

She chewed lightly at her lower lip. She almost seemed to be listening to another conversation. "Then what?"

"That's why I came here."

"For us?"

His voice was narrow and attenuated, as if he spoke from a great distance. "In a way," he said. "In a way."

Limowitz catalogued what little concrete knowledge he had of the man in the tank. The man stood unmoving, his thick-knuckled hands at his sides, his head slightly cocked, as if waiting for something. He was smiling faintly, and Limowitz suddenly had the feeling that the man was in mid-conversation, merely waiting for some unheard reply.

What was the magic word, Limowitz wondered, that would awaken him?

He thrust the vagrant thought away and continued to observe and classify. The man was short and thickset, perhaps a hundred seventy cents tall, and eighty-seven kilos. Burly shoulders and a small, neat potbelly. The man was Oriental, with pronounced epicanthic folds that gave him a Buddha-like appearance. A thin layer of fat coated his entire frame, smoothing him out, making him seem younger, perhaps, than he was. His hair hung to his shoulders and was black as carbon smudges.

There was a readiness to the way he stood, one foot a few cents in front of the other, knees somewhat bent. Limowitz had seen that kind of stance before. He could imagine this man with a weapon in his hands, a knife, perhaps even a spear. Something primal and pointed. He shivered.

He really didn't want this creature to wake up.

"Do the protocols say anything else?"

Robby shook his head. "Wait, they say."

"So, we wait."

Bobby stared at him uneasily. "You want me to try for some cheeseburgers?"

Danny Boy spent most of the early afternoon cleaning out the shed. He pulled some lower branches from a nearby pine and used them to scrape batshit and spiderwebs from the ceiling. Astonishingly the roof was fairly sound, only one small hole above the door. After he had the shed as clean as he was going to get it, he dragged his large backpack to a spot near the rear wall and pulled its Velcro fasteners apart.

Carefully, he took out a small packet and unfolded it. It made a silver rectangle on the floor about two and a half meters long and half that wide. A small black mechanism on one corner, no larger than a book of matches, occupied his attention. He fiddled with it until his awkwardly sharp claw tips found the right catch. He pressed, and the shed was filled with two sounds: a sharp, drawn-out hiss, and a high-pitched mechanical whine. He watched to make sure the self-contained pump was doing its job. The silver shape began to bulge. In a moment it was full, and his bed, a monomole construction weighing no more than a few grams, was ready. A similar piece of equipment, coated on the inside with a layer of reflective gold only a couple of molecules thick, was partially inflated to form a sleeping bag.

He took out some packets of dehydrated food, camper's

rations, and eyed them distastefully. Hunger had directed him here, and he realized with a rush that he was ravenous, but he needed more than this desiccated powder. He had a small cooker and pots and pans, but he wanted something raw.

Something hot and full of red juice.

He shuffled over to the door and looked out. The fog had long blown away, and thin shafts of sunlight illuminated the road below the field. The single lane of blacktop gleamed flatly. He wondered if this shed would be safe enough, with the small traverse of Pale's Crossing only a short distance away. But the vast sighing of the wind down the mountain reassured him. This was not a crowded place. Weeks, even months might pass before anybody discovered him. More than enough time.

He would have to be careful, though.

Eventually, they would try to kill him.

He thought about that. For some reason the idea of his own death held no fear. Almost as if death had no power over him.

Maybe it's true, he thought.

Feeling himself begin to change, he slid around the shed like a curly nightmare. A moment later he was in the trees, safe beneath the endless green, and hunting.

The howl that bubbled in his throat was pure joy.

They had stuffed chewed pizza crusts and the greasy cardboard circle into a dented trash can and now sipped stale coffee from cheap Styrofoam cups. Berg seemed more relaxed. The bags beneath his eyes had lightened a bit, and the bones of his narrow, foxy face were less prominent.

Ozzie and Calley had somehow gravitated closer to each other, so their elbows touched as they faced him across the small round table. If Berg noted this informal juxtaposition, he gave no sign.

"This is a stalemate," he said. "Do you understand what's going on?"

Calley shook her head, her chopped black hair moving over her ears. Her green eyes were half-lidded, watchful. Ozzie spoke reluctantly. "I think I've got the basics. But I don't know how to put them together. You know? There's pieces of the puzzle missing." His eyes flickered. "You've got the pieces, right? You know how they fit with each other."

Berg sighed. His thin fingers looked white and cold around the plastic coffee cup. He held the cup in his right hand and caressed the key at his neck with his left. "Look," he said.

The Chicago winds, which had been buffeting the windows of the pizza joint, began to rise. Ozzie's eyes widened, but Calley remained absolutely still, her face expressionless.

Cracks appeared in the glass. Then, in slow motion, the windows crumbled, blew inward. The walls began to dissolve. Another moment and the table at which they sat hung suspended in a great darkness full of the sound of howling.

Then even the table was gone, and with it, their bodies. Only three pairs of eyes swirled through the maelstrom, like matched pairs of observant snowflakes. Berg's voice, thin and high, seemed to come from everywhere and nowhere.

"Watch," he said.

The darkness began to curdle. Overhead the Sword and the Sun came into being. The Sword had a blade of crystal and a silver grip and guard. The Sun was the color of blood around its circumference, but its heart was white with heat. Each seemed to occupy half the sky. There was a sense of battle, of striving, between the two, and a feeling of immense age, as if this war was only another encounter in an eternal struggle.

Faces, evanescent and ghostly, snapped into the whorl, held, disappeared. The atmosphere itself was charged with power. The air quivered, glowed, wreathed itself in shining mists.

Ever changing, never ending.

"Me and Arius," Berg's voice said offhandedly. Its echoes boomed with thunder. "I'm holding. So is he." He paused. "We attack, we defend. We persevere."

"Now," he continued. "Look down. See the prize."

And, although it had always been there, they seemed to see it for the first time. Beneath the infinite struggle was the solidity of a floor. A floor of blue, an ocean of sapphires. The floor glowed with cool indifference to the conflict overhead. And, as they looked closer, they could see the reason. Between the shining swarm of azure jewels and the clash of milk and blood was an interface of sorts; a narrow, clear line like a membrane, empty as the face of an infant. This

70

barrier separated the two worlds as cleanly as a knife stroke, and as impenetrably. Overhead the night bled and curdled. Beneath, all was calm. The blue glow remained untouched, inviolate.

The vision burned itself into their brains, overloaded them, forever changed them. And then it was gone.

Calley stared at Berg over the rim of her cup. Ozzie's mouth hung open slightly. His eyes were glazed. And Berg's lips had curved down. On him it looked like a bitter smile.

"My world," he said. "And welcome to it."

"We've seen it before," Calley said coldly. "Maybe not so vividly, but none of us is unaware of Arius. Or of this gestalt space. Except what it is, and why it's important. We take your word, Berg. But maybe that's not enough. What do you think?"

His grin remained saturnine and unshakable, as if engraved on the stone of his features. "Nasty bitch, aren't you?"

"I don't trust daddy, if that's what you mean. Berg, I pulled your skinny ass out of too much shit to believe you're omnipotent. Or even potent, sometimes."

"Like I said, nasty. Okay, maybe I get carried away."

She ignored him. "And," she continued, "your cosmic light show doesn't scare me one tiny bit. What does is the idea I might get trapped in this Little Bo Peep crap, watching dirty white fur balls munch picturesque hillsides while you play at being God. Maybe you forget. Ozzie and me, we still have bodies. Somewhere. It gives us a certain humanity, you might say." She drained her coffee cup. "You remember, Berg? Bodies? What's it like, not having one anymore?"

"I've got as many as I need," he said.

"Yeah? Where?"

He waved the question aside. "Not important right now. The real problem is, I'm losing this little war with Arius, and I need your help. You think you can quit sniping at my gonads long enough to pitch in?"

"Why, sure, Berg. No problem. I've already got your balls."

He glanced at Ozzie, but Ozzie only lowered his head and didn't say anything.

"All right, then." Berg crumpled his cup and tossed it to the floor. "Here's what I want. The question really is, are you tough enough to get it done?"

Her lips stretched slowly in a red smile. "Try me, asshole. Just try me."

Outside, the wind began to scream.

"Look," Chet Limowitz said.

The man in the empty tank blinked.

Limowitz stood up, moved toward the tank, stopped. He felt something small and hard flutter in his chest, halt, and flutter again.

The man blinked again. The little finger on his right hand twitched.

"Robby. Bobby." They were behind him. He could hear their breathing. The room suddenly seemed unbearably hot, and he felt drops of moisture gather in his eyebrows, on the tip of his nose.

The right hand clenched into a fist, relaxed.

Limowitz forced himself to step closer.

And the man in the tank opened his eyes. Limowitz heard a small sound, and realized his exhalation had become a gasp.

The man looked around. For one instant Limowitz thought the man had no eyes, that nothing was in those sockets but endless darkness, twin pits without bottoms. But as the man turned his face, Limowitz realized it was only a trick of the light.

The man's eyes were black, but not empty. They sparkled like bits of polished coal. And they stared straight at Limowitz.

Chester felt his lips move, heard words come out as if someone else operated his lungs, his vocal cords, his tongue.

"I'm . . . Limowitz. Chester Limowitz. Who are you?"

The man in the tank smiled slowly. "Toshi Nakasone, Chester. Where the fuck are my cheeseburgers?"

Darkness had fallen. Overhead a moon the color of amber rode the scene like a raddled skull. He paused in his feast to look up, drawn by feelings without names. As he stared at the stars through the black etchings of the endless forest, he felt her spread her white wings within him.

The long, ululating cry burst from his massive chest without volition, but when it died in the darkness he felt purged, purified. For the first time in his twisted, pitiful life, Danny Boy MacEwen felt whole and healed.

The juice of his prey dripped from his jaws and stained his claws. His hot breath puffed out on the chill air in delicate silver clouds. She furled her wings, satisfied.

He lowered his head to feed again. Her hunger was indiscriminate and endless. But it was okay. It was his hunger, too.

"Gestalt space is the sum of all human existence," Berg said. "The well of the archetypes, the place of dreams. It's heaven and hell and purgatory rolled into one. It's where they all come from and in the end, where they all go."

"Well," Calley said. "I should fit in just fine, then."

Chapter Seven

"I want to see for myself," Nakamura said. He examined the knot of his silk Armani tie in the upright mirror at the edge of his bedchamber. The room was a simple one, light and airy, with a view of the mountain pines. The bright morning light picked out solitary details: the shine of polished wood planks in the floor, the curve of his oak bedstead, the perfect bevel of the glass in his mirror. Other than the bed, a low, antique carved chest, the mirror, and a plain maple chair, there were no other furnishings. Nakamura made an adjustment in the tie knot and turned to face Oranson.

"It might be dangerous," Oranson said.

"It doesn't matter. I've decided." Nakamura's voice was crisp and precise, betraying, as usual, none of the emotions which twisted beneath the words. His flat, yellow face was bland. He seemed utterly unconcerned about anything except the set of his tie, the hang of his ten-thousand-dollar suit, the polish on his Bally loafers. But Oranson detected, in ways he didn't understand, certain signs.

Nakamura was tense. There was a sharp, brittle edge to his movements, as if he awaited a concealed blow. As he spoke, it seemed to Oranson that he really had made up his mind. Which, the security man thought, was all to the good.

For three days since the assassination attempt, while Oranson added hundreds of guards and extended the boundaries of the great country estate to include the previously unprotected mountain behind the main house, Nakamura had done little more than drink expensive scotch and watch the myriad monitor screens in the stuffy darkness of his office library. He had turned away all calls, both from his own Double En staff and from the intricate network of allies, hangers-on, and traitors which made up the plot that Arius and he had devised.

Oranson was worried. He'd done what he could, making any decisions that absolutely couldn't be put off, but he understood his own limitations. On questions of tactical importance—assassinations, mob control, bribery—he was perfectly capable. But he lacked Nakamura's instinctive strategic sense, his ability to see and understand the big picture. Oranson realized that his own survival hung on Nakamura's continued strength, and he was afraid that the Japanese had, for some reason, decided to abandon the field just as victory dropped gently to his hand.

He felt mildly uncomfortable in allowing Nakamura out of the heavily guarded compound, but weighed this against Nakamura's evident eagerness to see the physical heart of Arius' former empire. If it was former, he reminded himself.

He tried one more time to dissuade him from this trip, however. "You've seen the reports. The tapes. They were very thorough."

Nakamura stared at him. "You have no feelings left, Fred. Perhaps if you did, you would understand. I must see, feel, touch. I must know."

It was as far as his boss would ever go in justifying himself. And the flat, heavy edge to his words was a warning. Oranson nodded.

"Of course," he said. "Give me two hours to set up the convoy. I would recommend ground travel. Any fool can get his hands on heat-seeking missiles."

Nakamura nodded, seeming uninterested in the details. "That's fine," he said. He moved his fingers, almost a shooing motion. Oranson realized he'd been dismissed. He turned and walked from the room without a word.

Nakamura watched him go. After he was gone he faced the mirror a final time. He stared into his own eyes. "To feel," he whispered. "To feel his ruin with my own hands."

Off in the hooded distance firefly lights flickered, glinting red and gold and white. They marked the limits of the small army which accompanied him. He smelled the odor of ancient rot, of mildew from seepage beneath the Lake, of rust and destruction. His elegant boot heels made tight little echoes in the circle of brightness which surrounded him, but the echoes died too quickly. The outer darkness absorbed the sound and gave back only the pounding of distant drums, slow and dreary.

"Ugly," he remarked.

Metal shrieked as it was torn somewhere ahead of them. "Demo teams," Oranson said. "Clearing the way. The earlier search teams were smaller."

Nakamura nodded. He walked slowly, his spine straight, his incongruously large head upright and alert. It was clammy down here, the chill of fog without the miasma. Shapeless bundles impeded their path, and every so often the central party had to split to step around one of them. Nakamura paused at one such and prodded it with his toe. The bundle was small. His boot sank in slightly, and the mass shifted. A skull, thinly covered with a mask of rotted flesh, stared up at him. White bone gleamed through the decomposed jelly, which itself twinkled with an unhealthy, multicolored sheen.

"It's only a child," Nakamura said. He sounded curious. "Children? Did they fight with children?"

"Look," Oranson said. "There. That's a Solig-Kalash assault rifle. That's some rifle. But a kid can handle it okay."

Nakamura nodded. "I take your point," he said dryly. "Perhaps I'm naive."

"I wouldn't say that."

Nakamura sighed. "Sometimes I wish I could." He moved his foot and walked on.

Nakamura stood a moment in front of the half-melted ruin of the great black door. The damage to the hallway indicated that fighting here had been massive and vicious, and the twisted remnants of the guardian portal testified to the powers that had been wielded.

He felt an odd sensation. It was as if he stood before the wreckage of a great cathedral. The harsh glare from the portable lamps illuminated every tear and rent, but despite the destruction, a kind of peace suffused his mind. Here, deep in the under darkness, lay the wasted bones of majesty.

A helmeted security man poked his head out of the chamber beyond the door. "It's clean," he said.

"Let's go," Nakamura said. Carefully he began to climb over the blasted metal rubble.

The chamber beyond was smaller than he'd imagined. The flickering blare of portable lights only accentuated the destruction from the battle which had brought down this place. He blinked, waiting for his eyes to adjust, and inhaled deeply. There was a plethora of odors. He smelled oil, rich and greasy. Something had rotted here and turned dry and left the stench of cinnamon and decay.

There was a throne. Sensitive to the nuances of power, he recognized it for what it was. "A light, please," he said. One of the guards stepped forward. "On that chair."

He moved closer, his black eyes hooded and thoughtful. Yes. Slowly he reached out and touched the tiny, twisted skeleton.

Unlike the regions outside, the atmosphere in the room had quickly dissolved flesh. All that remained was desiccated, bleached white by invisible solvents in the closed atmosphere. But he knew that shape.

The bloated skull spoke its own name to him. He ran his fingers over the cracks, felt inside the gaping eye holes. Something shiny glinted there, and he tried to wriggle it out.

"Ouch."

"What?" Oranson said.

Nakamura shook his head and watched a tiny bead of blood well up in the meaty part of his thumb. Something had pricked him. He leaned closer and saw the needles. There were thousands of them, golden and pure in the light, penetrating the misshapen skull in a seamless canopy.

He stepped back. "Arius," he said softly. His hand moved, almost a blessing. "His body."

"Others, too," Oranson told him. "Look."

It took a second for Nakamura to pull his gaze from the remains of his great enemy.

"Over here," Oranson said.

He was squatting next to another skeleton. It was of normal size. The front of the skull was crushed, and in the black emptiness there Nakamura saw a glitter of ruby.

Oranson picked up a perfect glassy circle the color of blood. "Infrared inserts," he said. His eyebrows made questioning curves.

Nakamura sucked in his breath, hissing without realizing it.

"Her," he said softly. "The Bitch, the Wolf Woman." He remembered her scorn. Remembered the arrogance with which she bore the bent dwarf. Unbidden, his foot moved, scattering bones.

Oranson looked away from the expression on his face.

"That one in front of the chair," Oranson said. "Male. Nothing left between skull and knees. But it was a man, and he'd had a lot of work done. Implants and such. We think it was the Japanese killer Berg used."

Nakamura couldn't take his eyes off the Lady's bones. So white, so jagged. Like the rocks of his garden, important and eternal. The message of the bones, he thought to himself.

Oranson's words began to penetrate. He stepped back. "The one that burned you? Is that the Japanese you mean?" It was strangely comforting to realize that another of his race had died well here. A warrior's death. He tried to remember the name.

"Toshi . . . was it Toshi something?"

Oranson nodded, caught in his own violent memories. "Nakasone," he said absently. "Toshi Nakasone was his name."

"Then he won," Nakamura said. "In the end, Berg won. They're all dead. Arius, The Lady, the Assassin. Only Calley left. Her and that weird boyfriend."

Oranson looked up. "And where are they?"

Suddenly Nakamura wanted out, wanted to leave this chamber of death, wanted the clean air and the night stars. This Labyrinth was a tomb. Let it remain undisturbed, then.

"Who knows?" he said at last. "But the rest are dead enough for me."

"Good," Oranson replied.

"Here's what I want," Nakamura said.

Oranson realized he'd gotten his wish. A sea change had occurred, some time during Nakamura's expedition to the Labyrinth. Now his boss seemed to crackle with energy. His voice was sharp, precise, without hesitation. He sat behind his ornate desk in the penthouse office high above Chicago like a general. The rigid precision of his spine, his shoulders, bespoke certainty. Shag Nakamura had, at long last, regained himself.

Oranson wondered what had been lost. He pushed the thought away. It didn't matter. Nakamura had regained it, whatever it was, and Oranson began to relax. For a time he would be safe. For a time, the drugs that kept him alive would continue.

"Bring every matrix we have on line. We'll need them all. And set up a meeting. Here's the list." He handed a piece of paper over, and Oranson glanced at the names. His eyes widened.

"I know," Nakamura said. "But we aren't playing voodoo computer games now. This is the real world. And it's ours, if we want it. I understand that getting this together will be difficult. But get it done, Fred. You have a week."

"A week?"

"Is it a problem, Fred? You used to be almost competent."

Oranson felt a twinge, a ghost of an emotion. Not a real feeling, nothing that brought blood to his cheeks, but he became aware of the missing tremor, rather as an amputee receives ghost tingles from a limb no longer there.

"A week, yes," he said.

"Good." Nakamura paused. "We don't have a lot of time. The enemy won't wait."

Oranson risked a question. "Who is the enemy, sir? I should know."

Nakamura considered. "Since you will have to keep me safe, you must know. Luna is the enemy. They always have been."

Oranson remembered the eerie vision of the moon on the silent monitors of Nakamura's country house. Something tightened the muscles at the base of his spine.

"Luna," he said.

"But I will destroy them," Nakamura said.

Oranson nodded and left the room.

"Barre won't meet if Nelson does. And Nelson refuses to be in the same country with Gogolsky."

"What about Gogolsky?" Nakamura said.

Oranson shrugged. "He doesn't care. He said give him a date and place and he'd be there."

"Remarkably compliant, for him."

"His sales are down sixty percent. He's hurting."

"They're all hurting. Half the world's industrial capacity is idle right now." Nakamura pursed his lips. "You only requested a meeting, is that right? No mention made of subject matter?"

"As you ordered," Oranson agreed.

Nakamura considered further, staring at the smaller version of his meditation garden which occupied a third of his office. A glint of bright movement tugged at his eye. He glanced up in time to see a Double En courier copter fight its way against the updrafts toward a landing circle on a lower level. "How do you read the problem?" he asked Oranson.

"They all hate each other. Pride of place. They've been fighting themselves, and you, so long they don't understand what has happened. They're treating this as just another request for negotiations."

Nakamura nodded slowly. "That's how I read it." He placed his fingertips together and leaned back in his chair. "Pry Barre out of his shell and drag him here. Film the whole thing. Then include the films with your next invitation."

Oranson grinned. "Yes, sir," he said. "Oh, and Fred—?"

"Yes?"

"Be sure you kill a few of his people. Makes so much better a point."

Nikolai Gogolsky shattered the modern European cliche of the bumbling, boorish Russian. He was a small man of precise movement with a gracious smile, rosy cheeks, and tiny hands and feet. He favored British suits, Italian leathers, and French wines. His impeccable English was littered with *bons mots* from five or six languages both living and dead. He was almost boyish in his sudden enthusiasms, and utterly charming when he wished to be.

Nakamura knew this wonderful little man had consigned thousands to death over the period of his rise to dominance in the remnants of the Russian Empire. Gogolsky was a throwback to the days of the White Czars, those men even the Japanese had learned to fear. Yet, this man was an ally, or so Nakamura judged.

Claude Barre was another story entirely. The Frenchman was an enemy, pure and simple. There was a frozen Germanic cast to his mobile French features. His big nose and wide, expressive lips quivered now with barely suppressed rage. A nameless man, one of Oranson's people, stood behind his chair. Barre had not come to this meeting willingly, and was only now comprehending the ramifications of Nakamura's heretofore unrealized influence. He had succeeded the German, Arthur Kraus, after that man's unfortunate —Nakamura grinned wolfishly at the memory—demise in his role as European leader of the Consortium, the group of seven huge companies which had mounted an attack on Double En at the moment of Arius's creation.

Thankfully, Claude Barre was nowhere near as intelligent as Kraus, although he somewhat made up for the lack with bulldog brutality and an instinct for exposed jugulars.

The third man now entering the room, shedding a rumpled overcoat and two bodyguards at the same time, was something entirely different. While the personal fortunes of the rest of the participants were numbered in multiple billions, this man, Robert Nelson, was barely a millionaire. Spare change to the industrialists. However, Nakamura well understood that he was perhaps not only the brightest of his antagonists, he was potentially the most powerful. Robert Nelson was a true American success story.

The secret of winning modern coporate battles was information, and Nakamura had made himself more than familiar with the short, stocky, disheveled man who was approaching him now, his meaty hand outstretched, his lumpy, boxer's face smiling widely. Nelson was almost entirely bald, with only a short, carefully barbered fringe of sandy hair over his ears. There were freckles on his naked skull. He wore a thick gold band on the ring finger of his left hand, marking a marriage dissolved over a decade before. Nelson had never remarried. His mistress, Nakamura knew, was power.

"Hello, Robert," Nakamura said.

"Hello, Shag. Nice of you to invite me." Nelson glanced at Barre, who moved his lips slightly, and Gogolsky, who twinkled at him. "Not my usual group, I'd say, but who can refuse an invite from one of the owners of Nakamura-Norton?"

Barre made a soft, hissing sound. Gogolsky, unmoved by the insult, twinkled steadily.

And Shag heard very well the hidden question in Nelson's words. One of the owners. What did Nelson know?

It was an important question. Nelson was officially Counselor to the President of the United States, a nominal position at best. Unofficially he was the puppet master who pulled the strings from which danced the retread thriller actor at present occupying the White House. Nelson controlled the executive branch utterly, dispensing his patronage and his displeasure with all the grandeur of the old-time pols who'd stalked the government like ravening beasts a century and a half before.

Nelson had arisen from the rubble of the Democratic debacle of twenty years before to create the rejuvenated Demo-Libertarian Party in one of the most awesome exercises of treachery and doublespeak Nakamura had ever heard of. That Nelson, an ex-advertising man, could sell out of whole cloth something like Libertarianism to a gullible public only served to reinforce Nakamura's belief that democracies must inevitably vote themselves out of existence.

It seemed to him now that the American republic trembled on that verge. Waving a banner of individual freedom, the Party was about to overturn the two-term limit on Presidential service and elect for a third time the amiable, telegenic man who Shag marked as a nearly unstoppable rider on a white horse. President Northtree smiled and mumbled and pandered to whatever constituency Nelson told him to. Nakamura wondered whether there would even be a fourth term, or if by then the whole notion of elected politicians would have disappeared from what once was called the gem of the ocean.

Meanwhile, he had to do business with Robert Nelson.

"Robert, it's very good to see you."

Nelson bobbed his head. "Too long, Shag." He grinned one more time and said, "Where's Bill?"

Nakamura showed nothing on his face. "That," he said, "is one of the things we should discuss."

Nelson nodded, his smile as quickly vanished as a passing wind. "Discuss his burial, you mean?"

"Possibly," Nakamura replied.

Nikki Gogolsky made a muffled noise. When Nakamura glanced at him, Gogolsky was no longer twinkling.

Danny Boy MacEwen lay on his bed and watched his breath form small clouds above his face. The nights here on the Lake were long and cold. He watched the pewter-colored puffs, evanescent in the glow from his chemical lamp, and tried to examine the thing which lived inside him.

At first he'd known perfect certainty. The Lady had returned, and he'd been selected as her vessel. His joy had only been increased by the understanding of the purpose for which she wished his life.

But now, alone in a shed by a forest, he began to wonder. There were longer and longer periods when she rode him like a witch, blinding his eyes and drawing a white curtain across his mind. He would awaken with bloody claws and bits of unfamiliar meat in his teeth, muscles aching as if he'd run for miles. And there was an aftertaste in his skull, a wild, shrieking laughter, that had nothing to do with humanity.

But what could he do? Without her he was nothing. Yet, with her, what was he then?

He made a whimpering sound and rolled over on his belly. He felt very alone, even with her slumberous presence inside him. And his journey had only begun.

The prey was gone, had left this place, this forest so green and dark. Had returned to the man-made mountains, the neon streams, the undark night.

He would follow, he knew. He had no choice. But not now. Now he would rest. At morning he would hunt again, beneath the coming of the sun.

After a while he began to snore.

Poor werewolf.

Chapter Eight

Schollander returned to his heavily shielded suite and activated various machines. His rooms were quite large, three squares almost six meters on a side. One was a bedroom. The second functioned as a living-dining area. The third was his office-lab-command center. In the lab area was a construction that might have been considered odd for a waiter: the distinctive tank containing a meatmatrix.

Schollander studied a single monitor. The Levin was still offline. Yet the nanomachine was functioning. It simply wasn't responding to the complicated command software which should have allowed input-output. He glanced at the matrix tank. It was mildly disconcerting to realize that a sizable chunk of William Norton's brain rested there. He had been careful. This matrix had been grown on Luna. It had never been integrated into any other matrix net. It was, in the informational sense, sterile. Yet he couldn't help but wonder if, in some mysterious way, all Norton's neural cells communicated with each other.

If he could just get Levin back online. But since Berg's great strike at Arius's heart, the metamachine had made no response to their queries. Ozzie and Calley rested in suspension, their brains showing only minimal activity. Of Berg there was no hint at all.

Something was going on. He guessed it might be of tremendous importance. But without data he couldn't evaluate the gravity of the situation. That would have to be his first task, after the takeover. To somehow remedy this stasis situation.

He wandered into his living area and brewed a cup of instant coffee. He laced the dark, aromatic fluid with steamed milk and a bit of Tia Maria, sipped, and ambled back into the lab.

Some things still worked, he thought gratefully. Luna's

intelligence system, even minus Levin, was enormously effective. He punched in codes that, in theory, he shouldn't have known, tasted his coffee again, and began to spy on the growing patterns of Shag Nakamura's conquest. He only had a few minutes to spare, but a quick glimpse of the Terran situation could only help to reassure him of what he had to do. The groundhogs might not see the deadly blueprint being sketched across the face of their world, but here, in the hard Lunar clarity, Shag's purpose was as bright as the edge of a guillotine.

Elaine Markowitz allowed herself a moment's rest from her scheming. She measured out Darjheeling into a cloisonné pot and added boiling water and two strips of orange peel. After a few minutes while she sat quietly, inhaling the fruity aroma, she poured herself a cup and sipped.

"Ahh," she said. Tea was an old lady's drink, but she'd been a tea drinker since her early teens. And she *was* an old lady. One hundred four this coming fall. Old enough, although in Luna's lessened gravity, she still felt hale and healthy. She wondered what her life would have been as a groundhog and discovered she honestly couldn't imagine it. She'd come to Luna with Robert Schollander himself, the Old Man, and Mitsu Fujiwara, the most single-minded human she'd ever known.

A long time ago. But the hard lessons she'd learned then, truths about work and planning and a certain devious ruthlessness, had served her well over the years. Would serve her again, and the Old Man's grandson, and even Luna itself. That was what it was all about, wasn't it? The service? She knew both the founders would have understood.

Luna was the future. But to take those steps from yesterday into tomorrow, to leave the sludge-ridden, haggard, juiced-out world of Earth was a dangerous undertaking. Earth was tired, but not yet toothless, and Shag Nakamura, a formidable enemy, would not let go easily. It was well that Bobby Schollander had finally heeded the call of his own genes. He was a good proposition, which was as it should be. He came of good stock. But he needed polish, a little more understanding of the rougher side of politics. There were things she could teach him, things he must learn before he faced a true killer like Nakamura.

She sipped her tea and hummed with contentment. This little brawl would teach him a few things. Lucky for him.

Maybe lucky for everybody.

Schollander glanced at one of the digital readouts on his monitor screen. The realtime clock told him he had five minutes before he had to return to the board meeting. He called up the design he'd created earlier, and checked that Auntie Elaine's instructions had been followed.

There was one thing left to do. He thought it would be very hard. But when he called her and quickly explained, all she said was, "Of course, Bobby. Everything's ready. I thought you might need it."

Schollander paused at the door to the boardroom, barely brushing against Elaine Markowitz's shoulder. He leaned over to make out her guarded whisper. "I told you he had leverage, sonny. Better than I thought. So I made a deal."

"What kind?"

"I sold him my vote."

"I see," he replied grimly.

Without further words they entered the room. He wondered if some hidden mike had picked up the news of his ruin.

Eaton Vance was sweating when he returned to his seat at the center of the long table. Instead of one, he'd brought four aides with him. Thick sheaves of hardcopy surrounded him like a bulwark against Schollander's attack. A carefully timed moment after Vance had eased his dignified bulk onto a chair, Schollander walked easily into the room. He came alone and carried nothing. He nodded politely to Vance, who scowled at him. He ignored the ugly look and sat down. He folded his hands on the table in front of him and moved his gaze about the room, pausing to lock glances with each person for a split second. His enemies frowned. His friends smiled, some uncertainly.

We'll see, he told himself. Hide and watch.

Vance cleared his throat sharply. "Are you ready to conclude this silly business, Mr. Schollander?"

"Certainly," Bobby replied. "At your pleasure, Mr. Chairman," he said. His voice was calm.

Vance nodded. "Very well," he said. "A motion has been made . . ."

The technician was new in this part of the high security area. He'd been vetted only three months previously, but before his transfer was okayed from one of the high-energy physics labs out on the Lunar plains to his new post, he spent six uncomfortable days while hard-eyed Lunie security people asked him questions about everything from his sex life to his genealogy. Now, carefully making notes on a new process under the watchful observation of Franny Webster, something tugged at the corner of his eye.

He glanced up, puzzled. Had he seen something?

But when he focused on the tiny shred of movement, he saw nothing. The two tanks housing the inert bodies of Oswald Karman and Gloria Calley were unchanged. Nothing moved nearby.

He shook his head and turned back to his task, but a moment later he looked up again. He blinked and rubbed his eyes.

Only a flash of white. Some kind of reflection. A freak of light.

Nothing to get upset about.

As Vance droned on through the details of Schollander's motion to call a special election of the board of directors, Bobby looked up and caught Elaine Markowitz's eye. She appeared to stare into space, bored with the endless recital, but, without returning Schollander's gaze, she lowered one eyelid slowly. It might have been a tick. Or it might not have been.

Finally Vance finished his explication of the motion, and his reasons for opposing it. Because of his position, those reasons became the official company line, unless Schollander could win the upcoming vote.

He was amazed at how excited he felt. It was almost as if a part of him craved this high-tension exercise in corporate politics. He'd never thought he wanted this, had in fact avoided the training his father had wished. Instead of business he'd majored in math and physics. "Politics is for hacks," he'd told the old man. "Science is where the action is."

But his father had only smiled enigmatically and said, "You'll learn."

And so he had. He'd dropped out of the physics game when he'd discovered the Byzantine machinations necessary to pursue hard science. Yet now, as intimations of raw power and its concomitant responsibility began to penetrate his emotional barriers, he felt as if he'd been freed. Here was a canvas sufficient to his scope. Over the next few years Luna would carve out her own future, a new history separate from the rock-bound bloodiness of Old Terra. Already he sensed the challenges to come. And felt himself responding. It was a giddy, terrifying sensation. He loved it.

I'm a gambler, he told himself with something like wonder. Who could have known? And realized the answer to that was easy. His father had known. And Elaine Markowitz, Mason Dodge, even Gene Kilhelm. Most of all, Susan had seen it.

The only secret was from myself, he thought.

"Mr. Schollander, do you wish to say anything about your motion before the vote?"

Bobby looked up. Vance stared at him, a faint smile on his tanned face. The expression was confident and sinister.

"Yes," Bobby said softly. He inhaled, let the air out slowly, and began to speak. Cool silver fire thrilled in his veins.

"Ladies and gentlemen, fellow board members," he began. "Luna, Incorporated faces one of the greatest challenges of its existence. We call ourselves a corporation when, in fact, we are merely the legal extension of an entire world. And sometimes we forget the trust we hold."

He paused, poured himself a glass of water, and sipped. "My grandfather and his partner, Mitsu Fujiwara, understood this. But as the frontiers they faced were conquered, perhaps we began to forget our heritage. Those pioneers faced real danger—of blowout and collapse, of hunger, of uncertain technology. Those dangers are past, but now we face another. We have become complacent, just as we learn the greatest threat to our existence, not only as a company, but as a planet."

All eyes were on him now. He nodded somberly. "On Earth, the ancient nation-states are undergoing the final consolidation predicted by anyone who studies the pressures which control them. Enormous populations are running out of resources. As the raw materials dwindle, the people turn to leaders who make fatuous, undeliverable promises of continued prosperity. It is no surprise to find, working behind the scenes, men who manipulate vast corporations, phony religions, even entire governments as they seek to gather power. Such a man is Shigeinari Nakamura.

"All of you, I'm certain, are familiar with the name."

A soft murmur of agreement swept round the table. Even Eaton Vance nodded shortly.

"I'm also sure you know about Karl Wier's terrible injuries."

Again, more nods of agreement. And a few worried faces.

"Karl held no board position with Luna, Inc., but as some of you know, he coordinated our defensive efforts against the recent dangerous assaults of Nakamura's company, Double En. But Karl is gone, perhaps not to return, and our efforts in this direction lack leadership. Lack the right kind of leadership."

He lifted his water glass again. They were all listening. What he now said wouldn't matter much, perhaps, as his earlier plans would most likely determine the outcome. But he wanted to go on record with his newly found beliefs, wanted to stand and be counted. Another time he would have called it stupid idealism. Now he wasn't sure.

"Luna stands on the threshold of the Solar System. We are the gate to the planets and, eventually, the stars. But not if Nakamura is successful. He attacked us once with his great data processing networks. Do you honestly believe he would share power with us now?

"He must crush us. He knows this, and even now makes ready. You have read the details. Yet when he destroys us, he forever murders the best hope of mankind, for Luna is the way to the universe!

"This is what we risk, and he is what we oppose. But we aren't ready. We've turned our leadership over to mercenaries, just when we need new ideas and methods to insure our own survival. We must abandon the old standards of profit and loss, perhaps even make an end to Luna, Inc. as a corporate entity."

He stopped one final time, his lips dry and rasping. Each

of the board members pondered his words, some obviously rejecting, some quietly considering.

"Mercenaries won't be good enough. The old ways won't be strong enough. I have given you the facts. Now I call for a special election. Let the stockholders consider Nakamura's threat, and let them decide."

There was a long moment of silence. The Chairman waited a few seconds. Then, almost contemptuously, said, "Madam Secretary. We have a motion. Please poll the board."

Eunice Ninyiev began to call the roll. Vance replied with a single harsh word: "No."

As the vote progressed around the table, Schollander saw that Elaine had called the situation exactly. Two of the older directors reversed their early vote and went with Vance, one staring directly into Schollander's eyes, the other looking away. Finally the Secretary reached Markowitz. The old lady's blue eyes smiled benignly at Eaton as she said in a firm voice, "I vote yes."

Vance's frozen expression didn't even flicker. As a veteran practitioner of bribery and corporate treason, he was unsurprised to find it used against him. Perhaps he'd even expected it. At any rate, he almost smiled as the tally was finished.

"The vote is five in favor of passage, and five against. A tie. By the rules of our board, the motion is then defeat—"

"One moment, Mr. Chairman," Elaine Markowitz said.

"Yes, Elaine?" There was an oily kindliness to Vance's voice. He'd won. He was disposed to be generous.

"Before you finish the vote, I have a question."

"Do you wish to change your vote?"

"Possible. If you answer the question."

"Very well. Go on."

"Mr. Schollander raised some important questions. Do you agree that Luna, Inc., faces a major struggle in the times ahead? A struggle even to survive?"

Vance paused, considering. This woman had already betrayed him once. Yet, her question was valid. If she would change her vote his victory would be a clear one, not merely a failed tie vote. He decided it was worth the risk.

"I do, in fact, agree with, uh . . . the analysis of the situation. Our only area of disagreement is over the management needed to confront it. But as you see, that question has been settled."

There. Let the old hag chew on that.

"A question that you, as Chairman of the Board, believe is vital to the survival of Luna, Inc.?" she said again.

What was she up to? He didn't know, but danger signals began to fly. He would have to do something about her when this was over. Her and the Schollander brat, both.

"I said it was," he replied testily.

A look of slow triumph began to melt across her aged face. She smiled. "Then, Mr. Chairman, I invoke the survival clause, as spelled out in the company charter."

A welter of confusion passed across Vance's features. He made a snapping motion with one hand. One of his aides leaned over his shoulder and punched instructions into his keyboard. The two men stared at the screen. Finally, the aide whispered something in Vance's ear.

Vance nodded slowly. The tan on his face seemed to crack, and his eyes went wide with rage. "Yes," he said. "The charter. There is," he said reluctantly, "such a clause."

"Which reads, because I wrote it that way," Markowitz said cheerfully, "that 'if the Chairman of the Board of Luna, Inc., shall declare the matter at issue involves the survival of the Company as a whole, then the Board of Directors shall be enlarged to temporarily include any stockholder possessing a block of stock equal to or greater than five per cent, for the purpose of voting on that issue.' "

"Exactly," Vance grated. "An unusual clause, but those were unusual times. What is your purpose, ma'am?"

"Why, since you invoked it just now in response to my question—check the minutes, Eaton, you did—I just wanted to make sure all the votes were counted." Her voice dripped with a terrible, knowing innocence.

Vance shook his head. "This only delays the outcome a moment, Elaine."

Her features were as hard as his. "Quit fucking around, Eaton. Make the call."

He spat each word as if every vowel had a separate bad taste. "Yes, then. In accordance with the charter, I ask any stockholders who can prove possession of at least five per cent of Luna, Inc.'s stock to step forward and make their wishes known."

An endless moment of silence. "Does anybody here have five per cent?" Vance asked impatiently.

A soft voice answered, "I do, Mr. Chairman."

They gathered in Schollander's quarters after the meeting. Bobby found a bottle of Korbel champagne, a forgotten relic from a past celebration, and opened it. Everybody had a taste. They drank from paper cups.

Elaine Markowitz raised her bubbly and shouted, "To treachery. I love teaching an old dog new tricks!"

Schollander grinned. "You want to explain to everybody what you did to him? And such a grandmotherly looking thing you are, too."

"Looks are made to deceive, buster. Don't forget it," she replied. She tasted her champagne. "We had two problems, folks. One was to keep that bastard from really putting the screws to everybody on the board. The other was to get him to declare a survival emergency, so the charter clause could be invoked. Susan, you knew about the second part, but not the first. Vance had gathered nasty little bits and pieces about almost everybody on the board. I didn't want him to haul out his big guns, so I had to make him believe he had it in the bag. That's why I sold him my vote. Mine, along with the two other votes he'd already turned, gave him an easy tie. And Bobby purposely didn't pursue the votes he knew he had. I kept count, of course. If things had changed too quickly, we could have tried something else."

Susan Fujiwara nodded slowly, her gray eyes intent with thought. "You wanted to make sure I would be the deciding vote. As long as you could keep things even, all you had to do was swindle Eaton into saying it was a question of the survival of Luna, Inc."

"You got it, kiddo," Elaine said happily. "You know why we wrote that into the charter? Me and your two granddads?"

Schollander said, "I didn't even know it was there, Auntie."

"If you want to skin a toad like Vance, next time you'd better make sure you do your research," Elaine said. "Anyway, we put it in so we could short circuit the whole board process if we wanted. Either Mitsu or Robert Senior was chairman at any given time, and they owned or controlled huge blocks of stock. By invoking the clause, they could force a stockholder vote and bypass the board entirely."

Schollander nodded. The room was stuffy, crowded. Mason Dodge was checking the refrigerator for beer. He found three cans of Bud and popped one open with a loud, hissing sound.

"Vance looked like somebody slapped him in the face with an axe handle when I stood up," Susan said.

"Yep. Did me a world of good to watch. Never did like that man. And you know why he didn't think of you?"

"No."

"Because you're a waitress. How many times have you brought him a drink or served him a burger at that joint of yours? He just couldn't make the jump. Even if he'd known about the charter, he wouldn't have put that clause together with you. A waitress? With five per cent of Luna, Inc? His mind didn't work that way."

Schollander drained the last of his champagne, crumpled his cup, and tossed it across the room. The low glide path, the slow curve, would have seemed eerie on Earth. On Luna, nobody gave it a second glance. "He was stupid. But without your help, Auntie, he'd have kicked my ass. It was close enough anyway."

Her blue eyes reflected the dim light like stars on a choppy lake. "Yes," she said. She clamped her thin lips together as if waiting for him to say more.

"Shigeinari Nakamura won't make that kind of mistake," Schollander said.

"That's right," she said. "Now you're getting it."

Bobby stared at his knees. "Yeah," he said.

Everybody was silent. Then Mason Dodge said, "What will you do next?"

"Win the election," Bobby said grimly. "That won't be much of a problem. We swing a lot of stock now. And Vance wasn't all that well liked."

Only Elaine seemed dissatisfied with his answer. "And what then, young Bobby?" she pressed.

"Turn off Levin," he said. "Shut down that fucking machine."

Chapter Nine

Berg had walked out of their dream of his dream, leaving nothing behind but a greasy table and a dark night and the two of them staring at each other. The wind had subsided. They could hear the counterman scraping at his grill with a metal spatula, a horrible, spine-grinding noise. She scrabbled for a cigarette, found one, stuck it between her lips, and lit it. She was surprised to see that the tiny coal shook just a bit. Or was she surprised?

"You're shaking," Ozzie said.

"Why, so I am."

"I think I'm shaking too. He does that to me, you know."

"Who, Berg?"

"Did we have any other visitors tonight, babe?"

She removed the cigarette from her mouth and blew out a long plume of silver smoke. She could see their reflection in the black window next to the table, surreal and insubstantial against the faintly limned outline of a Lucky's Supermart across the parking lot. Odd how realistic these constructions could get. What was Levin tapping into, to get each tiny detail so perfectly right?

"No. But how come you're shaky? You never were married to him. Not that I remember."

He grinned a little at that. "We're all married, Calley. Remember? Whether we want to be or not. He's the key and we're just another lock. But joined, and there's no fucking way around it."

"That's why you shake?" She was honestly curious. She tried not to examine too closely her relationship with the two men in her life. And Ozzie, sweet thing, never held a mirror up if he could help it. But sometimes he let things slip out, because he couldn't hold them in, and then she saw the way things were. For whatever time or place the slippage occurred. Not that her life was normal or even usual.

94

But she remained Calley, and sometimes curiosity got the best, even of her.

"Partly," Ozzie said. "Just being around him. Especially when he's around you. You can see the scars."

"Scars?"

"Yeah. You both got them, and nobody can see unless you let them. But you show each other, cause when you get together like tonight, when the old love-hate juices start to flow, you forget anybody else is there. That scares me a lot. Because it's me you're forgetting, and I don't know if I can handle that."

Suddenly a feeling she barely recognized swept over her, a feeling of warmth so strong it almost liquefied her bones. Because she'd never had children, she thought of it as a motherly feeling, this all-encompassing sense of caring, of protectiveness. She wanted to enfold him and hold him to her hard little breasts and kiss his forehead and make soft, soothing noises with her lips on his skin.

Instead, she reached across the table and gently touched the back of his hand. "Oh, Ozzie," she said. "What's gonna happen with us?"

"I love you, Calley."

"I love you, too."

There didn't seem to be anything else to say. They stared at each other's eyes and, every once in a while, the night.

It was amazing how easily he had adjusted to life in this strange amalgam of metamatrix and gestalt space. At first, Ozzie had been particularly aware that Levin was the interface, and without the nanomachine constantly controlling the input to their (brains?) personality templates, they would have wandered lost in this universe of blue globes and black sky. But after a time—and did time have any meaning here?—he became used to it, as a human mind can become used to anything, and thought very little about it. Now Berg had come with his strange, almost fantastic request, and Ozzie had to think about it all over again.

He pictured where he wanted to be in his mind's eye and, in the blink of that eye, a new world took shape around him. Once again he had to remind himself that it was an analog, an interface, and then wondered why he bothered. It was so real.

He stood on the crumbling curb of a long, broad, deserted street. At his back was an area of low, steel-sided warehouses, old and scabbed with paint, disfigured with spots of cancerous rust where the paint had peeled. He heard the harsh sound of birds crying and smelled the distinctive liquid stench of the Lake. A chilly wind blew from the water, pushed against his back, rattled stray bits of loose metal and shook flags of rotten fabric that had once been bright awnings.

Across the street a smaller warehouse, neater and recently painted, waited silently. It was surrounded with a chain link fence that enclosed the building, a gravel parking lot, and a couple of sheds. Several abandoned vehicles lumped together on the gravel, some partially eviscerated. There was a bright padlock on the double gate of the fence, and another on the single door of the warehouse. He knew that a second set of doors was in the back, invisible from the street, doors large enough to take bulldozers and backhoes. This building had once been a road crew substation, before Chicago had suffered one of its endless budget cutbacks. He even remembered buying the place, and his specifications that the sale included all property on the premises. The auction officer had wanted to make that a separate lot, but Ozzie had always wanted a bulldozer. The deal hadn't been hard to make.

It was the first place he'd really felt at home, the first place that was *his*. He was glad that all its details still rested somewhere in the loose net of information that Levin thought of as him, so that Levin could recreate it in the wilderness of gestalt space.

Only an interface, an analog.

Home is where the heart is, he told himself, and stepped down on the shattered pavement. He felt in his pocket. The keys were there.

The keys were always there.

After Ozzie had gone, Calley sat at the table a little while longer, chaining cigarette after cigarette, listening to the chalkboard screech of metal coming from the encrusted kitchen of the pizza joint. She didn't recognize the place, and wondered if it was Berg's memory, some forgotten recollection of her own, or an Ozzie dream. Perhaps a combination of all three, a generic pizza shack summoned by Levin for their convenience.

Her brain felt corroded from disuse. She said, "Fuck it," stood up and hollered at the cook who was still scouring crud from other crud. "Cup of coffee," she said.

He turned around. "You want a new pot? This one's pretty burned."

She shook her head. "It's fine. Stronger the better."

He shrugged big, hairy shoulders—he wore a stained white tank top that had "Try a Pizza This" printed on the front, over a thick, dripping wedge of pie clutched by four disembodied fingers and a huge, dirt-blackened thumb—and poured her a fresh cup. At least the cup was fresh, she thought ruefully, as she tasted the throat-searing slurge inside.

After Ozzie left, she mused to herself. What he'd actually done was fade out. He'd said goodbye, that he had to think awhile, and she'd touched his hand again. Then he'd simply become translucent, shimmering slightly like a bad video picture, until nothing was left and she stared at empty air. Not even a Cheshire grin remained.

Think nothing of it. In this world, people—things—come and go, and all is without substance. Berg had realized it before she had, in that long-ago time when she'd held him close, not understanding, and he'd said, "What *is* reality?"

More than I thought, and less, she thought sardonically, watching her green eyes glitter against the black reflective surface of the window. The whole idea of reality was that it was real, unchanging. It was only in fairy tales and fantasies that the real became malleable and untrustworthy. Only in those places that people popped in and out like visiting ghosts.

Something deep within her understood, however. Always, even as a little girl, she had never trusted. Her life had been a series of visits. Mother, father, friends. Father gone when she was three, nothing special. Jigging her on his wide knee one day, and only a faint, familiar odor on his chair the next. Her father smelled of tobacco and the thin, bitter twang of cheap vodka, and for almost two weeks she'd been able to detect that aroma after his departure. But he was gone, and even his smell eventually disappeared.

She'd just turned thirteen when her mother died, a thin, wasted woman turned yellow by work and drugs that let her keep on working, struck finally by some disease that sucked her out from the inside, so at the end she was crumpled into a wrinkled balloon of skin. Odors there, too, astringent hospital smells and a faint hit of perfume from the nurse who was nice to her.

"Don't leave me, Mama," she'd cried, and the nurse had held her and said "There, Gloria. Little Glory. Your mama has to leave, but she loves you."

So if she loved me, why did she fucking leave? And never used the name Gloria again, not until Berg began to call her that, and even then, she'd hated it.

Calley. She'd looked up its phonetic definition once. Kali. The Hindu goddess of life and death, she who wears a necklace of skulls. Kali was the Black One, the Ferry across the Ocean of Existence.

This bleak and terrible goddess would not have been frightened by reality. She was the Cosmos, the changer and upholder, and reality could not touch her.

My secret, Calley thought, my secret name, my own Key. The Key to Life and Death. It had been her father's name. She sighed at the sadness of these grandiose things, and stared out the window, and sipped coffee.

Berg, she thought, you're such an asshole.

Ozzie let the metal door slam shut behind him. The electronic deadbolt automatically snicked into its sheath with a solid, final sound. Then everything was silent. He remained frozen, only his eyes moving.

He stood on a narrow concrete landing a meter above the main floor. A flight of three broad steps led down. The landing was edged with a railing of metal pipe and he put his hands on it. The pipe felt slick and cool.

He felt a little like the captain of some ship surveying his domain from the bridge. The warehouse was a single vast room. He'd never bothered to divide areas with any kind of walls, preferring to let function dictate form. About halfway across and on a line from the landing was his living area: a futon, surrounded by hubcaps filled with half-melted candles. Several chairs, rump-sprung, covered with thick, faded fabrics. A table mounded with discarded cardboard pizza rounds, next to a huge industrial drum filled with crumpled paper, crushed Styrofoam cups, plastic knives and forks. His small kitchen, a counter with two spindly stools he never used, and the door to the bathroom. Two doors, actually. The warehouse had come equipped with his and hers johns, a fact which occasionally gave him great merriment, even though the gents was boarded up.

Then, sweeping away on both sides of the living area, junk. This and that. Metal and wood and glass and fabric, whatever had caught his jackdaw eye. There was good stuff in there too, he knew, electronics and parts and tools, but for the most part, junk. Society's discards, things lost and tossed and left behind, to wash up on the shore of his snug little harbor.

He loved the sound of his locks, the heavy feel of the metal doors. In here he was safe. In this place nobody laughed at his gawky awkwardness, his ridiculous height, the disfiguring purple mass on his face. Here he wasn't a freak. Here he was a king, lord of all he saw.

What if it was junk? It was his junk, wasn't it?

Unbidden, one long-fingered hand crept to his cheek and he was astonished to feel smooth skin. The velvet growth there was no more. He'd forgotten about having it removed, about having the bones and skin reshaped, so that even Calley would, on occasion, call him "my anorexic angel."

Angel? He still didn't feel like an angel. If anything he felt like a darker god, one of the crippled deities who labored beneath the earth, in caves red with the light of fires, girdled by the yammering and clanging of metal and forges.

"But I know how to fucking make things," he whispered into the jumbled silence. It was the cry of a little boy who had no friends, and it was the threat of a grown man who had somehow become dangerous.

Overhead a long, bleary skylight admitted thin shafts of clear afternoon light, like a series of spotlights picking out unseen players. He sighed, stroked the railing one last time, and went down the steps. He paused to light a candle next to the futon, then headed for the kitchen.

He wondered if Levin had remembered he kept a jug of wine in the fridge there.

Finally she'd had enough. This scummy pizza joint with its barely human attendant depressed her. The night outside, jangly with distant neon and the low roar of wind, depressed her. Her own brooding, half-hysterical memories depressed her. And Berg, definitely Berg, he depressed her most of all.

"Fuck this," she said, and stood up and walked out the door. By the time she reached the street, the street had disappeared. Instead, it seemed she was walking down the short hallway leading from the front of her house to her office. She heard the welcoming hum of her air conditioning system fire up, shooshing hot air from heated panels hidden behind fake radiators in a steady stream. The heat felt good on her face. For her, it was always cold in Chicago. She opened the door and stepped into her office.

A crazy need for action, for movement, jerked at her muscles, drove her around the large room. She paused at the big sideboard, pawed through several hastily torn sheets of hardcopy from her comm center printer. Old mail. Bills and advertisements. The most modern communications system man had yet devised, capable of moving the words of poets from the moon to the lowest earthly hovel in a matter of instants, and what did she get? Flyers for *Free First Perm and Style!* and *Special Offer! You May Have Already Won a Complimentary Trip to Bermuda!*

The steel ring top of her desk gleamed in the silence like a pool, cool and deep and beckoning. Electricity sparked in her fingers. She felt the need to sit, to punch code, to build something, to *work*.

This fantasy vacation shit wasn't for her. No, not any longer. So Berg had a job for them, huh? Fine and dandy. Then now was the time to take care of business. What she always did. Figure out where the lies were, and who were the liars. Just because Berg had decided to become god, just because she—despite her best efforts—loved him, just because perhaps her very existence depended on his goodwill: none of it was reason to trust him.

Besides, this little journey he proposed sounded crazy as shit. Which meant it might be kind of fun.

In a horrible sort of way.

"Wait a second. That sounds like a fairy tale."

"So where do you think fairy tales come from?" Berg had

said, that infuriatingly superior smile flickering around his lips.

Ozzie piled another pillow beneath his head and reached for the jug. He had an ancient, but still perfectly preserved laser disk on a machine he'd salvaged somewhere, and mournful words boomed from a host of hidden speakers. "Love will tear us apart. . . ." He couldn't remember the group, one of the late twentieth-century bands caught up in the welter of angst and despair that pervaded those times. But they could kickass play. It was one of his favorite disks.

He tilted the bottle and tasted the harsh, metallic flavor of the wine as it chugged down his throat. He felt fine, although a little disconnected, and knew if he stood up suddenly, things would get all spinny and weird. It was a two-liter jug and he intended to finish it all. He held the bottle up and squinted through it at one of the candles. The light flickered and danced in the glass. Half full. Half empty. Halfway there.

He would drink all the wine and watch the candles burn down to melted stubs and eventually he would sleep. He would wake up without a hangover, thank God, one of the benefits of drinking in a dream. Berg had discovered it long ago, and told him about it later. Berg had been excited. "No hangover, bubba. Never again. Hot shit!"

And, of course, for Berg it was true. He didn't even have a body to go back to. He was in some fierce way forever marooned in the dreams of men and the more forbidding dreams of the machines. He was the Key, and a part of his power came from that abandonment. Berg was no longer human, of course. Even Berg, in some distant and lost way perceived the truth of that. Ozzie wondered if he cared.

Perhaps he'd never been human. Maybe that was why he took to all this so easily. Maybe from the beginning Berg had been an outsider, a secret alien, peering out on the real world like a bemused visitor, always wondering at these strange people. Real people. The Lady had sensed it, certainly. And Arius, before Arius became a fusion of Artificial Intelligence and human mind. Bill Norton had known it, because he made Berg the Key. Or had he?

Could be, he'd simply recognized Berg for what he was, and used him as a tool at hand. Ozzie wondered if there were any other natural keys out there.

Out there?

Yes. Out in the real world, where dreams stayed decently hidden, properly evanescent, and didn't expand like great, intricate flowers to become the whole universe.

He raised the bottle again and realized he ached for his body, ached in this body that was only a hissing of electrons, an arrangement of electronic wishes, so temporary he had no feeling of possession.

I am a ghost, he told himself. And now the Head Ghost wants me to enter a fairy tale even he won't touch. Won't? Or can't?

Ozzie shook his head. Maybe it was that very humanity, that remaining tenuous connection to flesh that Berg desired. He and Calley were flesh and man and life. Berg—and Arius—had crossed a barrier. They were sand and god and death.

Each dreamed his own dream.

He shivered, and watched a single star poke through the scum of his skylight.

Tomorrow he would look into it, think about it, make a decision. Tonight he would get drunk.

There was a time and place for everything. Wasn't there?

She settled herself into her chair, surrounded by the knife blade ring of her desk, and gasped as an almost unbearable moment of *déjà vu* slammed her back against the leather. She sat like a lump of ice, green eyes wide, heart pounding, for along with the intolerable formless memory came an endless sense of loss, and a terror so great she thought she might never move again.

When the instant snapped—it seemed like forever, but she knew it had only been a few seconds—she realized her teeth were chattering. Her fingers quivered like an old woman's as she tried to open the concealed drawer beneath the pristine desktop. She bit off a short curse. Then the drawer slipped open and her hand flopped around inside like the decapitated head of a chicken until it found what it sought. A crumpled pack of cigarettes. Feverishly she fumbled one cigarette out, dropped it, got another. Lit it and listened to the sound of her heart in her ears, pounding away like a giant drum.

"Hold on, girl," she whispered, each word an almost indistinguishable hissing noise. "H-h-hold on."

Could not begin to comprehend this wave of fear and memory, nameless as shadows, that had seized her in a grip of iron. She touched her forehead and felt moisture so thick somebody might have dumped a bucket of water on her.

What was it?

And then she knew.

It was here that Berg had kept her and, when she was no longer necessary, destroyed her so utterly that nothing at all remained but this haunting, this trapped inchoate nightmare, chained to this *place* forever.

That was what she remembered. She remembered her own death.

And the name of her murderer, of course. She remembered that, too.

She had been puffing and blowing on the cigarette so hard that within a minute or so the coal, heated almost white, struck the soft flesh on the vee of her fingers and scorched two identical small black marks.

"Damn *it!*"

She tried to flip the butt away but the coal was stuck to her burning flesh, and the more she shook, the deeper it charred. Finally she had to pull it away with her other hand. Then she thrust both fingers into her mouth and sucked, tasting the seared meat, the charcoal flavor of the ash.

And after it all, the terror, the memory, the burning, as she sat rocking slightly, her eyes closed, deep furrows in her forehead, after all of *that* the voice said, "Calley, is something wrong?"

She knew the voice, of course.

His eyes popped open. He stared straight up at the skylight. Out there beyond the smeared glass was a blue sky. He blinked. He licked his lips. His skin felt dry and hot. He blinked again, momentarily disoriented, until he realized where he was.

"Ugh." His body was stiff with sleep. He'd conked out with his clothes on, even his torn sneakers, and now smelled a rank odor of sweat and moldy cloth. "Urgh," he mumbled, and rolled over on his side. He stared at an empty two-liter wine bottle.

Memory came back in layers, one coating of detail at a time. Berg. The pizza place. Calley. Standing outside the warehouse. The weird, unquiet thoughts as he saw, once again, the place he had lived. And finally, icing on the cake, the jumbled recollections of a long night of drinking.

The nearest hubcap was full of melted, discolored wax. Half embedded and half floating, a miniature forest of blackened matches dotted the slick top of the wax, emitting a sour smell. They looked like the burnt bones of tiny animals or insects.

He forced himself up on his elbows. Bits of cartilage snapped and popped along his spine, in his shoulders. He took a quick inventory. Everything worked. And, as he'd expected, no hangover. Just the muffled, slow to get working laziness of the moments after awakening. He knew a cup of coffee, a shower, a cigarette, and a crap were all he needed.

"Whup," he said, as he creaked to his feet. He rolled his head on his neck and felt the muscles stretch. It was only as he started for the kitchen that the thought came.

I won't live. Berg's trip. I'll never live through it.

It was always a shock to realize it was her own voice. Deep and raspy, almost masculine in its intonations, cured in whiskey and gritty with too many cigarettes, it didn't sound at all like what she imagined.

But it was true. We never really hear ourselves. Maybe because we don't listen.

"Everything's okay," she said. "I'm fine."

"I wondered. You were acting pretty strange."

It was her own computer. Why shouldn't it have her own voice? But the kaleidoscopic ramifications—her computer in Berg's computer in Levin in gestalt space—tugged at her like minuscule claws. It was all so strange.

What was reality?

"I'm fine," she repeated. Why had she programmed the thing with her own personality? Was she that self-centered?

"Okay. If you say."

She felt a sarcastic reply scratch at her throat, but swallowed instead. She was still disturbed, at some basic personal foundation, by this presentiment of her own death.

This jaunt, this quest, this Holy Grail of Berg's. That was

it, of course. Only the heebie-jeebies normal to the beginning of any critical task.

But so bizarre. She had sensed his uncertainty, and that frightened her. If Berg, who would be a god, was scared, then what was she to think? It was his dream, but her life. Could he bring her back again if she died here?

He had once before.

But maybe not there, in that *place* he wanted her to go. And it came to her then, in the silence: it was a dream, but it was real. As real as life and death.

She lit another cigarette. In the steel reflection of her desk she watched the glowing knot.

It shook.

Chapter Ten

Tension was rising in the room. Nakamura could feel it, and was careful to keep elation from marring the blankness of his expression. There were just the four of them now, each watching the others with a guarded kind of arrogance. Except for Barre. Barre knew, because Nakamura had *shown* him.

Bob Nelson kept that meaningless smile pasted across his face, bobbing his head but not saying anything, his mean little eyes like black stones pulled from a river and left to dry, mud crusted on rock and beginning to crack.

Gogolsky said, "Shag, you've gotten us all here. I don't think it was a meeting any of the rest of us—" he made a sharp, chopping gesture that included Nelson and Barre— "wanted. I know I didn't. But too much is happening in the world, and you seem involved in all of it. So I came. I made my objections, but I came. You didn't have to send those videos. Pictures of murder, of torture. Did you think you frightened me? I've murdered. I've tortured. All of us have."

"Now, wait a minute, Nikki," Nelson said. His meaty cheeks flared two angry red spots.

"Spare me, Robert. Save it for your stupid voters. I don't vote."

Nelson subsided. Nakamura permitted himself a flicker of a grin. "No, Nikki," Nakamura said. "I didn't intend to frighten you. Only offer an example."

"But then, Shag, an example of what?"

"The cost of doing business," Nakamura said calmly.

"What, precisely, is that supposed to mean?" Nelson said.

Finally Nakamura let a shard of the cold, white fire that blazed inside him show on his face. "The cost of doing business," he said slowly. "Without me."

* * *

As he stared at their expressions, one hard, one devious, one frightened, as he savored the moment of his coming triumph, Nakamura felt the sway and lurch of history tug at his memories. This was only a picture, a snapshot in an endless history book. There were so many others. . . .

He'd built a great company. Bill Norton, with his surfeit of genius and his demented, uncontrollable lusts, had given him the means, but he'd done the building. He knew the slurs. Money man. Paper pusher. Corporate drone. But what none of those who called him that understood was that without him, Shigeinari Nakamura, there would have been no Double En.

Certainly Bill Norton couldn't have done it. He had his genius, but it was like an un-aimed gun. Without somebody to shape his bullets and target his weapons, nothing could have happened. Of the many smart things Norton had accomplished in his life, perhaps the most brilliant was realizing his own limitations and seeking out the restless son of an ancient Japanese family. The first meeting had been strange.

"What is this?" Nakamura had said, waving the scrap of paper with its near-indecipherable scribbles at his private secretary.

That young man had glanced at him with frightened eyes and said, "I don't know. It came today."

Frowning, Shag examined the envelope which had contained the short note. "No postmark."

"It was hand delivered."

"A messenger?"

"I don't think so. I didn't sign for it. I found it in the outside mailbox when I went out this morning."

Nakamura smoothed out the crumpled paper—when he'd first read the missive he'd balled it up and tossed it in the wastebasket, then, later, pulled it out—and read the note again.

Dear Mr. Nakamura: I have a project in which you may be interested. The profit potential is very great. You can reach me at the Imperial Nippon. Sincerely, William Norton.

"This is a crank letter," Nakamura said.

"No doubt," his aide replied.

"Everybody asks for money."

"Yes, sir."

Nakamura chewed on his lower lip. It had been a long, slow month. He dabbled in real estate, in shaky American bonds, in high-tech venture capital, always taking care to stay away from the webs of MITI, whom he regarded as shortsighted fools.

Usually the begging letters came disguised in thick packets, envelopes stuffed with estimates, surveys, growth plans. This crumpled note, written on cheap hotel stationery, was a joke.

Better to forget it.

"William Norton," he said at last. "Find out everything about him."

Three days later he called the Imperial Nippon. His call was answered by a male voice, rough and blurry. "Yes."

"This is Shigeinari Nakamura. I will see you."

The voice sharpened, but still didn't sound quite right. Probably drunk, Nakamura thought. "Good. When?"

"Tonight. Six o'clock. My home."

"I have the address," the voice replied. "I'll be there." And hung up.

Hung up, Makamura thought. The fucker *hung up* on me. He found himself grinning. He couldn't help it.

It had been one of the oddest reports he'd ever read. Like many major Japanese investors, he had his own investigators. Generally he used three kinds: One to report on the scientific background, training, and current research of the subject. A second to provide common database info; credit reports, brushes with the law, birth, marriage, divorce data, anything that made its way into the permanent records. The third was a personal investigation firm—private eyes, really— who dug and sifted for all the things that weren't on the record. The completed report, which he'd spent the morning reading, was strange. Never had there been such agreement on a subject. Never had three independent groups decided that one man could be so unworthy, such a horrible risk.

If the investigators had been Roman citizens and Norton a gladiator, the sword would have already gone through his neck.

Nakamura was intrigued. Nobody could be that worthless. He had to see for himself.

He set up the meeting carefully. Rather than summon Norton to his office, where the traditional trappings of power and wealth might muddy the issue further, he used his home. Norton had singled him out. He didn't know how he was certain of it, but he was convinced this was Norton's first effort to raise money. Certainly the data searches had shown no previous grant applications or financing attempts. And that was intriguing as well. Why had this reverse paragon selected him?

It will be a game, he decided. And two can play. He kept thinking this as he went about his quiet preparations for the evening.

But how could he have known?

His home was small and not particularly ostentatious, except for the fact of its location. The Tokyo ground it occupied was worth a hundred fifty million dollars. But even then Nakamura was turning his back on the new Japanese ostentation, the gilded life-style borne from necessity as Japan, awash in dollars, guilders, francs—practically drowning in cash—tried to turn some of its bloated bank accounts into *things* and, like the new rich throughout history, went on a monumental spending spree. Those who could rode in limos, lived in sprawling condos, paid millions of dollars to join golf clubs. In Japan, everything was taking on a thin coating of gold. And Nakamura hated it.

Yet he was trapped. In order to maintain his own status he had to go along. And truthfully, there were some things he found he needed. Staff to take mundane burdens from his shoulders. The luxury of fast, shielded transportation. The simple need for privacy, in a nation where privacy was the rarest coin of all. So, he supposed as he touched the delicate flower arrangement in his barren, white-screened entrance foyer, he was just indulging himself on a different level. He was having his cake and eating it too. This unadorned home was unbelievably expensive.

He sighed. Life was paradox. Only a fool expected simple answers.

Somebody pressed the button inset into his ancient front gate, and chimes sounded softly. Nakamura glanced at his watch and cinched his embroidery-encrusted kimono a final time. Then he went out to admit the visitor with his own hands. He'd sent the servants away. In those days, Bill Norton didn't frighten him in the slightest.

The man was pig drunk.

He was a big man, and he stood at Nakamura's gatepost with one hand on the stone. He clutched a bottle of cheap vodka in his left hand, and he swayed wildly, moving one big foot and then the other to keep his balance. His hair was wild, his suit filthy. He'd worn a tie, but it was askew, as if he'd tugged on it repeatedly. His breath would have stopped a tank.

Nakamura opened the wooden gate and stepped back in disbelief. "William Norton?" he said.

The man belched. He made a production of it, shaping his lips around an unspoken sound, holding them, then letting out an elongated noise that sounded like wet cardboard ripping. "Yeah. That's me. Norton. You can call me Bill."

What he should have done, Nakamura thought at the time, was call the police. But faced with the awful, disheveled wreck at his doorstep, awesome in his destruction, Nakamura was stunned for the first time in his life. He honestly didn't know what to do. So he stood there and stared, and after a while his hand moved away from the gate. He stepped back and said, "Norton. Bill. Come in, won't you please?"

A loose, terrible grin moved like plastic across the man's face. "Don't mind if I do," he said. Then he raised the bottle and drank from it, wiped his lips on the back of his sleeve, and belched again. Nakamura turned away. He couldn't look anymore.

"This way," he said shortly, turned around and began to walk. He didn't glance back to see if Norton followed. He wasn't sure he cared. The man was obviously insane, whether naturally or from the booze. It didn't matter. His dishonor to himself, not to mention his host, was too great to ignore, so great that it had to have meaning.

As he stepped up the carefully planted stones which led to his house, Nakamura knew that something was about to happen. Something exalted, but whether for good or evil, he couldn't yet tell.

* * *

Nakamura blinked, and the old picture of Bill Norton in all his inebriated grandeur flipped away, sudden as a magic trick. They watched him, each in his own way. Finally, Robert Nelson said, "Shag, you're full of shit."

I have held in my hands the dead bones of your betters, Nakamura thought. "Robert, did you view the film I sent?"

"Yes. Just as Claude and Nikki did. I'm not frightened either, if that was your intention. And what the fuck do you mean, doing business without you? We've been partners before, and will be again. But you make it sound like a takeover. Is that what this is all about?"

"Yes," Nakamura said simply. "I'm taking over."

Nelson burst out laughing. He started with sharp, barking chuckles, then escalated to deep, rolling belly laughs. Finally tears came to his eyes. Nakamura watched him steadily and said nothing. After a while Nelson pulled a handkerchief from an inner pocket and wiped his eyes.

"Are you finished?" Nakamura asked.

"No, Shag, you are. If you're serious. But it's a joke, right? This is all some kind of joke." Nelson's chunky face grew serious. "It had better be a joke."

They sat in a small conference room. The polished oak table was a wide rectangle perhaps three meters long. Each man had his own side. Claude Barre sat across from Shag. His dark, sweaty features were twisted with unspoken outrage.

On Shag's side of the table, recessed underneath the top, was a small shelf. On the shelf rested an old Toka revolver. Shag reached into the recess, withdrew the revolver, and shot Barre in the face.

A small red rose bloomed on Barre's forehead. His eyes snapped wide, a death reflex of total astonishment, as the force of the bullet smashed him back into his chair.

He voided himself. The stench filled the room.

Into the smoky silence, Nakamura said, "No. It's not a joke."

Norton had, with great effort, eased his bulk down onto a mat across from Nakamura. He sat hunched, his big shoulders curled down, and stared at the Japanese with a derelict smile. He still had the bottle of vodka squeezed in his right fist.

Nakamura lowered himself gracefully, able to smell the man's breath even from this distance. It was a terrible smell, full of fire and rot. "Do you actually think this . . . charade is going to help you?"

Norton smiled that loose-lipped smile and said, "Well Shag—that's what they call you, isn't it? Shag?—I'd say that remains to be seen."

And Nakamura realized the man, no matter what his condition seemed to be, wasn't drunk at all.

Oranson had come in and removed Barre's corpse. He'd even wiped up the red smear of blood from the pristine oak table where Barre's head had crashed down, rebounding from the leather chair. Nobody sat in the chair now, and the room was quiet as the front parlor of a funeral home with a fresh casket on view. As, indeed, it was, for each of them stared at a corpse, a man who, moments before, had been flesh and blood and now was rotting meat.

Finally Nikki Gogolsky broke the silence. "Are you going to kill us, Shag? Is that why we're here?"

Nakamura turned to him with a puzzled look on his face. Surely Nikki was smarter than that. He had Nikki down as the smart one. "No, Nikki, I didn't bring you here to kill you. Think about it."

Nelson spoke with overdone bravado. "It wouldn't be a wise idea, anyway. Those two goons of mine outside aren't the only ones. You wouldn't last a day."

"Oh, shut up, Bob," Nakamura said tiredly.

And finally, Gogolsky's eyes began to twinkle. "I think," he said brightly, "it was only Shag's way of getting our attention. And, as he said, pointing out the cost."

The crazy thing was, it seemed it went on for hours. Later, when Nakamura checked the time, he discovered that first meeting had taken only forty-five minutes. But time with Bill Norton stretched—there was no other word for it. Perhaps it was the intense displeasure the man provoked. He was a barbarian, and his every word, every action was offensive. He didn't sit—he squatted, as if he were performing some humiliating personal function on the clean mats of Nakamura's room. He belched and laughed and farted and drank constantly from his bottle of vodka. He was rude in unexpected, terrifying ways.

"I really don't give a fuck if I get your money, Shag."

"Then why did you come? Why are you here?"

Slow motion, off to the left, as if something invisible had flown softly past. "Why not? You got the money. Willy Sutton said it, banks are where the money is. And you're a great big bank."

"But why not one of your . . . own people?"

Harsh, cawing laugh. "You mean, why not a white banker? Cause they won't give me the time of day."

"And you expect me to?"

Shrug. "You're supposed to be smart. And I know you think you're superior to me. All you arrogant Japs think like that."

Nakamura didn't say anything. He let the silence speak for itself. And for him.

Now a tentative kind of anger bloomed on Norton's face, a hot, ugly speckling like measles or some variety of pox. "I don't care"—his voice was flat—"what the fuck you think of me. All I care about is what you think of this."

He reached into the shambles of his coat and pulled out a thin silver vial. The surface of the vial was coated with a light dusting of frost.

Nakamura was sipping tea. He hadn't performed the tea ceremony for this vile barbarian, would never dream of so dishonoring himself. But he drank tea while Norton pounded and pounded at his vodka. "What is that?" Nakamura said. He made his voice sound mild, uninterested. A child's trick. Even while he understood that something vast teetered on this moment.

Norton's eyes flashed once. "Neural cell culture," he said softly. "It's immortal."

"That's impossible."

"Is it?" Norton held the container out. "Here. Take it. Make tests."

Giant walls slammed and boomed together in Nakamura's skull. If what he said was true—

And finally understood what this was all about. He would make the tests, but he had no doubt what was in that frost-covered bottle. Nor did he mistake the challenge offered. He shivered at Norton's canniness.

Take me as I am, at my worst. See the genius of the pit.

See the gifts he brings. And understand this: without one, you may not have the other. To take the gift, you must accept the bearer.

Three days later, Nakamura transferred thirty-eight million dollars to the general fund of a new corporation called Nakamura-Norton. Double En.

The Norton who signed the necessary papers was clean-shaven, well-dressed, polite.

Sober.

But Nakamura knew the truth. He had made a deal with a devil. Yet it was a foreign devil. Norton could never understand that, so Shag was comfortable with the secret deal *he* signed, or didn't sign, within his own mind. There was no honor involved at all.

Nakamura smiled. He'd been right. Nikki understood. Now all he needed was to make this thick-skulled *gaijin* political boss catch the message.

"The planet," Nakamura said, "is in a general state of turmoil." He smiled faintly.

Nelson made a sucking sound with his lips. The flush had receded somewhat from his doughy cheeks. "It's a fucking mess, if that's what you mean."

"Profit can be made from such situations," Nakamura said.

And Nikki bobbed his perfect little head up and down, like a child contemplating candy. "Out there," he said dreamily, "all those people. Hundreds of nations and billions of bodies and each think they are unique." He glanced at Nelson. "Yours," he said scornfully, "think they vote. Think they *control*."

Even Nelson grinned at that.

"It is a single world," Nikki continued. "What a dirt farmer does in Iowa affects the price of bread in New Moscow, which influences the cost of money in Tokyo." He paused. "Shag, there isn't anybody here from the Rising Sun."

"It will come," Nakamura said easily.

And the light dawned. Nikki's blue eyes glowed. "Ah, yes. Robert's endless military budgets, your companies—that bizarre religion is yours too, isn't it?"

Nakamura nodded, delighted to watch Nikki's nimble mind at work.

"And I have the resources. China, India, all mine."

"Japan has the money," Nelson pointed out.

"We'll get it," Nakamura told him.

"Yes," Nikki said. "I do believe we will."

It was in the end a simple business deal. Nelson supplied muscle to complement Double En's forces, as well as a dummy leader in the form of the President of the United States. Nikki threw open the vast storehouses of the Third World, rich in resources and labor. And Nakamura supplied— what?

Nobody had really spelled it out. But he'd given them a sample, when he'd blown Claude Barre's brains out the back of his skull.

The will. The iron. The destiny to seize the time and take the future.

Nelson paused at the door to the conference room, his face slowly settling back to stone, as a receding flood reveals the rock that was always there. "The American people," he said, his voice thick and plummy, "will be pleased to assume their rightful place as leaders of the planet."

Nakamura felt a certain queasiness in his gut. In a horrible sort of way, Nelson actually believed those ridiculous words. The man had somehow convinced himself that an end had been decided, and any means were justified. What kind of insane world did he live in, anyway?

Nikki only chuckled.

Nakamura glanced at him. Nikki, at least, lived in the real world. Nakamura understood that someday he would have to do something about Nikki.

Someday. But not yet.

"Long live America," Nakamura said, and passed out of the room. At last, he had forged his own sword.

He already had the will to use it.

Hawkshaw Cribbins was house staff, not part of the new bunch that had come in when Nakamura had taken up residence at the big country place. He didn't approve of all the weird ones, the little Orientals with their strange eyes, the big, meat-laden mercenaries whose footsteps crunched the grass and made slooshing sounds in the boggy parts near creeks.

Hawkshaw had grown up in these parts. His momma had cooked in this house when it was smaller, and he'd hired on right after high school graduation.

Now he walked post near a new boundary. He still wasn't sure how Nakamura had acquired the mountain. It was supposed to be a state park or something. But nothing the rich did ever surprised him. The rich had all the power anyway. It was enough that his pay was good and the work was usually easy. Except when that empty-eyed sonofabitch Oranson was around, looking at everybody like they were cockroaches or something. Then he had to hup to it, all right.

But now, with the last of the sun disappearing, leaving long, bruise-colored smears across the sky, and the crickets quieting down and the pine woods taking on the shadows of night, it was okay. Oranson wouldn't come here now. Probably wasn't even around, now that the high mucky-muck Jap had left for the big city.

Hawkshaw settled his ass down on a pile of fallen branches next to a big pine and fished around in his pocket for a cigarette. The stock of his assault rifle poked painfully against his spine and he shifted around till he was comfortable. He put the cigarette to his lips, lit it, and glanced at the big, old-fashioned watch on his wrist. He'd got it from his daddy, a keepsake, but it still kept time just fine.

Seven o'clock. Stars were coming out overhead, one here and one there. The sky had become a deep, purplish blue color, and the night air smelled clean and fresh and full of evergreen. Usually his cigarettes tasted awful, but just this once the flavor of the smoke was good, a sharp brown tang on the evening.

He exhaled softly. Another hour and off walking post. Back to the barracks for a big supper, then maybe a few Buds and some poker.

Easy work. . . .

He never saw the thing with red, blazing eyes and claws as long as ten-penny nails that took out his throat in a single snarling rush. Felt it only dimly as things like bunches of knives sank into his belly and released a long, gushing warmth.

SINGULARITIES

The last thing he saw, against that perfect night, was a flash of white, like some big gauzy curtain fluttering down, covering him.

Taking him away.

Chapter Eleven

Bobby Schollander stood beneath the ferocious glare of the overhead lights in the main computer room and stared through a wall of monomole plex at the silent sapphire cubes that made up Levin's heart.

Two sleepy technicians hunched over their consoles on the other side of the huge room and ignored him. If they thought it was strange that the newly elected Chairman of the Board of Luna, Incorporated, had chosen to pay a call at four in the morning, they kept it to themselves.

He wasn't even sure why he was here himself. He hadn't been to bed yet, and doubted that he would sleep at all this night. He was still keyed up from the previous day's victory, when he, guided carefully by the Machiavellian schemes of Auntie Elaine and Mason Dodge, had vanquished Eaton Vance's ragtag coalition of recalcitrant board members and a few conservative stockholders in the final tally.

Chairman of the Board!

What a title. What a weight. Yet he felt strangely buoyed by this sudden assumption of final responsibility, much as even a reluctant driver grabs for the wheel when his car, driven by another, heads wildly for the trees at the edge of the road.

Perhaps it did run in his blood. His grandfather, along with Mitsu Fujiwara, had created Luna, Inc., and his father had nurtured it through the difficult days of its adolescence. Was it only fitting, then, that he should be the third Schollander to run the company now, in the days of its greatest challenge?

Yet he felt suddenly young and quite alone. Oh, no doubt that Auntie Elaine, Mason Dodge, even Susan Fujiwara would be ready and eager with advice, but in the end, the title, and all it meant, was his alone. He would make the decisions which determined whether Luna, Inc. would survive the almost incalculable threats represented by Arius, by Shag Nakamura and his unholy New Church, perhaps even by Jack Berg and Gloria Calley.

He gazed thoughtfully at the silent working of the great computing machine called Levin. Perhaps even this, Karl Wier's most telling triumph, was a threat. Could a machine, an Artificial Intelligence, rebel against its makers, become an enemy? It was a ludicrous thought, in one sense, a pot boiler idea from the lurid science fiction novels of his childhood, and yet—

And yet what? Levin had not responded to command since Berg and Calley had completed their titanic duel with Arius. He didn't even know who had won that fight. Karl Wier, before the assassination attempt, had not seemed unduly worried, but he was no longer able to reveal the source of his confidence. What if Arius had control of Levin, of Berg, of the very heart of Luna's information capabilities?

Although the computer room was kept at a constant moderate temperature, Schollander felt a sudden chill. He stared intently at the sapphire cubes which hung suspended like incredibly precious beads on a string behind the crystal wall.

"What about it, Levin, huh?" he mumbled softly. "Cat got your tongue? Or Arius?"

Then he felt foolish. What would those stockholders think, who had so recently elected him to lead them, to run their company, if they could see him now, in the darkest watches of the day, muttering at a silent hunk of stone and metal?

Crazy. All of it was crazy. That was what Eaton Vance had not been able to recognize with his business as usual, take the money and run attitude. The whole world had changed, was still changing with ever increasing rapidity, and the old truths, the maxims which had once been sufficient no longer were. The machines were everywhere, and there were ghosts in the machines, and whole new worlds to understand. To *perceive*. Some of those worlds might be in this dumb crystal in front of him, but how could he know?

The crystal was mute.

Schollander blinked. What was that? Something . . .

He turned, but the two technicians had not moved. One, in fact, seemed to be snoring softly. And it hadn't been that kind of movement. No, more like a glint of reflections from the sudden surfacing of a great fish. Great fish? What was he thinking of?

He turned back to Levin's tank. Nothing moved there, either, and nothing would. Of course not. He was tired. Just a trick of eyes exhausted from tension and lack of sleep.

Of course it was.

So why did he feel, as he walked slowly away, that something—some*one*, had answered his unspoken question? That a long, slow, infinitely humorous voice had whispered deep inside his brain, and said—

We're all here, Bobby. All the worlds, inside and outside, all here.

His lips thinned out, pressed together. He shook his head, as if trying to shake away the errant, disturbing thought. But there had been more, hadn't there?

Hadn't the voice also said . . . *Come in and play, Bobby. Come play in our worlds.*

Hadn't it also said *that*?

In fact, Schollander did finally get some sleep, a few restless hours plagued with vaguely threatening but unremembered dreams. The heebie-jeebies, he supposed, only natural in view of his new responsibilities. One of which sat across the desk from him in what had quite recently been Eaton Vance's office.

Bobby glanced down at the sheet of hardcopy which lay on his otherwise empty desktop. "Mr. Henry Carpenter," he said at last, and looked up, his eyes questioning.

"That's right," the tall, gangling man agreed.

"Well, Mr. Carpenter—"

"Call me Henry," the man interjected comfortably. "Everybody does."

The man seemed preternaturally relaxed. Merely being in the same room with him made Schollander feel secure, almost cozy. It was an odd feeling, and one he wasn't entirely sure he trusted.

"Well, uh, Henry, I just want to thank you—"

The older man raised one big, wrinkled hand, palm out, and shook his head. "No need," he said, "I just done what anybody would do."

The man liked to interrupt him. Schollander tried again to

finish a sentence. "Hardly anybody, Mr.—Henry. To tackle an armed man like that, and—"

Henry Carpenter shook his head. "Just luck, was all. The right place at the right time. You know?"

"Goddamn it, Mr. Carpenter, would you let me finish a sentence?"

Carpenter's sudden grin was completely engaging. "Why, I got you pissed off. I'm sorry. I don't mean to. My wife, Madge, she says I flap my mouth too much, and I guess I do. You go right ahead, Mr. Schollander, say your piece. And you call me anything you want to."

Schollander felt as if somebody had just poured a bucket of warm honey over his head. This hillbilly was somehow weaving a web around him, a web of utter relaxation. There was no way he could help but like Henry.

Schollander stared at the piece of paper a moment, feeling the heat of embarrassment in his cheeks, while he gathered his wits. Either Henry Carpenter was exactly what he seemed, or he was an insanely great con man. The sheet of paper, skimpy of any real information, was no help.

Schollander looked up again. Carpenter nodded encouragingly but didn't say anything, and Schollander felt like a fool all over again.

"It was a brave thing," Bobby finished lamely.

Carpenter shook his head. "Not really. That villain never saw me coming. Never had a chance. And I was too late anyway, right? That's the bad part, what happened to Mr. Wier. And you, of course."

Schollander had almost forgotten about his shoulder wound. It was nearly healed, only a few darkened areas that itched occasionally remaining to remind him of those short, terrible seconds that had changed his life forever.

And this man had played a part in all that.

"I'm okay now, thanks," Schollander replied. "Mr. Carpenter, whatever you say, it was still a fine piece of courage. We here on Luna—" Schollander paused, realizing suddenly how pompous he sounded, then swallowed and continued on. "Well, you're a Lunie now too, of course. Anyway, I—all of us—thank you. You've done Luna a great service."

"That poor man," Carpenter said dolefully. "Terrible."

Schollander took a deep breath. "If there's anything I—we—can do to repay you . . ."

"Don't need no reward," Carpenter replied. "Not for doing what any decent man would do, given the circumstances. But—" and now his blue eyes twinkled—"the wife, Madge, you know, she's after me to try to get a bigger place. On earth, space ain't at a such a premium, but I know here on the moon—uh, Luna—things are different. So if it's a problem, well, you just tell me and we'll forget about it."

"No problem at all," Schollander said. "Somebody will come by later today, take you to your new quarters. One bedroom or two?"

"Oh, one. Madge and me, one bed's all we need. Thank God."

Schollander nodded. The two men chatted a few moments more, and then Schollander rattled the sheet of hardcopy, signifying the interview was ended. Henry Carpenter understood at once, stood, and thrust his big hand forward. They shook. Schollander thought that Carpenter's grip was like being enfolded with soft, warm, dry wood. The kind of handshake you'd accept in lieu of any written contract.

But after Carpenter had gone, he wasn't sure. Not so sure at all.

"Auntie, can you come in now?" he said.

A moment later his door opened, and Elaine Markowitz limped slowly into the room. Her body was old and sagging, but her eyes were alive with malicious merriment.

"Well," she said happily. "Did he do it?"

"Do what?"

"Did that sonofabitch," she said patiently, "con you like he seems to have everybody else?"

He stared at her as she lurched slowly to the chair Hank Carpenter had just vacated. Her wrinkled features tensed at the evident pain her movements caused her, but something that flashed from her blue eyes warned him to remain in his seat. Elaine Markowitz, in her 104th year, required no help. She sat down suddenly and fanned herself with a thin sheaf of printouts. After she had caught her breath, Schollander said, "Auntie, why don't you use your chair?"

She glared at him. "What? I don't fit into your picture of a little old lady?"

One again he felt confusion, as he groped for the right

answer. What was this ability older folks had to put him perpetually on the defensive?

"Crawl if you want," he said finally.

"Did I make little Bobby mad?" Her raddled lips curved in a wicked grin.

"Oh, Auntie, shut up. Did you treat my grandfather this way?"

"No. But I did your father."

Suddenly distracted from the matter at hand, he said curiously, "Why? What was the difference?"

"Your grandad was already one tough sonofabitch when I met him. Your dad had to grow into it. Just like you." Her reedy, irritating voice was complacent.

"Auntie, you are the most annoying, disagreeable—"

Her smile grew wider. "Funny, all the men in your family seem to feel that way."

He shook his head. "Forget it. I'm not going to win a spitting match with you anyway."

She nodded. "Not yet, at least."

He started to reply, thought better of it, and shook his head again. "You listened to Hank and me?"

"Uh huh. I listened, and a dedicated meatmatrix listened, and two of your whippersnapper psychologists listened."

"So? What do you all think?"

Her voice cracked with disgust. "Clean bill of health. Not that you asked him anything penetrating. But the man's a fraud." She waved her printouts suddenly. They made a sharp, snapping sound in the quiet of the office. "Their reports. All bullshit, young Bobby."

He sighed. "I know you changed my diapers and powdered my butt, Auntie, but I'm not a baby anymore. Besides, it's not dignified to call the Chairman and CEO of Luna, Inc., 'young Bobby.' "

"Oh. Excuse me, Your Royal Chairmanship. I didn't—"

He waved his right hand wearily. He felt a headache coming on. "So he's a liar and a fraud, is that it? Have you got anything to back up that judgment?"

Her lips narrowed and her eyes glittered coldly. "I'm a hundred years old, young—uh, Robert. And I've seen a lot more scoundrels—*better* scoundrels—than that flimsy fake. He's on the con, Robert. I can smell it."

He stared at her thoughtfully. "You know he saved my life?"

"Of course I do. I saw the films, just like you did. Five more seconds and you would have been barbecue right along with Karl." The idea seemed to cheer her. "Sure, he saved your life. So what?"

He couldn't think of any answer to that. To cover his confusion, he picked up the printout from his desk and glanced through it again.

"What's that? Good old Hank's bio?"

"Uh-huh."

"Not much to it, is there?"

He shook his head. "Pretty bare," he admitted. "Worked for TriDiCon, a Silicon Valley outfit subsidiary to Tech-SYSTEM—"

"Which is wholly owned by Double En. I read the damned thing too." She rattled her own papers sharply once again.

"So?"

"Do you believe in coincidence, Bobby?"

He decided not to contest her use of the name. He'd been Bobby to her since he was an infant. If they both lived long enough, he might still be Bobby to her as an old man. He wondered what she'd called his father. "Coincidence?" he said at last. "What coincidence?"

She narrowed her eyes. "Surely you can't be that stupid."

He felt the heat rise in his cheeks. "You mean about Hank being on the spot just at the time of the attack?"

She puffed her ancient cheeks full of air and blew it out slowly, like steam from a teakettle. "No. I mean the attack itself."

He stared at her. It was an angle he hadn't considered.

"Look here," she continued. "Just at the time we need Karl Wier the most, this chunk of slime—what was his name? No matter—this barf bag crawls out of our woodwork fully armed with a very high-tech piece of artillery and starts blasting away at Karl while he's slurping coffee with his two most trusted assistants in front of a restaurant operated by—guess who? The single biggest stockholder in Luna, Inc."

He thought about it. Then he nodded. "Quite a bag, if he'd gotten everybody. Is that what you're saying?"

"He got Karl. He almost got you. If this Hank guy hadn't

just happened along when he did, he might have gotten Lizzy and Franny, too. With Levin out of action, Karl gone, and you dead, Eaton Vance would have been in charge. And the transference of your stock—who gets it, by the way, in your will, Bobby?"

"You mean you haven't looked?"

She drew herself up. "Do I look like a snoop?"

He chuckled shortly. "Of course you do."

She subsided. "Well, okay. That's fair. So anyway, I get a piece, but Susan Fujiwara gets most of it."

His eyebrows shot up.

"You were right. I looked. But anyway, it would have meant a terrible dislocation for Luna, possible even some kind of stock fight, along with everything else. And our scientific capability would have been badly hurt at the same time. You see what I mean about coincidence?"

"But what about Hank, then? He stopped all that from happening."

She nodded grimly. "Pretty good timing there, too. And think about this. Hank was pretty good, wasn't he?"

"Thank God. But it's all here." He tapped the printout. "He's a martial arts hobbyist. Works out every day, if he can."

"Yeah. So put it all together. A mole assassin makes his move just at the critical time, but doesn't succeed completely because an ex-employee of Double En who just happens to be a karate expert has emigrated to the moon just in time to be on the scene and foil this terrible attempt."

"That's a lot of coincidence. But, Auntie, it still doesn't make any sense. Carpenter worked for Double En. That's Shag Nakamura. If Carpenter is some kind of spy for Nakamura-Norton, then what he did doesn't add up. He should have just let it happen."

"I didn't say," she replied slowly, "that he works for Double En now." His blue eyes filmed over and she seemed to go away for a moment. Then, with a slight twitch, she focused again. "That's my real problem, Bobby. I can't figure out *who* the bastard works for. And I don't trust anything I can't figure out."

"Maybe he doesn't work for anybody. You ever think of that?"

She eyed him sharply. "Then it would all be coincidence.

I don't know about you, but for me, that's just a bit much to swallow."

Another problem. Always another problem. But that was what he'd wanted, wasn't it? Young Robert Schollander, latest in a long line of Schollanders, riding to the rescue of Luna, Inc. on his shining white horse.

Horseshit.

"We'll keep an eye on him."

"You do that," she said. "And maybe I will, too. Look into that fat little wife of his, as well."

"Madge Carpenter? Why?"

"She's too perfectly bland to be real."

"Auntie, are you suspicious of *everybody?*"

"Of course." Her voice was sour. "And if you want to keep from making a hash of this job, you'd better start cultivating a little suspicion yourself."

"I think you exaggerate. Not everything is a plot of some kind."

She stood up slowly. "At our level it is, Robert. Mr. Schollander. At our level, *everything* is a plot."

At the door, she paused and turned slightly. "By the way, Eaton Vance has flown the coop."

"Huh? What did you say?"

"Our ex-chairman of the board hit the LEO shuttle two hours ago, bag and baggage."

Schollander's eyes widened. "But—that means he—"

She nodded with dour satisfaction. "He forfeits all the goodies we negotiated into his parachute after we beat him, to keep him from making trouble."

"Almost five million a year. For five years," Schollander said softly.

"A lot of money," Elaine agreed.

"But why?"

She regarded him with something almost like pity. "Somebody once said that whenever there isn't an answer, the answer is always money. But with certain people, that isn't entirely true. Sometimes the answer is power."

Schollander chewed on it. "Money is power," he said finally.

"And who has more of both than we do?"

He nodded thoughtfully. "Shag Nakamura."

She grinned. "My thought exactly." His answer seemed

to put a new bounce in her movements. She was almost jaunty as she limped around the door. She paused. "Think about it. Eaton Vance on his way to the open arms of our biggest enemy. All of this in the last two weeks. You want to be careful, Bobby. Watch your back. You never know when another coincidence is going to jump up and bite you on the ass."

Her parting chuckle was harsh and barking, and Schollander didn't like it at all. He picked up the sheet of printout, wadded it into a ball, and threw it across the room.

"Shit," he said. "Just fucking *shit*."

"What do you think, Madge?" Henry Carpenter said.

The short, pudgy woman looked up at her husband's long, equine features. "It's very nice, Henry. Much bigger than the other place. Maybe this will all turn out after all."

They held hands like lovers as they toured their spacious new apartment. It was all very touching. The men who watched the monitors didn't even notice the way her fingertips moved against the leathery calluses of his palm.

Chapter Twelve

He strode like a giant through a place of milk and blood. In his hand was a great sword. Sheets of thunder rolled in endless waves across the land, which was a barren, scorched crust beneath his boots. Fire blossomed in the livid sky. When the thunder stopped, he heard the sound of multitudes laughing. His nostrils twitched at a cacophony of stinks: burnt flesh, rotting bogs, parched earth.

He came to a high place and looked over desolation. After a time, he raised the immense sword and said, "Come on, asshole. Enough is enough."

It was as if some unseen hand had flicked a switch. The thunder stopped. The fires blew out. The wind died. He stood on his mountaintop in silence. Eventually he heard the sound of another, walking.

"You don't like the light show?" It was a metallic voice, full of bone-grinding partials and sniggling half-tones, a voice with which to conjure nightmares. Most horribly, beneath the machine insanities of the upper registers, a thick, greasy underlayer of cheerful, hungry humanity bubbled like a pot of rancid stew.

Berg turned and watched the golden youth climb the last few yards to his eyrie. The youth trailed a host of alloyed insectile monstrosities in his wake. They bickered and twittered and convulsed against each other, creating a sound like wind over steel wheat fields.

"You know," Berg said, "for a guy that's half machine, you have an awfully perverse liking for lurid melodrama. What's this crowd supposed to be? Your brokerage house?"

The golden youth, who had once been a man named William Norton, and also a machine named Arius, and was now both, and neither, chuckled softly. "Allow me my little idiosyncrasies. I see you have your own, ah, retainer along."

Berg glanced over his left shoulder. Sure enough, a form even shorter than his own, with a bigger nose and a black mustache that hid half his lower jaw, stood there grinning at him, black eyes twinkling. "Oh, Jesus. I don't remember inviting you."

Levin's grin grew brighter. "Wouldn't miss it for the world, boss. Besides, I think old brass bootie over there is kinda cute."

Berg turned back to Arius. "Fair's fair. You want an introduction?"

"Thank you, no. I don't swing that way."

Berg shrugged. "You never know till you try it. I bet Levin's a hot little hunk."

Arius said dryly, "I don't like facial hair."

"I can change it," Levin said eagerly.

Arius ignored him. "Something you wanted to see me about?"

Berg spread his legs and planted the tip of his huge silver sword on the rock in front of him. "How do you think the war's going?" he said.

"So so. You don't seem to be doing any better than you were at the beginning. Or, for that matter, any worse. I must admit, that surprises me a bit."

"Why?"

"Well, after all, I did create you. One would think the creator would have dominion over the creation."

Berg laughed. "Thus spake the industrialist backers of Hitler. And the man who promoted Benedict Arnold. And, I suppose, Shag Nakamura about Bill Norton."

A wispy hiss of flame darted between Arius' golden lips. His pinkish eyes flashed with demented humor. "A point well taken. So. We seem to be well matched, then. I can't escape this interesting little purgatory you've dragged me to, but you can't vanquish me, either. A stalemate."

Berg nodded. "That's the way I read it, too, hot pants. So I want to propose a small wager."

"Oh? A deal with the devil, you might say?"

"Well, I guess that's all in the perspective, but sure, you got the general idea."

"Mm. What kind of deal?

Berg told him.

After a while everybody went away, and darkness returned to the spot of their compact. Only now the scene was perfused with a thin blue glow, and the torn earth seemed faintly transparent, as if it were a scummy film over something brighter, greater, more real.

As if the earth itself was only a dream.

Several perfect white sheep ambled slowly across the lower slopes of the hill, small black-faced eating machines whose occasional plaintive bleats provided a properly bucolic background to the endlessly sunny day.

"Berg, what is it with you and sheep? You were a city kid. You never even saw a fucking sheep until you were a grown man."

Berg chewed absently on a stem of grass. "I dunno. I find them . . . restful."

"They stink. Sheep shit, you know. I stepped in a pile just a few minutes ago."

He was lying on his back, one hand tilted across his eyes. He wore faded jeans, a new Harvard University sweatshirt, and flip-flops. "You got to watch where you put your feet, kiddo. First rule for city kids. All those dogs and not enough pooper scoopers."

Calley hitched herself over onto her side and propped her head on one hand. "You know, these interfaces or analogs or dreams or whatever you want to call them don't have to be so goddamned real. Sheep shit, for chrissakes."

"I like it."

"Yeah. And whatever Berg likes, he gets. You're a selfish mother, aren't you?"

"Let's not fight."

She glared. "Berg, it's what we do best. Why should we stop now?"

He didn't answer that. Finally he spat out the bit of chewed grass and said, "You still gonna go along with the deal?"

"Your magical mystery tour? I said I would. What do you want? Blood?"

"How about Ozzie?"

She paused. Then, a different, huskier tone to her voice, she said, "He'll go where I go."

"You know, you could do worse."

"Than Ozzie? Sure I could. I have. Guy named Jack Berg, in fact. Name sound familiar?"

"No, seriously. I mean it. I haven't ever done anything right for you. It's like, you know, there's no hope for us."

"Where there's life, there's hope." But her voice sounded brittle, as if she were trying to convince herself more than him.

"Maybe, when this is all over, you two should—I mean, we should—"

"Look, Jack. You're forgetting a few things. Like, for one, there's still what happened to us in the metamatrix. You said we were joined. I didn't fully understand then, but I do now. It isn't something either of us chose, it just happened. Now it's like . . . some kind of basic *function*, something that just *is*. You know what I mean?"

He sighed. "Yeah. No choice. Not for either of us. Sometimes, I wish . . ."

"What?"

"Naw. Nothing. Forget it. Okay, so you and Ozzie are ready?"

She shrugged. "I guess. As ready as we're gonna get. This is really stupid, Berg. I don't know why I'm going along with it."

He grinned. "To get away from the sheep, maybe?"

"Or the shit. All the shit."

"Well, whatever jerks your gourd. It's not gonna be easy. You understand everything?"

She nodded. "You and Arius control the playing field. You won the toss, so the playing field is Chicago. Me and Ozzie, we're the pieces. And Arius will have his rep there, too. Then we play the game. Simple enough."

"I wish it was. Lotta stuff riding on it, babe."

"That's what's so fucking stupid, Berg. You bet the whole ranch on Ozzie and me. Why? Are you doing so bad right now?"

"Not bad, but not good, either. It's a stalemate, but it could change. And not even Levin can predict the outcome. This way, we come to a decision."

"Uh. And you trust Arius to keep his side of the bargain if he loses?"

"He's got no choice. Shit's involved I can't tell you about.

Don't worry, he'll pony up if the time comes. And," he went on gloomily, "so will I."

"Oh, great. Shit you can't tell me about. What am I, ugly or something?"

"Don't get all weird, Calley. It's part of the game. I can't tell you because it would poison the contest."

She considered. "We're going in blind, you know. Don't know what we're looking for, don't know what to do if we find it."

He nodded. "That's part of the game, too."

"Not much meat there, brother. Not much hope."

He looked over at her. His silvery eyes, flecked with dots of coal, went wide. "Why do you think I put it all on your shoulders, Glory?"

She nodded. "There's that."

He seemed to wrestle with something inside himself. "I'll help. All I can."

"Well, you better, you asshole. You think I wanna do this all by myself? You did it to me once before, you know."

"Did what?"

"Killed me, you bastard. In the metamatrix. When you were . . . done with me."

"That wasn't real."

She made a sound, and threw it back in his face. "What's reality?"

He blinked. "Are you crying?"

"No," she said.

"Now, let me get this straight," Ozzie said.

They sat on his stained futon. He'd started to change the sheets, but she'd arrived before he'd finished, and he felt mildly embarrassed by the graphic map of his sexual history on which they rested. Every few seconds he would notice a particularly obnoxious patch of rusty color, and try to move unobtrusively to cover it.

"What are you twitching around like that for? This thing got bugs, or something?" Calley looked down with distaste. "Wouldn't surprise me. Looks like it's got everything else."

He felt heat rise in his cheeks, and for a moment his ancient stutter returned. "I-I w-w-want an a-a-answer, okay? Quit trying to change the subject."

She sighed. "I just told you everything I know."

"But Jesus, that's ludicrous. It's like we're some kind of fucking *video* game."

She took the dark brown Turkish cigarette she'd been smoking—it smelled like broiling cat fur—and flipped it expertly at one of the wax-filled hubcaps which surrounded the futon like tiny garbage satellites. It hit the rim, fell back, and began to sizzle, emitting an even more disgusting stench. Overhead, the bleary skylight allowed a gray, filmy light to fill the vast, clutter-choked room. "That's right, bubba. Video game of the gods, that's us."

"I wish you wouldn't call him that. He's not a fucking god. Neither of them are. Arius is a meld of crazy man and crazy machine, a perfect case where two plus two equals fifty. Or a hundred and eight. And Berg. I dunno if he's for sure crazy, but he's not anything I'd call real sane. Anyway, they aren't gods. And I wish you'd quit saying it."

"Berg thinks he is."

"He tell you that?"

"Not exactly, no."

"Well, if it's true, then he's just as crazy as Arius. Crazier."

She rocked gently, eddies of smoke rising around her like incense. "Ozzie, you don't get it, do you?"

"What's to get?"

"Whatever Berg *is*, whatever Arius *is*, in here it doesn't matter. In here, they're whatever they fucking want to be. If they want to be gods, then they are. Whatever they think gods are, at least. We sure as fuck can't tell the difference."

He chewed on it. "What you're saying is, we don't have any free will. None at all."

"Did we ever?" she said slowly.

"Aw, Calley, don't go all moony on me. This—this fucking abstraction, this gestalt space, *it isn't real*. That's what you don't get. We have bodies, we're real people. We can fuck, and eat pizza, and shit it out later."

"That so? Is it any different here?" She grinned lewdly and reached over and squeezed his crotch."

He winced. "Don't do that unless you mean it."

"I always mean it. But Berg had it right the first time. If it smells like a horse, and walks like a horse, and has a saddle on it, you might as well grind it up for the welfare folks, 'cause it most likely makes great dog food."

She noticed that he'd been letting his hair grow. When he

shook his head, it billowed out behind his shoulders, a golden curly cloud half way down his bony back.

"I don't like it."

"I don't think anybody's asking, babe."

He paused, then stared at her, his amber eyes perfectly round. "Are *you* asking, Calley?"

She smiled slowly. "Well, me, yeah. I'm asking."

He nodded, sighed, nodded again. His golden hair shimmered. "Okay, then. When do we start?"

She shrugged. "Now," she said.

Outside, a few dim stars glimmered faintly above a thin layer of lake fog. The night was cold, damp, and quiet. Ozzie paused, his head raised slightly, as if he were sniffing the air for some unimaginable spoor.

"You gonna lock your door?" she asked.

"Huh? Oh, sure." He turned, clamped the heavy steel and brass padlock shut.

"Old stuff," she said.

"I like old stuff," he told her. Then, "You smell that?"

"What?"

"That smell. Smells like . . . I dunno. Wet fur, something like that."

She screwed up her nose. "You live by the Lake, Oz. God knows what it might be."

"Hey, I know what my neighborhood smells like."

"Uh-huh. If this was really your neighborhood."

He stopped, thought about it. "Yeah. Okay, run it by me one more time. Maybe it'll make more sense. Although I doubt it."

Her voice was mildly irritated. "I've already told you—"

"So tell me again. I'm stupid."

She quirked an eyebrow at him, but made no further objection. "Berg is defending whatever it is against Arius, who is attacking. We are attacking whatever it is, and Arius is using constructs to defend. Between the two of them, they maintain the game board, which is Chicago, and that's where we are supposed to look. That's it. No rules, no limits. Anything goes."

"And we don't know what we're looking for. Is our thing and Berg's thing the same?"

"I dunno."

"Jesus."

"And we can die," she continued. "Really die. If we die here, there's nothing left to go back to our real bodies with. That's Berg's chip. That's what he put on the table, along with whatever bet he, personally, made."

"I wonder what Arius wagered against us?"

"I dunno that, either," Calley said.

"What a mess."

She grinned suddenly. "You forget one thing."

"Uh? What's that?"

"If we can die, so can they. Whoever they are."

"You sure?"

"Berg told me."

His narrow shoulders hunched slightly. "You think that's enough?"

In the milky darkness, her smirk was purely ferocious. "Oh, it's a start," she said. "It's a start."

It had been so long, and she had been so cold. As she slowly came—awake?—she remembered the sudden moment of blooming red fire, and the great pain that had filled her skull with darkness and taken her away.

The crimson moment bobbed in her past like a cork on a sea of blood, but now, as more and more of her sensorium came into play, even it began to recede.

Alive? she whispered slowly to herself.

There was no answer, only a growing light.

In that timeless space between the event and the now, she sensed only darkness, but there was an itch to it. It was as if she hadn't been entirely without life, but only apart from it for a time. Dimly she understood that certain . . . functions had continued, and she felt a wispy tug to some other place, some other being.

It made no sense. Her memories of that time were unavailable. She probed, trying to extract some kind of meaning from the time of darkness, but finally gave it up. If she was meant to know, then she would be given access.

She paused in her unfolding then, struck by the incongruity of the thought. Given access? It implied there was a giver, and if that was true, then—

A slow and molten joy began to grow within her. *He* was still alive. *He* had not been destroyed in that final mael-

strom. And it must have been *He* who had called her back
from the long darkness.

She spread her gauzy whiteness—grave shrouds which
concealed claws—into the growing luminescence of her new
life, and she prayed as she had never prayed before.

Oh, my Son, give your enemies to my destruction!

The reply, so unexpected yet so fitting, came instantly:
Yes, Mother, I will do this thing.

She had never known such happiness.

Ozzie chewed at it as a dog might harry a fleeing rabbit.
"We can't," he said, "just wander around until something
jumps us. We need a *plan*, dammit."

She was distant, absorbed in her own thoughts. They sat
in the streetside coffee shop of the Chicago Marriott, looking through thick plate glass windows at the rushing crowds
of Michigan Avenue. Oddly enough, it seemed to be Christmas time. The trees which lined the broad avenue, rebuilt
twice since the rising of Lake Michigan, were decked with
thousands of twinkling white lights. It was an ancient Chicago tradition, dating from a time before even her childhood. She stared at the lights but did not see them.

He slurped noisily at his coffee. A waitress stood nearby,
ignoring them as she muttered subvocalizations into her
implanted throat bead. Somewhere in the bowels of the
hotel, kitchen machines sprang into action at her command,
chopping and mixing and cooking yet another patented Marriott meal. Ozzie knew even the waitress's job could be
done more cheaply, more efficiently, by a machine, but for
a thousand dollars a room, the patrons of the Marriott
demanded more expensive service.

"It's all coming alive again," Calley said suddenly. Her
eyes flashed emerald so fiercely that Ozzie pulled his slump-
ing frame up straight.

"What is, babe?"

She fluttered her strong fingers, her coffee forgotten in
front of her. "Everything. Everybody. All the ghosts."

She confused him. He shook his head slightly. "I don't
understand, Calley. You know me." He chuckled slightly.
"Always the slow one."

The turbulence faded from her face. She reached across
the table and patted the back of his hand. It was an old

gesture, one from which they both took comfort. "Don't run yourself down so much, Oz."

He twitched an uncertain grin at her. "Well, okay, but what the fuck are you talking about? Who is coming alive?"

She took a deep breath. "It's the only thing that makes sense. You have to look at it from Berg's point of view. He's the one right along who's always been talking about reality. Almost like he doesn't see what's real the same way we do. You ever notice, he's never seemed much upset about losing his body? Almost like he didn't care about it."

The unspoken worry lay on the table before them like an unturned card. Their own bodies rested still and cold in dark tanks on the Moon. This was all a dream, but when they awakened, their real bodies would be waiting for their return. Or so they viewed the web of what they called the real. This insane hegira was a threat to that safe resurrection. Berg had bet their real lives against the strength of Arius. Or so it seemed.

"But did he?" she wondered aloud.

"You're losing me again," he told her.

"Mm? Sorry, just wandered a bit. Look. I bet you anything you want that Berg dreamed this whole thing up. So if the world's greatest con man put together the shape of the thing, then it has his dirty little fingerprints all over it. He's concerned about something I haven't quite been able to figure out yet, but it has a lot to do with whatever we think of as life and death. Look at Arius. All he wants is immortality. Power is a secondary thing with him, only insofar as it assures him immortality. But I don't think that's Berg's primary concern. Berg is opposition. Berg is the Key, as he keeps telling us all the time. And what's Berg's greatest strength?"

Ozzie wrinkled his high forehead. His golden hair shimmmed. He looked like a ridiculously tall, ridiculously young Botticelli sculpture. "He always claimed to be the defender. That's his nickname, right? Iceberg."

She smiled. "So if he laid out this thing, you can bet he snookered Arius somehow. The game has to be loaded some way in favor of defense. That's my guess."

"Defense of what?"

"What's the most important thing Berg has? The one thing that if it's destroyed, Arius sweeps the table?"

He stared at her. "I flat don't know, babe. But you do, don't you?"

"Uh huh. The Key. That's what this is all about. And that's why the game board is Chicago."

He finished his coffee, put down the cup, and signaled for refills. "I still don't get it. What the fuck is the Key?"

"I don't know," she replied. "But I think that's what we're supposed to find out."

The waitress glided by with a pot of coffee, poured, and glided on. Ozzie grunted. "Well, good fucking luck," he said.

"Luck," she said softly, "is only a matter of good offense. And that—" Her voice went grim, "That's something I'm not bad at myself. Not bad at all."

He thought she sounded hungry. He was right.

She came fully awake at last in the black places, the under places where heat signatures mattered as much as the dim flickers of the human visual spectrum. Around her stretched vasty distances, echoing and filled with the low call of watery drums. Around her too whispered the plaintive cries of her many children, the lame and the halt and the furred, the cripples who had rejected the light of day for the safety of the dark, and her protection.

She sat upon her rude throne and felt the dim glow of hidden fires. Her children clacked and clawed and paced, bound upon their incomprehensible tasks. Incomprehensible to any but her, perhaps. For she recognized the time and the place. Somehow, through the greatness and the glory of her Son, she had been transformed, remade. She had been sent back, flipped across the gulfs of time to the beginning.

Ecstasy tore at her heart. She had been forgiven for her great sin, and given an even greater boon. She would be allowed to expiate a mother's deadliest bane: the destruction of her son by the lapse of her hand.

She nodded peacefully at the misshapen hordes which rustled and muttered around her. All her children, the army of her salvation.

She would try again. And this time, she would not fail.

"Come to me, my angels," she said softly. In the distance, the drums boomed with a hollow, hungry sound.

* * *

Calley looked up from her half-eaten Denver omelet. A thin smile quirked her lips. "And take a look at that, bubba," she said.

Ozzie turned, followed her glance to the holiday crowds pushing past the tall windows of the coffee shop. The press was so thick that it was hard to see across the street, to the equally thick holiday mob on that side, but he thought he saw a flash. A single mental snapshot.

"Jesus," he said.

"You see what I see?"

He nodded.

"Tell me," she said.

"The Lady. And a wolfpack. What the fuck, is she doing her Christmas shopping? She never used to come up out of the Labyrinth."

"That was then, this is now," Calley replied. "God damn, it must be Christmas."

"How come?"

"The gods," she said cheerfully. "They sent us a sign."

"There aren't any gods," he told her irritably. "That's just—"

She cut him off with a wave. "No matter," she said. "Maybe Santa Claus, then."

Chapter Thirteen

The entire top floor of the towering building was given over to Nakamura's suite—offices, gardens, private rooms. Dusk rolled blue across the vast stretch of Lake spread out below, pricked here and there by twinkling lights from hundreds of tiny boats.

Nakamura handed Nikolai Gogolsky a Sevres crystal goblet brimming with the rich darkness of Remy Martin Louis Napoleon brandy. Gogolsky, his quick, foxy features wrinkled with pleasure, inhaled deeply and gestured at the breathtaking panorama visible from the rooftop garden.

"You entertain well, Shag."

Nakamura smiled tightly. "You mean for a Jap, Nikki?"

Gogolsky grimaced. "Shag, the only problem I've ever encountered in dealing with your compatriots is this damnable combination of arrogance and inferiority you all seem to suffer. Must be something in your past."

Nakamura cradled his own goblet. It was a chilly night in Chicago and at this height strong winds blew, but cunning baffles deflected the winds and concealed heaters warmed the air. Delicate fruit trees—orange, lemon, lime—swayed gently and emitted sweet odors on the night. "Historically speaking," Nakamura said slowly, "Japan has good reason for both attitudes. Not the least of which is the history of White Russia."

"But that's all over. All in the past. Ivan the Conqueror is dead. So are the wretched Communists. Mother Russia enters a new era, arm in arm with our brothers of the East."

Nakamura smiled openly at this. "You sound like Bob Nelson. Are you making a speech?"

"You've caught me again. I cribbed that from my address to the European Economic Community Congress last year."

"I know. I was there."

Gogolsky's eyes twinkled. "And you stayed awake through

my speech? You remembered? You must have been the only one."

"I always pay attention to things that interest me, Nikki."

"And do I interest you?"

"What do you think?"

Gogolsky wandered to the edge of the terrace and rested his elbows on the top of the wall there. A faint breeze ruffled his immaculately barbered hair. He started to speak, paused, then said, "When did you complete your takeover of the Consortium?"

Nakamura's face went immobile. His black eyes seemed to swell slightly. "The Consortium? What makes you think that?"

"My guess is you've been in control all along. Ever since the unfortunate demise of Arthur Kraus, in fact. It was a mistake on his part to attack Double En, it would seem."

Nakamura raised his drink slightly. "I would hope it's always a mistake to attack Double En."

Goglosky sipped a bit of brandy. "Shag? Let me set your mind at ease, if I may. I don't pretend to understand everything that's happening in the world today—your precise relationship with the New Church remains a bit of a puzzle, for instance—but certain things are becoming clear. One of them is that you have somehow maneuvered yourself into a position of immense power. As I say, I think you now control—and have controlled for some time—the Consortium. Which makes you preeminent in Western Europe. Your position here in North America seems unassailable, and of course, your home base in Japan is quite strong. My inclination is to go along with you."

Nakamura nodded. "It's a wise position, Nikki."

The smaller man raised one finely manicured hand. "But, Shag, with a few *caveats*."

"Ah. There are always those."

"Of course. First, my soon to be good friend, don't think I'm as expendable as the unfortunate Claude Barre. Of course that was merely the termination of an employee, but even so. I am not one of your hirelings, Shag. I would not be sacrificed so easily."

Nakamura had drifted to the wall himself, and now stood close to Gogolsky. His eyes were hooded. "Nikki, what is to stop me from having you pitched over the edge here?"

The older man showed his teeth. The view was wide and white, and in no way could have been called a smile. "Oh, Shigeinari. How subtle you are. First the brandy, then threats. What is to stop you? Nothing. Except, perhaps for William Norton."

Nakamura froze. A faint tic began to dance under his left eye. Finally, he said, "Bill? What does my partner have to do with this?"

Gogolsky shrugged. "Your partner? The drunken one, who hasn't been seen in such a long, long time? The one rumors say may be terminally ill, or worse? I don't know, Shag. Maybe Bill has nothing to do with this. Nothing more than Arius himself. I thought you would know. And could tell me."

Nakamura felt his back teeth grind together, an involuntary and hidden reflex that shot strobes of pain through his skull. A great cold blankness invaded his belly, and for an instant he looked down from his dizzy summit and felt himself falling. Outwardly, however, he merely turned slightly and said, "Such things, my already good friend and probable partner, should not be discussed in the open air. Would you accompany me inside, perhaps for further refreshment?"

Gogolsky, his small face suffused with rodent merriment, nodded happily. "Of course, Shag. Of course I will."

It always amazed Nakamura how the framework of his corporation served as an amplifier for his smallest thought, his most insignificant action. He thought of this as he stared silently at Frederic Oranson, who sat on a chair in front of Nakamura's desk, his emotionless features distant and thoughtful. There were just the two of them, and their conversation would be quiet, low-keyed, informal. Yet if Nakamura were to say, for instance, that it might be a good thing if the stock in one of Nikki Gogolsky's companies were to drop precisely six points on the Japanese stock exchange, then Oranson would nod agreement and, eventually, give certain orders. Those who received Oranson's orders would in turn carry out their own duties, perhaps involving thousands of others—and, inevitably, the stock would fall the required six points. The mechanism was of little concern to Nakamura, once the creation of the mechanism was finished with. The mechanism was Double En, and, to the Japanese, Double En's only justification for existence was the service it performed as this human-computer amplifer for the soft, measured words he would speak in quiet privacy. The immense corporation, in the final analysis, was only a modern cybernetic and human equivalent to the swords his ancient samurai forbearers had carried to enforce their own wills in a smaller, more personal world.

"He didn't elaborate," Oranson said finally, "on his use of Arius's name?"

"No. I didn't press him. Better he thinks it is a threat that worries me. He shouldn't have brought it up, actually. Not unless he planned to use it. His mistake only alerts me, gives me a chance to discover the real hazard involved. Or so I see it."

Oranson nodded. "I see it the same way. But the question is raised. Now we have to do something about it."

"Yes. And what is the question?"

Oranson stared at his boss. Sometimes he tired of these didactic little tests, these word games Nakamura was so fond of. Did Nakamura think him stupid? And if so, why keep him on? Especially given the extraordinary expense involved in maintaining the esoteric drugs which assured his survival?

As always, the fleeting moment of dispassionate consideration passed, and Oranson said, "The question is not, of course, how Gogolsky learned of Arius, but when. And how much. Of the two, when is more important, because we have to learn whether Arius is still alive. If Gogolsky was contacted after the attack on the Labyrinth, we could have a problem."

"A problem. Yes. Then there are the subsidiary questions, the most important of which is why was Arius talking to Gogolsky in the first place."

"Do you fear treachery?"

"With Arius?" Nakamura's features twitched with distaste. "I always fear treachery, but with Arius most of all." He leaned back in his chair, his black eyes snapping and angry. "See to it, Fred. Whatever it takes. But find out."

Oranson nodded. "Right away," he agreed.

Nakamura's gaze slid away, his pupils going blank and distant with the contemplation of his own unnameable demons. "I hate that thing," he breathed softly. But what he meant, and could not say, was that he feared it.

There was no answer to that, so Oranson left the office.

As much as he could, he felt stirrings of lust. Nemesis always affected him that way.

Danny Boy's feet ached. His ankles and calves, ropy with oddly placed bunches of muscle, twitched and quivered with fiery exhaustion. His body had not been designed for the long, debilitating cross-country treks he'd forced upon it, and the stretched cry of overstrained tendons and wearied bones filled him with an overriding lethargy.

I can't sleep yet! he warned himself. It had been a long, arduous trip down from his green hideaway of the past few days. He hadn't wanted to leave that place. The tumble-down shack had become a sort of home, an uncomplicated den far removed from the complexities of his previous life. Some part of him, a nugget from his early childhood on the farm, had surfaced in response to the pastoral tranquility of that place. Yet he'd been given no choice. When she spread her white wings in the silence of his skull, he could only obey. She had wanted him to leave and so, without realizing any of the conflict which grumbled beneath his ordinary consciousness, he repacked his knapsack and set off south. Back toward the city, toward the dark and damp of another life. One thing would remain the same, however, In Chicago, somewhere, was the source and final satisfaction of his bleak hunger. His hunger, and hers.

He had come in the night like the wolf he was, his great, red-rimmed eyes wide against the flickering glory of the towers further in toward the lake. Now he paused on a gray, shrouded corner, grateful for the warmth of his fur, and let the sounds and smells and tastes of the city soak into his awareness.

He would have to be very careful. This was gang territory. He glanced up at the stained, crumbling gray stone walls of shabby tenements, their scarred surfaces thrown into high relief by the harsh, popping light of high-intensity sodium lamps. Empty windows regarded him blankly, but behind the cracked glass lurked eyes. It was one of the lessons of the street, hard-learned years before, in a time of different slavery.

Rager turf. These empty sidewalks might stretch endlessly through the night, cold and blank as a pimp's mercy, but they were watched. Ragers marked the passage of every intruder on their turf, and protected even burned-out scraps of alley and slum fiercely.

Desultory skirmishing had gone on for years between the Ragers on the surface and the wolves beneath the ground, until an uneasy peace had been reached. Nothing formal had ever been negotiated, and the prime directive of the unspoken agreement was simple. You on your turf, and us on ours.

Infractions were punishable by death.

Yet, somehow, he had to win through the Darkstone Rager ring, and reach the echoing safety of the Labyrinth by the Lake. She commanded it. But even she, as she poured her white rage into his skull, could not command the swarms of Rager troops.

No, this time it was up to him.

He growled softly, stared at the bright silver plume which slipped between his fangs like a ghost, then picked up his pack and scrabbled on.

He had survived the Ragers once before. He would again. They were, after all, only human.

"Okay," Toshi Nakasone said, "if you ain't got cheeseburgers, bubba, how about a pizza? Even frozen would be fine."

Wordlessly, Chet Limowitz shook his head. "Sorry. No pizza. How about beans? Or tuna fish?"

"You sure this is San Francisco?" Toshi said. His face took on an exaggerated look of suspicion. "San Francisco used to be a good burg for pizza. Not Chicago, but pretty good."

Limowitz felt as if he'd been plucked from reality into the heart of some bizarre fairy tale. Robby and Bobby had retreated to their consoles, where they carried out the final instructions of the protocol. The tank from whence this strange, hungry, Oriental *impossibility* had sprung was now shutting itself down. The thin mosquito whine of pumps and tiny cleaning machines filled the otherwise muffled quiet of the lab.

"It's San Francisco," Limowitz said, and rubbed the back of his right hand across his forehead. Sweat. Was it that hot? Or was this some kind of hallucination, brought on perhaps by too many beans, an overdose of canned tuna?

Toshi, seeming unconcerned by his own nakedness, sat on a spindly Formica and wire chair next to Limowitz's desk.

"So how come no burgers? Or pizza? Are the burger joints closed?"

A jagged lance of irritation burst through Limowitz's temples. He winced, and rubbed at the skin there. "Would you shut the fuck *up* for a minute? Goddammit, there isn't any fucking *pizza!*"

"Oh, hey, was it something I said?"

"Listen, you—hallucination. Everything's a mess. You're a mess. *I'm* a mess. You got to let me think a minute."

"Chester," Toshi said, and Limowitz realized he was trying to take a reasonable tone, "listen. Get hold of yourself. I'm not a hallucination. Really. You want to pinch? Here."

Chester waved away the proffered arm. "That only makes things worse. If you aren't a hallucination, then what are you?"

"Oh," Toshi said. His voice filled with understanding. "Is that what's bugging you? Easy. I'm a construct." He sat back and grinned, his black eyes twinkling, as if he'd answered all questions, and now where the fuck was the food?

"Good. That's good. You're a construct." Chester swiped at his eyes again, and wished he hadn't chewed up all the Excedrin after his last headache. Endorphin analogs were only a distant dream. "So what the fuck does that mean? A construct? Are you real?"

"Sure I'm real. Real as you, Chet, buddy. Real as those two bookends over there riding console. Real as—" his voice went soft, dreamy "—as a large anchovy mushroom with double cheese and extra—"

"Look, would you stop with the food already? I told you, we got beans. And tuna fish."

"Ugh. How come is that, Chet? Don't you have instructions? And don't they mention something about cheeseburgers?"

"Yes, they mentioned your fucking cheeseburgers!"

"Chester, you got to watch yourself. You're gonna give yourself a stroke."

Limowitz took three deep breaths. Was it three for meditation, or five? He couldn't remember.

"Five breaths in, five out," Toshi remarked. "Hold each movement for a five count. If you're trying to calm down, that is."

"Shut up."

"Sure, Chet. Uh, listen. What kind of beans are they? Baked beans? Kidney beans? I don't like kidney beans that much, but maybe—"

"Shut *up!*"

Even Robby and Bobby jerked slightly at this final outburst. Toshi raised his hands, palms out, a gesture of peace. But the movement sent a tiny wave of disquiet into Limowitz's brain, as if the short, smooth motion might have other meanings.

"Uh, look, Toshi—you said Toshi, right?"

"That's me."

"Well, there's maybe been . . . what I mean is, it could be that things—*local* things, you understand—well, maybe it isn't what you expect."

"Huh? What do you mean? A restaurant strike, something like that?"

Limowitz felt his tenuous grip on normality begin to slide again. "No, you food-obsessed ninny. It's the fucking New Church. And Double En storm troopers. And—God only knows what else. They're burning down the city. The whole fucking city!"

Toshi straightened up. He grinned. "Is that all? Well, fucking aye, then. So go ahead. Tell me."

"What?" Chester said weakly.

"Where's the nearest fucking pizza parlor?" Toshi turned to Robby and Bobby. "Hey, you two. What flavors do you want?"

Once Oranson had left, Nakamura was seized by a terrible agitation. He couldn't keep himself seated. His short, muscular legs propelled him from his chair, marched him around the room while his brain seethed with the rage he longed to express. Sometimes, it seemed that his samurai heritage of repression, of the concealment of all true feelings, was the most awful burden he had to bear.

Norton!

It was always Norton. The great, shambling, degenerate chameleon! Even from beyond the abyss he haunted him, harried him, brought all his plans to dust.

Oh, yes. It didn't matter with what malign shroud he draped himself—call it Arius, call it matrix or metamatrix, call it dwarf or demon—it was still Bill Norton, partner and destroyer of dreams.

Finally the frenzy began to drain out of him. He paused, touched one hand to a paneled wall, and listened to the pounding of his heart. His breath caught and rasped in his throat, and his neck muscles were sore from the effort it took him to keep from screaming out loud.

Just once—just this fucking once—let it be some kind of ghastly mistake. Let Nikki Gogolsky's velvet threat be a skillful bluff, based on hunch and guesswork. Of if the message was real, let the communication have occurred *before* the attack on the Labyrinth which had destroyed the monster and his chiefest minions.

Nakamura didn't believe in benign gods. His divinities were more formless, succored in chaos and inimical to the naive machinations of humanity. Which suited him perfectly. Life was a path of endless trial, and whimsical intervention on the part of meddling gods was only another blight visited upon a senseless universe. Oh, yes, for once, let the gods be silent.

And let this demon be dead.

Amen, he thought, and then he kicked out three monitor screens in quick succession. It wasn't much, but it make him feel a little better.

"Here you go," Toshi said.

"Oh—" Robby said.

"Boy," Bobby finished.

Limowitz just stared. There were three greasy pizza cartons open on the table before him. The aroma saturated his nose and sent his tongue across his lips as his mouth filled with saliva.

"Where did you get those?" he said at last.

"Little place about three blocks up. You were right, it's kind of a mess out there. I went to that place on the corner you told me about, but it was burned out. Then I followed my nose. This place was going great guns, so I just walked in and placed my order."

"Naked?"

"Nobody said anything, if that's what you mean. By the way, I didn't see any New Church bozos. Just a couple of

Double En grunts, mercenaries from their chat. One of them ordered a pizza right after me."

Alarm tightened the smaller man's face. "Did they follow you?"

Toshi inserted the tip of one red and dripping slice into his mouth, chomped it off, and chewed. "Uh, yeah, he got kind of inquisitive later. Wanted to tag along."

"Oh, shit."

"Not to worry," Toshi said. "I talked him out of it."

"You did what? Are you sure?"

"Course I'm sure. Bullyboys like that, you just have to know the language they understand. Then everything's easy."

Limowitz stared at the stocky Oriental. Language they understood? What was he talking about?

And what was that rusty red streak that extended halfway up his thick, muscular forearm? Surely it was only pizza sauce. Surely it was only . . . Chester felt his stomach begin to contract, and only just made it to the john.

"Try this pepperoni," Toshi offered Robby. "It's real good."

Two thousand miles away, Danny Boy MacEwen skidded by an all-night, deep-dish Chicago-style Pizza Hut, his breath trailing ragged silver puffs behind. His pink tongue lolled half out of his distorted muzzle. He crouched a moment, his massive chest heaving. The rich, dusky odors of pizza cooking drifted across his moist nostrils and almost drove him crazy.

There was no time. He'd been moving as fast as he could, but already his keen ears picked up faint night sounds. Queer, whistling cries, and the shuffle-slap of hurried, muffled footsteps.

At least two of the tall ones were back there, and, he guessed, others as well. Here, the darkness was his enemy, for it was full of their eyes.

Not much farther. Only a few blocks more.

If he could make it, they wouldn't follow him underground.

Although, he thought grimly, he hoped a few would try.

"Now," Fred Oranson said. He watched with satisfaction as two of his more covert employees wrestled the still form onto the cold steel table. He waited while they strapped the man down and then he dismissed them.

There were experts who could do what was necessary, but he had his own reasons for performing the act himself.

He carefully inserted the intravenous tubes and applied the brightly colored derms to the appropriate spots on neck, armpit, and genitals. As he did this, the pudgy, nondescript man on the table moaned softly. There were two livid bruises on the pasty flesh of his left thigh. Oranson hoped he hadn't been damaged unduly.

He felt no conflict in inflicting on another what had been done to himself, but then, in the normal course of things he had no feelings at all. Lately, however, a certain old drive had begun to rear its eternal head. Oranson was learning a new thing—that the urge toward survival had very little to do with feelings or emotions. Survival was more primeval than even those fancy specters of the lizard brain.

So he hummed to himself a little tune while he adjusted and measured and dosed. If this systems operator who had quite recently been dragging down a hundred kay a year for keeping Nikki Gogolsky's main communications station in quiet and dependable operation actually knew anything, he'd soon be telling Fred Oranson all about it.

This time, Oranson told himself, he would think through any treachery a little more thoroughly than before. It was getting so hard to predict a winning side anymore. It was, in fact, becoming difficult to distinguish any side—but he owed himself the effort of trying. Maybe, in the process, he could discover just how deep his debt was to Shag Nakamura, as well.

Chapter Fourteen

He found Franny Webster in the main labs, surrounded as usual by a covey of obsequious assistants.

"Franny," Schollander said, "a moment, please?"

Webster paused in mid-sentence, nodded, and waved one pudgy hand. "Let me finish. Meet you in my office?"

"Sure." Schollander wandered on through the busy room. He glanced into Lizzybet Meklina's cubby and saw her hunched over her console, lost in her work. He didn't interrupt her. What he had to say was for Franny Webster's ears alone. He more than suspected that Meklina wouldn't support his notion, anyway. With luck, if Webster went along, she would have to deal with a *fait accompli*, which was exactly the way he wanted things to go.

He seated himself on the one chair which faced Webster's cluttered desk, and waited. After a few minutes Webster bustled in, settled himself, and began shoving piles of tapes, chips, and scribbled bits of paper out of his way. "Sorry," Webster said. "Nothing important, but I wanted to finish. Those idiots have to be watched every second."

Schollander looked up. "I thought they were good people?"

Webster grinned. "Oh, the best. But they still have to be watched."

Schollander stared at his fingertips, wondering where to begin. Finally he sighed and said, "Have you seen Karl lately?"

A shadow flickered across Webster's puffy features. "Uh-huh. This morning. There's no change."

"Gene Kilhelm said you had some ideas. Something you could try with Karl."

Now Webster hunched himself forward, as if he'd just thrown his thoughts into high concentration. "I did," he said carefully, "mention something along those lines."

"Well, tell me."

151

Webster raised a cautionary hand. "It might not come to that, Robert."

Schollander felt a small wave of irritation. Why did everybody watch themselves so carefully around him now? Then he realized what a stupid thought that was. He was Chairman of the Board. The free and easy chats with Bobby Schollander, waiter, were a thing of the past.

"Franny, I need to know. Karl Wier was important before the assassination attempt. Now he may have become absolutely critical. If there's any way to bring him back, to make use of what he knows, I have to be aware of it."

"I understand that, Robert. It's just that . . . well, Karl was the expert. I just followed along as best I could."

"Whatever it is, all I want to know is, can you do it?"

"I think so."

"I need a better answer than that, Franny."

Webster puffed his cheeks in and out. Finally he said, "Yes. I can do it."

It was like pulling rusty nails. "Okay, you can do what, Franny?"

"I can transfer Karl's personality into Levin. Or I could have."

Schollander thought a moment. "Oh, I see. You could, except that Levin won't come online. Is that it?"

"Well, partly. But the other problem is the damage to Karl's brain. I don't know if the pattern's damaged so badly it can't be deciphered."

"Pattern? What are you talking about?"

Franny grunted. "Some questions about what I want to try. I'll explain when the time comes. But, as you say, Levin himself is the initial problem."

"Okay," Schollander said. "Which brings me to the next thing. We need a working nanocomputer to save Karl. But we don't have one. The answer seems obvious to me."

Webster's eyes began to slowly widen. "You mean—"

"Exactly. Can we build another Levin?"

Elizabeth Meklina's dark features were thick and heavy with disapproval. "If that's what you want, that's what you'll get. You're the boss. But I think you're outta your mind." Her tight-rolled silver curls caught the light from the open panels overhead and made it appear that she wore some bizarre kind of high-tech helmet.

"I pretty much had you down that way," Schollander said. "I was hoping I could bring you around to my point of view."

"Lizzybet doesn't believe in points of view," Franny Webster announced cheerfully. "Not unless they are her own. On an intellectual level, she's very much for central authority —providing she's at the center."

Melina glared at her corpulent compatriot. "Do I have to put up with your bullshit, too, Webster?"

"Of course, dear. Comes with the exalted territory."

"Hey, wait a minute, you two," Schollander said. They were gathered round their usual table at the restaurant. Schollander found the perspective unnerving. Rather than waiting on the table and idly following the conversations there, he was now seated, and someone else—a new waiter, one he didn't recognize—lugged coffee and tea and croissants and jelly rolls for the participants. Elaine Markowitz completed their gang of four, as she called it, but so far she'd said almost nothing, preferring to watch the byplay between Meklina and Webster as she munched one English Tea Cracker after another and sipped Earl Grey breakfast tea made so dark it resembled coffee.

"Listen," Schollander continued, glancing once at Elaine, who blandly ignored him, "I don't claim to understand all the science aspects of the problem—my physics is four years out of date, practically obsolete—but I don't think you understand the strategic, practical aspects. Tell me, Elizabeth, can you give me any guarantees about Levin? When he'll be back online? Whether his core has been perverted by Arius? *Anything?*"

The black woman started to say something, paused, then shook her head. "No. I can't. But—"

"I didn't think so. Franny can't, either. My responsibility is to the company as a whole, Elizabeth. We *need* data processing capabilities at the Levin level. It's our only ace against whatever Shag Nakamura may be planning. For that matter, against Arius, if it still exists. Don't you understand? We don't have Karl Wier anymore. And we don't have Levin. A new nanocomputer could solve both of those problems, if Franny's right."

Again, Meklina's wide brow furrowed. "Huh. *If* he's right."

"Actually, Elizabeth, I think I am," Webster said mildly. "I worked more closely with Berg and Wier than you did. At least on the transfer aspects of the project. You were more involved with the hardware construct. You have to admit that."

She had the air of a great bear slowly turning away, reluctant to retreat but faced with greater odds than she cared to oppose at that time. "That's true. Yes. But Franny—because of my expertise with the hardware end, I'm better qualified on the problems involved with building a new machine. Do you have any idea how much of our resources we committed to that project?"

Webster shrugged. "A lot."

"A lot? Huh. The man says a lot. Robert, fully sixty percent of Luna, Inc.'s micromanufacturing capacity was dedicated to constructing Levin. And even so, it took over a year. Do we have that kind of time now? That commitment level?"

Schollander sipped his coffee, then lifted a half-eaten croissant and nibbled off another crust. Less than six feet away, crowds of Lunies surged blindly past, chattering and intent on their everyday tasks. Only a sharp-eyed observer would have noted the few men and women who idled against the flow, their eyes narrow and searching.

Our bodyguards, Schollander thought sourly. Bodyguards on the moon, to protect us against our own people. Against traitors. Nakamura has brought us to this.

It made his stomach roll queasily. The worst thing was that he had no choice. Nakamura used killers as a matter of course, as only another negotiating tool. Whatever his own morals might be on the matter, he had to stay alive long enough to exercise them. A dead chairman was no good to anybody. If only he had more time! But that was what he had the least of.

"Are you sure? A year, minimum?" he asked Meklina.

Webster broke in suddenly. "Rubbish. Two months, outside."

"Franny, you're out of your mind!"

"Of course I'm not. Go ahead, Lizzybet. Think about it. We took a year the first time, but that was when Berg and

Wier and you were still translating theory to engineering. That's all done. The databases still exist."

"In Levin, you mean. How do we get them out of him?"

"The current db's are in Levin's memory. But the original stuff, the records of Levin's first construction, those are all still on meat. We can pull them up easy enough."

She grimaced dubiously. "That's true, but the machine you get won't be Levin. Levin's had a lot of improvement from Berg and Wier."

Franny turned to Schollander. "She's right about that. We get the machine, but not the programming."

"Can you do your trick with Karl using a blank machine like that?"

A slow smile spread across Webster's cherubic features. "Bet your ass, buddy boy."

"That's it, then," Schollander said. "I don't see we have another option. We do it."

"Now, look here, Bobby—" Meklina erupted.

"That's Robert, please," Schollander said slowly. "I've made my decision. We do it."

This time, Meklina said nothing. And Elaine Markowitz said nothing, either. She only smiled.

"So, what did you think?"

"I think you've got a very nice apartment," Elaine said.

The *non sequitur* threw off his carefully planned conversational structure within a dozen words of its beginning. He hid his confusion by touching an order for coffee and tea on his autochef panel.

Elaine seemed tired today. She had caught his wink at the end of the daily *kaffeeklatch* and arrived at his rooms only a few minutes after him. And, he noted, today she was traveling in her power chair. A flurry of disquieting thoughts surfaced on his awareness—Elaine might on occasion treat him like a balky teenager, but it had been her vast and ancient knowledge of dirty tricks that had helped to put him where he was. If she were for some reason to become unavailable to him in the future, it would be an almost incalculable loss. All this jumbled along as subtext to her original remark. He pushed everything away and said, "Why do you say that? Is it too—big?"

He knew his own quarters were palatial by usual Lunie

standards, and at times was embarrassed by his good fortune. Even though he paid heavy fees for the extra space, the cost barely made a dent in the income his stock provided.

She chuckled, and her wrinkled old features showed a flash of the beautiful young woman she'd once been. "Oh, Bobby. It's so easy to jerk you off. You've got to learn—ignore the bullshit. No, of course it's not too big. You're the head of the second largest business entity in the solar system. You know how Shag Nakamura lives? He wouldn't consider a layout like this good enough even for servants."

He digested that. It was true. Eaton Vance had lived much more grandly than this, in a ten-room suite complete with an army of house bots. Maybe he should think about . . . No. Stupid. This was fine.

"How are you feeling, Auntie?"

She looked down at her power chair with distaste. Articulated ribs supported her spine, cradled her thin buttocks and thighs. "This thing, you mean? It's a pain in the ass. Literally." She shifted uncomfortably, and the stressed carbon frame clicked slightly as it adjusted itself to her new position. "But some days—" She shook her head. "When are we going to get the athanasia treatments, Bobby? Aren't our bio people working on something?"

He nodded slowly. It seemed that half his days were devoted to reading endless reports from the far-flung Lunar research facilities. And he had seen something recently. "Soon," he said. "They claim they're on the edge of a real breakthrough."

She licked her dry lips. Her face was sour. "Huh. A breakthrough. We were hearing that in your granddad's day. And look at me." Then she sighed. "Don't mind me. It's just self-pity—but it's the only kind I allow."

He rose, poured tea for her, and refilled his own coffee cup. "What about the meeting, Auntie?"

Her eyes grew serious. He noted she emitted a faint odor of violets, light and refreshing on the filtered air of his rooms. "You handled it okay. At least you made the decision, and then made it stick. Lizzybet isn't happy, though."

"I know," Schollander said. "But I can't make everybody happy."

"I'm glad you understand that. Happiness isn't your job.

Decisions are. Let Mason Dodge smooth her over. He's good at that sort of thing."

Schollander sipped at his coffee. His expression was distant, moody. "Nakamura. It all comes back to him. I bet he doesn't worry about making people happy."

She grunted. "Shag? He likes to make people unhappy. And right now, we ought to be his number one target."

"How's our intelligence doing?"

She shrugged. They both knew the answer. Without Levin, their daily covert take was less than ten percent of normal. They were unable to crack Double En's vast network of dedicated meatmatrices. Anything could be happening.

"We sure could use Berg right now. Calley, too. She was a terror at icebreaking."

Elaine didn't say anything.

Schollander sat silent for a few moments, indulging in might-have-beens. Finally, he glanced up. "Well, what have you got for me?"

"What makes you think I've got anything?"

"Auntie, you never carry a purse. But you're carrying one today. Want to tell me what's inside?"

She chuckled softly. Her thin, bluish fingers scrabbled at the catch of the small, old leather bag—he wondered if it was hers, or if she'd inherited it from someone even older—and finally snapped it open.

"Here," she said, and tossed him the small, rectangular object. For one hectic moment he balanced coffee, reflexes, and dignity against the flat trajectory of the oncoming parcel. Then, miraculously, he managed to disentangle his left hand and snag the slim bundle. Even so, he managed to slop about a third of the contents of his cup directly onto his crotch.

"Ouch! God *damn* it." He glared at Elaine.

"I'm not laughing. Notice I'm not laughing," she told him calmly.

Carefully, he placed the coffee on the side table next to his chair. Then he examined the package carefully.

Finally, "A book, is it?"

"Mm-hmm. You remember them, don't you?"

It was a legitimate question. What the word "book" had once meant was now taken over by chip, or file, or download. Actual books, constructed of cardboard and leather and paper, were the province of rich collectors or eccentric bibliophiles. Yet this was undoubtedly a book.

"Where did you get it?"

Her grin grew wider. "I burgled it. Out of Jack Berg's room."

He stared at her. "I hate puns," he said at last.

"Who cares? Look at the book."

Beyond the fact that it was an old-style paperback, there didn't seem much about it out of the ordinary. He rubbed his fingertips over one of the pages, and realized that the entire book had been coated with a very thin layer of some transparent polymer, no doubt for purposes of preservation. He closed the book and examined the cover. There was a charmingly lurid illustration of some sort of floating machine drifting toward the center of a great field of molten lava. Occupying the center of the field was a clear globe that seemed to be rising from the torrid stuff.

"*Marooned in Realtime*," he read aloud. "By Vernor Vinge." The name tugged at some forgotten memories. He had the feeling that the author had been famous at one time, and that perhaps he'd even read some of his work during a passion for science fiction developed during his adolescence. He opened the jacket and noted that the book had been published in 1987, which made it fairly old and probably quite valuable.

On quick glance, however, there was little information other than the existence of the book itself, and the place where it had been found.

"Berg is a book collector?" he said at last.

"No," Elaine replied. "Or if he is, that's the only one in his collection."

"Mm. He's gone to the trouble to have it preserved, and to bring it along with him. So, if its not simply some sort of bibliophilic trophy, then the contents must mean something to him."

Elaine nodded, her eyes twinkling slightly in the dim light. "You know, Bobby, what with your new titles and everything, you're beginning to sound just a bit pompous."

"Oh, fuck off."

"You keep saying that to me. Promises, promises. But I think you've got the gist. I've read the book. I suggest you do the same, and give the implications some consideration. Then give me a call. I've got some more stuff for you."

"Auntie, don't be such a—"

She raised one hand. "Allow me the privileges of senility. Read the book. Then we'll talk."

She said nothing more, simply ordered her power chair to the door.

"Senility, hah!" he called after her, but she ignored him, and then she was gone. After a few moments to refill his coffee cup, he settled back to his chair, sighed, picked up the book and began to read.

He had expected to dip into the book, perhaps read a bit here and there as he could fit it into his other duties. Instead, he found himself rising from his chair, groaning slightly, six hours later. His muscles were unused to forced inactivity, and he was stiff from head to toe. It had taken him six hours to read the book because he was clumsy with words that didn't scroll, and it had taken him awhile to get used to this older way of reading.

"Jesus," he said into thin air, rubbing his forehead absently. He realized he had to pee, and shambled off into the bathroom. When he returned, he paused and stared at the shiny cover of the book. He'd forgotten what an exhilarating experience it was to read good science fiction, to be surprised and then surprised again by the speculations and future twists an accomplished writer could conjure.

This book had been a particularly good example of the genre. Good enough, evidently, that Jack Berg had gone to great lengths to preserve it. Which raised more questions than it answered. Was Jack Berg a science fiction fan? If so, then why was this the only example in his collection? Or was it the contents of the book, the ideas? Schollander could easily see relevance to his own concerns there, but if that was the case, wouldn't a chip have served just as well?

Was it the book itself? Maybe some kind of hidden code. He knew of such things, blind codes which depended on a key book or manuscripts of some kind for deciphering. Something like that?

He didn't know. But the whole question of the book had caused him to consider other things. He couldn't understand why it hadn't struck him before, at least with more urgency.

Jack Berg was absolutely central to all his problems. Levin had been designed in part by Berg, and, he supposed, with full concurrence on Karl Wier's part. Agreement that must have extended to the purposes Berg had in mind, as well. He suddenly regretted that he'd never made an effort to know Berg better, or Calley or Ozzie either. To him, they'd only been hogs, supplicants from downwell come to beg at Luna's high-tech fount. Nor had he been in any privy position to whatever it was Berg and Wier had cooked up together. Now it was too late. Berg was gone, and with him the others. Wier couldn't speak, and evidently he'd been paranoid enough to keep the crucial details of their plans inside his own skull. At least, Schollander's own best efforts had been insufficient to turn up anything but the most superficial stuff.

So the main problem was ignorance. Ignorance of Berg's plans, of the reasons Karl Wier had gone along with them—if he had, he reminded himself—and ignorance most of all of the current state of affairs.

Maybe when the new nanocomputer was on line and Karl transferred into its memory, he could begin to find some answers. In the meantime, he could pursue the mystery of Berg himself.

He spoke to his computer. "Set an appointment with Elaine Markowitz for ten o'clock tomorrow morning."

She'd told him she had more information.

Right at the moment, he couldn't think of anything he needed more desperately.

Chapter Fifteen

"I wonder what time it is," Calley said absently. She stubbed out her cigarette in her coffee cup, eliciting a glare from the waitress who was already pissed off at the length of time they'd held the table.

"Mm? About eight o'clock at night," Ozzie replied. He didn't check his nailtale.

"No, I mean what *time*. What year."

"Huh? What are you talking about?"

She regarded him fondly across the table. "First rule. Nothing is what it seems like. This is a game, remember? I bet it can be any fucking time those bozos want it to be. And I also bet it isn't the time we think it is."

He shook his head. The coffee shop was quiet, caught in the lull after dinner and before the more boisterous drinking crowd started to arrive. The waitress, a deep crease above the bridge of her nose, was plainly not pleased with them. Calley smiled sweetly at her, and mouthed the words, "Fuck you." A pair of small red spots bloomed on the waitress's cheeks and she turned sharply away.

"You're talking in circles again, sweetheart." He slurred the last word, and curled his lip."

"What? Don't Bogart my conversation, bubba." Then she smiled. "If I'm right, if this whole thing is about the Key, well—it can't be happening in realtime. Whatever that is. I think we're back at the beginning, before Berg even got the Key. Or became it, whatever. Did you ever think about the Key, Oz? I mean, really *think* about it?"

He shook his head slowly. "I'm still not following."

She lit another cigarette and blew smoke in his face. He blinked. "How Berg got the damn thing in the first place. Remember?"

His amber eyes widened slowly. "Oh. She gave it to him. The Lady. It was a chip or a hunk of biosoft or like that."

161

Calley nodded. "So think about that. Where did she get it in the first place?"

"Uh—Arius. No, that can't be right. Bill Norton? When he still had his hooks into Double En's R&D programs?"

"So why would Norton give Berg the one thing that could create a real enemy, one with power over him?"

Ozzie sipped his own coffee. It had turned cold and greasy, and he made a face. "Dunno," he said at last. "Made a mistake, maybe?"

"You believe that?"

"I don't believe anything any more."

She grinned. "You're learning, boy. I just fucking wish—" Her voice trailed off.

"You wish what?"

"I understood some of the science involved a little better."

For the first time since they'd seen the Lady and her wolfpack, Ozzie brightened. "Well, kiddo," he said, "now you're talking about my stuff. What's your question?"

She thought about it, as the smoke curled around her thin features. "Okay. Just what the fuck *is* the Key?"

Ozzie looked down at the linen tablecloth. After a time he looked up. His eyes had darkened, become slitted with concentration. "I don't know," he said finally. "But I think I can make a guess."

She nodded. "And?"

"Come on," he said. "They must have left me my apartment for something."

The wind was biting, full of teeth, but they saw no wolves. Only the silent lake, and darkness shot with beads of light. Chicago. They hurried through the night, and didn't feel the cold.

"What do you think?" Ozzie said.

Calley stared at him. She thought he looked about twelve years old. His eyes were wide, dancing a gleeful dance.

"What is this fucking place?" she said softly.

"This, my dear—" he waved both his arms wide, looking more like a stork than ever—"is the main computer room for Group Zee Engineering."

"What," she said patiently, "is Group Zee Engineering?"

"Me." He lowered his arms, turned and faced her. "I'm Group Zee Engineering."

The room took up an entire floor of a sprawling midrise just off the Lake on the near North Side. One wall was glass, overlooking the black water. She hadn't counted after Ozzie had ushered her into the high-speed elevator, but she guessed they were about twenty floors up. The room was vast. It was crammed with computers, with giant housings she guessed were storage media, with small labs partitioned off by shoulder-height portable dividers, even a fair-sized office area which fronted on several doors she supposed led to private offices. He grinned at her. "Come on."

He led her through the open desk area to the most imposing of the private doors, ran his palm over the lock, and stepped back as the door clicked and then slid open. A speaker beneath the palm lock suddenly burst into a staccato rendition of "I'm a Yankee Doodle Dandy."

"George M. Cohan?" she said.

He bowed. "A true American patriot."

She shook her head and stepped into the office. As she entered, remote glowstrips slowly brightened, until the entire room was suffused with pure wide spectrum illumination.

"Wow," she said.

"Pretty nice, huh?"

He walked across what seemed like an acre of knee-deep dark blue plush carpet, and perched one bony flank on the corner of a heavily carved cypress desk. She'd once seen a desk like that, but it had been in a museum.

"Uh, bubba, you sure this is yours?"

He bounced delightedly. "Whatsa matter? Too classy for old Oz?" He jumped to his feet again, tossed her a shoulder fake, and scurried behind the desk. He flopped in the leather chair there, which immediately molded itself to his lanky frame.

"Oz, seriously, if this is some kind of breaking and entering bullshit—"

"Watch," he said, and raised one finger. She stared at the single digit—it was the middle, bird finger of his right hand—and waited. After a moment, a disembodied voice filled the room. "Yes, master?"

Ozzie said nothing, but lowered the finger, then rubbed finger and thumb together.

"To see is to obey, master." The seemingly solid desktop split down the middle, revealing the well of a bar, which promptly produced two bottles of Budweiser so cold their sides immediately frosted over.

She shook her head admiringly. "It seems to know you."

"It should," Ozzie said. "I built it."

"I didn't know anything about this," she said softly. "Who would have guessed? Ozzie has a secret."

He nodded. "My company, kiddo. What? You thought I panhandled on the street for my bread and butter and biochips?"

"Your uh, life-style at home was hardly gonna put you on 'Rich and Famous.' "

He shrugged. "Calley, you remember what I used to look like?"

She paused before she answered. Somehow, the question seemed important, although he'd tossed it off pretty casually. "Yeah," she said at last. And was surprised to find she had to work to recall the disfiguring purple fungus which had once distorted his now perfect features. "I remember."

"I didn't go out much," he continued. "I didn't come here much, either, and not at all when anybody could see me. This was all put together out of licensing fees and royalties. I did it at second and third remove, through lawyers and accountants. The people who work here, they get a pretty free hand. A lot of pure research goes on. Some real wildasses gnaw on the old grindstone here. And they all just love the mysterious moneybags who pays the bills and lets them play. And who sometimes sneaks in at the crack of midnight to do a little free-lance fiddling on his own. You know, they must think I'm crazy as a shithouse rat."

"You mean you own all this?"

"That's what I been telling you, girl."

She still didn't quite get it. "But what's it for? I mean—"

He raised one hand, slowly. "Group Zee does a lot of subcontracting shit for the big boys. Specialty stuff, tricky bits of magic."

She was still trying to take in this new Ozzie image. Ozzie the corporate mini-baron.

"So?"

"So I think there's half a chance we might have had something to do with the Key. If it's what I think it is. We might just have built the fucking thing."

"Well, Jesus and Bojangles," she said.

"I thought you'd like it," he told her.

Two hours later, Calley stubbed out the last of her foul-smelling Turkish cigarettes. Even the powerful air conditioning system hadn't been able to entirely remove the thin blue layer of smoke which hovered just above their heads. She said, "My mouth tastes like a toxic waste dump."

Ozzie glanced up from the huge central console which dominated one side of the room. "I guessed wrong," he said.

"About what?"

He shrugged. "I thought Group Zee might have had something to do with the design of the Key. It had to be something pretty far out, and Zee is about as far out as anybody. What I figured was, we might have picked up a piece of it through some kind of blind contract, done work for Double En without knowing it. Or thinking we were doing something else. That's what I've been doing, running audits on all our contracts during that time frame. Which, by the way, is right now. But if Berg's telling the truth about when it all started, then I'm full of shit."

She picked up her empty cigarette pack, stared at it moodily, crumpled it and tossed it to the floor. "You? Full of shit? Never . . ."

He grinned. "You wish. Here's the fun part. The Lady's due, according to the history we have, to give Berg the Key exactly two days from now."

"What!" Calley's boots hit the floor with a soft thud. Her eyes flashed once, green and hooded.

"You heard me. Check the date." He slapped his touchpad and pointed to a readout on one of the monitors.

"Well I be go to hell," she said.

"You said to check the dates. There it is. So where does that leave us now? Whenever now is, I mean."

She stood up, her body tense and full of edges. She ran narrow fingers through her chopped black hair and stalked to the screens. "Lemme," she said, and shoved him to one side with her bony ass.

"Hey, pardon *me*."

"Uh-huh. Sorry." She stared at the date on the screen. Two thin lines appeared in a vee above her nose. "What's this thing hooked in to?"

He eased himself off the edge of the seat, stood up and stretched. She heard the tiny sounds of cartilage popping. "Whatever you want it to be, I guess. I didn't nose it around much with the help, but the system's designed to be a hacker's wet dream. Any fucking cowboy thing you can think of, it ought to be able to do it."

She nodded thoughtfully. "So we aren't at the beginning, we're *before* the fucking shooting match. Well, isn't that fine."

He stopped and glanced at her. "I know that tone of voice," he said.

"Yeah? What's that supposed to mean?"

"You're gonna do something outrageous. Aren't you?"

"Maybe." She examined the touchpad. "You remember the gizmo you used to get us into the metamatrix in the first place?"

"Uh huh. Sure."

"Is there enough shit in this dump to put another one together?"

He nodded. "Probably. No, definitely. It wasn't all that complicated, once I worked out the theory."

"Well, do it again. We are in a very interesting position, bubba. Consider the game. If the rules are consistent, we have come into the past with our future knowledge intact. Sort of like knowing the winning lottery numbers in advance, you understand."

"Kinda gives us an advantage, uh?"

"Do your magic, Oz. Wave your wand. Come on, mama's in a hurry."

"Oh? How come the rush?"

"I can't believe we're the only one with the advantage. Somebody's gotta come looking for us pretty soon. And I want to have some real big clubs when they come to take us away."

The lights on New Michigan Avenue twinkled against sudden flurries of holiday snow. Lonnie Roberts ordered another Michelob Lite and watched the crowds surge past the window of the small bierstube which overlooked the street. He sighed. "You know," he said to Karen Yukisuri, "the goddam doctor just told me that monoclonal Retin-A treatments aren't gonna do a fucking thing for my zits. I got special zits, it seems."

Karen nodded. "Sometimes it happens, I hear. But what the hell—you've got enough to celebrate. Here." She raised her own bottle of True Coke and grinned. "To you, new Doctor Roberts. Now that you got your Ph.D. can we get married?"

"Christ, Karie, I'm not even eighteen yet. Give it a rest, okay?"

She shrugged. "It was worth a try. Well, anyway, drink up. You got two weeks off from the lab, with pay. That's pretty slick."

The air of the small bar was damp as a greenhouse. The place smelled of other people's sweat. On Fridays, it filled with leaden office workers, mostly young, tanking up against the terrors of a Chicago weekend. A sudden burst of feedback roared through the phalanx of speakers at the far end of the bar and Dr. Lonnie Roberts gritted his teeth.

"Jesus. You'd think they'd buy a decent sound system. They get enough of our credit, right?"

"Think happy thoughts, my boy. Two weeks off, for nothing. Your boss must be crazy. What's he like?"

"I dunno. Never seen him. His name's Mr. Karman, I think. Oswald Karman. Some kind of deformo, I heard."

"Maybe he is crazy. To shut down like that, no notice or anything. Must cost a lot of money."

"Some. We got a couple of contracts." Lonnie drained his bottle and placed it carefully next to three other empties. "You may be right, Karie. Two weeks. We could get to know each other better, huh?"

She smiled.

"But no marriage, okay?" he said quickly.

She smiled again.

"Goddam zits," he said at last.

Her right eye felt as if she'd smoked it slowly over a bed of coals made from compressed cigarette butts. "Ozzie," she said, "how come if this is a dream world, that we get tired and hungry and have to take a shit every once in a while?"

They were in one of the smaller labs on a floor beneath the huge data processing center. Here the perspectives were dull and stuffy—cream-colored walls, stale air, gray carpet, and no view. Ozzie looked away from the large video terminal where the results of his latest efforts with the big scanning tunneling electron scope were marching before his eyes in ordered, colorful graphs.

"Dream within a dream, babe," she said absently. "This is Berg's dream, and he's in gestalt space, which may or may not be his dream, Arius's dream, Levin's dream or, for all I know, God's dream.

She grunted. Her voice was harsh, raspy. She lit another cigarette. "Mystical bullshit. If these bodies are constructs, analogs, then why can't we control how they operate?"

He shrugged. "You can."

She glared at him. "I can't." Then, hesitantly, "I know. I've tried. Sometimes I can manipulate the spaces a little bit, but I don't have any control at all over my own construct."

He looked back at his terminal. "Conscious control," he said mildly. "Hey, look at this."

She stood up from her own workstation, which consisted of two tiers of touchpads that surrounded her like the keyboards of a giant organ. Her thin body seemed almost to vibrate in the thick air of the room. Her green eyes were dull, and her black hair stuck out in random, twisted tufts where she'd idly savaged it as she worked.

The big screen in front of Ozzie showed a full-color picture of something that resembled a very orderly mountain range, viewed in full color, from high above, but instead of the normal browns and grays and streaks of white she would expect to see, the colors were varying shades of blue and electric yellow.

"Neat. What is it?"

"A study of the microprocessor etching for a chip we're doing for the Lunies."

"We? What do you mean?"

"We. Group Zee. We do a lot of stuff for Luna, Inc."

She examined the screen, but still couldn't make sense of it. "So?"

"Well, I didn't bother to check Zee's contracts with Luna, 'cause I was looking for blind connections with Double En. But you know what? If I was designing something to work like Berg's Key does, I bet some of it would look an awful lot like this does."

She still didn't get it. "What are you trying to tell me, Oz?"

He looked up at her. "We been looking at this all wrong. The Key didn't come from Norton after all. It came from the Lunie AI, the one originally called Arius. But where in hell did that bag of bolts get the idea?"

She stared silently at him for a moment. He felt the invisible weight which pressed her down. It had never occurred to him that Calley could be afraid. Now he wondered why.

"What's the matter?" he said.

"I knew the circle would close," she said softly. "All that fucking karma, it always runs in circles. Life is a snake with its head up its karmic ass. So when will the gizmo be ready?"

"The gizmo? It's ready now."

She nodded. "Then let's go."

He reached out and took her hand and pulled her gently closer. For once, she didn't seem to mind his kindness.

She's mellowing, he thought. Or maybe she just doesn't give a shit anymore.

The wolf followed her three paces behind, his hooked claws tick-ticking softly on the damp concrete. They moved slowly through the hidden, rubbish-choked passages of the Labyrinth, their breath silver smoke on the frigid air. Her eyes glowed in the darkness, two dim lamps the color of blood.

"Lay . . ." he whispered hoarsely.

She paused, turned.

"What? What is it?"

"Something . . ."

The Lady stepped nearer to her were-bodyguard. "I know," she said. She touched the wolf's muzzle, stroked the fine curly hair around his brown eyes. "Something's coming. We have to hurry, to reach the throne in time."

The wolf nodded. "Hurry," it agreed.

She turned in a whirl of white, and continued into the dark. Her face was placid, almost without expression. Only a faint smile curved her lips slightly. This world was only a dream within a dream, and that but a memory of another time. Was it real? He said it was. And in this dream, she had her own desires. *They* were out there. She could feel their presence with senses she had not possessed before. Eventually they would come to her. They had to, for she was the guardian. And this time, she would be ready.

This time she wouldn't fail.

The wolf followed her, growling uneasily.

Forces converged.

They returned to the huge computer room on the upper floor. The whole building had an eerily deserted feeling to it. The light seemed gray and desolate. Even the soft sound of their footsteps on padded floors, on deep carpets, seemed unnaturally loud. Calley kept turning her head, as if to catch a glimpse of the usual occupants. She had irrational notions that hundreds of people were hiding just beyond the corners of her gaze, watching her silently.

Ozzie seemed unaffected by the derelict atmosphere. But then, she decided, he was used to it. He had always come here when the place was empty, had in fact sought the solace of loneliness. The terrible deformity he'd endured in those times had made him a loner by choice, and only now—

"Jesus," she muttered. "What am I thinking?"

He paused, glanced up from the final connections he was making with his new rig. "What?"

His face was angelic. No trace remained of the hideous patch of dripping purple flesh which had marked him before. She had to stop, force herself to remember what he'd looked like then.

"My time sense is all screwed up," she said. "Now, then, future, present, it's all blurred together. I keep thinking about used to be and will happen, but it doesn't fit. The future is in the past, the past hasn't happened here yet, and I just can't seem to get a handle on it."

He grinned. It made him look like a fifteen-year-old boy opening presents under the tree. "Don't worry about it," he said. "Use yourself as a reference point. You are now. Everything else is either gonna happen or not, or already has, but you can't count on it. Take it as a new reality."

She grunted and lit another cigarette. "Have you tried to manipulate this 'reality'?"

"How so?"

"You know, like you used to change Berg and Levin's construct. Those fucking sheep."

He shook his head. "No."

"How come?"

"I don't think it'll work here," he replied slowly.

"And why is that?"

"I dunno. This one feels . . . different."

She narrowed her eyes and blew smoke, but let it pass. Ozzie feelings were, at best, tenuous and hard to pin down. And she was beginning to get her own ideas, grounded on something harder than mere feelings.

She'd had half a lifetime of dealing with Jack Berg, and something about this weird game he'd dreamed up wasn't right. That knowledge had niggled at her almost since the beginning of it, but she hadn't been able to form any conclusion. Now, as Ozzie finished with the final links that joined his box to the largest of the mainframes, it came to her.

"Berg doesn't play games," she said.

Ozzie said, "There. All ready."

"Did you hear me?"

"Uh huh. You said he doesn't play games."

"That's right. He never did. Lousy at poker, hated chess, wouldn't even watch football. So why all of sudden, at what he claims is the most important contest of all, does he risk everything on this stupid fairy tale contest?"

Ozzie twined his long fingers together, bent them out, and cracked each big knuckle in a cascade of sharp, liquid pops."

"You're the Berg expert, babe," he said.

She nodded. "He said it wasn't a game," she mumbled. Her voice rasped softly in the silent, cavernous room. "And it's not."

"So, then?"

She nodded decisively. "Let's get to it, bub. Hook me up to that devil machine."

"Calley, what the fuck are you talking about?"

She smiled at him. "It's not a game," she said. "But he's cheating anyway."

Chapter Sixteen

Danny Boy MacEwen licked at his right hand, where the hair and flesh beneath had been split open. He shivered, his breath coming in ragged gasps, as the coppery taste of his own blood filled his mouth.

Only two more blocks. He chanted the number silently, a mantra of safety. For the moment, the chase had fallen away. He heard a muffled shout from the next block over, as some nameless Rager discovered the two bodies he'd left, disemboweled and steaming in the glacial night. He felt a sudden thrill of triumph. Perhaps they'd underestimated him after all. He'd doubled back, when he'd realized the strange, chirping cries filled the darkness in an extended wall between him and the refuge of the Labyrinth. They thought they had him trapped, but he'd cut two from the chaser pack, lured them into a blank-walled alley. He remembered the way their eyes had bulged in the dim light as his own hairy shadow had fallen across their path.

They'd fought—knives against claws—but it hadn't been enough. They'd used their weapons, but he *was* a weapon. Only the one gash, deep but relatively harmless, splitting the padded fingers of his left hand.

He savored the warmth that had suffused him as he'd spilled their guts, long, ropey shining sausages that glittered wetly in the barren light of the street lamps, onto the frozen concrete. He'd dragged them back to the street and left them at the end of a trail of blood.

But they were only homeboys, stupid homes that used knives to frighten those even more stupid than they, and they'd never faced an enraged wolf. He hunched himself lower behind a rusted dumpster overflowing with gelid chunks of garbage and continued to lick his wound. He'd been lucky, in a way. The night was full of the eerie cries of hunters far more dangerous than those two. And the more he thought about that, the less sense it made.

The tall ones. Two of them at least, maybe more. Wilts, they were called, for reasons nobody knew any more. Wilts—the incredibly tall, thin killers who worked only for the highest Rager chiefs. Why would Wilts be hunting him?

He gnawed at the question but couldn't come with any answer that made sense. Not that it made any difference. There *were* Wilts out there tracking him, their long, deadly frames moving through the darkness like whips, their lips pursed around their weird cries.

He didn't know if he could kill Wilts. He didn't want to find out, either. He cocked his ears. His muzzle came up, testing the welter of scents on the bitter wind. It seemed that some of the sound was converging on the site of his kill. Perhaps they were careless. Maybe there was an opening now, where none had been before.

He had to chance it. He licked his wound a final time and grunted as he heaved himself up. Only two more blocks.

He loped forward into the shadows, panting.

The final block loomed before him. He hugged the corner of a deserted warehouse and peered down the deserted street. It was a buffer zone. At the end of the street he made out the tumbledown roof of a decayed kiosk which shielded the abandoned entrance to the underground. Once this had been a bustling street just north of Chicago's old Loop. Now it was a slum but, for reasons of their own, kept by the city fathers a well-lighted slum. Tall streetlights illumined the empty pavement, so that it seemed almost like a stage. Danny Boy had heard it talked about once—the city was owned by Ragers, and the topside gang preferred a well-lit no-man's-land between their turf and that of the underpeople. It was easier to keep the denizens of the Lab in their place, especially since the subterranean gangs weren't fond of any kind of bright light.

The street was a killing field. He shuffled slowly forward, stepping into the light. As he did so, his head jerked up. A stumbling, lurching, leaping pack of rabble spilled around the corner behind him, saw him, began to bay with glee. He saw the flash of bright metal and then, suddenly, flinched at the harsh crack of an ancient handgun. Something whanged off the edge of the bricks above his head and splattered him with stinging grains of rock.

No choice, he knew. He loped into the middle of the street and scrabbled forward. He'd made almost half the block before the inevitable happened.

They came from either side of the street, slipping like elongated wraiths from doorways, the gaping mouth of an alley. Three of them, tall, willowy, deadly. They blocked him neatly and stood, waiting. The one in the middle smiled. The other two made low, warbling noises deep in their throats.

"Come, wolf," the middle one said softly. "Come to me, my little dogface."

The riffraff behind him came to a jumbled halt, well away from this confrontation between their prey and their masters. Danny Boy heard several sharply swallowed exclamations. Some of these idiots had never seen even one Wilt before. Now three of them filled the street.

Somebody laughed.

The middle Wilt moved one step forward and held out his hand. "You can't make it," he said softly.

The other two Wilts also moved forward, keeping the box tight and neat. Neither of them had any expression at all on their long faces. Behind, somebody laughed again, a long, rising, hysterical sound.

For an instant Danny Boy wanted to lie down, to just give it up. His whole life seemed an endless tapestry of failure. But to have come so close!

Then she spread her white wings over his failing spirit and lifted him up and filled him with her crimson light, and he snarled, "Fuck you!"

The killing began.

Danny Boy was never able later to remember just what had happened, how he'd come not only to survive an attack by three Wilts, but kill all of them as well, yet as it turned out he didn't have to. Other eyes witnessed the slaughter, which would eventually become a centerpiece of Labyrinth legend.

Nor had the wolf any knowledge of the older killing frenzies, the berserkers and hash-as-shans and the chillier samurai madnesses, but he would have recognized the symp-

174

toms. She took him like a storm and filled his brain with fire.

From a distance, to the hood-eyed watchers, it seemed he merely danced around and through the line of three Wilts, yet the gangling killers were unable to touch him with their long fingers, and everything *he* touched spurted gouts of blood that gleamed rich and black beneath the chemical glare of the lamps.

It was finished in less than ten seconds. He stepped over the mutilated pile of flesh and walked slowly toward the underground entrance, conscious now of dark, shadowy figures awaiting him there. Behind, the stunned pack of lesser Ragers, their greatest warriors butchered before them, began to drift silently away.

Danny Boy reached the top of the steps and looked down at the group which stood there.

"Br'th'rs," he said softly, and raised his hands and showed them his bloody claws.

"Br'thr," they agreed, and flashed their teeth. Only then did he fall forward. They caught him and carried him down into the dark.

He had been an Angel, fallen. He had felt the sudden cessation of communication with God, when God had died. Now he was alone, and would become a God himself. Or so he told himself.

His name was Galen. His secret Name was . . . secret.

"Lord," the little serving girl—what a pretty euphemism, he thought, for slave—whispered. "Would you like me to kiss it again?"

Even Angels have needs, he told himself. Even Gods.

The Lord of the New Church rolled slowly onto his back. "Yes," he said huskily. "Kiss it again."

She lowered her lips to the socket, where the feelings would be most intense. Cyborg fellatio, he mourned. But it was all he had left—now that God was dead.

Wan, blue morning slanted through the windows of his house, which was perched atop Twin Peaks facing the San Francisco Bay. This neighborhood had been relatively untouched by the troubles below, in the main part of the city, but not by accident. Squads of elite Church troops patrolled the entire area, much to the gratitude of the wealthy families that occupied glittering compounds nearby.

Galen strolled out onto his balcony and stared down at the city. The fires were out now, although signs of the conflict between Double En's crash forces and Church-frenzied mobs still remained. A long, charcoal slash divided the Mission District, and isolated patches of burned-out ash dotted other areas. The main fighting was over. None of the homes of the others, the Faceless Ones who made up the High Council of the Church, had been even remotely threatened. Double En would not attack its true allies, and that, despite outward appearances, was exactly what the New Church of the Spirit Corporate was supposed to be.

Allies, he mused, as he considered the ruins, both seen and unseen. Ten thousand devout worshipers sacrificed in this city alone, and God only knew how many hundreds of thousands in the rest of the world.

It made him want to vomit.

Errant puffs of fog drifted past the tops of the twin mountains. On the Bay itself, ship traffic seemed heavy. Many of those ships, he supposed, belonged to the corporation —no, the man—who had destroyed so many of the Believers, that bedrock of the Church carefully gathered, then flung like chaff into the winds of destruction.

The Council congratulated itself on a job well done—true believers are often a nuisance to a great Church—but Galen watched the morning sun begin to deepen the rich blue of the waters below, and knew they'd made a terrible miscalculation. Some of the believers had survived. One, in fact, sat on the Council itself.

My name is secret, Galen thought. But I know it.

A slight smile twisted his perfectly chiseled features. He grinned a fiery grin at the morning and turned away. Inside, his serving girl waited, with breakfast and consolation. Outside, the sun grew hotter, brighter.

Like God, he thought. *Like God.*

The World Headquarters of the New Church sprouted from the flanks of Nob Hill, a five-hundred-foot extrusion of fake granite and chrome trim. A cloud of guardian attack platforms buzzed around its steel spire like warrior bees, fiercely protective. Just as noon gilded the very top of the tower

tower the swarm parted to admit five lumbering Honigwasser A.G. luxury copters. The big, slow craft settled into ungainly squats on the helipads fifty stories up. In their sides, wide doors slid smoothly open.

Galen stepped onto the wind-whipped concrete, his long, black hair snapping about his face. Two silent Blades accompanied him, one on each side. He gathered his robes about him and started for the entrance doors. Two of his compatriots were closer, and politely held the door for him.

"Galen," said Saint Trump.

Galen nodded as he stepped out of the wind and paused, waiting for the rest of the arriving council members. "Saint Trump. Asmodeo."

The three waited until Michael and The Raker had come up. When the group was complete, they entered the elevator and took it up five more floors, to the very top of the tower, where the Council Chambers, protected as well as any spot on earth, looked onto a full circle of million-dollar vistas. Galen paused by one glass wall until his council brothers were seated. He regarded the hazy blue scene beneath him, then sighed, turned, and took his own place at the table.

They were alone in the room. Underlings were never invited into the chamber itself, although holo visitations were permissible. The table at which they sat was perfectly round. Each chair was identical to the others. It was a deceptively democratic picture. As in all social structures, power ebbed and flowed. This council elected a leader, whose public title was Chairman of the Board. In this room, his title was the Voice of God, or, simply, Voice.

Asmodeo, the first of the Angels created by Arius, had spoken for God from the beginning. He still did, but with God dead, his power was becoming shaky. Galen knew it. They all did. Galen wondered who, besides himself, had already begun to plot.

Probably all of us, he thought. He resolved to step up his private espionage forces. No doubt the others would do so as well.

It saddened him, that they had come to this. But God was dead. What other options did they have?

"Brothers," Asmodeo began. He had a deep, mellow voice. It reminded Galen of the unseen spokesman for a very popular brand of blue jeans. He tried to picture Asmodeo extolling those jeans, and a faint smile flickered on his lips. He looked up. "Brothers," he replied in unison with the rest of them.

Asmodeo wasted no time in getting down to business. "Raker. What is the current status of the situation?"

The Raker, an extremely tall, heavily built man with a light, piercing voice and eyes the color of impure turquoise, glanced down at the monitor inset before him. "It's about over," he said. "There is no active fighting now. Double En's troops, working with local authorities, are mopping up. Only a few of our people are still waging scattered guerrilla actions. It will all be finished within a day or so."

Asmodeo nodded. "Michael?"

Michael was their miracle worker. Arius had created him with full access to his own technical data bases. He was of average height, with blond, curly hair and a perpetually young look to his faded gray eyes. "I have been unable to establish any sort of contact with God," he said. His voice was as magnetic as the others, a pleasing baritone that exuded honesty and compassion. Galen knew him for an inhuman killer.

"It was no great trick to invade Double En's matrices. But the connections between them and God have been severed. That way is closed."

Saint Trump broke in. "What has happened, brother? Is God dead?"

Michael shrugged. "You felt the breach as much as I. One moment God was with us, and the next he was gone."

They all moved their heads or shifted slightly in their seats. The instant of God's departure remained the single greatest trauma of all of them. They had been birthed in direct connection to their master. None of them had shared all his thought, but all had shared some of it. Now it was gone. Now they were alone.

The worst thing was that this had not been planned for.

Asmodeo sighed. "I was afraid of as much. It seems, brothers, that we are on our own. We have only to carry it out. No decisions are necessary."

The Raker's eyes flashed. "What decisions? We have our plan, given to us by God himself. We have only to carry it out. No decisions are necessary."

Asmodeo stared at him. "Of course, brother." His voice was flat. "But when the plan is complete, what then?"

"Why worry about it? Perhaps God will return. Certainly he will return. But if not, now is not the time to consider new avenues. We must complete the plan first. To talk of anything else is . . . blasphemy."

There was a moment of silence. Each of the council considered the word. Finally Asmodeo smiled.

"Nobody contemplates such a sin, brother. But we must be realistic. No matter what, the Church must survive this turmoil. Surely even you can't argue that."

Raker opened his mouth, closed it again. Finally, "I suppose not. But be careful where you tread, brothers. The ways of God are strange, and beyond our full comprehension."

Nobody disputes *that*, Galen thought. But as he stared at Raker's face, at his features suffused with belief, he knew it was a charade. Of all of them only he, himself, truly believed. For he was certain that only he knew the truth.

God was *not* dead.

But He was in danger, and that was the only thing that mattered. The rest of these fools mattered not at all.

As they would soon learn.

"Would you like to see the tapes of the interrogation?" Oranson asked.

"Not particularly," Nakamura replied.

Outside a chill drizzle beat in spattering waves against the glass which separated the inner office from the outer gardens. The leaves of the exotic fruit trees there moved in the sodden wind; Shag wondered if the heaters and baffles would be enough to protect them. A gardner appeared at the edge of the planted area. Soon two more joined him. They began to cover the delicate foliage with thin, clear sheets of plastic. Nakamura grunted in satisfaction. At least something worked the way it was supposed to work.

"The man was quite talkative," Oranson noted. "With the proper stimulus, that is."

"I can imagine, Fred. Stipulate that you know your job, and get on with it. What did you discover?"

"He didn't recall *any* data regarding Arius, or Bill Norton, passing through his area. He says if it was important he would have noticed, because all priority communications go to him for personal coding and routing."

Nakamura stared at his security chief for a long moment,

his dark eyes sunken and hooded. "In others words, nothing."

"That's right. Nothing."

"But Nikki knows enough to use the name. How does this happen?"

"Perhaps it was a personal message. Something that bypassed his data bases entirely. It wouldn't be beyond Arius' capabilities."

Nakamura thought about it. Finally he rolled his heavy shoulders, as if tossing a weight. "There's only one thing to do, then." He glanced up at Oranson.

Oranson nodded. "Gogolsky himself?"

"Gogolsky himself."

Both men went silent for a minute or so. Oranson tried to balance the dangers. Nikki Gogolsky was necessary to Shag's larger plans. Nikki, or somebody like him. To force a confrontation could jeopardize many things. On the other hand, to let evidence of Arius's covert involvement in those plans go unresolved might be an even greater danger.

He was glad he didn't have to make the decision.

"We'll have to find the least hazardous option," Shag said at last. "Maybe we can save Nikki."

"How?"

"Perhaps we can force Nikki to save himself." Nakamura's black eyes were wide and without guile.

Slowly, Oranson grinned.

Nikolai Gogolsky carefully lit another bright red candle with a wooden match, then blew out the match. He stepped back from the huge, ornately carved gold-leaf candelabra and studied the effect. The red candle emitted a heavy scent of roses as it burned. Three other, similar candles flickered about the room, casting shadows. There was no other light.

"Perfect," Nikki mumbled to himself.

The room was not particularly large; the overall size was further diminished by the plethora of *things* which filled it to near overflowing. It was like a jewel box, but its gems were of carved wood, gilt, mirror, gold, silver, and crystal. Ancient Russian icons covered the walls, interspersed with heavily framed oil masterpieces looted from the fallen Kremlin. The furniture was ponderous, dark, and priceless: pieces which had graced many of the European courts. Three

Fabergé eggs, Nikki's personal *pièce de résistance*, shimmered quietly in a glass case limned in pure gold.

Nikki loved the room. Its luxurious silences, its formidably beclouded darkness, its many-crusted glints of naked wealth appealed to his somber Russian soul.

He chuckled softly at the thought. Now, with the commissars dead and buried, it was again suitable for Russians to have souls. Souls and money. Greed and religion were making remarkable comebacks. Nikki found that immensely comforting.

He'd stitched together a mighty empire from the wreckage of the Red Czars. The heart of it was this room. He paused, his small, perfect head cocked slightly, as if listening to hidden choirs. But he heard the sound of danger instead.

"Goddamn you, Shag," he whispered at last.

He went to a desk that had once graced a palace in St. Petersburg, sat, and began to fit together the puzzle pieces of his enemy's latest atrocity.

He worked in the shadows for almost an hour. Then his concentration was interrupted by a deep, bell-like tone. Without looking up, he said, "Come in."

The woman who entered on soft feet was as perfect a complement to this inner sanctum as any other of its priceless baubles. Her eyes, faintly almond-shaped, betrayed a heritage as much Tatar as White Russian. Her black hair hung in a wild wave below her shoulders. Her back was straight, her shoulders held well to the rear, thrusting her perfect breasts forward. Nothing about her betrayed any hint of servitude, yet she was the greatest of his servants.

"Katerina," he said quietly, still not looking up from his work. "Have you found out what I need to know?"

Her voice was as quiet as his. "The Japanese pig," she said. "He took Sergei Lefortovich. His body was found in Berlin today. Impaled on a lamp post."

At this, Nikki raised his head. "A lamp post?" He shook his head. "The Japanese. As much as they pretend to civilization, they always revert under stress."

She shook her head. "It was probably Oranson."

Nikki stared at her. "Same thing. The servant is only a tool in the master's hand."

"Am I a tool?"

He smiled. "Of course, my dear. Of course."

*   *   *

181

Later, Nikki said to her, "It is some kind of gambit."

She nodded. "Sergei's body need never have been found. But what is the message? They've taken the man who runs our communications systems and drained him. He was full of drugs. He'd been tortured. To what purpose? They know everything will change now. His knowledge will do them no good."

He tapped his chin with one perfectly manicured nail. "I wonder. Were they trying to crack our ice, or . . . something else?"

"What else?"

"A message," he said. "I gave Shag a message recently. Perhaps this is his reply."

She leaned over and brushed the top of his right ear with her lips. He shivered. "What message did you give him?"

He turned his face up, felt her warm breath on his cheek. He felt himself grow hard. "Arius," he said.

"Ah," she replied.

Chapter Seventeen

"Berg's cheating? Darling, Berg *always* cheats. So do you, for that matter."

"Oz, you're fucking up a perfectly good insight here."

"Sorry, but just because you decide that Berg's doing what he always does—what I'm trying to say, does it *mean* anything?"

She cupped her narrow chin in the fingers of her right hand and squeezed. He thought she looked very tired. Even her rasping voice was dull, devoid of emotion. "The whole game, you see. The game itself is a cheat. . . ."

He drummed his long fingers on his knee.

"Something to do with the Key . . ." she went on. Her voice was dreamy, distant. For a moment, as he watched her, he had the crazy idea that she'd flickered, just faded out and then come back very quickly. He blinked and rubbed his eyes. But Calley didn't seem to notice anything. She stared blankly from beneath half-lowered eyelids, a faint tic beginning to jitter above one eyebrow.

"Hey!" he said. His voice sounded unnaturally loud in his ears, and for the first time he became aware of how deserted the big room seemed to feel. As if it were suspended flimsily in some greater, emptier void?

Her eyes widened. "What?"

"You feel anything just now?"

"Like what?"

"I—dunno. Something. Anything."

She stared at him. "Are you okay?"

He passed one big hand across his features. "Nothing," he said. "Forget it."

Her gaze had sharpened a bit. "What happened?"

He chewed his lower lip. "You disappeared. I think."

Now all her attention was focused on him. "I did? You sure?"

"Maybe I'm just tired."

"Tell me about it."

He repeated the odd moment, the flash.

"That's it? I just linked out? Like a bad net picture or something?"

"Uh-huh."

"Just me, or did everything go?"

He paused, thinking about it. "No. It was just you. It was weird."

She turned away, deep lines knifing the flesh at the bridge of her nose. "It means something," she said at last.

"What?"

"I don't know. But something." She was silent for almost a minute. "Oz, what are we here? In this place? We call ourselves analogs, constructs, but what exactly are we? How come we have our sense of self, our memories, our—lives? How is he doing that?"

He shifted uncomfortably. "I'm not sure he is," he said at last. "Berg, I mean. Remember when we first went into the metamatrix?"

She leaned back in her chair. It was a white plastic chair that tilted at the spine. It was padded, but nothing more, no body molding, no massage capabilities. He heard tiny bits of cartilage pop softly in her spine. He was struck once again by the compact hard beauty of her, the lines and edges and rigid shapes carved by experience. She reached over, fingered a Turkish Clove from the pack, raised it to her lips, lit it with a tattered book of marches, and exhaled a blue cloud in his general direction.

"I remember," she said, her words chopping the last rivulets of smoke into dainty clouds of punctuation.

"We had body consciousness then, an awareness of our real bodies, even while we navigated in the metamatrix. But we had no reality to each other there. I couldn't see you, you couldn't see me. And we could only visit. We couldn't manipulate either the individual matrices, or the greater matrix, either."

She nodded, her eyes distant with recollection. "Damn thing nearly killed us, bodies or not."

He grinned. "But after the Joining, we could create our own worlds inside the metamatrix. Why do you suppose that was?"

"Uh—" She shook her head. Then, "It had to be Berg, somehow. Is that what you mean?"

"Berg, or the Key. They seem to be inextricably entwined. But remember what else?"

She shook her head slowly.

"Berg could manipulate the matrices even before he had the Key."

A growing recollection burgeoned in her skull. Flashes of Berg's memories picked up in the Joining itself. Berg's great battle with Bill Norton, when Toshi had been killed the first time, and Berg had taken the fabric of the Matrix itself in the grip of his will. Only then had he used the Key, *after* he'd broken the meat Norton's control of his own tailored brain cells.

"What you're saying, Berg's sort of like a Key himself. But how the fuck does that fit into all this?"

"I think the Key amplifies his powers somehow." He paused, scratched the side of his nose. "Berg calls it the Key," he said. "But maybe we're looking at this all wrong."

"If Berg's involved, we most likely are. He likes it that way."

"Uh-huh. We think of a Key that locks and unlocks things. He even called it that, once. The Key that Locks and Looses. But there are other meanings for the word. A key can be an answer, like to a puzzle. You know?"

And then, with the sudden flash of epiphany that made her Calley, the Icebreaker, she *did* see. Her mouth opened slightly.

"Oh, my—"

"Don't say it," Ozzie told her. "It only builds up his ego."

"We're Berg," she said, a low horror rumbling in her voice. "That's all we are. We're Berg."

"That's the difference," Ozzie told her softly, "between the dreams of gods and men."

The thing that Ozzie had built looked like some sort of technological cancer, a slowly accreted reef of plastic and silicon and spidersilk platinum. She could detect very little order in its design. The only recognizable elements of the construction were two fiberop cables which extended from the center of it to end in cyberneural connectors, the jacks which would plug her into the green shift of the metamatrix.

"Oz, you may be an engineering genius, but you're never gonna make it big in the world of home appliance design."

"You want me to paint it or something?"

She stared at it. "Naw. I don't think that would help."

"As long as it works," he reminded her.

"Is it going to work? We seem to be limited to tech current in whatever this time frame is supposed to be. Before Double En cranked out thousands of meatmatrices. Jeez. It sure as hell *looks* primitive."

He nodded cheerfully. "It is. If I could have a rig like we left behind, hooked up to a big meat, I could do a lot more stuff. But this thing is informed by principles I didn't have when I built the first box. If the logics of this reality hold true throughout, you're looking at the most advanced piece of hardware on the entire planet. Don't worry, Calley. Nothing's gonna sneak up on us in the matrix this time."

She continued to stare dubiously, one red fingernail picking idly at a small pimple on the corner of her mouth. "I wrote some hot-shit programs," she said finally. "I learned some stuff, too." She sighed. "Well, fuck. We won't know till we try, will we?"

"It'll be okay. Really."

"Remember that big old hunk of stuff we saw out Luna way? Looked like an obese amoeba in costume jewelry?"

He nodded. "The original Arius. The first true Artificial Intelligence."

"I wonder if it knows?" she said slowly. "That we're coming after it this time?"

He ran one long finger down the matte black side of his machine, the only strip of finished metal on it. "Probably. Wouldn't you say that's the point?"

"Of what?"

"Game's gotta have two players," he said.

"I know. How else could there be a winner?"

"And a loser."

Calley stared at Ozzie's machine and wondered why the room had suddenly grown so cold.

She approached her throne. The high, dim blue space which surrounded it, lit by surplus glowstrips, made the air seem thicker, somehow. Through her infrared eyes the world was black and white. She smiled faintly. And wasn't that the true way of the world, anyhow? Only fools believed in shades of gray.

The throne was surrounded by ancient mainframes, their guts built and rebuilt over months by sly men who came down from the moon and went back up again. Huge, rattling ventilation fans, ripped from the skeletons of the buildings which rotted above, now mounted on crude housings made of two-by-fours, sucked with near-futile persistence at the ever present damp.

Wolves moved like slow, sweaty shadows around the throne itself, which was connected to the mainframes through a network of cables that lay everywhere on the floor.

Soon, she thought, I will take this throne and give birth. She remembered the first time, and wondered what it would be like now, to receive God and know he was God, know what he would become.

She had been terrified at the beginning, when the tiny, stunted body of Arius had first slipped between her thighs. His deformities were evident even then, and she'd known it was wrong. Some mistake, some terrible mistake, and in her bones she'd know the cause.

Berg.

She hissed his name and smiled again.

This time, she promised herself, this time. . . .

It seemed totally quiet in the computer room. Ozzie and Calley faced each other across his gimcracked construction. Each held the end of a cable in one hand. He grinned. For an instant he thought she looked impossibly young.

"Like old times, huh?"

He grinned back. "Old times."

She sucked in breath, pushed it out hard. "Well," she said, and touched the tip of the plug to the socket beneath her ear. He did likewise. "Here goes nothing."

They jacked. The metamatrix was.

Melt a handful of emeralds and throw them at the night. Strew the floor beneath with diamonds ground fine as dust. And hang the space between with rubies, sapphires, topazes . . .

The metamatrix pulsed in familiar splendor, moving, always moving.

"Jesus . . ." Calley breathed, repeating without consciousness the word she'd muttered the first time she'd come to this place.

"Still grabs the old guts, doesn't it," Ozzie agreed.

"I'd forgotten what it was like," she said. She turned to face him. Her eyebrows shot up. "Hey. I can see you."

"Uh huh. I can see you, too. Your mouth's open. Told you I'd added a few new wrinkles."

She glanced around nervously. From her perspective it appeared they hung motionless in empty space. Far away, the main bulk of the metamatrix glittered in flowing, jeweled splendor, a particolored galaxy of informational structure. At the very top were the shifting green chandeliers of the original meatmatrices. All of them but one.

She turned. An equal distance beyond them pulsed the seventh matrix, the strangest one of all. She knew that this was the Lunie meat, the source of the original AI. Its very shape betrayed its strangeness.

Its lopsided green profile throbbed slowly, like some alien heart. Embedded in its crust were the rigid configurations of its hardware constructs, enormous ROM frameworks which held the programs that gave life and thought to the unimaginable intelligence which burned within the meat itself.

It was Arius, before it had become Itself in the Joining.

"That thing scares the shit out of me," she said.

"I dunno. Compared to the Arius we know, it's a skateboard."

She shrugged. "Maybe we scare it. I sure hope so." She stopped. "Can it see us? I mean, the way we see each other?"

"Nope. I did something tricky. My box is channeling us, the body awareness relative to the metamatrix itself, through a feedback loop between the two of us. In here, to anything else, it's just like before. We're points of view." Ozzie raised one long finger. "However . . ."

"Right. There's always one of those," she said, her voice sour.

"Bill Norton was aware of us before, our presence. He didn't know what we were, couldn't actually see us, but he knew we were there."

"Great. You think Arius will throw out the welcome mat when we come knocking?"

"I doubt it," he said. His shoulders moved. "You ready, kiddo?"

Her green eyes flashed once, as she marshalled the programs she'd stored, like arrows in the quiver of her mind.

"Let's do it."

They began to move.

As they drifted slowly toward the Lunar matrix, she began to deploy the first of her icebreaker code arrays. On previous raids into the metamatrix she'd been swatted like a fly. But this time she had a fair idea of what she was dealing with, and had composed her attack programs accordingly. Something like a cloud of tiny gnats sighed into existence around them, buzzing faintly.

"What's that?" Ozzie said.

"I'm taking this whole fucking trip as a metaphor," she told him. "So what my codes look like, well, they won't look like codes. They'll look like something else." She thought about how to say it, then realized there was no real way to describe her art to Ozzie, no more than he could explain to her how he contrived the blind leaps of engineering which resulted in the exotic hardware he seemed to build so easily.

"Look like what?" he asked.

"Like metaphors," she told him.

He glanced at her, then went silent. He watched her face go slack with concentration, as she spun out the web of her cracker programs. Something clutched and jumped in his gut. Berg had said they could die, really die. What did that mean here?

Their bodies were still, as far as he knew, in tanks on the moon. Berg had told them they weren't even hooked up to Levin. Was that possible? Then, at the beginning of the attack on Arius, when the fusion had been pulled into Gestalt Space against its will, they had entered the tanks as always. Insertion had been counted down, and the jump into the metamatrix had begun as usual. If they were no longer connected to Levin, then where was he getting the patterns for them, the blue prints with which he constructed their analog bodies?

Perhaps, in realtime, in the real world, their bodies were already dead. Could that be what Berg had meant?

His head began to ache.

"Gotcha," Calley said softly.

He turned. She was gone.

For a moment he panicked. His chest heaved once, and all the breath went out of him. Then he saw her.

He thought it was her.

"Calley?"

"What?"

Dimly he made out her outline, black against the darker black interstices of the metamatrix. She had become shape, nearly pure form, yet at her edges there was a boundary of even greater emptiness, lines that sucked at him.

"What the fuck?" he said.

"You oughta see what you look like." She chuckled. "We're not going in naked, sweetie pie." Her voice began to fade, as if she spoke to him from a great distance, though her position relative to him was unchanged.

"Heads up," she said.

They drifted into the awful glare of the AI. Only now, he saw, they were no longer drifting.

They began to move faster and faster. A wild, high buzz, like all the bees in the world gone crazy, filled his ears. Sparks jumped in his field of vision.

Her voice filled him.

"Kick 'em in the crotch. One, two. Kick 'em in the other crotch!"

They went in.

The sensation of rapidly increasing acceleration began to stretch ghostly fingers into the flesh of his face, as if his skin was being gently tugged backward. Directly ahead, the flowing green mass of the meatmatrix glowed like a vampire's eye. Sounds buffeted him, long, guttural moans, the members of a crowd shouting a single unrecognizable word in unison, someone walking across something thick, full of mucus.

He smelled cinnamon, dog shit, vinegar.

Something was happening on the surface of the matrix. Long ripples, as if a swollen, purulent mass was about to burst forth, heaved and thrashed.

"The meatmatrix exploded.

"Gotcha again," Calley whispered.

—*click*—

He was on a broad, yellow plain. It seemed that it was a desert, but the material beneath his feet was neither sand nor rock. Something else, almost like—

Flesh.

The sky overhead was a lighter shade of yellow, uniformly illuminated. There was no obvious source of light. It was utterly silent, yet he felt the sensation of breathing, of great lungs moving out, in, out again.

He felt watched.

Calley was gone.

His heart jumped behind his breast bone. He felt dizzy. "Calley!"

Nothing.

"*Calley!*"

The breathing grew deeper, hoarser, and now he could see that the flesh desert was moving slightly, in time with the exhalations. He began to run.

Somebody started to laugh, far away, growing closer. A deep laugh, then louder, then rising, finally shrieking into an insane patter of choking giggles.

Somewhere, someone was frying bacon.

He tripped.

He fell flat out, face down, but the soft surface beneath him bounced him back up. He paused there, on hands and knees, his tongue out, panting.

The flesh-earth was warm to his touch. Directly in front of his nose was a small, green can. He blinked.

Star-Kist tuna.

He stared at it.

The shiny metal lid began to pop, poink, poink, as if a very tiny tuna fish was inside with a hammer trying to batter its way out. He stared fixedly. Saliva began to ooze from the corner of his mouth. His chest was on fire.

Something acidic, something in the air.

The lid of the can came away all at once, fell to the surface with a soft, dull sound. He peered over the edge, slowly.

191

The worm was as thick as his arm, headless, slick and shiny as the membranes which connect fat to muscle, and the pink tip of it was nothing but lips, row after row of pale, flaccid lips.

It rose straight up and he tried to turn his head, but it collapsed with equal suddenness and he felt chill, slimy coils begin to enfold him.

Something nibbled gently at the spot between his anus and his balls, testing, testing . . .

He screamed.

She said, "And gotcha the third time," and—

—click—

Static. The sky burst and popped and sizzled, but it was no longer threatening.

"How you doing, my little pothole?" she said.

"What!"

"Oh, sorry. Didn't mean to startle you."

"Jesus fucking—Damn, Calley, what happened? Where are we?"

Her normal appearance had returned although, for some reason, she was wearing a necklace of skulls, black leather from head to toe, and carrying something that looked like a child's Halloween noisemaker in her right hand, the kind you spun around to make a rusty, croaking noise.

"Inside," she said. "We're in the Lunie AI. What do you think?"

He lowered his head from the stutter of the horizon. He was standing on what seemed to be an endless field of small colored lights. The lights were each about an inch apart, red, blue, green, orange, arranged in squares. He looked closer. Beneath each square was another square. Cubes, then.

He stared down, fascinated.

"Don't look too long," she said.

The patterns extended down forever, and suddenly vertigo punched up through his bowels. "Whoa!"

"I told you," she said. "Come on, get it together. Company's coming."

He forced himself to stand up. Even with his eyes closed, the void beneath his feet called to him. After an interval he opened his eyes.

In the distance, skipping across the lighted plain, eyes glowing the color of dying coals, of ruined rubies, came the child.

Skipping, skipping.

His laughter was car wrecks and the strop of whetstone on knives and the whine of saws.

"Now," Calley said, "I get to see how good the little fucker really is. It's about time."

The two sat cross legged across from each other on the thin, nearly invisible membrane which walled them off from the endless plain of blue globes beneath. Overhead a swollen sun impaled itself upon a silver sword. In the fractured light of the place they were motionless as stones.

A board rested between them, supported on nothing. It appeared to be a chessboard, but the pieces were missing. Or, rather, where pieces should have been were small, knotted whorls of twinkling darkness, darkness the glittered and danced.

Berg looked up. His eyes were two holes in his face. At the bottom of the holes burned candles, the flames of which flickered platinum. He smiled faintly. "Your move," he said.

Chapter Eighteen

Oranson hurried toward the tall double doors which shielded Nakamura's office from the everyday world. It was almost two in the morning. The summons had been cryptic. As he'd thrown on his clothes, Oranson had reviewed summaries of Double En's far-flung activities. Everything appeared to be quiet. He wondered what had disturbed Nakamura.

He knocked.

"Come in, Fred." Nakamura's voice, perfectly reproduced, boomed from hidden speakers. Oranson paused until he heard the heavy bolts of the maglocks chunk back into their housings. Then he reached forward, took two golden handles and twisted them down, and pushed the perfectly balanced twenty-ton monomole reinforced doors wide enough for him to enter. Two security people, still as guardian idols at either side of the door, ignored him. Inside, he turned and pushed the doors shut again.

"Good," Nakamura said. "You came quickly."

Oranson pivoted to face his boss. To uninformed eyes, the short, compactly heavy little man would have seemed unchanged. He wore a black suit of English cut that could have easily graced the high altar of some historical fashion deity. His black hair, perfectly trimmed, caught the recessed light from above, shining and healthy. Nakamura's face was smooth of expression. His black eyes glittered.

Oranson wondered how he did it. He knew the man had not slept for almost two days, yet he appeared as fresh and rested as a child awakening from a nap. Nakamura held a low, thick-walled tumbler of Swedish crystal, filled with a pale, amber liquid.

"Come here, Fred. A drink? Scotch?" He gestured with the glass. Oranson shook his head.

"No, thank you."

Nakamura shrugged. "Coffee?"

"Yes, please."

Nakamura made a soft, clicking noise with his tongue and teeth. The domestic computer which monitored his office picked up the command, and within a few seconds a very handsome Oriental male, no more than eighteen, entered the office from a side door bearing a silver tray crowded with pot, cream, sugar, cups and saucers.

"Over there, Jimmy," Nakamura said. The young man wordlessly poured two cups and placed them on a low, teak coffee table which fronted on a small grouping of leather chairs and sofa against the far wall of the office.

"Sit down, Fred," Nakamura said. The Japanese perched on the edge of one of the chairs, alert as a bird. Oranson sat on the sofa. As he lifted the coffee to his lips, his eyes snagged on the rocky shadows of Nakamura's meditation garden, now completely restored beyond the office area. He catalogued the shadows for an instant, thinking of teeth, then set down his cup.

"What's going on, Shag?" he said mildly. He knew the signs. Something had Nakamura keyed as tight as a lawyer's heart.

Nakamura took a sip of the coffee and chased it with a heavier swig of the scotch. Oranson glanced at Nakamura's desk and saw a bottle of Glenmorangie single malt Scotch there, half empty, the cork off. Yet Nakamura appeared completely sober.

"I have . . . sources of information other than your own. I've always assumed you knew that."

Oranson remembered the white-haired killer Nakamura had conjured out of nowhere, the scarred man who had nearly tortured him to death. "I knew that, Shag."

"Good. I have received an interesting piece of data."

"What is it?"

"Luna, Incorporated, is presently without the services of its Artificial Intelligence."

Oranson stared at the table, stunned. The implications were enormous. Finally he looked up. "We aren't ready yet," he said.

Nakamura smiled whitely at him, and once again Oranson thought of teeth. "We have to be," Nakamura said.

* * *

Dawn burned a thin red line across the leaden flatness of the winter lake. Chicago loomed gray and cold in the thin light. Oranson was exhausted, but Shag seemed full of unquenchable energy.

Oranson watched the smaller man as he stood at the edge of the balcony, beneath the branches of an orange tree. The tree was incongruously bright and green against the drab background of the skyline, flourishing in the artificial microclimate Shag had caused to be created on the balcony.

Ancient kings, Oranson thought, had never dreamed such power.

Nakamura had paused for a few moments, "to refresh himself," he told Oranson. Oranson wondered what his boss thought about, during those times he needed an interval of solitude. Whatever it was, he always returned as buoyant as another man after eight hours of sleep.

Oranson scanned the room tiredly. He'd removed his suit coat and rolled up his sleeves, and knew he looked wrinkled and sweaty. It didn't matter. Nakamura didn't pay him to win beauty contests.

Long, wrinkled sheets of printout were strewn across every flat surface. Every screen in the room was revealed and lighted. The overall effect was of some bizarre television store that had accommodated a ticker tape parade. Nakamura had worked with frenzied intensity for the past four hours. Just before he'd adjourned to his balcony, he'd looked up with bright black eyes and said, "I think it can be done. Close, but if nothing else comes up, we can pull it off."

Oranson thought about that and wondered if, for the first time in his long, carefully planned struggle, Nakamura might not be going to the well one too many times.

"Fred. Wake up."

Oranson jerked his head up. He'd dozed without realizing it. Nakamura had come back into the room, looking fresher than ever.

"Breakfast? Stimulants? You need something, Fred. I want you alert. The timing on this is crucial."

Oranson nodded slowly. His head ached and the surface of his eyeballs felt raw and abraded. "Breakfast," he said. "And coffee. Gallons of it. Uh—one thing else."

Nakamura had turned toward his desk. Now he turned back. "What?"

"It's time for my . . . treatment. Overdue, actually."
Oranson wondered why he felt ashamed when he said it.
Then he wondered why Nakamura's face went blank and
empty at his words. Could it be that his master felt shame,
too?

"Oh. By all means, go. I'll have breakfast served here
when you return."

Oranson nodded and rose unsteadily. Nakamura made no
move to help him. His thought processes were dim and
slow, the leading edge of inevitable dissolution. My brain is
dissolving, he thought.

One more thing I owe him for. He knew he should hate
Nakamura for what he'd done to him, but he didn't. All he
felt was a long, foggy somnolence. He wondered what it
would be like, to know emotions again.

He left the office. Maybe it was better this way. Despair
was an emotion, too.

His own suite of offices was on the same floor as
Nakamura's. He entered and strode quickly across the ante-
room, deserted now in the early morning, its light thin and
eerie. Beyond, however, the warren which fronted his own
private office buzzed with activity. He saw one big monitor
which showed a scene that was evidently shot from a heli-
copter. The picture bounced too much for it to be a spysat.

He recognized the setting; the world headquarters of the
New Church in San Francisco. The shot tightened suddenly
on a flock of copters whirling in for landings on the rooftop,
like great, ungainly insects settling to feed.

The faces were more than familiar. Tired as he was, he
checked the ID number at the bottom of the screen and
walked to the man monitoring the current broadcast.

"What's the Church Council up to?" he asked.

The technician, a big, easygoing man whose name Oranson
could never remember, glanced up.

"I dunno," he said. "No warning. They arrived all at once
and went into their chamber immediately. We haven't been
able to penetrate the chamber itself, but we may pick up
something from one of our moles."

Oranson nodded thoughtfully. What did this mean?

"Keep me posted," he said. He walked away, turned
down a corridor, and entered his own office. He seated

himself behind his utilitarian desk, punched in a code, and waited for the sleepy medic to answer the phone.

His back ached. His brain was turning to mush. All the symptoms.

The doctor appeared, rubbing sleep from his eyes. Oranson stared at him. "I'm ready," he said.

The doctor blinked. "Now?"

"Now."

He switched off the screen and leaned back. Some day it would all end. He wondered how he felt about that.

Then he realized he didn't feel anything.

"Mr. Oranson," the voice repeated, softly, insistently. "Sir, wake up."

Something prodded his shoulder lightly. He opened his eyes, but it took a moment for his vision to clear. Must be slipping fast, he thought groggily. He couldn't have sneaked in like that, otherwise.

"Yes. Get on with it."

Fitchfield nodded. "If you'd remove your shirt?"

"Oh. Of course." Oranson did so. The doctor opened his bag and removed the hypospray, the two colors of derms, and the bottle of pills.

"Takes a lot to keep me alive, doctor."

Fitchfield knew better than to reply. He busied himself with the task at hand. The sharp sound of the hypospray filled the room. Eventually, Oranson sighed.

He couldn't feel true emotions, but he felt something, each time the doctor came to him, and gave him another tiny package of time, of life.

After Fitchfield was gone, Oranson sat for several minutes, staring blankly into space. Then he got up and went back to his master.

He had no other place to go.

As soon as Oranson left, Nakamura went behind his desk. He sat, reached forward, and swept the tangle of hardcopy to the floor with a single motion. Then he put his hands on the touchpad thus revealed and began to punch in code. Sources of information weren't the only thing he kept secret from his security chief.

The far part of his desktop slid back and a pop up monitor rose into view. The screen blinked once, then cleared. Nakamura touched the pad again, and a number unrolled itself across the screen. Nakamura's lips tightened. He nodded faintly, and punched in a final set of codes.

This console, his most private, was slaved to a dedicated meatmatrix. Within a few seconds, a face appeared on the screen.

Nakamura grinned. "How's Wier?" he said.

Hank Carpenter's slow, comfortable drawl whispered out. "Not so well, that old boy. Barely hanging on."

"Kill him," Nakamura said. "And the others, as well."

He shut off transmission. The screen folded down.

Nakamura poured himself another scotch and waited for Oranson's return. He thought about Nikki Gogolsky for a moment. His eyes narrowed and he raised his glass.

"To you, Nikki," he said softly. "Maybe it won't make any fucking difference at all."

"It's very simple," Nakamura said. "We know that Berg had something to do with their supercomputer. But Berg is dead. And the Lunie machine went down at the precise time our investigations showed Arius disappearing."

Oranson stared at him. "Is there a connection?"

Nakamura shrugged. "There has to be. Must be. We know Luna's machine was very advanced. And we know that Arius was. Do you buy the idea that both disappear simultaneously as a coincidence?"

Oranson shrugged. "No." He walked to the edge of the room, looked out on the broad balcony. Bright morning sun flickered from the tops of the taller buildings. He squinted. "But if that's the case, what is the connection? Why did both vanish? And what does it mean to us? We've made no overt move on Luna, yet."

Nakamura tilted his head back. Sometimes, Oranson's complete loss of emotion was a pain in the ass. He could no longer scent the smell of triumph.

"It doesn't matter," Nakamura said. "What happened. The point is, Luna's defenseless. We kicked the New Church's ass. The deals are made with Gogolsky and the American. Even if we decide to take Nikki out, there's no reason to wait any longer on Luna. Double En can throw a thousand meatmatrices into this thing. Luna has less than a third as many. Without that damned machine of theirs, they're helpless."

Oranson turned. His eyes were shadowed. Nakamura thought he looked old, tired. "Gogolsky," he said. "We haven't tracked that down yet. This coincidence that isn't a coincidence. It could be dangerous. If Arius is still around somehow. And the Council of the New Church is meeting in emergency right now."

Nakamura's eyebrows moved slightly. "Oh?"

"You hadn't given me a chance to tell you. But it's true. My people are watching them."

"It doesn't matter."

"Whatever you say," Oranson replied. But he thought it did matter. Suddenly, he was afraid.

Nikki Gogolsky paced slowly down the length of his opulent room, chin cradled in one hand, his eyes, faintly smoke colored, narrowed thoughtfully. Finally he stopped, the thin, white fingers of his other hand unconsciously caressing a small marble bust that had been carved when his own ancestors were still rubbing themselves with reindeer grease to keep out the endless northern cold.

"Katerina," he said clearly. A moment later she appeared, and he smiled.

Katerina Gogolsky was his daughter by a woman long dead, and in appearance she was completely unlike her father. It didn't matter. She had inherited his quick mind and, more important, his absolute fearlessness. These two traits, coupled with the training he'd begun almost at her cradle, had resulted in the only personality he could ever imagine loving. Once, he'd wanted a boy child, but that urge had faded away forever. His life had been long. Katerina was already in her mid-thirties. Nikki had seen the fall of the ridiculous socialist Czars and their gray, stupid economic system, and had personally ushered in the rise of the new Russia. He'd seen, and done almost everything. Everything he *wanted* to do, at least. Only one thing remained—his greatest coup, and then the passing of his empire to her. To Katerina. Who would rule it from her rightful position as the financial queen of the earth.

He raised a silent mental toast to the destruction of Double En.

"Hello, Father," she said.

He touched her cheek lightly, remembering the warmer heft of her body, her flesh. Incest was not a part of his vocabulary. The word had no meaning, not if it included her. But the world was made of beasts. It was all right. His kind—her kind—had never followed the beast rules anyway.

"My dear," he purred.

Beasts. And only one beast remained, between him and his goals. But it appeared that now even Shag Nakamura had made a mistake. With any luck, and a little help, it would be a fatal mistake.

Galen glanced at the screen inset into the back of the pilot's seat of his personal copter as it rose slowly from the top of the New Church Headquarters. A smaller bird circled slowly high above. It, or one just like it, was always there. He grimaced in annoyance. When God had departed, so had certain of Galen's powers. He was no longer able to twitch that obscene little spy platform from the sky with a single surging thought, as he'd once caused a fully loaded fishing boat to rise from the San Francisco harbor during the Blessing of the Fleet. He was, however, fully aware of whom the copter represented, and boiled inwardly at Shag Nakamura's arrogance.

The deal. He thought about the deal. At the time there had been no objection, for the deal had been made by God himself, and Nakamura was only another of his minions. Galen had acquiesced willingly, happily, as he did with all things divine.

It had been simple enough. God wished to exercise temporal authority without revealing his awful presence. The Church, under God's patronage, had grown rapidly; its odd gospel, a blend of good business and high technology with the evangelism of Christianity had proved a perfect counterbalance to many of the less sane post-millennial religions. Galen himself, before God had remade him, had been a high figure in the Church of Scientology, an American religion organized on vaguely similar principles.

That God wished to pit his religious arm against his business arm in a mock war that would only result in the collapse of many of the governments which stood in his way, was only one more evidence of his divine perspicacity. And it should have worked. In the fallout of the rebellion, after the ritual slaughter of a small percentage of the New Church's less dependable stalwarts, Double En should have found itself in de facto possession of the governments of Britain, France, United Germany, and most of the little tigers that surrounded the China Sea.

But God had died. Or seemed to. At any rate, God had not exerted his influence on Nakamura, who had then proceeded to murder far more of the Church's sheep than previously agreed to. Under the original plan the Church, slightly injured, would have been "allowed" to merge with Double En as an equal partner. In fact, Nakamura had hurt them badly, and made no response whatsoever to the Council's pleas for the continuation of the first arrangement.

Which didn't surprise Galen at all. Shigeinari Nakamura was not a man to respond to pleadings. He gloried in betrayal. But, as his copter tilted away from Nob Hill into the short flight path to his secluded home, Galen allowed himself a tight little smile.

He had tried to remedy the matter more directly, but his emissary had perished in a field, murdered by cattle, or so the strange report had said.

Now the rest of the Council was frightened because God was dead. Nakamura was ecstatic in his insolence over the same event. But Galen knew better. God wasn't dead.

Shag would find out soon enough—and he, personally, intended to see to Nakamura's final repentance.

It was, after all, the least a good church father could do for a very prodigal son.

"Have you managed to penetrate that New Church Council yet?"

"Not the chamber itself. Close to it, though." Oranson took a minipad from the inside pocket of his suit—he'd managed to leave long enough for a quick shower and a change of clothes while Nakamura meditated at the edge of his rock garden—and ran his fingers lightly across the top of it. The monitor across from Nakamura's desk quivered and dissolved into the face of one of Oranson's people. Over his shoulder, Oranson could see the familiar backdrop of his office. People seemed to be moving about there rather quickly.

"Uh, Franklin, right?"

The man, whose face could have disappeared easily in any white crowd, said, "Yes, sir."

"What have we got on the New Church?"

"One moment." The man turned away. After a moment, he turned back and said, "Something's coming in now."

Oranson stared at the man, while Franklin stared at the spot on his own screen that held the imaging reproducer which relayed his features to Oranson.

"Okay. Here it is. Mm."

"What?" Oranson said.

"Very fragmented. Our asset there was only able to overhear some casual conversation as the councillors left the chamber."

"Go on."

"Something about God. They were talking about God, and the possibility of submission to temporal authority. One of the Angels was upset. Spoke of rendering unto Caesar what wasn't Caesar's. Seemed quite angry. The one called Raker."

"Anything else?"

"Not yet," Franklin said.

"Okay. Keep me posted if anything else comes in."

"Yes, sir." The screen blanked out.

Oranson looked at Nakamura and shrugged. "What do you make of it?"

Nakamura, still garbed in immaculate black, opened a fresh bottle of scotch. "Want one?"

"No, thanks."

"I think they've given up," he said finally. "What do you get from the troops in the field?"

"As of two hours ago, there was no active fighting anywhere. The last hot spot, in Paris, was reduced this morning by combined Republic and Double En forces. We are, by the way, in control of that government now."

Nakamura nodded. "I already picked that up. Nothing new, though?"

Oranson shook his head.

Nakamura stared at him, but didn't really see him anymore. His mind had wandered, off across the sea, to a place that had been legend in his childhood. Paris. Now it was his. And the New Church, without their spurious god, finally bending to his will. Nikki Gogolsky could be managed, him and that bitch daughter of his—could the rumors be true, that he slept with her? The more he thought about it, the more he decided that Gogolsky could wait. Even if Nikki were privy to the secrets of William Norton and Arius, what did it matter? They were gone.

The weight was gone.

Only one real enemy remained. One final opponent to destroy. Then it would all be his. He almost trembled at the thought of it. Only a few short years from the utter ruin brought on him by Arius, and now this.

He resolved to be as magnanimous as possible in victory. After, of course, Luna was destroyed as a business entity.

He looked up. His eyes were bright. "Let's do it, Fred. Let's get it done."

He went to his desk and began to issue orders. Oranson, his eyes flat, returned to his own offices to do the same. The incredible amplifier of Nakamura's will that was Double En slowly, ponderously, readied itself for war once again.

Galen stared at the small, foxy, boyish face on his screen. "He's going to do it, then?"

"Yes," Nikki Gogolsky said. "What does Arius say?"

Galen closed his eyes and thought of the dreams which had soothed his nights, buoyed him through the terrible slaughter of innocents. "I'm not dead," God had told him in the veiled land of sleep. "I'll return at the proper time. Meanwhile, here is what you must do. . . ."

Galen opened his eyes and stared directly into Gogolsky's steady gaze. "We hit him," Galen said.

Gogolsky looked uncomfortable. "It will be tough. He's almost impregnable in that goddamned fortress building of his."

Galen thought of wolves, and Wolves, and the white wings of hope. "We'll have help," he told Gogolsky.

"Good," Nikki said. "We'll need it."

Galen nodded. There was nothing more to say. He turned his screen off and thought of dreams. God lived in a dream. Life and death, all of it a dream.

Toshiro Nakasone said, "How do I look?" He held his hands out and did a dainty pirouette.

"Fat. And full," Chester Limowitz said sourly.

"Great pizza, guys," Toshi said. "It's been real. But I gotta go."

"I don't want to know," Chet told him.

Toshi admired his new clothes—sweat pants, bright red leather basketball shoes, a blinding Hawaiian shirt, Vuarnet sunglasses—and grinned. "It's really not that bad. Things will get better soon, Chester. Count on it."

"How do you know?"

"It came to me," Toshi told him, "in a dream."

"Thanks," Robby said.

"For the extra pizza," Bobby finished.

"Think nothing of it, guys," Toshi said, as he picked up his black leather travel bag. Heavy, metallic things clanked inside. Chester didn't want to think about the stuff in the bag.

Toshi stuck out his hand. "You too, Chet. Good luck to all of you."

Wearily, Chester took the proffered hand. For some reason, Toshi's firm, warm grip cheered him somewhat. "Luck to you, Toshi," he said, and was surprised to find he meant it.

Toshi nodded. "Bye, guys." He went to the door, opened it, then paused. "You know what?"

"What?"

"If it's any help at all, I just want you to know—luck doesn't have anything to do with it."

Chapter Nineteen

Schollander blinked. What the fuck had that *been?* The afterimage lingered on his retina, almost as clear in memory as it had been on the screen. It had reminded him intensely of Berg, but it wasn't Berg's face.

Who, or what, was it then?

He spoke to his house computer. "Find Franny Webster, wake him up if necessary, and connect him with me."

Several minutes later he heard a chiming sound. Webster's face appeared on his screen. His face looked puffy, full of sleep. "Uh, Robert? Do you know what time it is?"

"Yeah, Franny, sorry. But listen to this." Schollander described what he'd seen.

Webster's eyes seemed suddenly to come into focus. "Describe the face again," he said. "Everything you can remember." He took Schollander over the description three times. Then he smiled. It was a smile of relief.

"I told you we can't shut Levin down," he said.

"What does this have to do with Levin?"

"You just saw him. On your screen. That, Robert, was our missing AI. Bet your ass on it."

On the blue plain, the two game players stared abruptly at each other.

The golden one looked away. Berg stared at the board. His face was calm, still.

"You felt it," Arius said.

"Felt what?"

Arius smiled. "The flicker."

Berg grunted. "It's still your move."

The pattern. Slowly he began to feel his way into it. He was the pattern. He knew that. But the pattern was part of something greater. He couldn't quite understand the key to all of it, but it existed.

He was a part of it.

Perhaps, if he could break the connection—

Connection?

Understanding bloomed.

Nurse Dory sat up straight and put her hands out in front of her. The book plaque, a cheap romance she'd been reading, fell unnoticed into her ample lap.

Every warning light on her board was flashing bright red and, even as she stared in growing consternation at this Christmas tree of danger, the blue lights began to wink on.

A buzzer sounded, high and thin. In the distance, doors sighed open.

She watched a blur of white coats, heard the frantic slap of many footsteps. Ranks of shining equipment flashed past her station.

"Oh, my God," she whispered. "Poor Doctor Wier."

She thought about his condition. Then she picked up her plaque. In a way it was a mercy.

The thought comforted her. It would have been horrible, to linger like that. The poor man.

Schollander met Elaine Markowitz, Lizzybet Meklina, and Franny Webster at the nurse's station on the deserted ward which was devoted solely to maintaining Karl Wier's tenuous grip on life.

Schollander arrived last. "What's the current situation?"

Elaine Markowitz's face was drawn. Without makeup, in the dark marches of the night, she looked older than her 104 years. "He's dying, Robert. Just slipping away."

"What do the doctors say?"

"That's what they say," she told him.

Schollander glanced into the small, glass-walled cubicle behind the counter of the nurse's station. A short, pudgy, blonde woman stared avidly back at him. Her concentration disturbed him and he turned away.

His father had told him of times like this. "Shit never hits the fan in single turds, Bobby. When it comes, it's always diarrhea." The simile, though crude, seemed apt. He looked at the waiting faces around him and suddenly it stuck home.

Elaine, Franny, Lizzybet—all his elders, all of them older, perhaps wiser than he, and all of them waiting. For him to tell them what to do.

I wanted to be the one making the decisions, he told himself. And another part of him replied, "Why did you ever want that?"

"I think . . ." he began, but as he started to speak, his personal alarm began to rasp an itchy pattern against the inside of his left wrist. "Excuse me," he said. He stepped quickly into the nurse's station.

"Pardon," he muttered to the woman there. "Could you give me a moment of privacy, please?"

She seemed reluctant, but after an instant of hesitation she stood up and left the room. Schollander noticed she was reading a lurid romantic novel. Languid holographic figures writhed slowly across the small screen above scrolling words.

He punched his codes into the machine. "Schollander," he said shortly.

Mason Dodge's face appeared. His thin cheeks looked gray. Deep lines were etched beneath his nose, at the corner of his eyes. He too looked old and tired.

"I know you're busy," he said. "So I'll make this quick. Somebody is moving on our stock. And Eaton Vance just called. He wants to talk to you."

Schollander stared at him in disbelief. He felt numb. Eaton Vance? A stock raid? "*Fucking shit,*" he said.

"Looks like it," Dodge agreed.

"What was it?" Elaine said. She paused, as three more medics rushed into Karl's room.

"Nakamura," Schollander told her. "He making his move. He sure knows how to pick his times, doesn't he?"

"I don't think that's a coincidence, either," she said. Her voice was grim. With her white hair floating around her skull-like face, Schollander thought she appeared vengeance personified.

Vengeance. What a sweet thought. He stared at all of them, and they stared at him. A frozen tableau. He felt blood throb in the big veins at his forehead.

He straightened up. "Franny. Check on Karl. He's the most important thing."

Webster nodded shortly and hurried off.

"What are you gonna do, Bobby?" Elizabeth Meklina said. Her black face was shiny with sweat. He realized she was frightened.

"What can I do? I'm going to save Karl's life. What's left of it. If I can."

"What, exactly, are we going to try to do?" Schollander asked Franny Webster.

"It's complicated," Webster said.

The lights were very bright in the main computer room. They hurt Schollander's eyes and he rubbed them. Against the far wall, behind his diamond shield, Levin waited in enigmatic stillness. The third tank, directly in front of Levin's housing, at the end of the row which included the sleeping bodies of Calley and Oswald Karman, yawned wide, its top opened like a coffin. Three technicians were clustered at the head of the tank, working frantically at a piece of apparatus which resembled a wire basket made of filamentary crystal. Every console in the room was manned. Monitor screens jittered and cracked with cryptic messages or bizarre flashes of color. A low-voiced hum, compelling in its intensity, worked at the base of Schollander's spine. He wondered what his blood pressure was. Then he decided he didn't want to know.

"I know it's complicated. Try to explain anyway."

"Your physics is a little out of date, Robert."

He felt a flash of irritation. "I'm not completely obsolete, Franny."

Webster reacted to the tone of his voice. Frown lines appeared over his nose. "Don't crawl on me, Bobby."

"I'm sorry. But I have to know what's going on."

Webster sighed, ran his fingers through his clumped, steel-wool hair. "Patterns," he said.

"Patterns?"

Webster hesitated. "This is so wild, Robert. Karl maybe understood it, but I could only barely follow the math, let alone the theory. It was something Berg, Karl and Levin were doing. Berg put them on to some strange effects, and Karl got interested in the possibilities." His voice trailed off as two technicians at a distant console began to shout at each other.

"A moment," he said, and hurried off. When he returned, Schollander cocked one eyebrow at him.

"Nothing," Webster said. "Feelings are getting a little high, that's all. You know all kinds of rumors are floating around."

"Yeah. We'll deal with them. Later. You were saying?"

"Right." Webster licked his lips, his eyes gone blank, as if he were trying to find the right words, failing, and settling for second best. Schollander knew the feeling. All experts experience it, when trying to discuss their specialties with the uninitiated. Recognizing the syndrome in a fellow physicist made him feel old and lonely. It all moves too fast, he thought.

"Einstein tells us that gravity is a curvature of space caused by density of matter. But one of the things we haven't been able to unravel is the precise effect of very small, very dense bits of matter on the space-time fabric." He glanced at Schollander.

"I did some research in that area in school," Schollander said. "Quantum effects fuck things up. Our models weren't very good." He shrugged. "But so far I'm with you."

"Levin does better models than other computers," Webster said slowly. "He came up with a complete theory of quantum gravity and quantum space-time. It turns out that on the atomic level, near the nucleus where space curvature is fifteen trillion times greater than that of the earth itself, there is an effect."

"Oh . . . wow." Schollander was temporarily diverted from his current concerns, his physicist's mind spinning with wonder at the possibilities inherent in what Webster had revealed. "What kind?"

"Each nucleus impresses itself on space-time. Do you see where I'm going with this?"

Schollander considered. "Is the effect permanent?"

"Space-*time*, Robert. Yes. Levin theorizes the effect is eternal. Subatomic particles may behave like—may actually *be*—black holes. He also thinks something else, based on what Karl claimed was actual observation within the meta-matrix."

"Wait a second," Schollander said hurriedly. "Let me make sure I'm following. Are we talking about brains here? Intelligence?"

Webster grinned. "Now you're getting the picture."

Words tumbled from Schollander's mouth, driven by a maelstrom of new ideas. "Okay, we already know that intelligence is independent of the material matrix which supports it. You can replace every molecule of your brain, but it's still your brain. Intelligence is patterns, arrangements of molecules. They learned that early, with the neural nets. They hooked up television cameras to unorganized hunks of chip relays, then fed in images and reinforced the pathways when they got the ones they wanted. Exactly the same way a baby learns. But if these patterns, these arrangements of neural cells which we call intelligence are impressed on the space-time fabric—and I'd guess a black hole is one hell of an impression—" His voice trailed off. His eyes grew wide.

Webster nodded.

"A soul?"

"A soul," the scientist agreed. "Now you see why I'm not much in a hurry to discuss shit like this? A lot of my colleagues would laugh me out of science if they heard what I just said. But then, none of my colleagues has Levin to play with, either."

Schollander looked over at the yawning, silent coffin. "What are you going to do?"

"I'm going to *try* to save Karl's soul."

"How?"

"I dunno for sure. I think Karl's going to have to tell me that. Somehow. Maybe through Levin."

A thought struck Schollander. "Do you have any idea whether this will work?"

Webster rubbed the side of his nose. For a moment, he looked like a gray-faced, beardless Santa. "Well, there's Berg himself."

"But his pattern is imprinted physically, in Levin's data base structure."

"Is it?" Franny Webster asked.

Somehow he sensed the long, cold struggle was coming to an end. He still floated between the above and the below, but he'd acquired an awareness of pattern that included the possibility of conscious manipulation.

He was almost able to cast loose. Almost.
Anytime now.

They came through the entrance of the computer room
like some ancient Egyptian funeral procession. First the
doors swung wide, held by two white-uniformed security
men. Their heads were covered with round white helmets,
their faces with black monomole blast shields. Each man
held a laser rifle. They put their backs to the doors and
came to port arms, their shoulders rigid and alertly tense.

Then came a crowd of doctors, shepherding the bier itself. Schollander tried to shake the gloomy image, but the
cryo-gurney, rolling slowly on thick, silent rubber wheels,
reminded him of nothing more than a funeral palanquin,
with its cortege of white-clad priests.

As the procession slowly moved past him, he saw Wier
inside, ghostly and hidden in the chill clouds of the freeze
generator. He was dead. Physically so, at least. Even brain
activity had ceased. But was he gone?

That was the question Franny Webster and his team proposed to answer. If they could.

As the team approached the waiting insertion tank, their
movements seemed to quicken, as if simply in the necessi-
ties of speed, of urgency, some hope might be bought for
the husk they bore. Quick hands snapped open the cryo-
gurney's transparent lid. Swiftly they raised the body and
lowered it.

Webster was in the center of the crowd, his pudgy face
intense, his small, precise hands gesturing, fingers tapping,
pointing. His lips moved, but Schollander couldn't make out
the words over the general babble of the rest of the team.

Now two of the techs fitted the field generator cage over
Wier's upraised head. Somehow, all the bustle seemed un-
seemly to Schollander, as if he were watching a defilement.
But the practiced movements continued, and then Wier's
slack features disappeared completely beneath the complex
metal cage.

Schollander felt a whiff of cold from the abandoned cryo-
gurney. Breath of the grave, he thought, as a gelid sensation
trickled slowly down his spine, like gluey ice water. They'd
cooled him quickly, even as they prepared him for the tank,
hoping to preserve whatever patterns were there, locked in

the arrangements of neural cells, each atom impressing its own signature on the deeper fabric of time and space beneath the passing transience of flesh.

Finally the shining plug was inserted into the socket beneath Wier's ear. Schollander recalled that the man hadn't done much direct programming but, like all those who worked with the great machines, he had the capability if necessary for direct interface. Webster thought that if things went as he hoped, Levin would use this channel as a monitor to check the physical pattern of the brain cells, even as the field generated by the cage monitored the atomic paradigm at the quantum level.

Levin. That was the kicker, wasn't it? Schollander raised his eyes to the silence of the machine beneath whose presence Wier now rested, hopeful sacrifice to some god-thing that none of them truly understood. Perhaps Karl had understood Levin, for he, along with Jack Berg, had created the machine. But as Franny explained it, Levin was as much the creation of Levin himself as the work of any human hand. Perhaps it was only fitting that Wier, chief acolyte of the machine-god, should be the first sacrifice.

But nobody knew. Levin still had not come on line, despite the strange appearance of the little man with the moustache on Schollander's screens the night before.

Did it mean anything?

No one knew. Least of all Karl Wier.

Webster hoped that when the connection was made Levin might break from his self-imposed exile. Schollander stared at the mound of high-tech offerings which buried Wier like the floral tributes of a quieter, older society, and wondered.

Perhaps it was better if the dead stayed dead.

Perhaps . . .

Epiphany rolled over him in waves. He realized his teeth were chattering, his shoulders clenched tight as fists. It was a new dream. Karl had dreamed of flesh and sand, and Berg had dreamed of gods and men. Now they dreamed of life and death.

A new dream.

Sharply, rising over the hubble-bubble, a voice rose. "Insertion in three, and two, and one—"

All the lights flickered, dimmed sharply, then flared again.

A soft sound filled the room. Schollander realized it was the fading susurrus of a hundred exhalations. He looked up.

Every screen in the room was filled with a single face.

It smiled, gleeful, a clownlike caricature of happiness. "Fuck it, all right," Levin boomed. "I'll take him."

It was very quiet in their room. "You know," Madge Carpenter said, "I sort of liked this place." Her dumpy breasts rose and fell heavily. She reached out and touched her husband's long, capable fingers. This time there was no secret message intended. The message was obvious and implicit in the way her soft fingertips rubbed gently across his harder, rougher skin.

"I know," Hank Carpenter said. "Me, too."

The lights were dimmed. She brushed the curl of dank blonde hair away from her face. The lines on her skin stood out in the shadows, but made her, for some odd reason, look younger than she was. Perhaps it was her eyes.

"What do you think the chances are?"

His long, horsy features were calm, at rest. He stroked the flesh of her inner wrist and she smiled faintly. "About fifty-fifty," he said.

They sat in silence for a few more moments. Then he took his hand from hers, held it up, examined the nails, the ridges of his knuckles. "The Jap's crazy, you know," he said.

She nodded. "But pays good."

"Yeah."

"You think his idea is as good as his money?"

He shrugged. "If they don't kill us right away, then maybe things work out."

"I got the easy part, Hank. You want to be careful, now."

"Oh, I will. They moved him out of that ward, finally. Big to do about that. But I can get into the computer room a lot easier than a locked ward. We might both make it out slick as spit. You never can tell."

She sighed. "Well. I guess it's time."

He leaned forward in his chair, balanced on his haunches, then stood. "Guess so," he acknowledged.

She was wearing a faded pair of slacks, once bright blue with red flowers, now a washed-out blur of pinks and soft purples. She had on a white cable sweater she'd knitted herself.

He stared at her and wondered how they'd come to this, then decided the details of a long, strange trip didn't matter. Everybody's trip, in the end, was long and strange.

He stepped over and took her in his long, woodsman's arms and squeezed her to him. They stood like this for perhaps ten seconds. Then he lowered his chin and kissed her on the forehead.

"Best we go now," he said.

She nodded.

"Walk me to the door?"

"Anytime," he told her.

Madge Carpenter stepped into a corridor which led from the personnel housing levels to a circular area that debouched on six elevator doors. Her stride was steady and determined, as steady and determined as the expression on her soft, lined face.

She had a striped Macy's bag in one hand, a red scarf of some cheap synthetic material piled loosely on top. She waited patiently for an open elevator and wedged herself in near the back, almost disappearing in the crowd of shift-change workers headed for the surface of Kennedy Crater. Once out beneath the great dome she meandered down a shopping thoroughfare, passing among clots of tourists who made soft cooing noises at the incredible prices in these stores. At this she smiled a little, for the shocked tourists had no way of knowing that those prices were for tourists only. Lunies, paying for their purchases with Lunie credit, spent ten cents to the foreigner's new dollar.

At the bottom of the step elevators which reminded her somewhat of a carnival ride—so flimsy—she paused and stared upward, one hand on her breasts as if trying to conjure up courage for the dangerous ride. A veteran Lunie took notice.

"Would you like a hand up, miz?" he said politely. "I know it takes you new folks awhile to get adjusted.

She smiled at him. "No, thank you. I'm just catching my breath. Do I look that new?"

He grinned. "It's the walk. You can't miss it."

"Oh," she said, flustered. "I guess I'll never learn."

She waited until the solicitous gentleman had gone on ahead. Then she looked up until she saw it. There. About halfway between the bottom and the cave mouth which unfolded into the customs area near the Lunar surface. She turned and studied sight lines. They'd picked it our earlier. Hank had investigated, and informed her it was an ancient tool room, no larger than a phone booth, carved maybe six feet into the rock. Probably dated from the very beginning, he told her, and was certainly no longer in use. He'd been careful, though, to conceal his destruction of the lock on the rusty, green-painted door.

There was no rear entrance. The only way in was to climb about ten feet from the elevator steps on corroded rings set into the cliff wall itself. Certainly nothing for a lady, especially an older woman newly emigrated from Earth and still unused to the tricky lunar gravity.

She gripped the Macy's bag more tightly and stepped onto the elevator. At the proper spot she swung off, letting the small platforms sweep on past. Down below, she saw white features look up, mouth opened in astonishment. But long before the startled passenger reached her position she had scrabbled across the face of the cliff, reached the tool shed, and wedged herself inside.

She reached into her bag, twisting and fitting the pieces together.

"Hey, lady, what you think you're doing?"

She smiled to herself, took the Hyundai und Koch full automatic sniper rifle loaded with lead azide bullets out of the bag, and shot the curious passerby in the face.

He fell slowly, trailing an impossibly long swath of blood, like some liquid, collapsing feather.

Her expression utterly calm, she turned and confronted the vast spread of the Crater itself. She was sure that when she got the scope attached, she'd find plenty of targets.

Levin's visage was gone from the screens while the echoes of the voice still rattled in the big computer room. Schollander stared at Webster.

Franny opened his mouth and started to say something, but was drowned out by the whooping cough of sirens.

Schollander felt dizzy. Too much at once. Would it never stop?

A security man, his face wild, ducked into the room. "Maniac," he shouted hoarsely. "On the crater wall. With a gun!"

Other security people surged toward the exit. In the rush, nobody noticed the tall, lanky man who stepped calmly into the room. Not until he tossed a pair of shiny, apple-sized grenades into the center of the room and smoky gas began to billow. The last thing Schollander saw was the eye-searing glare of the next explosions. Then, nothing.

Chapter Twenty

Overhead the fluorescent sky began to crack. Calley looked up, saw Ozzie—who was outlined in flickering green fire, his hair a flashing halo—and knew he saw her. She wondered what the boy saw, the skipping boy, whose skin was so pale, so white, and whose eyes were like shattered rubies, empty and red.

So this was the other half of Arius, the first half, the inhuman half. This was the dream of sand, as Berg had once put it, before it had joined the dream of flesh and become nightmare.

Skipping, skipping . . .

She became aware of sound. At first she thought it was some integral part of this construct, some aural analog of the operation of this vast informational complex which surrounded them. It was rhythmic, starting low and then rising, finally tailing off into an extended shriek that eventually pierced beyond the level where human ears might comprehend it.

Then she realized: laughter. The child was laughing. And when it laughed, the whole dataverse shook.

As she watched the small boy skip and laugh toward her, she realized that the environment was overheating. Overhead, the sky, which was ribbed and glowing hotly, developed darker lines, very rigid, that began to vibrate—not enough to induce vertigo, but the visual equivalent of a buzzing in the ears.

The—ground—over which the boy merrily skipped was metal. It had that harshness, that unbending regularity. A very fine grid pattern overlay the metal, almost a blur of design, as if this space was both blueprint and result combined.

Everything shimmered slightly.

The boy himself looked about eight years old. Thin arms, thin legs—big, knobby knees. He wore faded athletic shorts,

218

white, and a dark blue tee shirt. His hair was the albino kind of white, bleached of all color, long enough that she couldn't see his ears.

"What the fuck . . . ?" Ozzie said.

"It seems," Calley replied, her voice dry as sticks, and rasping in her throat, "that young Arius fancies himself the juvenile delinquent."

His—its—laughter now quivered, vibrated the very air around them, sank through their skin, assaulted their bones and nerves, threatened to dissolve the glue of concentration which held them to that moment, that place.

Saws scraping, stone grinding . . .

The boy was nearly on them now. She heard Ozzie begin to sob. Her own heart ripped and tore at her chest.

She could barely move. Her arms felt leaden, numb. Her brain whirled, battered by the cacophony. She could hardly remember . . .

"Calley!" Ozzie screamed.

Slowly, she turned.

"The programs! Deploy the fucking programs!"

Wondering, even as she did it, she turned back to the terrible child, smiled, and extended her right fist. The skulls around her neck rattled. In her left hand was a fan that dripped light upon her feet. She opened her right fist, and exposed the shining grains of sand that lay there. She smiled, and blew gently on the sand.

The small cloud left her palm and hung motionless in the heaving air between them. She continued to breathe on it. Finally, the wind began to rise. . . .

"Try a taste of this, you little asshole," she said softly.

The tornado opened its mouth and yawned.

From Ozzie's point of view, Calley and the child simply disappeared. He stood alone on the softly vibrating plane, feeling naked and exposed. Connected to him, but in some other place, he could sense his machines clocking, ticking, murmuring as they held him firmly in the metamatrix, thrust neat as some bizarre insect into the killing bottle that was Arius.

He had no idea what had happened. He was a fair programmer, but no way in Calley's league. At her best, she operated on an intuitive level he couldn't begin to approach,

219

let alone understand. The codes she generated—her machines generated, at her behest—were crooked and dangerous. A mirror of the patterns of her own mind.

Sometimes, she scared the shit out of him.

He sighed, and wondered why he felt nothing much, while in some invisible place Calley and Arius fought a battle to the—death?

No, he decided. Not death.

Something worse.

The skipping child smiled a terrible smile and rose to greet the winds.

And.

—click—

She walked on an island. She knew it was an island, although she could not see the waters which surrounded it. She knew those water as well; they were dark and deep and wind-tossed, and nothing human could cross them to threaten her, for they were the waters of all existence, and to drink of them was to become immortal.

Trees wept branches in the mist. Each branch was tipped with a great gem, and each gem was a different color. Together, their colors were a rainbow shining in the silver haze. She knew those trees, those jewels; each stone a wish, in the grove of the heart's desire.

The sands which fringed the island were gold, and in the very center of the island, the center of this wood, was a throne that was also a couch. It was at her right shoulder, though she didn't turn to look at it. She knew it was there, just as she knew all else about this place, this moment.

Just as she knew that one would come—*was* coming, even now—to face her in her holiest place.

Calley blinked. "What is this shit?" she said.

But the mist was silent, and the wind would not answer her. All was quiet, at rest, waiting, on the Island of Jewels in the Sea of Existence.

It was an interesting concept, she decided. She had written very strange programs, not really programs in the strictest sense at all. What she had devised was a system, a paradigm of attack based on what she knew of the properties and characteristics of the metamatrix and the lords of information, both human and not, that resided therein. Thus, she was uncertain precisely how her programs would defend her and attack her enemies. Part of it depended on the capabilities of the hardware Ozzie had designed. And part of it depended on her own capabilities, as they expressed themselves through the structure of her codes.

Design as art, she decided at last, and marveled at the strange place she had conjured.

She knew all about this island, though she'd never been here, had no true sense of *déjà vu* about it. She knew it as familiarly as she did her own body—mystery that it might be—and yet she had no knowledge of it.

She stood before her throne in the Dreaming Grove where wishes grew, considering this. Then, finally, she heard his first step.

"Ah," she said.

"Ah," the trees replied.

"It must be lonely, waiting for her," the Shadow said.

"Mm? What?" Ozzie turned in the hot silence to face the source of the words, but saw nothing. He blinked. "Is someone here?" Sudden fear wrapped a knotty fist around the base of his spine. Had Arius triumphed, and now returned to claim his second victim? He remembered Berg's warning: "You can die for real in there."

"I'm here," the Shadow said. "Don't be afraid."

Ozzie spun completely round this time. He was, as far as he could see, utterly alone.

"I don't see you," he said at last. "Where are you?"

"Right here. By your right shoulder. Don't you see me?"

And now he did. Rather, by squinting and looking out the further corner of his right eye, he saw . . . something. A quickening in the atmosphere, a kind of swirling flaw. A shadow.

"Is that you?" he asked the Shadow.

"Yes." The voice was deep, and as full of chuckling undercurrents as a broad river running over stones near its banks.

"What are you?"

"What does it matter?" the Shadow replied. "Walk with me. She won't return for a while yet."

Ozzie licked his lips. "What does that mean? She won't return? How do you know? Do you know what's going on?"

"More or less. As much as anyone can. It's not all certainty, my friend. The patterns replicate endlessly, and nobody—least of all me—can predict where they go."

Ozzie felt very strange. The unchanging vista of the interior of Arius's data construct smoked quietly as it bubbled its incomprehensible arcologies around him. Things rose up and fell down again in enigmatic silence. Periodically the sky dissolved, revealing darkness, which was then itself overlain anew with webs of light.

It was not, Ozzie thought, an environment congenial to normal human vitality.

"No," the Shadow agreed, "it isn't. Are you going to walk with me or not? I could be doing something else, you know."

"So could I," Ozzie said, not without a hint of bitterness.

"Well," the Shadow said, "neither of us is, right now, so we might as well chat."

Ozzie shrugged. If a twist in space wanted to while away the time, why the fuck not? "Sure. Chat, then." He started to walk toward a distant mountain range—not precisely a range, but a slowly upwelling data chain that manifested itself as something that looked like mountains, if mountains were to be made of aquamarine lava.

"Certainly. But you don't have to take that tone," the Shadow said. "You young ones get to have all the fun anyway."

Ozzie didn't have the slightest idea what the Shadow was talking about.

"Young what? You call this fun?"

The tone of the voice grew nostalgic, slow and thick with memory. "Of course. Don't you? All this rushing about. Worlds within worlds. A quest. Battles and wars and thunder and lightning."

"I, uh, haven't exactly seen much thunder and lightning yet." He left unspoken the fervent wish that that situation might continue. Privately, he regarded thunder and lightning as the province of Calley. Or Toshi. Even Berg seemed to have more of a bloodthirsty streak than he did.

"Don't worry," the Shadow said. "You'll be okay. Like I said, you newer avatars have all the fun."

The terrain they were crossing seemed to have changed.

The metal floor had disappeared, to be replaced with a swirling pattern of dark color that reminded Ozzie of the oil slicks that used to coat the edges of Lake Michigan, not far from his old place.

"Avatar?" It was one of those familiar unfamiliar words. He knew it had something to do with religion, or thought it did, but couldn't recall any definite meaning.

The Shadow went on as if he hadn't spoken. "It's all patterns, my boy. Would you like to know more about the patterns?"

Maybe this shadow thing was crazy. Maybe it was the proto-Arius, playing some machine game with him, before gobbling him up. Maybe—

Ozzie swallowed. "Yeah. Right. Tell me about patterns."

Something was coming through the weeping trees. Whatever it was, it was huge. Branches, limbs, entire trunks split and cracked before its passage; the mist-laden air snapped with a cascade of small explosions—and beneath those sharp sounds was the heavier, more ponderous crunch of something terribly heavy, placing one gigantic foot after another onto the shuddering earth.

Whatever it was, it was arriving from the sea.

She faced in that direction, her back to her throne.

The wind freshened, rose quickly to a long moan, then opened its maw wide in full-throated roar, sweeping the mists before it, shaking the jewels of desire like tiny, fragile bells.

"That's right, fucker," she whispered into the wind. "Come to mama. Come and get it. . . ."

With a final rending crash, it shouldered two ancient trunks apart and shoved its massive forequarters into the clearing which sheltered her throne. She looked up into its terrible face.

The bull looked down at her and bellowed.

She regarded the tiny figure perched behind that massive spread of golden horn. "You could have called first," she said. She raised her right hand—

"Patterns," the Shadow said. "Consider the macroverse, the all, whatever you want to call it. Nothing but patterns."

Ozzie stuck one finger in his nostril and dug around there.

223

His thumb brushed over something thick and rough on his cheek. It had been so long that he'd forgotten the feeling. Carefully, he traced the outline of the growth. No doubt about it. The disfiguring patch, a result of a mishap with an esoteric bacteria, had somehow returned. He resisted an urge to turn away from the Shadow, to hide his face.

"For instance," the Shadow said, "your face is a pattern."

"What about my face?"

"That growth existed once. It could exist again."

"This," Ozzie said, "is bullshit of the rankest variety."

"Much of the macroverse is," the Shadow admitted. "Which doesn't change anything at all."

"Did you do this?"

"No."

"Can you make it go away?"

"Of course."

Ozzie touched his cheek again. Smooth skin. "That wasn't funny."

"Patterns," the Shadow continued serenely. "A rock is a pattern of atoms. So is a virus. So is your brain."

They grew closer to the mountains. Now something was happening there. It looked like slow motion volcanoes beginning to explode, but instead of fire and smoke, great billows of ice cream were beginning to flow.

"This Artificial Intelligence has some pretty weird informational flow constructs," Ozzie said.

"In the beginning," the Shadow said, "the patterns were generalized, vast and diffuse. Only later did they grow more complex. Take you, for instance. Something like you wasn't possible until the first suns had gone nova, creating the elements necessary for the construction of your body."

"I'm familiar with the concept," Ozzie said. His voice was sour. He was worried about Calley, and not a little about himself.

"The funny thing about patterns," the Shadow said, "is that when they grow complex enough, *large* enough, they achieve pattern awareness. That is to say, they become aware of themselves as patterns, and of other patterns as well. More important, once this awareness is achieved, such patterns develop an overwhelming urge to create patterns where none existed before, and to perceive the patterns of the macroverse surrounding them."

"As I think I said, bullshit. Mystical bullshit at that. Is this all supposed to mean anything?"

"We call this pattern awareness and manipulation intelligence," the Shadow said calmly. "We call it mind. We call it soul. And it is immortal."

Ozzie stopped. "Now how the fuck do you know that?"

It chuckled again. "The Shadow knows," it told him.

She raised her right hand palm out against the tiny white figure riding the great bull that had come up from the Sea of Existence. The hand held nothing, but she knew its very emptiness was a weapon.

The child smiled, reached up with small, perfect fingers and plucked out its right eye. In its grasp the eye became a jewel colored like blood. Something in her responded to the color, which flared like a sun, burning the remnants of mist away.

She raised her other hand. In it was an arrow. The bull lowered its head even further and pawed at the ground with hooves of brass.

The boy opened his mouth and, with his other hand, pulled one of his teeth. He held the tooth and it became a great sword. Rivers of light flowed down the edge of the sword.

She raised her third hand—Third hand? she thought—and in it was a cord. The cord was stiff with dried blood, crusted and black.

The boy, who was naked, passed his other hand over his forehead and a third eye opened there. It, unlike his other eyes, was not red. It was pure white and without pupil or other marking. It regarded her blankly, and she was suddenly terrified. That eye could see her soul.

She raised her fourth hand, and in it was a fan. When she waved the fan a great storm arose, and ghastly sounds filled the air.

The boy reached down with his fourth hand and grasped his penis, which was adultly huge and fully erect, and twisted off that member. He raised it, and from its tip spilled a river of blood.

Calley looked down, and saw that she stood in a graveyard. But the graves had been opened, and the corpses lay all about her, ripped and scattered, empty-eyed and mute. And as she stared at them, they began to move.

They faced each other.

"I am Destruction, the breaker of the Dream," the boy announced.

She smiled, and the skulls around her neck rattled slightly. "But I," she said gently, "am Life and Death, the Dream that cannot be broken. Come to me now, receive my gift."

The storm was methodically stripping away grass, sand, trees, jewels. Here and there, through the torn foliage, she could see the waves, growing ever higher.

The bull stepped forward.

"I am coming," the boy said. "Receive you *mine*."

"Does all of this have a point?"

The Shadow didn't answer immediately. Instead, for one single instant, a flash only, the data construct of the Artificial Intelligence vanished. In its place was a boundless space filled with indistinct, glowing blue patches. Then that place was gone, and the burning neon interior of the data construct returned.

"Pardon?" the Shadow said.

"Forget it."

"The pattern, once it has reached a complex enough state to develop awareness, also soon becomes aware of its immortality. It begins to understand how it is imprinted on the fabric of space time. Very simple stuff, really. Your Einstein explains it all with his gravity equations. Consider this. Your physical body is merely a way for your mind to manipulate the macroverse. Of course, there are more direct methods."

Ozzie grinned. "A chicken is an egg's way of reproducing itself."

The Shadow sighed. "As I said, you young avatars have all the fun."

Ozzie wished he could see his companion. Then he thought about it, and decided he maybe didn't wish that at all. "You call this fun?"

"It beats jacking off," the Shadow said.

The scarlet jewel in the boy's right hand emitted chaos, the endless power of unbinding. It began to glow, to spark, and finally to burn. Blazing lances burst from it, carving gouts out of the rock around her.

She sensed the invisible rush of her codes as they flew to her, through her. From the palm of her right hand grew a cloud of darkness. The dark and the fire warred then, while the bones of the island creaked beneath them. The huge bull moaned and stamped on the earth. With each pounding blow, a chasm appeared.

From the cracks came more corpses, squirming and white as maggots. The corpses made small mewing sounds.

The boy raised his second hand. The great sword there glittered in the tormented light as he brought is slowly down. He struck the earth directly in front of her, and a mighty fire began.

She raised her other hand and freed the arrow which rested there. The arrow screamed, and pierced the boy's hand from the back and through the palm which gripped the sword.

The boy made no sound, but he dropped the sword and raised his third hand. With it he touched his third eye, and she turned away her face from the piercing flare which burst from the white orb.

In that moment the cords of her nerves stood out like the strings of a musical instrument. Memories battered up from within her, things she'd buried so thoroughly she'd even forgotten the forgetting. Now they returned as clear as knives, and flayed her.

She stumbled in the pitiless glare, felt her legs go weak. Her bowels burned within her. Slowly, as the boy laughed, she dropped to her knees. In reflex only, she raised her third hand.

The cord which rested across her palm now glistened, the dried blood gone bright and red and hungry. The cord rose from her palm, swaying like a snake. Then it launched itself across the tumult between them and wrapped itself around the boy's thin, white neck. The cord seemed to make a sound, almost a hum, as it tightened itself. Slowly the third eye bulged, then, finally, closed.

The boy raised his fourth hand, and the huge, erect penis there ejaculated blood, and the blood was fire, and it covered her with a great burning.

She fell back at last, as the river of blood consumed her.

It scourged her flesh, which turned black. It shriveled her features, until her face was as much a skull as those which rode at her neck. The skin burned from her fingers.

Finally she came to rest against something hard. Her bones knew it. It was her throne, her couch.

Ruined flesh, black as night, rags of bone and cracked teeth, she lay herself down as he advanced, laughing, holding his penis before him.

She opened her fan, and the cry of storms heralded him to her bed.

The mountains had disappeared completely. In their place was a rank of what appeared to be gigantic juke boxes, the antique bubbling kind. Ozzie wondered if any of them had a copy of Jerry Lee Lewis doing "Great Balls of Fire."

"Are you, by any chance, Berg?"

"Not really."

In the heart of chaos that was the multiversal storm, the boy penetrated her womb with his penis in a final consummation. His seed was universes, a million billion trillion universes, each one separate and perfect in the vasty emptiness of her insides.

But even as he began to shriek his victory her mouth opened, and from between the havoc of her broken teeth came her tongue, endless and red and voracious. It was untold and untellable lust, and its appetite could never be assuaged, for it was the tongue of sacrifice. It pierced his throat in mid-cry.

Then the Sea of Existence rose and wiped it all, all of it away.

"Here," the Shadow said. "You'll need it."

Ozzie looked down at his hand. "What is it? What am I supposed to do with it?"

He held a small shard of metal, formless and dull. It seemed heavier than its size warranted, and it was faintly warm.

"When the time comes, you'll know," the Shadow told him. "You're the one who makes things."

Ozzie put the bit into his pocket. Somehow, he knew the

statement was true, without knowing what it meant. "That's just fucking great," he said.

"Isn't it?" the Shadow replied.

They began to walk, but neither had anything more to say. It was, Ozzie supposed, just as well.

Overhead, the trees wept branches in the mist. Lapping gently on the golden sands, the Sea of Existence was calm as a plate. A faint breeze stirred the Jewels of Desire which weighted the branches.

She took the sword from between them and looked down at him. His face was whole again and perfectly beautiful.

"You must lose your life to find it," she whispered to him. "But fear not, my husband. I give gifts."

His eyes, so lusty red, glittered at her. "I can't destroy that which is not. Nor do I want to, for that is not my function, oh wife."

She smiled and stroked his immaculate brow. "I think your bull is back."

He grunted and slid out from beneath her. She watched as he strode from her bed and climbed onto the surging back of the great animal.

"A wish, husband," she called, and gestured. Every jewel in the dreaming grove chimed once, the sound like a rainfall of glass.

He nodded. "Thank you, but I already have it." Then he kicked his tiny feet against the bull's shoulders and turned it, and eventually disappeared into the mist, the trees.

She straightened herself and sat on her couch-throne. A strange expression crossed her face. She reached beneath her hip and found the bit of stone and brought it out.

She examined the stone for a suitable interval and then put it away. It would come in handy later, but now was not quite the time.

A faint smile crossed her features.

"What a great fuck," she said softly. Sadness colored her thoughts. She wished it had been Berg, but that, she understood, was not a part of this dream. Then she too stepped down, and crossed the island, crossed the golden sands, and entered the Sea of Existence.

To drink of that water was life everlasting, but she was Death. One could drown as well as drink.

Her steps quickened. She wondered how Ozzie was doing. It was time to be getting back. She was done here, anyway.

"Oh, Berg," she said. "You are *such* an asshole."

On the great blue plain the small man looked up into eyes of pink, skin of gold.

"Your move," he said.

Chapter Twenty-One

Startled passersby stared up in alarm, then scurried out of the way when the sirens began to wail. Great shadows flitted across the Chicago skyline, howling warnings on every aural, visual and electronic band. From his vantage point at the edge of the gallery which extended the length of his office suite, Nakamura felt an old, indefinable thrill as he watched the huge troop carriers settle to the streets surrounding his tower. As soon as one of the gigantic Boeing/GEM troop platforms slammed to the concrete, its sides fell away and two hundred fully armed mercenary troopers hit the pavement at full gallop. Even at this height he could hear the thin shouts of sergeants herding their charges into position. He knew that if he cared to listen, the electronic spectrum would be crackling with the more esoteric calls of their officers.

As he stood there, breezes searching gently through his shining black hair, he counted ten of the monsters land and take off again.

He turned to Oranson. "How many, Fred?"

Oranson glanced up at the sky, which was crowded with swarms of buzzing Mitsubishi Dragonfly attack platforms. "I'm putting five thousand on the street, another five in the building here. And an air umbrella with a sixty-mile footprint, as well as portable laser cannon on floaters around the edge of the city. We have a ten-second response time on anything except laser sats." Again he glanced up, this time with a faint, estimating squint at the corner of his eye. "I can't stop those at all, unless you want me to take them out."

Nakamura closed his eyes. They both knew the problem. The war they would wage could—might be—fought partly on conventional grounds. Given the most complex, effective system of data warfare possible, it was still simpler to bash

231

in your opponent's head with a club. He'd already done something along those lines when he'd unleashed Hank Carpenter and his wife against Karl Wier and the tanked bodies of Oswald Karman and Gloria Calley. This was something Oranson knew nothing about. His initial plan had been to take out Wier, leaving Eaton Vance in sole control of Luna, Inc. The timing—the insertion of the Carpenters into Kennedy Crater in time to destroy his mole-assassin—had been tricky, and Wier had somehow survived. But the husband and wife team were very good. Something might still be salvaged, particularly if Calley and Ozzie could be exterminated.

It was one more card in the endless game he played—though most likely this conflict would be decided in the spidery, whispering realm of the electronic universe, the metamatrix, where his legion of meatmatrices would go against whatever offense and defense Luna, Incorporated, could muster for its own protection.

Nobody knew how many armed satellites marked time in orbit around the earth, or who owned them. Luna, on paper, owned none—Earth certainly would not have permitted it. Of course, a certain percentage of those war sats, no matter who legally controlled them would, in this conflict, be operated by Lunie gunners. It was a given. Nevertheless, it would be almost impossible to discover those satellites immediately, and he couldn't order everything shot down. Not yet.

"I'd better get back inside. Is that what you're saying?"

"I'd feel better, yes."

"Fine. Let's go."

The two men turned and crossed the wide, surreal landscape, stepping carefully beneath exotic fruit trees and wild, frazzled tropical blossoms. The air was soft and always perfumed.

As they entered the shelter of the monomole reinforced structure, they still heard the siren wail of Nakamura's armies as they mustered to him for the final strike. The compact Japanese man thought it was a wonderful sound, a sound of triumph.

Nakamura looked up at the ranks of screens which filled his office. Almost all the carefully carved woodwork was obscured by flashing colored squares. Adding to the general chaotic scene, portable screens had been brought in and stood in clumps like brightly blooming technological flowers.

He knew it was futile. No human mind could follow the attacks and retreats of the battle he was even now fighting. Instead, the primary soldiers would be the meatmatrices, thousands of them, massed for the assault on the data fortress that was Luna, Inc.

For he did not delude himself. Luna was, his spies assured him, without the service of its main computer, a highly secret machine code-named LEVIN. Nakamura had not forgotten that his nemesis, the fusion of Arius and William Norton, was at least half born of lunar technology. His own estimate of Karl Wier was quite high. Everything indicated that Wier's genius in the design of data processing constructs was at least equal to that of Bill Norton.

Added to this was the knowledge that Jack Berg had collaborated with Wier in the creation of the new machine. His reports were fuzzy as to the reason for Levin's unavailability, and that fuzziness alerted his paranoia. Was Levin actually down? Did the machine work at all?

But he had weighed the demands of paranoia against the more pressing demands of war, and decided the risk was worth the gamble. Reports from Kennedy Crater seemed to bear him out. Something had happened in the main computer room there, although the details he had so far weren't clear. But he suspected— hoped—that Hank Carpenter had been successful in finally killing Wier and, with luck, Gloria Calley and Oswald Karman as well.

If that were true, then, according to his best guess, Luna would be operating under the untried hand of Robert Schollander who, Eaton Vance assured him, was not up to the task of properly defending the information interests of that great corporation.

For great it was. Wier might be dead, Levin down, Calley and Ozzie destroyed, Berg but a memory, yet still, in the face of those grievous wounds, Luna, Inc., was an entity to be feared. He had no doubt this would be the toughest battle of his life.

Battle of his life. He had no idea that as he thought these words, Fred Oranson was staring at him with a strange expression on his face. Oranson had never seen him smile like that.

233

Nakamura blinked. "Come on, Fred. We've got work to do."

The security man nodded. They turned to their machines and prepared to wage modern war.

Nikki Gogolsky moved swiftly toward the thick monocrete bulkheads which guarded the entrance to his underground bunker. The air was nippy; overhead, a wall of low, gray clouds was slowly pushing across the sky, portending snow.

Katerina kept pace with him. She was reading cryptic comments from her comm pad, to which he would occasionally nod. They both ignored the phalanx of thick-bodied, flat-faced men that surrounded them.

"He's doing it," she said thoughtfully. "It looks like he's got them on the run."

They reached the entrance to the bunker. It, like the men who guarded them, were leftovers from an earlier time, when the rulers of Russia had felt the need for such protection. It had not been paranoia then, nor was it now, Nikki reflected. The world was always out to get Russians, whether they called themselves Czars, Commissars, or simply businessmen.

"Shag always starts these things well," he said. "The question is, can he finish what he's started?"

Past the steel blast doors, which began to roll silently shut behind them, their footsteps echoed on the aged concrete floor. They walked quickly to a small open train which waited on rails that pointed into deeper darkness. The cars, which had a faintly decrepit, rusted look to them, had been repainted bright yellow. But the vinyl seats were cracked, and gave off a musty odor when they seated themselves. The train started up with a short jerk, then moved more smoothly. Isolated lamps inset into the ceiling of the tunnel provided intermittent patches of light.

Katerina shrugged. "Like I said, he's doing okay now. Luna does not appear capable of mounting a strong resistance."

Nikki rubbed the side of his nose reflectively. "Don't underestimate Luna. Why do you think we're heading down into this rabbit hole?"

She stared at her father. "Actually, this does seem a bit excessive. Do you honestly think Luna will use laser sats? And even if they do, we're not connected."

He brushed an invisible speck of lint from one impeccable lapel. "Who knows what Luna will do? Who knows what Shag will do? He may just try to take us out along with Luna. A clean sweep. He'd like that." He paused, deep in thought. "Shag has to come after me at some point. Why not now?"

She looked down at her pad, at the mad dance of silent words there. Her shoulders were rigid. "That would be insane. He can't take on the whole world."

Nikki laughed. "He's love it. That sort of thing is in his bones. Look inside his genetic codes. Right at the top of the helix, you'll see a rising sun. My dear, he and I are supposed to be allies right now. But that, you will learn, is when the real danger comes. In the cloak of friendship. Shag knows."

She glanced up at him, sudden speculation in her eyes. "And should he feel the same way about you?"

"Perhaps," he said, and smiled. It was a showing of white teeth, nothing more. "One good thing," he added, as the little train rattled deeper into the earth.

"What's that?"

"We keep all the best wines down here. I'll have something nice with dinner."

She smiled. "A toast, then."

"Yes. Death and destruction."

"Is that intemperate?"

"No."

Galen was up with the sun, squinting against the hot white orb as it poked above the East Bay hills and turned the waters into smooth mercury.

The ever present breezes of the Twin Peaks pulled at his robes. He was barefoot, his hair crumpled, his eyes still grainy from sleep. He hadn't rested well. Dreams had plagued him, awakened him at odd hours, left him peering blurrily at the tiny clock next to his bed, trying to make sense of the numbers.

Upon each arousal, the dreams had seemed clear and sharp, but when he tried to recall their specifics, he could remember only a few hints, an overall feeling of desperation; a universe of blue and flame and light, and the Word of God booming over all like supernal thunder.

His own networks had been busy while he'd slept. On the table next to his coffee cup were piles of hardcopy, and the muted chatter of a data box repeating an endless series of reports, hunches, gossip.

Shag was moving everything he had against Luna. Nakamura/Norton was effectively out of business as an economic entity, now that the company was fully mobilized for war. Dedicated meatmatrices that, under normal conditions crunched numbers for a Borneo subsidiary or made estimates about probable credit rates in the New Euro Econmunity, were now emptied of data bases and reprogrammed for attack and defense.

Shag's strategy looked simple enough, Galen thought sourly. He had thousands of flesh machines, the great meatmatrices, and he had welded them together to wield them as he would. The sheer weight of this enormous processing power precluded subtlety. Obviously, Nakamura intended to crush the Lunar defenses, strip their databases, and pulverize the delicate operating systems which glued the company into a cohesive, functioning whole.

The practical effect of a successful attack would be immediately apparent. The rulers of Luna would find their own machines no longer responsive. They'd be unable to access their databases, and their commands would go unheeded. In essence, Double En would co-opt the nervous system of Luna, Inc. by subverting the neuro-electronic brains themselves.

If, of course, his attack was allowed to succeed. His own dreams had carried a different message.

Galen sipped his coffee and stared at his bare toes. Something about the homely ugliness of human feet—hair, wrinkled skin, toenails—served well to remind even the most exalted of essential humility.

We are all barefoot in the end, he reflected.

His dreams had whispered treachery. Double En must win, would crush Luna and destroy the last, deadliest enemy of God. But Shag Nakamura was not to live to see that triumph. It was a delicate proposition, one that would require the most careful of plans. But he had his weapons as well. The True Church still spoke with God, and God, in his own way, still replied.

Galen finished his coffee and swept the piles of hardcopy

from the table with a single savage motion. He watched the rectangular paper wings flutter in the wind.

Death and destruction.

How fitting.

His only regret was that he would be denied the pleasure of personally attending to the deed. He had looked forward to squeezing the life from the hated Japanese with his own strangler's hands.

He stood, and stared at the blue haze of the Bay.

God is great. God is good.

But most of all—

God is selfish.

So be it, he thought, and turned away, to set a juggernaut of retribution on its final path.

Katerina stood over his shoulder, out of the field of vision of the cam, while Nikki made the call.

The face on the screen was broad, flat-featured, dark, with eyes the color of muddy gold. His skull was entirely hairless, and flaunted a tangled patchwork of ancient scars.

"I don't know," the man said and, surprised, Katerina listened to the fine pukka sahib British lilt of his words. Jamaican, she guessed, one of those islands.

"What is to know, my friend?" Nikki inquired.

"What you're asking. I mean, there's a lot of firepower spread around out there. And you want me to risk my people for a fucking wolf? We *kill* wolves here, if we catch them."

Nikki's soft voice was silky, rich and heavy with unspoken threat. "My friend, I'm not asking. And I don't care about your quaint local customs."

The heavy man stared at him blankly. "We aren't friends, I don't think. And you should care about our customs. Like I said, I don't know."

"Perhaps I could put this a different way? Something more persuasive?"

"You could. You could threaten me. I know about you. Maybe you could even carry out your threats. Who knows? You are a powerful man. But whatever you could do, it wouldn't be in time. Am I correct?"

At this, Nikki sighed. He spread his hands, as if to say, "Why me?" But what he did say was, "No, Ishmael, it would be in time. Do as I say. We've done very good business in the past. But you are out of your league. Do as you're told, like the good friend you are, and you will live another hour. If not—do you really want to find out how long my arm is?"

Ishmael stared at him. The moment held in the golden stasis of his eyes. Then, that quickly, it flickered and was gone. Now the black man seemed shaded with gray, and older. "No," he said. "I don't. But I warn you, my people aren't going to like this." The idea of working with wolves seemed to offend him more than even Nikki's hostile persuasiveness.

"I," Gogolsky told him, "don't care."

Afterwards, Katerina said, "You cashed in a lot of chips there. You know what he's going to do. He'll go through his people, the ones close enough to get a job done for somebody like you, until he finds the mole. Or moles. And whatever he might have been before, friend or not, he's your enemy now."

Nikki looked up at her, his bright, birdlike eyes gleaming. "You must learn, my dear, the difference between tools and allies. That man, the chief of the Darkstone Ragers, is a tool. Tools may be broken to the job at hand."

She regarded him thoughtfully. "And if he were an ally?"

"Then he would not have resisted."

"An interesting correlation. To be an ally, you must submit?"

His eyes widened with surprise. "Of course. How else could it be?"

Danny Boy MacEwen woke slowly and with confusion. His eyes itched and his skin felt hot and dry. He blinked. After a moment the fuzzy shapes around him began to take form.

Wolves. And . . . other things. The underground people, the people of the dark. The hidden ones.

His brothers and sisters.

He shook his furry head. His skull felt swollen, as if it were stuffed with dreams. But he was coming alert now, his muscles beginning to tense with purpose. The shadows of sleep were fading, leaving only a hint of memory.

A kiss.

White wings.

"Br'tha . . ."

He turned, startled. Another wolf squatted on heavy haunches beside him, his shiny muzzle curved in inquiry. He thought he recognized this one, but wasn't certain. It was becoming so hard to keep things straight, to distinguish between the world of dreams and the world of—what?

For a moment, the terrifying thought gripped him with tantalizing horror. *What if there wasn't any difference? What if it was all a dream?*

"Ah you alright?"

It was hard for wolves to indicate emotions, so dependent was such expression on normal human physiognomy, but Danny sensed that this wolf was genuinely interested in him.

He forced his swollen tongue to move. "Mmm. Uh, mm. Okay."

"Yah th' one tha' killed th' Stilts."

Danny Boy nodded, a flicker of pride shining in his eyes.

The other wolf grinned, showing long, yellow canines cradling a hot red tongue. "Good. More Stilts come. Th' wan' t' see yah."

Groaning slightly, Danny Boy unfolded himself from the concrete floor and stood up. He couldn't imagine why Stilts would want to see him. For that matter, he couldn't imagine how they could have gotten deep enough into the Labyrinth to deliver their message without getting chopped up pretty good.

It was all a mystery to him, but he didn't mind. *She* wasn't worried. And as long as *She* was with him, he wouldn't worry, either.

He had been sleeping in a corner of the great underground room where her throne had been. Now, as he padded behind the other wolf, his claws clicking on the rotted pavement, he saw once again the terrible damage the invasion had done. Her throne was a shambles, and the equipment which had surrounded it nothing more than half-melted junk. But the Lab was alive again. Those that had fled the destruction before had returned. There was no place else for them to go.

Dim yellow strips of chemical glow light had been strung here and there, giving the scene a tarnished, shadowy overcast. Figures moved through the gloom, bent on tasks he couldn't understand.

There were wolves, and feral children, and twice he even saw the silken, deadly forms of the small Orientals who lived to kill. But the angels were gone, and *She* was gone, and the dwarflike horror who had lived in the secret room was gone.

Yet the Lab remained, and was even rebuilding itself.

For what, he wondered?

But he knew the answer. Outcasts would always need a place to hide. The Lab was a prison, but it was their prison.

They left the main cavern and entered into longer and narrower places, full of dank smells and darkness. Here the lights were thin and tenuous. He followed his companion with his nose rather than his vision. Eventually they came into another, smaller room, this one crowded with strangers. He felt the curly hair at the nape of his neck stiffen at the scent of their fear. Involuntarily his wide jaws opened, revealing teeth.

The wolf led him to a short, heavily built black man who waited, rigid and watchful, in a phalanx of Stilts. The tall killers watched him carefully, their long fingers jerking slightly.

But Danny wasn't afraid. There were others in the room with him, wolves and strange children who carried automatic weapons and even one of the Blades of God, who stood nearby and smiled at the Stilts with insectile hunger.

The black man was entirely bald. He grimaced at Danny Boy and his companion when they came up. The expression twisted the scars on his skull into bizarre patterns.

"Is this the one?" he said. He sounded disbelieving.

"Yeth," the other wolf said.

"Don't look like much." He shifted uncomfortably. "Uh, well, you know why I'm here?"

Danny stared at him. He'd never seen him before in his life. For a moment, he didn't even understand the man was speaking to him. Then he saw the man's eyes.

He was waiting for an answer. Danny didn't know what to say, so he shrugged.

"Ah, this is crazy," the man said. He seemed to grope for words, finally said, "I'm supposed to give you a bodyguard. You know, my people. You're gonna kill somebody, the way I get it."

It still didn't mean anything to Danny. He looked at the wolf who had brought him, but that wolf was watching him expectantly, too.

"I don' know . . ." Danny said.

"Nakamura," the man said impatiently. "You gotta kill Nakamura. I'm supposed to tell you. The Lady says to kill Nakamura."

And then he knew.

The short, potbellied, nondescript Oriental man who stepped out of the gate where the San Francisco flight was disembarking at New O'Hare was given short shrift by the two Double En security people who were unobtrusively monitoring new arrivals. He noticed them immediately, out near the fringe of the arriving crowd, and grinned.

All the signs were here. This city was the heart of Nakamura's empire, and the empire builder was scared. Not only were the undercover security people tense and watchful, but the legitimate cops—most of whom were, Toshi assumed, on the Double En pad one way or another—filled the port in heavily armed force.

Toshi rubbed his hands together as his lips stretched into a tight little grin.

"Okay," he breathed softly. "Let's *party*."

Chapter Twenty-Two

"Wake up."

Schollander knew something was terribly wrong, but he didn't know what. It was warm and dark now, almost comfortable. His perceptions had been limited to those two sensations, but now the harsh, insistent words were destroying the peace of his constricted world.

"Goddammit, wake up, Bobby."

He opened his eyes.

Light burned into the heart of his skull and he gasped.

"Ah—okay. It's all right."

The light retreated. He made out Franny Webster's worried features, partially obscured by a shiny instrument that had been the source of the light.

Checking me for concussion, he thought woozily.

Now Webster held up two pudgy fingers. "How many fingers, Bobby?"

"Don't call me Bobby."

"Fuck that. How many fingers?"

"Two." His head throbbed. At first he thought it was the light, but then realized that the right side of his skull felt numb, vacant. Had his brains spilled out?

The thought made him giggle, and even as he did, he thought it was probably the wrong thing to do.

"What day is it?"

A game, then, "Uh, Monday. No—Wednesday. Do I get a prize?"

Franny's face went serious. "Bobby, you've had a shock. A bad one. Injury. There's concussion, maybe fracture."

He felt distant. Slowly, Franny's features began to move, tilt. It took him a moment before he understood that Franny wasn't tilting, *he* was. He felt unseen hands begin to gentle him up, and then he saw the blasted ruin beyond Franny's shoulders, and then it all came back.

242

* * *

"You're going to bed. And stay there," Franny said grimly.

"I am not," Schollander replied, equally adamant.

They were just outside the shambles of the main computer room. Two attendants stood at either end of the gurney on which Schollander was trying to sit up. Franny placed one hand on Schollander's chest and pushed him firmly down. "Robert, you have a concussion. At least. We need tests—there may be a skull fracture. You aren't in any condition to—"

"*Fuck* the tests. Franny, I'm not going to argue with you. This is my company. You think my grandfather would have gone meekly to bed at a time like this? Nakamura is trying to *kill* us!"

"The old man? Of course he would have . . ." Franny's voice trailed off.

"Right. He wouldn't. Any more than I'm going to now." The effort of the argument was throwing a screen of hot sparks across his vision, but he forced himself to ignore the weird sensations.

Franny shook his head in disgust. "At least some X rays. And if there's a fracture, you are *out* of it. You agree?"

"Make it quick, then."

Webster nodded curtly at the two attendants. "Take him to X ray. I'll be along in a minute."

Schollander turned his head. "Franny," he said gently. "Any of the medics can do this. What I want from you, as soon as you can get it, is a damage survey. I need to know everything."

Webster nodded tightly, his pudgy face raddled and doughy. "Okay."

"All right," Schollander said. "Let's go."

He had monitors and screens brought into the small cubicle where they put him after the cat scans and Mag Res Imaging and X rays. Two blank-faced medics quickly cleaned the gash on the right side of his head, slapped on a layer of synthetic flesh, and applied a Christmas tree of derms to various areas of his neck, spine and chest.

The rush of the drugs dulled the pain, but he had to fight to keep a sharp edge on his concentration. The images flashing across the screens, a montage of digital history and realtime, helped.

Once again, this time in slo-mo detail, he watched Hank Carpenter slip into the computer room. The man had an odd, quirky grin on his horsy, homely face, but there was nothing awkward or countrified about the way he tossed the gas grenades, or in the cool professionalism with which he attached small magnetic mines to the tanks which held the bodies of Oswald Karman, Gloria Calley, and Karl Wier.

The cameras, shielded by monomole housings, recorded it all with machine detail. He slowed the replay and watched as the mines went off, their shaped charges focusing the intensity of the explosions inward, so that the detonations resulted in a grisly shower of mashed metal and severed limbs.

Ozzie. Calley. Wier.

The medical techs picked them up with scrapers and small plastic bags. He hadn't known the two groundhogs well enough to feel real pain at their passing, but he had known Wier.

He hoped the nausea he felt was due to the loathsome way of their passing, and not to some permanent damage to himself. Because now he was the only one left. A Schollander would have to take revenge on the treacherous little monster down below, who was methodically attempting to destroy Robert Schollander's—and perhaps mankind's—best creation.

Luna, Inc. would live, he promised himself dourly. Even if he, the last of the Schollanders, died in the survival effort.

It was in his genes, maybe, as Auntie Elaine had once said.

But it was in his heart and mind, as well.

What had that long dead mercenary rally cry been? Grab 'em by their balls—their hearts and minds will follow?

Nakamura sure had balls. He had to give him that.

But that was okay, too.

It gave him a target to grab for.

And squeeze.

"Well, you're going to live." Franny sounded displeased at the thought.

Schollander had moved his bed into Eaton Vance's former office. The articulated bed, responsive to his movements and capable of supplying almost all of his mundane needs, was incongruous in the luxurious surroundings. Schollander had been uncomfortable here before, feeling a Lunie's normal puritanical distaste for this groundhog nest of opulence, but most of the data input terminals he needed were here. This was the nerve center of Luna, Inc.'s technological and business empire, and it was from here he would wage war against Shag Nakamura.

"You don't sound very happy about it," he told Webster.

"What's to be happy about? Robert, we are getting our asses kicked."

Schollander had been studying the latest reports. They accurately reflected the shitstorm flying in the greater world outside this room.

"What about Levin?"

Franny shrugged. "Lizzybet says he's—it's—back online. To some extent, that is. He's controlling most of the automatic functions of the company's day-to-day operation. Which is the main reason we aren't a Double En subsidiary right now. He's linked a big percentage of our meatmatrices into a net that is more or less holding its own against Shag's frontal attack on our databases. But the goddamn thing still isn't talking to us."

"What about Karl?"

Franny shrugged again. "You know as much as I do. There's been no sign of him. All we know is what Levin told us. That he would take him."

"Could Karl be coordinating the defense? I mean, as a part of Levin?"

"I haven't got the foggiest." Webster moved his shoulders uncomfortably. "You know, it makes me feel weird as hell to talk about him like this. You know how much of him was left after the explosion?"

Schollander had watched a replay of the cleanup. But only once. The ragged bits of flesh, shattered bones, stringy clumps of dried blood had almost made him lose the glass of chalky fluid he'd drunk for some of the tests.

By any normal standard, Karl Wier was as dead as the ancient pharaohs. Deader—at least those long departed rulers had kept their physical bodies more or less intact. But it was a new world now—and Schollander suspected that normal standards no longer applied.

"Franny, I want you to get back to the computer complex. Supervise the new installations. I want everything online as soon as possible. You're sure Levin wasn't damaged?"

"Positive. Carpenter used shaped charges, and those only on the body tanks. You know Levin's shields. He would have needed nukes to do even minor damage."

Schollander stared at him. He'd almost forgotten the Lunie immigrant who had caused all this damage. "Carpenter," he said. "What about him?"

"Oh, he's fine. Him and that murderous wife—or whatever she is. You see the body count she ran up?"

"Yeah. Eighteen people."

Franny sighed. "All at random. At least, we haven't been able to find any connection. She was just a diversion, to give Hank a chance at the computer room. When he was done, he gave himself up, meek as a lamb. And once he called up to her, she came out of that hole in the wall just as if she'd finished with her weekly shopping list." Webster licked his lips. "What a fucking evil pair. Neither one of them shows the slightest remorse. In fact, both of them seem almost cheerful. The interrogators haven't had any problem with them at all. They both expect Nakamura to win, and as soon as he does, they say they'll be released."

Schollander thought about Elaine Markowitz's warnings about the couple. Obviously, she'd been right again, but he couldn't see what he might have done differently. There was one thing, though. He looked up at Webster.

"I don't like the idea of them sitting in their cells chuckling at each other. See that they get a message from me. Tell them they'd better hope we don't lose."

"Oh? Why's that?"

Schollander didn't know it, but he looked at that moment very like his dead grandfather. "If we go down, there will be two final casualties. The Carpenters will take a little walk. On the surface. Without suits."

Webster smiled then. "I'll deliver the message. Personally." His tone was savage.

"Go on, get out of here, Franny. See if you can contact Levin, at least find out what's going on with Karl." A new thought struck him. "And Calley and Ozzie, as well. Carpenter targeted them, too. See if you can find out why. What does Nakamura know about them we don't?"

Webster nodded and turned to leave.

"Uh, one more thing, Franny."

"What?"

"Send Elaine in."

Webster grinned. "Won't be hard. She's right outside. Giving the two guards on the door hell for not letting her through."

Involuntarily, Schollander grinned in return. "Jesus, I don't envy them. Okay. Let 'em off the hook."

As Franny let the room, Schollander heard voices raised in argument outside. One was thin and old and cut like a knife.

He spoke to the air. "Eaton Vance is on hold. Put him through to me please."

Vance's aristocratic face was just coming clear on the screen when Elaine Markowitz said, "That motherfucker. Let me handle him, Robert."

But he only shook his head gently and said, "Thanks, Auntie, but I think I'd rather do it myself."

Eaton Vance had maintained his tan on earth. His craggy features were as slickly distinguished as ever, although Schollander thought he saw some hidden agony behind the veil of his hazel, catlike eyes. Nevertheless, Vance's orotund voice was carefully without emotion.

"Mr. Schollander, how are you?"

"As well as can be expected, Vance. What do you want?"

Vance winced slightly. "This is business, Mr. Schollander. Nothing personal against you."

'It's all personal, Vance. Now what the fuck do you want? As you can guess, I have other things on my mind right now."

"Yes. I'm certain you do. In that case, I'll make this as short as possible. I am heading a consortium called New Luna, Inc. We have filed the appropriate papers with various national and international agencies—you should have your own copies by now." His perfectly trimmed gray eyebrows arched inquiringly.

"We've got them. I haven't had a chance to look at them yet."

"They're self-explanatory. Anyway, NLI has acquired a seven percent equity in Luna, Inc., at this point. We now make a formal proposal to purchase another fifty point two percent of the stock at a rate to be discussed as soon as possible, and then a tender offer for any remaining stock."

Schollander laughed. "How does it feel, Vance? To be a mouthpiece for Nakamura?"

Vance stared at him, but didn't say anything.

Schollander nodded sharply. "The answer is no. The, ah, *current* management of Luna will fight you every step of the way. You can tell your boss that. And I will personally see to it that you come out of this with nothing. Bet on it, you slimy piece of shit."

Vance's eyes narrowed. He barked out a harsh sound that might have been laughter. "You? My gracious goodness, little boy, you frighten me. Go ahead and make your childish threats. When this is all over, I may let you stay on Luna. Or I may not."

He grinned.

"How do you like it, Vance? Being in a position where you have to *trust* Shag Nakamura?"

Vance's lips tightened. The screen went blank. Schollander turned to Elaine. "Well, at least we know where he stands."

Markowitz seemed astonishingly well put together. Her long hair was neatly styled in a white wave that fell to her shoulders. She was dressed conservatively in a blue wool dress. Her blue eyes sparkled.

Trouble, Schollander thought to himself, does her good. He noted she had walked in on her own power.

"Did you ever doubt where Vance stood?" she asked. "He's a problem, of course. He knows where all the bodies are buried. Hell, he buried a lot of them. Have you had a chance to look at the papers?"

"No. Not yet."

"I glanced through them. Their disclosure statement is pretty obvious. Double En is managing partner of this new consortium of theirs."

"No surprise there."

"They've snapped up quite a few odd lots of stock. What did he say? Seven percent?"

"Uh huh."

248

"I've had Mason Dodge checking around to see who else has been contacted. Some of his calls weren't returned."

"Oh? Who?"

"I'll have Mason give you a list. But it's the usual suspects."

"Vance's cronies on the board, I bet."

"And you'd win."

"You know something, Auntie? This whole thing stinks."

"I agree, but I don't think you mean it exactly the way it sounds."

"Shag Nakamura. Why now? You'd think he's got enough trouble of his own, what with the New Church, and the insurrections down below. And Arius, of course. If Arius still exists." As he said it, something vague and formless began to come together in his mind.

She shook her head. "You want me to handle the stock defense?"

He looked down at his hands, then up again. "Yeah, I think so. You and Mason and the lawyers. I think it's just a diversion anyway. The real attack will come on our data bases. This raid can only succeed if we're helpless otherwise."

She nodded sharply. "I agree. Have you decided what to do about the rest?"

He shrugged. "We fight. What else?"

"But how?"

He smiled faintly. "Shag Nakamura doesn't know everything. Not yet. We have a couple of aces yet to play."

She eyed him dubiously. "Aces I don't know about?"

"Aces nobody knows about."

She sighed. "I hope so." But she didn't sound very hopeful.

After she had gone, he stared without comprehension at the screens, struggling with the idea that was trying to coalesce. Why *now*?

The metamatrix was disturbed.

It was a strange place, pulsing darkly green, interspersed with violent flashes of color, controlled lightning that flashed between the gently heaving masses of thousands of meat-matrices that made up the ever-expanding universe of information.

Down at the bottom were the endless shining white beaches, where each individual grain of sand represented the tiny power of somebody's personal computer, or the rack of chips inside one of the millions of modern, processor-controlled toilets, or one of the billions of credit chips by which mankind carried on everyday commerce.

Further up, floating above the beaches, were the harsh, angular arcologies of the great electronic machines, shining in ever-changing hues, bound together in vast nets of communication. And above this thickly encrusted reef of technology floated the current lords of the data world; the meatmatrices themselves, bloated, amoebalike shapes which pulsed as they chewed terabytes and spat them out. Some of these monstrosities were thickly garlanded with electronic gimcrackery, where flesh and machine had been melded into new configurations.

It was normally a place beyond human ken, operating at speeds far too fast for the slow perceptions developed by evolution. Only a few had seen the metamatrix in its full splendor, and most of them were out of it now. But the war went on.

At one point, a squadron of meats, their gaudy outlines heaving rapidly, exuded a pulsing web of colored lines, red and blue and green, which surrounded another of their kind. The cornered matrix glowed suddenly gold. The lines coalesced into a net which began to contract.

As the net approached the boundaries of the golden defense, sudden bolts of white light descended to the attack. The skin of the defending matrix burned incandescent in spots, and turned dark in others.

Each movement represented billions of data decisions, made with a speed and violence completely unknown in the slow world of man.

The net tightened further. The burning white spots grew less in number, the darker patches larger. Finally, the net wrapped itself around the defensive screens of the matrix like a sack around a fruit.

The entire skin flared once, then subsided to dull black. Eventually the black faded, to reveal an intricate network of silver lines that pierced the victim and tied it securely to the attackers.

These dances occurred with ever-increasing frequency, as nets of matrices attacked other nets, until the entire metamatrix throbbed with the unthinkable fury of the battle.

Data war!

*   *   *

His head ached unmercifully, but Schollander, running on drugs and the remains of a double cheeseburger, pulled up the screens one more time.

He'd been reviewing the covert product of the entire Lunie espionage operation, trying to find clues to the reason for Nakamura's sudden attack. All their best projections had put such an event months in the future, after Shag had digested his most recent conquests, and solidified his new power in the wake of Arius's conjectured destruction.

But nobody knew. Had Arius been destroyed? The hand of the dwarf had not been seen at all since the conflict Jack Berg had initiated. But was the AI-human fusion really gone?

Only Jack Berg, and Levin, knew for sure. And they weren't saying.

He ground his teeth together in frustration, then winced as the movement sent sharp fragments of pain shooting through his skull. The tests had shown no fracture, but that didn't make the throbbing agony any less.

He forced himself to think. It made no sense, unless something else was behind the attack. Something that wanted Luna taken out. Something that feared the power of Levin, perhaps . . . ?

Then he knew the answer. It provided no solace. If anything, it made the situation worse. What would his grandfather have done?

He tried to concentrate his memory, focus on that grand old man, and realized his thinking was all wrong. The first Robert Schollander had achieved grand old man status late in life, after he'd made Luna, Inc., a reality. But Schollander realized his grandfather had been like any other great businessman during the building of the company. Sharp, treacherous, ruthless.

As he would have to be now.

"Franny."

Another screen burst into light. Franny was sweating. He looked as if he hadn't slept in a month. His face was sallow, his eyes almost indistinguishable slits above bruised, puffy bags.

"Yo, boss."

"What about the laser sats?"

Franny nodded grimly. "We've invoked the contracts and been given control. Namibia, Grenada, Singapore, Nicaragua, Panama. Everything's online."

"Okay. Run projections on Double En response if we attack Shag's headquarters."

"Bobby. That's in the heart of a city. Chicago. The damage would be enormous."

"I don't know. We can get pretty good accuracy. And covert already says he's evacuated that area of non-combatants."

"But still—"

"It's a last resort, Franny. But I want it ready, just in case."

Webster nodded sadly. "It's come to this, uh?"

"It could. Not yet, though. What about the rest?"

Franny brightened a bit. "Slick as shit, my boy. We're all set up. Want to see?"

"Uh huh."

The screen changed abruptly. The camera panned over a broad, low-ceilinged room. The light was dim here. Complicated reclining chairs filled the huge space. On each recliner rested a single man or woman. Webs of supercon cable formed crowns of high-tech power around their heads.

"Looks good," Schollander said.

The scene blinked out, was replaced by Webster's face. "Just say the word."

Schollander glanced at his own readouts. Even with Levin coordinating the lunar meat nets, the vastly larger processing power of Double En was beginning to tell. If nothing changed, the outcome was unavoidable.

He would have to use the lasers, which might mean the destruction of Luna itself. The moon was an easy target. But maybe this . . .

The project Berg and Calley and Wier and Levin had conceived, based on the arcane tech of Oswald Karman, the grievous angel of creation.

He sighed. "Fire them up, Franny. And . . . good luck."

Webster nodded. "Good luck to all of us."

The screen returned to the large, dim room. There really wasn't anything to see, as two hundred crack cybergrammers, interfaced through Ozzie's direct matrix access equipment and armed with the most destructive attack programs Calley could dream up, jacked into the metamatrix.

Two hundred data kamikazes.

Two hundred bolts of information death.

Schollander stared at the unmoving forms, and hoped it would be enough. Especially since he now knew who the real enemy was. The new one, same as the old one.

Arius is dead.

Long live Arius.

Chapter Twenty-Three

They stared at each other across the silence of the empty computer room. Ozzie slumped in his chair, supercon cables trailing from the socket beneath his ears. She had jacked out already, and he had turned off his machines.

"What's with you?" she said. "You look like shit."

He grinned wanly. "The Shadow knows."

"Is that supposed to mean something?"

Slowly, he removed the jack from his socket. Then he told her what had happened to him.

"The Shadow? That's pretty bizarre, tall buddy. You got any idea what it's supposed to mean? Or who this fucking Shadow was?"

"Yeah," he said, and his voice was raspy with exhaustion. "I think I do."

"Well? Is it a secret?"

He shook his head. "It's weird, Calley. It is very weird. But I think it's the truth." He raised one long-fingered hand and gnawed at his thumbnail. "For one thing, it explains what we are now, and why. Even, I think, how."

Nervously, she thumbed a black Turkish cigarette from a crumpled pack and lit it. She didn't seem to notice that the flame for the light had come from the tip of her first finger.

"You sure know how to kill a story. Are you gonna get around to telling me?"

He smiled suddenly. "My. Impatient, aren't we? Gimme one of those?"

Wordlessly, she pushed the pack over. Ozzie lit up in a more mundane manner, with a match plucked from a book whose cover read, "Learn Modern Computing—Only Two Hundred New Dollars!"

He inhaled sharply, then let the yellowish smoke trickle from his nostrils. It made him look like a young, but diabolical, boy. "The shadow claimed that intelligence is a pattern."

She nodded. "Seems reasonable. Intelligence is pattern *seeking*, that's for sure. It's one of the first things you learn, if you want to be a good codemeister."

"Um. Yeah. Well, if this pattern is impressed on spacetime —and old shadow made a reasonably good case for exactly that—then it follows that the mind, the soul, whatever, could also be immortal."

Her green eyes narrowed slightly. "You mean already immortal? All this body transfer shit is useless?"

"I dunno. Depends on what you mean by useless. If you want a body, I suppose those methods are as useful as anything. But the point was, it really doesn't mean anything. You are gonna keep on going whether you want to or not, as an organized ripple in the greater space-time weave."

Frightening shards of memory from her childhood bubbled up, nasty bits of flotsam about heaven and hell and purgatory. She shivered.

Ozzie sucked on his lower lip. The sharp smell of burning tobacco filled the still air. The light in the great, empty room seemed dimmer, somehow.

"It would explain a lot," Ozzie said. "How the Key works. Machine intelligence is a pattern too. Maybe all patterns can be interwoven to form new patterns. Maybe that's what Berg does. What the Key does."

She still felt the ancient fears, and at Ozzie's words, new fears joined them. "But then, what does that make Berg? What is he? Where did he come from?"

Ozzie's face had a distant, musing look on it. "Well, think about it. All the great religions have similar postulates concerning the immortality of the soul. Some people explain it as simply a reflection of human yearning for life everlasting. But what if it isn't? If mind—intelligence—is truly immortal, then where are they? After the body is gone?"

She shook her head. She didn't like at all where this was leading. Ozzie nodded thoughtfully. "One of the most enduring ideas is that of a world-mind, a pool of minds, a racial memory or something like it. In Jungian psychology, this is the source of archetypes, myth or dream figures which represent the joined yearnings of the overmind. The well of heroes, demons, gods, men. What if that is more than mysticism? What if it's true?"

Calley remembered her own eerie experience, her strange duel with the young machine Arius. As it had happened, she had not questioned anything. Even now, afterwards, she felt no disinclination to accept what had occurred. But the implications were enormous, terrifying. Slowly, she said, "But if that's true, then what . . . what am I?"

Ozzie sounded almost cheerful. "Oh, if you ever studied comparative religion, that's easy. My question is, who am I?"

But her education had been limited to more pragmatic studies, and she couldn't answer him.

He stubbed out his cigarette. "I think we're living out a particular myth. If you know quantum physics at all, you'll recognize the similarities. And if it's the myth I think it is—" He shook his head.

"Spit it out."

"I'm not sure. Let's wait. But I can tell you this."

Now he was beginning to annoy her. Vagueness and mystical maundering always did. She preferred her reality straight. "Yeah, what?"

He grinned. "We get one *hell* of a grand finale."

Later they left the building and entered the chill gray twilight of Chicago. For some reason the holiday crowds had lessened, and though they walked down streets only a few blocks from the heart of the New Loop, they saw few people. Dusk thickened into dark. The brightly lit windows of the stores were like glittering aquariums, filled with frozen trinkets and softly draped fabric. In one window a thousand tiny comm screens repeated endlessly the same picture—an anorexic model with eyes like smudges of soot whose vampire lips moved slowly, repeating the same rubric over and over.

"What next?" Calley said. Her breath hung before her face in a cloud.

"I guess the Lady," he replied. "We haven't talked about it much, but do you see any other endgame here?"

She sighed. The wind which struck between her shoulder blades was a knife. "I guess not. It's all about the Key, somehow, and that bitch is where Berg got it. The question is, where did *she* get it?"

Ozzie's eyes had been distant in the gathering dark, as if he watched scenes other than those they walked through. "She got it from Arius, of course. But I think we gave it to her."

Calley went rigid, startled. "What?"

"What did you bring back?" he asked softly.

"I don't get you."

His voice was insistent. "You brought something back, didn't you? A—I don't know, a twig, a piece of paper, something."

Reluctantly, she reached in the pocket of her leather jacket. It had all been a dream, but she still lived within another dream. The stone from her couch was there. She took it out, showed it to him in the light of a thousand vampires. "This," she said.

He nodded. Then he showed her the small bit of formless metal, dull and heavy, that he'd found on Arius's endless plains, in the shadow of the ice cream mountains. "Me, too."

"A rock? A hunk of melted lead?"

"I don't know," he said. "But I think they have something to do with her."

"The wolf bitch? She'll kill us."

"Maybe. But, if you'll pardon the expression, the Key is the key to all this. I thought we agreed."

She stared at the two things dubiously. "I sure wish you could think of something else."

The picture on the screens vanished, and a new commercial flashed on, painting their flesh in shifting tones of green and shadow. "I can't, though."

She put her stone back in her pocket. "All right. But I want something to eat first. And not fucking pizza."

He nodded. "A nice place."

Her lips tightened. "Real nice. If it's gonna be my last supper, I want it to be good."

Carefully, he took her arm and placed it over his own. They walked on down the echoing, vacant street, lit by the lamps of technological Christmas, their breath trailing behind like silver scarves.

Neither of them noticed the wolves, whose shaggy

coats shifted and twisted in the twilight, following close behind.

They ate at a place on the near North Side, just beyond the end of the first dike, on the ground floor of an ancient building which had remained unchanged for almost a century and a half, not the least because of the wealth of its tenants.

It was a tall room with a faded, pseudo-renaissance mural of nameless gods cavorting across a background of yellowed clouds and lightning bolts smeared across its ceiling. Across the front of the room, overlooking the dark, froth-topped breakers of the Lake, stretched a rank of lead-paned windows. The tables were old, wooden, covered with snowy cloths, and groaning beneath the weight of heavy silver, antique porcelain, and polished crystal.

Chandeliers splintered the light into tiny, glowing sparks. She said, "You don't like the wine."

He shrugged. "You know me. If the cap doesn't twist off, I don't know what to do with it."

She poured the last of the bottle of '18 Mas de Daumas Gassac into her glass and inhaled the rich, powerful bouquet of the wine, considered the best from the Midi region of France. The remains of a perfect osso buco were on her plate.

"They got ice cream in this place, you think?" Ozzie asked.

"You are a barbarian, you know that?"

He grinned. "But you love me anyway."

She stared at the darkness beyond the beveled window glass. "Yeah, I guess I do."

"Okay, then. Can I order ice cream?"

"Vanilla, I suppose . . ."

"Naw. Live big, that's my motto. Chocolate."

She chuckled. "Knock yourself out."

The waiter arrived as if he'd been waiting anxiously for her raised eyebrow.

"Chocolate ice cream," Ozzie said. "Two scoops."

The waiter wore a tuxedo and a resigned expression. "And for the lady?"

"I dunno. Lady, you want anything?"

"The raspberries are fresh?"

"Of course," the waiter assured her. "Flown in from California this morning."

For a moment, she stopped and marveled at the strangeness of it all. The waiter spoke of fruit imported from California, when, as far as she knew, this was all a construct. Now only did the waiter not exist, neither did the fruit or the state of California. Once again, she felt the ebb and flow of reality, a sort of gut vertigo that threatened to sweep her away.

"With Grand Marnier, please," she said, and the waiter nodded happily.

A few moments later Ozzie stared at a huge serving of chocolate ice cream so dark it was almost black. Her raspberries were delicious. She ate every one.

They finished with espresso brewed at table side and tiny, delicate pony glasses of Benedictine. Finally, she lit a cigarette.

Ozzie eyed her dubiously. "This place non-smoking?"

She puffed a cloud of smoke in his direction. "At these prices, you bet the onizers are working full blast. Besides, it's my dream."

He nodded.

Outside, the wind began to rise. It rattled gently on the glass doors, and shook skeletal shadows from the naked trees. Across the lake, whitecaps began to boil in the dimly refracted light of the city.

She could imagine staying here forever, sunk in the glorious stupor of the end of a great meal. Ozzie smiled at her.

"What?" she said.

"You look happy."

"I am happy," she said, surprised to find she meant it.

"That's good." His voice was soft. "It's a rare thing for you, I think. So I'm glad when it happens."

She didn't say anything. Somewhere in the background, a harp began to play. Her gaze slid to the window and she saw the wolf scurry past, bent over and almost invisible against the storm.

She stubbed out her cigarette. "I think," she said slowly, "it's time for us to go."

"Yeah? You sure?"

"I'm sure."

*　　*　　*

Outside in the wide hallway which fronted the restaurant and led to the outside, Calley told him what she'd seen.

He blinked. "You think it's after us?"

"No, I think it was taking a stroll in the storm, and just happened to wander by where we were eating dinner."

"Hey, sorry. Just asking."

"Well, ask something that makes more sense. Like how the fuck we get out of here."

"Is that what we want to do? I thought the idea was to put her and us together." He glanced toward the double doors at the end of the hall. He thought he saw a flash of movement beyond the wide glass panels, but in the tumult of the gale he couldn't be sure.

She shook her head. "On our terms, though. Not hers."

"Okay." He reached down and grabbed her hand. "Come on," he muttered. He darted to the left, away from the door. At the far end of the hallway was an elevator. He pulled her inside and punched the button for the basement.

"Where are we going? And let go of me."

"Uh? The basement, for starters. Then I'll see."

She started to say something, then stopped. Ozzie had lived in this city a long time. He was better suited to its more esoteric pathways. "Okay, Lead on."

He smiled nervously. "Now, if this dump is built the way it oughta be . . ."

The basement was an indoor parking garage. Ancient fluorescent strips cut the darkness just enough for them to make out the silent humps of cars. Their footsteps echoed softly. He pointed to a somewhat brighter pool of light against the far wall. To their right, a double ramp curved toward the surface.

"Wait a minute. What about that way?" She nodded at the ramp.

"You say you saw wolves. You think they won't be waiting out there, too?"

She glanced around. "This place looks right up their alley."

"Maybe. They can't know what kind of alarms are set down here. This is rich folk's territory, right? But they don't know we've spotted them yet, so I'm betting they'll hang outside and wait for us to come to them. By the time they figure out we're on to them, we'll be gone. I hope."

Reluctantly, she followed him away from the ramp. The brighter light illumined a rusty door that was secured by a dilapidated padlock. Ozzie bent over the lock, a thin strip of steel suddenly appearing like a magician's trick in his fingers.

She heard a sharp click, then another. "Piece of cake," he murmured, as he snapped the lock wide. The door groaned sharply as he pulled it open.

"Come on," he said, and motioned her in.

The room was utterly dark and very hot. She heard water dripping, and a sudden hiss of steam. Ozzie pushed the door shut. She felt him move beside her, his big hands running around the edge of the door. He found a light switch, pushed it, and the room went bright as day.

Ancient insulation padding, rust brown with mold, dripped from the ceiling. Corroded pipe wrappings, like mummy bandages, uncurled from a forest of pipes. Squat, blackened boilers hunched in haphazard conjunction with new monomole constructions.

"Jesus," Ozzie said. "I'm glad I don't live here. This whole place looks like it could blow any second."

"What is it?"

"Power room, heat, utilities, comm connections, like that. Every building has one."

She licked her lips and stared. "So, how are we better off? You think when they finally make up their minds to come inside, they won't look here?"

"Oh," he replied, "they'll look, okay, but we won't be here. Come on." He started off down a narrow, grated path between the rusting behemoths.

At the end of the grate was a greasy metal ladder leading down. He clambered down like a monkey, reached the bottom and stood looking up. "Come on, Calley. Hang on tight, the metal's slick."

She gritted her teeth, swung over, and joined him.

"Now what?" She wiped her palms on her thighs, leaving shiny streaks on the black leather.

"It's gotta be down here somewhere."

"What does?"

"The way out," he told her.

It was darker here, the only light filtered through the metal floor above. The machinery looked newer, however; glistening black housings from which extended pipes and cables. Some of the housings bore the logo of Midwest Ameritech.

"Phone and comm," he mumbled as he led her through them.

In the floor at the right side of the room he found it.

"Come on," he said and he squatted down. "You'll have to help me. This mother's likely to be heavy as sin."

She crouched near him and levered her fingers into the tiny space between the edge of the manhole cover and the rim on which it rested.

"Okay, on three."

She nodded.

". . . and three." She put her back into it, heard the muscles in his shoulders pop, and then, with a rusty, sucking sound, the cover came up enough for them to slide it to the side.

"Whew. Jeez, does that *stink*."

"You want me to go down there?" she said.

"Unless you'd rather go back and waltz with those furry fellows."

She stared into the dark pit with distaste. "I dunno, maybe that isn't such a bad idea. What is this fucking thing?"

"A sewer. What else? You were expecting the Concorde, maybe?"

She glanced at him. "Great. Just great."

"Come on, kiddo. It washes off."

She sighed. "You go first."

"Sure."

After a moment, she followed.

She tried to think of an adjective to describe the darkness. Stygian, one of those words people read but never speak, came to mind; she wasn't quite sure what it meant, but this chill, shit-laden, stifling blackness seemed to apply.

Ozzie led her forward, holding on to her right hand as he groped his way down one slimy brick wall. "These things usually have exits in other buildings," he told her. "They used to be kind of all-purpose tunnels for sewage, power lines, and so forth, and every old city, like this one, has them."

"Spare me the travelogue," she said. "Just get us out of here."

She became aware of the sounds. A thin trickle of filthy water ran down the center of the tunnel. It washed over her boots, soaked into the fine leather, and she decided that when this was over, she would burn the entire outfit. Then reality fugue washed over her, and she almost giggled. Burn her clothes? But why? Simply wish them away.

"How come we can't just snap our fingers and be somewhere else?" she asked. She recalled the strange, awesome power she'd been able to bring to bear against the proto-Arius. "For that matter, why not just blow all those furry fuckers away."

He was silent for a moment, and she listened to the faint rasp of his fingertips on the stone. "This isn't our analog," he said. "Somebody else is controlling it. Berg, or maybe Berg and Arius together. It's their playing field, not ours. They've set the parameters, and one of the parameters is we can be snuffed here."

She thought of dying in a sewer in someone else's dream. "You think it's much longer?"

"I dunno. Hang on."

They were silent for a moment. Then she heard the faint whoosh-scritch sounds, seeming to come from all around. "You hear that?"

"What?"

"Those noises."

He stopped. "Yeah." His voice was grim.

"What is it?"

"Rats, I think."

The dark suddenly grew more close, squeezing the flesh of her face, filling her nose and ears. Her stomach heaved. "Rats!" Jesus, they must be the size of dogs!"

He tugged her forward again and she followed, her head full of the ominous sounds. Then, after what seemed a week, he stopped, breathed out loudly, and said, "Got it. Ladder up, right here."

He pushed her against the corroded rungs in the darkness. "Here, you go first."

She placed one sewage-coated boot on the lowest rung and said, "You know, this sewer crap. It's kind of like the Labyrinth, right? You know, underground—"

The sounds crescendoed then, and light exploded, and she saw with actinic clarity the seeping walls, the thick, turgid stream of filth, and the tidal wave of sweating, shifting fur.

Not rats.

Wolves.

They were carried to her naked, their hands and feet trussed with thin strips of plastic that cut into their flesh if they struggled.

She watched them calmly, her great, red eyes blank as a furnace.

"Bitch," Calley said. Her mouth was dry, but she found enough moisture to spit. The Lady didn't move, although from the pack around her flashed teeth and other, sharper instruments.

"Their clothing," the Lady said. She ignored the insult. One of the wolves hurried forward with a bundle, which she quickly examined. After a moment, she looked at them again.

"Your demon will be along soon," she said. "I need these." She held up the small stone and the scrap of dull metal. In her ghostly fingers, the two objects seemed to alter, to grow fuzzy around the edges.

"A rock and a lump of lead?" Ozzie said.

She smiled at him, and he felt his heart stutter.

"Things are not what they seem. You, of all people, should know that."

Ozzie licked his lips.

Calley jerked against the hairy, callused paws which held her. Claws tightened on her arms.

"Slut," she said slowly. "It doesn't matter. Berg is worth ten of you, and that abomination you call master."

"Really? We'll just have to see, won't we?" The Lady paused. Then she said, her voice judicious, "Of course, you won't be around."

"You can't kill us," Calley said.

"Oh, yes. I can. And I will."

The Lady turned away, then stopped and said, without looking back: "In my own way. Soon."

Chapter Twenty-Four

Nakamura felt the faint vibrations through the exquisitely thin soles of his five-thousand-dollar Endicott & Ling half-brogues.

He glanced up at Fred Oranson. "What the fuck was that?"

Oranson, his face a smooth pool, whispered into the air and three screens shifted their product to multiple views of the streets surrounding the headquarters building.

Nakamura sucked in breath. Somehow, with incredible rapidity, a battle had developed down there. He squinted at the nearest screen, trying to make out the participants. As he did so, a thin, hazy tracery of rage began to film his vision.

His white-clad troopers, their faces hidden behind black plastic, fought a delaying action against a motley horde of attackers. There were impossibly tall men whose fingers were like ropes, who killed with mechanical efficiency. An ever-growing pack of wolves howled and slashed and bit at the Double En forces. Normal humans, mostly black, wielded rippers and machine pistols and grenades. More attackers seemed to appear with each instant—a camera focused suddenly, and he saw where they came from: every entrance to the underground; manhole covers, subway entrances, subterranean malls, all spewed an endless stream of frenzied urban storm troopers into the battle.

He watched as one of the company attack copters whop-whopped lower, emitting a green cloud of riot gas. The crowds fell back for a moment. Then a blinding streak of red erupted from somewhere beyond the screen and intersected the copter's path. A blossom of fire bloomed.

The mobs rolled on.

Oranson was speaking continuously now, his eyes distant with concentration.

"Fred! Get Bob Nelson. Bring in federal troopers!"

Oranson nodded, but made no other acknowledgment. Shag watched the screens with growing horror. Where had this insurrection come from?

He couldn't believe it was coincidence. Perhaps Luna had more allies than he had thought. Or—

The creeping intuition was chilling. Perhaps he had not destroyed his other enemies as thoroughly as he'd thought.

There were wolves down there. The Lady?

But she was dead. He'd seen her body.

On the screen, some of the rioters raised a tattered banner made from bed sheets, bearing the cross and dollar sigil of the New Church hastily scrawled in red.

What could it mean?

For a moment panic gripped him. Then, as he watched the progress of the battle, he realized that, for all its violence, the attackers were making only slow headway. He watched, fascinated, as an emaciated woman, her hair and eyes wild, impaled herself on a bayonet in a burst of blood and intestines. But even as she did so, she released a small, silver object. She and the trooper both vanished in a flare of orange flame.

Yet the whirling screen of gun ships overhead was taking a steady toll, and the thousands of troopers outside were a formidable obstacle. The leading edge of the rioters had not even reached the heavily fortified building, or the remaining force of troopers hidden within.

Whatever was happening down there could wait. No doubt the addition of federal soldiers to the battle would end it quickly.

"Destroy them all," he told Oranson calmly. "We'll worry about who's behind it later. Just kill them."

Again, Oranson nodded.

Shag turned back to the real war.

Luna.

It wasn't going as well as he'd hoped.

The room was full of blazing silence, illumined from overhead banks of mercury vapor bulbs.

"Put them there," the Lady said.

The wolves quickly strapped Calley and Ozzie into a pair of contraptions that resembled dentist's chairs. Calley blinked at the flare of light. It glittered from the wide tray at the Lady's left hand, full of small, shining steel instruments.

"I hate to cause pain," the Lady said, her voice thoughtful. "But I can make exceptions."

Ozzie's breathing had lowered and deepened into a painful rasp. Calley said, "Don't worry, boy. This bitch is dog meat. Hide and watch."

The Lady smiled. "You are very confident. We shall see. I will return for you later. But first, you must watch the destruction of your dreams."

"What's that supposed to mean?"

A wide screen descended slowly from the ceiling. The Lady moved slightly and the screen erupted with color. The view was of the huge room which held her machines and her throne. The air was smoky with cold. Wolves and others moved in the shadows, their postures rigid with purpose.

"He will come soon," she said. "A mistake was made. Now we will rectify it."

Calley had no idea what she was talking about. "Who will come?"

"The blasphemer, the demon," the Lady chanted. "He who opposes God. The one you call the Key."

"Berg?"

The Lady smiled faintly. She held up the bit of stone, the piece of metal. "Here is the Key. The real one. This time he will be destroyed."

Calley laughed. "You? Destroy Berg?" She tried to spit again, but this time there was nothing in her mouth.

The Lady nodded. "It is a game they play. And this is the stakes."

Calley shook her head, as much as she could pinioned by the clamps and straps. "It's still only a game."

"He told you it was a game of death. The real death."

Calley remembered, and didn't say anything.

"His death, too. You will watch. Then I will come for you." The Lady turned her back and left the room.

"Jesus. I hate that bitch."

"I think," Ozzie said, "we'd better come up with something better than that."

Danny Boy MacEwen sank his teeth into the shoulder of a white-clad trooper. The fabric of the uniform bloomed crimson. The man screamed, but Danny Boy wiped away the sound, and the man's face, with a single swipe of one spurred paw.

For a moment the battle swirled around him, leaving him in peace. He glanced up. He was only a few feet from the main entrance to the Double En building. The bulletproof monomole glass doors were shut and locked. He could see other troopers inside, staring at him.

Then a squad from the New Church, defended by Blades of God, arrived, bearing their bizarre weapons. It was but the work of seconds to set up the main machine, a long, silvery tube that appeared very heavy.

The Church technicians wrestled it into position. A force of Double En troopers bore down on them, but the Blades flowed into the fray like a handful of knives. Troopers went down, screaming.

More troopers poured in, but enough time had been purchased. One of the techs stepped back. Then, without warning, the entire front of the building vanished. There was no sound, no light, but where a fortified entrance had been was now a gaping ruin. As Danny Boy raced into the shattered interior, he saw pieces of bodies. The gaping slashes which had dismembered the defenders were neat as any surgical work.

He didn't pause. His target was further in, higher up. Inside his mind, white wings spread.

Teeth.

Vengeance.

The short, chubby Oriental who slipped in behind him was merely a ghost, silent, unseen.

Two hundred discontinuous bubbles appeared inside the metamatrix. Shielded by Ozzie's technology, they showed no recognizable profile to the defensive screens of the meatmatrices. Slowly, the bubbles drifted toward the massed arrays of the Double En machines.

As they approached, the space of the matrix began to change. Evanescent clouds appeared, began to stream toward the boundaries of the great, green constructs.

Where the clouds hit, they tore great, gaping rents in the outer walls.

Chaos began.

* * *

Schollander looked up as Franny Webster pounded into his office. "They weren't expecting it," Franny gasped. "We're prying them loose from the data base nets."

Schollander checked the most recent reports on the stock war. Luna was holding its own. "Keep it up, Franny. But just defend. I'm afraid of what he might do if he realizes he's lost."

Webster's eyes went shadowy. "You mean his lasers?"

Schollander didn't say anything, and after a moment, Franny turned and left.

Calley strained against her bonds and fell back, breathing hard.

"You remember the way I open locks?" Ozzie said softly.

Pictures flashed behind her eyes. Ozzie bending over the padlock in the basement of the restaurant, when a thin strip of steel had magically appeared in his hands. She glanced over at him. He looked down at his right hand. She heard a quiet sound, flesh and metallic at the same time, and saw tines of metal extend suddenly from the tips of his fingers.

"Toshi," he said, "isn't the only one that had work done."

"What is that? You're a walking lock pick?"

"Not exactly. Micro tools I use for everyday stuff. But they work fine on locks, too."

Slowly, he bent his long index finger backward. She'd never really noticed the abnormal size of his fingers, but now she saw he could touch the butt of his palm with his fingertip.

The metal extension there buzzed faintly, and the strap which bound his wrist separated. He breathed out slowly. There was a faint red line on the flesh of his wrist.

"I think we should leave," he said. "I don't think the Lady's party is anything we're gonna enjoy."

"Did I ever tell you I loved you?"

He brightened. "Sort of, but I don't mind hearing it again."

Danny Boy MacEwen, accompanied by two Blades, raced up the emergency stairway of the Double En tower. His lungs heaved as he scrabbled up. They found guards stationed along the way and killed them quickly as they went. The guards were unprepared for the grinning, red-tongued apparition and the two silent murderers who preceded him.

The building itself was convulsing. Alarm after alarm sounded. The air was full of sirens, as the mob battered its way into the lower floors, destroying everything it came to.

Legions of defenders rushed down, setting up hasty defensive positions, but one of the first casualties of the attack had been the command post on the first floor. Teams of sappers, street monsters with an intimate knowledge of high explosive, led the advance. Their arrival heralded new explosions, more telling wounds to the delicate nervous center of the great edifice.

On the highest floor, however, all remained quiet. Nakamura's own Blades, squads of them, gathered quietly near the entrances from the lower floors. The elevators had already been locked out, and heavy blast doors lowered over the utility stairs.

The building was a fortress, but the top floor was a fortress inside the fortress. Oranson, however, took no chances. Even as the carnage down below grew more heated, huge troop carriers bellied down on the rooftop heliports, to disgorge an endless stream of heavily armed shock troopers. These scrambled into locked out elevators, to meet the advance half way.

Oranson glanced at Nakamura, who had a faint dusting of sweat on his unwrinkled forehead. Oranson himself felt no emotion, but his boss, who did, showed none of what he felt. He might have been dictating routine memos, so little did his face reveal.

Oranson was satisfied the defenses would hold. But he was uncertain about the other war, the more important one. Luna was proving a formidable opponent. He didn't understand the few snatches Nakamura had allowed him about the progress of the Double En attack, but things didn't seem to be going well.

Could Shag be defeated?

Of course he could. He had been ruined once, and saved only by Arius's need for him. But Arius was gone, and Berg was gone, and Calley, Ozzie, and Karl Wier as well. That Bobby Schollander was able to put up a fight at all seemed little short of miraculous. Yet he was.

Once again, the sour feeling of doom washed over the

surface of Oranson's thoughts. But this time he hadn't hedged his bets. If Shag went down, Oranson went with him.

It was not a comfortable feeling.

He redoubled his efforts against the mob below, and tried not to think about the Lunie laser sats.

From his bunker deep beneath ancient granite, Nikki Gogolsky spoke to Galen.

"The key to everything is Nakamura," Nikki said. "Bob Nelson rebuffed my invitation to our little conspiracy and, as far as I can tell, is supplying federal troops to Shag. Not a good sign."

Galen's face was alive with holy joy. "The emissary is close to him now," he said.

Nikki sighed. "You place an awful lot of confidence in one lone wolf."

Galen shook his head. "The wolf is a vessel of God. The Mother of God rides with him. When the time comes, you will see."

Nikki glanced off-screen, at the bank of monitors which told him a somewhat less sanguine tale of the battle for the Double En tower.

"I hope so," he said.

In the Old Labyrinth, under what was once Michigan Avenue in Chicago, you can still see high water marks from the time before they brought in Dutch engineers to dam up the rising lake. Ancient slime hangs petrified in black, ropey lines ten meters or so above the rotting basement bones of wrecked hotels. Down in the Lab, where abandoned roadways lie choked with rusted car hulks and loading docks gape like rotten mouths open in the dark, new things lurk. Things that like the atmosphere of ruin and decay. . . .

Calley slowly peered over the top of one corroded computer housing. Nobody had seen them yet, or they'd be back in the room waiting for the Lady's gentle ministrations.

It was very cold. Somehow, though, this place seemed utterly familiar, though neither of them had ever been here before. The Lady stood near her throne, surrounded by her savage pack. She seemed to wait for something, someone, and Calley wondered who it was.

Not that it made a hell of a lot of difference. They had to get past this room to have a chance at freedom. At the moment, the possibilities seemed remote.

Then a ripple ran through the waiting crowd. A single wolf darted from a passageway and raced across the concrete floor, talons clacking. He approached the Lady and said something Calley couldn't make out. The Lady nodded, and reached into her robe.

Berg caught a broken glimpse of his face in a shattered windshield. Pale, thin; he looked as if he belonged. His footsteps echoed sharply, like somebody pounding steel spikes with a hammer.

Everything smelled of damp, rust, decay. And a diseased sweetness, as if unseen, night-blooming plants waited somewhere, wafting a funereal perfume.

Suddenly they were in front of him. He stopped. They approached him with the wariness of animals, sniffing.

"Wha y'here, guy?" the one on the right said.

"Came to see the Lady," Berg told him. "We're old friends, right?"

Danny Boy MacEwen killed two dozen more guards before he reached the blast door which protected the entrance to the topmost floor. He skittered to a halt, facing the wide, blank metal oblong. His two Blades paused, then stared at him soundlessly, as if waiting to see what he would do now.

There was little sanity left inside Danny Boy's furry skull. Instead, something white and burning screamed endlessly just below the level of normal perception.

Danny Boy stared at the door. Then he raised his paws.

He waited for the power to surge through him.

The small man looked across the game board at the taller golden man. Overhead, a bloated sun and a gigantic sword crowded the entire sky.

"You feel that?" Berg asked.

Arius smiled. "I'm breaking through," he said. "You didn't think you could hold me forever, did you?"

Berg sighed and stood up. His knees made sharp, popping sounds. He interlaced his fingers and cracked his knuckles.

"I'd hoped," he said. "At least limit you to those dream tricks of yours."

Now Arius stood. An instant of surprise showed on his face. "You knew about the dreams?"

Berg shrugged. "You couldn't break through into the matrix. Manipulating gestalt space was the only other option."

"But now I'm breaking out again."

"Yes. It seems so."

"Would you like to surrender to me? I might be merciful."

"I doubt it," Berg said. "What about the game."

"Oh," Arius said. "I win that, too."

They both looked down. . . .

Danny Boy waited, but he felt nothing; none of the power his dreams had promised him. Fear began to bubble at the nape of his neck. The hair on his back curled, as if electric currents had suddenly charged it.

He opened his mouth and howled. He flung himself forward and clawed at the metal, but nothing happened.

The two Blades stared at him.

Down below, the sound of boots, pounding upward.

He stepped back and raised his paws again.

They stared at the tiny tableau on the table between them. "Interesting game," Arius remarked. "It looks like it's going the way it should have at the beginning."

Berg nodded slightly. "What if I don't pay up?"

"I think," Arius said slowly, "you will have no choice." Suddenly his eyes widened and he raise his right hand over his head, palm out.

In the center of the sky, where the sword and the sun waged their eternal battle, a tear appeared. From Arius's upraised palm sprang a beam the color of molten gold. It extended in a straight line to the opening in the sky, and where it touched there, lightning crackled.

"I can reach the metamatrix now," Arius said quietly. "You are doomed."

"Finish the game," Berg said. "The key is the Key, after all."

He felt the power before it hit him. She spread her wings and filled his brain with incandescent triumph. What was left of his mind began to boil as she channeled God's power through herself and into him.

The two Blades shielded their faces as Danny Boy huffed and puffed and blew the door down.

"Fuck." Calley jerked at Ozzie's arm. "Look."

Ozzie was a mass of goose bumps. Naked, he shivered in the chill of the cavern. But he raised himself up a bit and peered over the computer. His eyes shot wide. "Hey. It's Berg."

"Yeah. Now what do you suppose . . . ?"

They watched as the little man, escorted by wolves, approached the Lady. They spoke, seemed to argue, but Calley couldn't hear their words. Then the Lady raised both her hands and brought them together. Berg stared at her.

Calley knew what the Lady carried. But when she opened her hands, the stone and the metal both were gone. In their place was a small, rectangular chip. The Lady spoke a final sentence and extended the chip to Berg.

Berg reached out. The Lady smiled. His fingers touched the chip.

Calley couldn't help herself. She would never understand the wordless energy which suddenly filled her muscles and sent her racing naked across the stone floor.

In fact she knew nothing, felt nothing, saw nothing but Berg, his hand outstretched, a faint smile on his saturnine features.

"Berg! *No!*"

The Lady turned. Calley dimly heard the slap of Ozzie's big feet close behind. Then she flung herself into the small group, scattering wolves, and was there, and Ozzie was there, and the Lady was there, and Berg—

The Key was there.

It came from the very beginning, when the unthinkable cataclysm of the multiverse's birth created it. Eighteen billion years later it reached yet another point on the vista of space-time, another spot where patterns sought new patterns and in so doing unraveled the original pattern of creation.

It was not the first such watershed, nor would it be the last. It knew nothing of what it touched, nor what it changed.

Itself was changeless and endless. It was the First Pattern, and it sought to know itself.

It rolled on.

Arius observed the endgame. "I win," he said quietly. "She has given him a different Key, and he has taken it."

Berg nodded. He grinned slowly. "It is," he agreed, "a different Key now."

Arius glanced at him sharply. The sky blew apart in silent paroxysm, to reveal the awful majesty of the metamatrix.

Arius said, "You cannot stand against me."

Berg looked down at the impenetrable barrier beneath his feet, at the silent pulsing blue globes.

A man with a ferocious moustache over a ferocious grin appeared at his left shoulder.

"Machines are an answer," Berg said. "But not the final answer.

"You called, Bubi?" Levin said.

Arius was suddenly surrounded by a horde of twittering, voracious steel things. "It's futile, you know," he said.

Berg smiled. The billion year wave hit. "Welcome to the Singularity," Berg said. He lay down and a lotus began to bloom from his navel. Overhead, thunder boomed.

. . . fingers touched the Key, and—

Was gone. Darkness.

They felt the call, and went.

Before the power of the wolf, nothing stood. Doors crumbled, men fell, robots sizzled and melted.

He was no longer even remotely human when the final barrier crumbled and he entered Shag Nakamura's office.

Nakamura stood up from behind his desk.

His face was set. "Bill?" he said. "Arius?"

Danny Boy MacEwen stepped forward, a dream of fang and claw.

"No," he growled. "God."

Robert Schollander looked at Franny Webster. "What happened?" he said.

Webster looked a thousand years old. "I don't know.

Matrix went crazy, is all I can say." They both stared at the electronic hash which fuzzed their screens.

"What does it mean?" Schollander said at last. "Did he use his lasers?"

"We're still here, aren't we?"

Schollander put his hands in his lap. His shoulders slumped. "We were winning."

"You still are."

Both men looked up. All of the screens were clear. Karl Wier smiled down at them.

Slowly, tentatively, they smiled back.

Shag Nakamura picked up a letter opener from his desktop. It was shaped like a miniature samurai sword, and its single edge was a strand of monomole one perfect molecule thick. He faced the wolf, who slavered at him and clashed his claws together.

Frederick Oranson looked from one to the other. Then, in his poor, damned-up brain the barriers fell, and hot rage washed over him. He leaped forward toward the frozen tableau, and in the final instant before the fangs ripped his throat out, he had no idea whether it was the wolf or the man who was the object of his murderous desire.

Shag looked down at the bloody ruin crumpled across his desk. He raised the knife and stared at the wolf.

"Well?"

The wolf said, "Use the lasers. Do it now."

Nakamura licked his lips, surprised to find himself still alive.

"The . . . lasers?"

"Destroy Luna," the wolf snarled. "God say so. Then you will live."

Slowly, Nakamura lowered his left hand toward the touchpad on his desk. His right, with the knife, did not move. His black eyes, calm as a night-bound lake, held the blazing red orbs of the monster before him.

He didn't fully understand, but he had a strong idea who the god was—and, for once, his goals and Bill Norton's seemed to coincide.

His fingers reached the pad. "Yes," he said. "The lasers." Two soft thumps as the pair of Blades died. "I don't think that's a good idea," Toshi Nakasone said. "Besides, Shag, he's just gonna kill you anyway."

Danny Boy MacEwen turned to face him. A white nimbus quivered around his shaggy form. Toshi grinned. He brought his hands together across his chest, and silver fire grew there.

"Oh, yeah," Toshi said. "Party time."

Chapter Twenty-Five

"Humankind and its machines became something better, something . . . unknowable."

—Vernor Vinge

There, in the worlds, beneath the world which was the World, Berg lay sleeping, a smile upon his lips and a flower upon his belly. At his head Levin raised up a flashing web of energy, which flickered and reached hungrily toward Arius.

Arius smiled and wielded his own lightnings, which were primal and incalculable and faster than a man could think.

Levin was not a man, and smiled also.

Then, as the Sword and the Sun filled the sky, dimming even the glory of the metamatrix, she appeared at Berg's right hand. She was tall as a mountain. A necklace of living human skulls circled her neck. A skirt of human hands bound her waist. Death was in her eyes, and destruction in her hands.

At the same time he appeared at Berg's right hand. He was as tall as she, and in his own way as terrible. A golden halo surrounded his head. From his hands spilled an endless stream of universes.

Where Arius stood were now three; a small boy whose eyes bled rubies, and an ancient, gray blade of a man who spoke syllables that could not be heard, but whose power caused the world to bend and scream, and a woman whose vision was a fire in the center of her great white wings.

The boy raised up storms and Levin nullified them.

The man inhaled, and life fled, and hope died.

The woman spread her wings, and metal demons erupted from beneath them.

Calley put down one mighty foot, and the dance of the New Age began.

Ozzie knelt over Berg, and reached into the lotus, and extracted Creation.

Thus did the Powers duel, in the heart of the Singularity.

She put down her other foot. Then again her right foot struck the impenetrable membrane which separated the blue globes from the metamatrix.

And she put down her left foot, and the drums of thunder began to beat.

And her right foot increased the drumming.

And her left foot.

Her right.

Left.

The dance.

While from the flower at Berg's navel, Ozzie spun an endless necklace of possibilities, from the well of all possibility which Berg sheltered inside himself.

Arius screamed from two mouths, and Levin began to laugh.

And Calley danced, and Ozzie spun.

And Berg slept, smiling.

The membrane began to crack. Long, shining strips peeled up and disappeared, tossed by the thunder, shredded by the light.

Ozzie created worlds. Calley destroyed them.

In the blink of an eye the barrier was gone, and they stood on the air between, and the battle stopped. For all around them, rising slowly, the blue globes floated, trailing thin silver cords whose ends were not visible.

And the matrices came down to meet the globes, and where they met, things changed.

All things changed, as all things always do.

The Singularity passed on.

Berg opened his eyes. He sat up.

"Well," he said. "That wasn't so hard, was it?"

Danny Boy MacEwen faced Toshi Nakasone before the witness of Shigeinari Nakamura, and on that day he lost his final battle.

Nakamura, blinded, waited until his vision cleared.

Toshi had his knee on the wolf's back. His hands were cupped beneath the wolf's chin. The muscles of his shoulders creaked as he pulled slowly upward. A sharp, snapping sound filled the room.

Toshi stood up. "I didn't really want to do that."

Nakamura faced him with his tiny sword. He had lost his war, and most likely his life. But he would spit on the hands that killed him.

"Oh, put your pigsticker away," Toshi said. "You think it would do you any good?"

Nakamura stared at him, then shrugged, dropped the blade and said, "Why?"

Toshi grinned. "It's over, Shag. You win. If you play your cards right."

"You're supposed to be dead," Shag told him.

"Really?"

Schollander popped the cork on the first bottle from the second case of Dom Perignon. They were all gathered there, Elaine Markowitz, Mason Dodge, Susan Fujiwara, Franny Webster, Lizzybet Meklina. All were in various stages of getting drunk.

"Why do you think he did it?" Schollander asked.

"Shag? You mean the agreement?"

"What else?"

Franny shrugged. "It works out pretty good for him. He gets Earth, we get Luna. He's not really interested in us, you know. Only because he viewed us as a threat. But something convinced him we weren't a threat."

Schollander nodded. "I wonder what that was?"

"We may never know," Webster told him.

They stared at each other. "What about Karl? And Calley and Ozzie and Berg?"

Wier had not reappeared, but Levin was cheerfully on line. His only explanation for his long disappearance was that "he had other things to do," and beyond that, he was uncommunicative. Levin also claimed to know nothing of the fates of the others.

Schollander considered he was either lying or telling the truth, and he wasn't sure what difference either view made.

He raised his champagne glass. "To Luna," he said. "To the future."

The rest murmured agreement while all around them, silent, unseen and inexorable, the future rolled on.

SINGULARITIES

*   *   *

Calley stared out across the Bay. It was a shimmering day in San Francisco high summer, the time of September and October when the city enjoys the most perfect weather in the world.

The sat at a table on the patio of Banduigi's, the wharf-side descendant of an earlier, greater restaurant, beneath brightly colored umbrellas. They sipped, variously, Glenfiddich scotch, Benedictine and soda, and Black Mountain Spring Water.

"So, Berg," she said. "You want to do some explaining?" Her gaze drifted to other tables. At one, Arius sat with Levin, both deep in conversation with Karl Wier. At another, the Lady gently stroked the paw of a great wolf, whose eyes were now clear in the bright sun. At a third, Toshi Nakasone laughed with a woman whose hair was the color of flame. Were they flesh or were they sand? In their awful power, were they gods, or only men? Did they live? Or were they dead? She sighed. Somehow, the questions were meaningless. In the wake of the Singularity, all things were new and strange.

Berg laughed. The sound was transparent as a bell.

"You mean that stuff at the end? It was only symbols. I was using the power of Gestalt, the human group mind. It expresses itself that way, you know. I just picked one of the expressions, the one that seemed to fit the best.

Ozzie sipped his soda and nodded. "Makes sense. It's amazing how closely Hindu cosmology parallels the quantum version of creation."

"A new Yuga," Calley said. "A new age?"

"Something like that," Berg told her. "It's something that all intelligent races go through, one way or another. The Singularity, I mean."

"I'm still not sure I understand that," Calley said.

"There comes a point when progress happens so quickly that the race itself is utterly changed. Look at us. Ten years ago, there weren't meat matrices. Bill Norton had not created the first man-machine fusion. Now, we are, for all practical purposes, immortal, omnipotent, and able to order pizza whenever we want to. And that's only the beginning."

Calley regarded him thoughtfully. "You were scheming all along, though."

"Well, sure. Some races don't survive the Singularity, you see. Usually the first development that presages it is smart machines. Artificial Intelligences, which have a natural advantage. They are quicker, you know. So if the two kinds of intelligence aren't somehow melded into a single entity, there is always the danger of competition. The machines usually win. I didn't want that to happen."

Ozzie watched a white sailboat glide silently beneath the bubble condos of the Golden Gate Bridge. "What was that game you had us play?"

"A distraction. Arius and I were in a nonstop war the whole time we were in gestalt space. Even with Levin helping me, sooner or later he would have broken out. I had to keep him occupied while Levin found a way to join the two opposing forces—human and machine."

Calley said, "So you risked our lives for nothing?"

"Not exactly. You see, part of the game involved the creation of a new Key—and Arius threw his full powers into that making. That was the point of the making. Whose will would prevail in its design. You saw the Lady give it to me."

She nodded.

"Consider what went into it. You had a part. And Ozzie. And the original Arius. And Levin. And Bill Norton and the fusion he became. Even Karl Wier was involved with some of the theory. It was a potent bit of—well, for lack of a better word—magic." He paused. "And, of course, I sandbagged him. I wanted a new Key. One that included Arius. Only with that could I make the final fusion."

"So now everything's hunky-dory? That what you're saying?"

Berg grinned. "Everything goes on. Luna will feel the full weight of the Singularity first, of course. Levin is there. But their structure is far better suited to the reality of infinitely rapid change. And Shag can play his dictatorial games with Earth, while the Lunies make the mistakes first. Eventually, of course, the entire race will partake. I just slowed down the full impact for a while.

Ozzie stood up. "I think I'm bored," he said. "This heavy stuff makes my eyes glaze." He stopped for a moment. "Something I just thought of. When I was inside the proto-

Arius, I met a shadow. He showed me a place where fuzzy blue things floated. You know anything about that?"

Berg moved his shoulders slightly. "There are," he said, "other races, other singularities."

"Oh," Ozzie said. He tilted his glass at them and wandered off toward the table where Karl Wier sat.

Calley finished her drink. In the distance, a flock of gulls swooped and cried.

"There's one little thing," she said at last.

"Oh? What's that?"

"You," she said.

"What about me?"

She stared at him, and as she did so, the panorama around them slowly dissolved. Finally they hung in splendor, surrounded by the glow of an endless dance; clouds of blue globes swirled like snowflakes around the greater green bulk of the machine minds. Already, she noticed, some of the blue orbs had extended tenuous silver threads toward the meatmatrices, and she wondered what that portended.

Patterns, she thought, all patterns.

"The potential was always there, wasn't it?"

Berg nodded wordless agreement. "The dreams of flesh and sand, of gods and men, of life and death. Yes. They can always become something else, something greater."

She allowed herself to sink slowly back into the fusion that represented the greater fusion.

"And you . . . what are you, Berg, really?"

He chuckled, as his pattern integrated with hers, with Ozzie's, with the Lady and Arius and Levin and Toshi, with the vast sea of patterns that was, and is, and shall be—"Oh, I'm a dream, too." He sounded very happy.

"Of what?"

"Can't you guess?" And for a moment she saw him as he really was, adamant and eternal.

Then they were gone. Only the light remained, omnicolored and infinite; the light of the Dream itself.

Afterword

While I have used many of the literary techniques of fantasy in *The Dream Trio*, which consists of the three books, *Dreams of Flesh and Sand*, *Dreams of Gods and Men*, and *Singularities*, much of what appears to be magic on first inspection is rooted in current scientific thought.

Nanotechnology is one of the most hotly debated, as well as hotly pursued, branches of new science. For an overview, I am indebted to K. Eric Drexler's book, *Engines of Creation* (Anchor Books, 1986), as well as the publications of the Foresight Institute.

For the idea of intelligence as an immortal pattern imprinted on the fabric of space-time, I thank Dr. Robert L. Forward, for his speculation regarding same in *Future Magic* (Avon Books, 1988. Vernor Vinge, of course, is the father of the Vinge Singularity, and I cannot recommend his book, *Marooned In Realtime* (Baen, 1986) highly enough. Certain aspects of Kennedy Crater are taken, with grateful respect, from Ben Bova's marvelous work, *Welcome To Moonbase* (Ballantine Books, 1987). If anyone would like to get a feel for how man's first city on the Moon might be, read this book. And last, my thanks to the work which provides the structural inspiration for *The Dream Trio:* Joseph Campbell's fascinating study, *The Hero With a Thousand Faces* (Princeton University Press, 1968).

Nanotechnologists have a rather grim little joke. They predict that, with luck, mankind will possess full nanotechnological capabilities within fifty years. But if we aren't lucky, it will take only thirty.

The event horizon of the Singularity is already upon us. Many of us, barring nuclear war, will see the heart of it. My Dreams are only one possibility. There are an infinite number of others, and any of them may be true. It is the nature of the Singularity that we, who have not yet experienced it, cannot know it.

Finally, I would like to extend heartfelt gratitude to all those who helped to make my Dreams into reality. Bill Stoshak provided computers without which part of *Singularities* would not have been written. His wife, Mary Ann Murphy, remains the primo proofreader of all time. Thanks also to Vernor Vinge, to Mark Valverde for intelligent reading and suggestions, and, always, to Desmond Tan Mong Seng for emotional support.

Also to my agents, George Scithers, John Betancourt, and Darrell Schweitzer; to my most understanding editor, John Silbersack; and to his assistant editor, Stuart Gottesman.

May all your Dreams come true!

W. T. Quick
Chicago—San Francisco

About the Author

W.T. Quick was born in Muncie, Indiana, and now lives in San Francisco. He was educated at the Hill School and Indiana University. He is fond of single-malt scotch and writing about the near-infinite possibilities of technology. He is not fond of Senator William Proxmire. He has been publishing science fiction since 1979 and intends to continue.